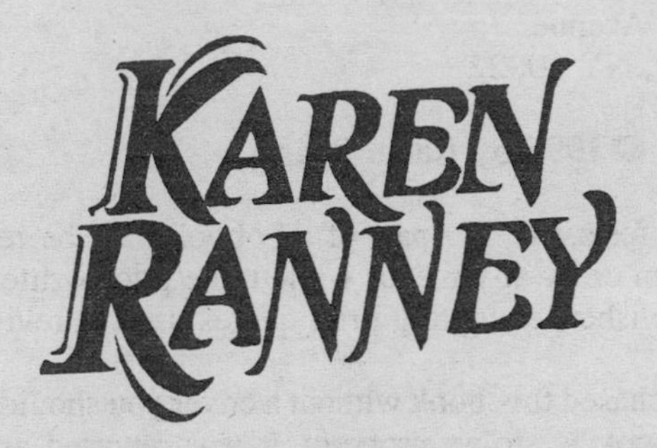

ZEBRA BOOKS
KENSINGTON PUBLISHING CORP.

ZEBRA BOOKS are published by

Kensington Publishing Corp.
850 Third Avenue
New York, NY 10022

First Printing: August, 1996
10 9 8 7 6 5 4 3 2 1

Printed in the United States of America

IT WAS SEDUCTION

He decided, he said, to call her Kat. "If I'm a tiger, dear Katherine, then you must be a member of the feline family also. Why else would we share such an affinity? Sleek Kat, purring Kat," he murmured, tracing a finger near the line of her jaw. That almost caress caused her to shiver as though ice had been brushed across her skin.

What female would not arch into his hands, and stroke the length of every limb? What woman wouldn't purr under his touch? It was a thought that, oddly enough, irritated her beyond measure.

In her bed at night, she could almost feel him next to her. She could imagine the arch of one foot as it slipped seductively up her bare leg, the band of muscle in his arm as he pulled her closer. She could envision his lips on hers, his warm breath slipping from between salted lips, a tongue teasing, darting, flicking. The rasp of new beard was almost real, as she could feel it skating across her throat, down her shoulders, and over taut budded nipples.

It was danger, it was magic, it was passion, and he had yet to touch her.

* * *

CRITICAL PRAISE FOR KAREN RANNEY'S *TAPESTRY*:

"Marvelous . . . guaranteed to steal your heart. A very special love story." —*Romantic Times*

"As intricately woven and beautifully crafted as its title. Ranney is certainly [an] uncommon talent."
—*Affaire de Coeur*

"FIVE GOLD STARS!" —*Heartland Critiques*

"Majestic." —*Rendezvous*

ROMANCES BY BEST-SELLING AUTHOR COLLEEN FAULKNER!

O'BRIAN'S BRIDE (0-8217-4895-5, $4.99)

Elizabeth Lawrence left her pampered English childhood behind to journey to the far-off Colonies . . . and marry a man she'd never met. But her dreams turned to dust when an explosion killed her new husband at his powder mill, leaving her alone to run his business . . . and face a perilous life on the untamed frontier. After a desperate engagement to her husband's brother, yet another man, strong, sensual and secretive Michael Patrick O'Brian, enters her life and it will never be the same.

CAPTIVE (0-8217-4683-1, $4.99)

Tess Morgan had journeyed across the sea to Maryland colony in search of a better life. Instead, the brave British innocent finds a battle-torn land . . . and passion in the arms of Raven, the gentle Lenape warrior who saves her from a savage fate. But Tess is bound by another. And Raven dares not trust this woman whose touch has enslaved him, yet whose blood vow to his people has set him on a path of rage and vengeance. Now, as cruel destiny forces her to become Raven's prisoner, Tess must make a choice: to fight for her freedom . . . or for the tender captor she has come to cherish with a love that will hold her forever.

With grateful acknowledgment to those individuals who help me make it through each day, gifting me with laughter, understanding, and friendship: Armida, Sandi, Lesa, Hilda, Eunice, Lou, Donald, Rosie, Penny

And with gratitude to those delightful friends who keep replenishing my supply of joy: Bill, Peggi, Flo, Laura, Yolanda, Carla, Tom, Anne, Trudy, Eura, Marilyn

And especially Pat Wood, for Saturdays, peonies and telling me when to shut up.

Trust me, I couldn't have done it without all of you.

Chapter 1

"No-o-o-o-oh! Dear God, no!"

The female scream was accompanied by the tinny screech of iron-bound wheels, the whinny of frightened horses, and the angry curses of the driver. The carriage lurched heavily to one side, before it righted itself in a groan of bouncing springs and straining leather.

The Dowager Countess of Moncrief hung on to the strap mounted above the window, constructed for just such a purpose, closed her eyes and sighed with the patience of a much-tried saint.

A soft moan made her open her eyes and just as quickly shut them again.

Only seconds had transpired since the carriage had stopped, yet her daughter Melissa was already beginning to demonstrate a fit of the vapors, her lace-edged handkerchief pressed against her mouth, her eyes wide and fearful. Melissa, it could be charitably said, was high-strung, a statement that always made her mother think of a high-stepping pony, or a springer spaniel with a habit of relieving himself on the carpet. The female scream outside the window had evidently triggered a like response in her grown daughter, not unlike a noisy puppy will provoke the yipping of the litter.

Melissa possessed the ability to irritate her mother beyond belief.

It was no wonder—it truly had been an awful day.

The countess had spent the majority of it vainly attempting to secure a nurse for her illegitimate granddaughter, an unprecedented action on her part—it was usual in most cases simply to ignore the blatant fact that one's children occasionally sired offspring outside the bonds of matrimony—but neither her good intentions, nor the fact that she had spent most of the morning interviewing candidates, had resulted in finding someone suitable.

She had seen five young women. Two would not be considered to oversee the kennels at Moncrief, they were so slovenly. The third determined that the position was beneath her; the fourth was a possibility, but did not wish to rusticate in the country. The fifth she did not care to remember but the lingering odor of gin made that nearly impossible. She sighed again.

"Oh, do be quiet, Melissa," she said to her daughter, who was showing all the signs of working herself into a fine case of ladylike delirium. She was trembling, and every few seconds she would emit little mouse squeaks of terror, despite the fact that the carriage was no longer rocking dangerously. In fact, it was not moving at all.

She gestured for Melissa to remain seated and opened the door, letting the three folded steps unfurl themselves to the street. It was not easy navigating her way unaided, but some voice of reason must prevail in the scene that met her eyes. John, assigned to be her driver on this hapless day, stood impassively at the front of the carriage, while a young woman pulled at his arm, gesturing frantically toward the rearing horses. Finally, unable to budge him, since he was a large, broadly built man who had no intention of moving, she flew to the rear team, grasped the halter of the nearest horse, and attempted to force him to back up. The high-spirited horse, straining at the bit and shaking his head wildly, was not cooperating.

"Please help me!" she yelled, while swatting at the horse. It showed the same obstinacy as its driver, refusing to budge despite her tugging on the lead. Nor did the crowd that had rapidly gathered make any attempt to aid her, either. Miriam stepped forward quickly.

"What seems to be amiss?"

The young woman stopped pulling at the team long enough to breathe deeply, glance at Miriam with an expression that could only be construed as disgust, and point to a brown bundle lying dangerously close to the legs of the rear team, horses bred for their beauty and their matched gait, not for their patience or safety.

"Dear God, what happened?" Miriam asked as she turned to John and motioned for his assistance. The slight gesture was enough to summon him without delay.

"Your driver happened," Katherine said, censure in her voice. Tears wet her flushed face but she didn't seem to notice, her concentration fixed on the sight of the carriage driver manipulating the frantic horses. Together with the footman, he managed to back the horses slowly away until their hooves no longer posed a threat.

"We must get help, John," the countess said, her voice holding a note that brooked no interference.

"But your Ladyship . . ." John began, years of service making him dare what others would not.

A single shake of the head and a slight smile were all that was needed to stop his protestations.

Katherine knelt beside the bundle just as the woman reached her side.

"Will he be all right?" Miriam asked in concern. The

wadded rags had been transformed into the figure of an emaciated child, his thin legs sticking out at an unnatural angle from the rest of his body.

"I don't know," Katherine said, her voice conveying real distress. Poor little boy.

John stood behind his mistress. He wanted to tell her that it wasn't his fault, that the child had darted in front of the carriage before he could do anything but pull frantically on the reins. It had been too late to stop their iron-shod hooves from striking the lad. It wasn't his fault.

Miriam was in no mood to assign blame. She simply wanted to help the child. She glanced at the people ringing the scene. No one came forward to assist, but they all stared as if this were a mummer's play, something to break the monotony of their day.

The young woman straightened and sighed. The dark glint of anger illuminated amber eyes.

"I fear both of his legs are broken," she said. "More than that, I do not know."

"I am deeply sorry," the countess said, words that separated her from a great many of her peers. It was not that Londoners were callous, nor was it that members of the ton treated life without regard. They simply did not see the wretched conditions that surrounded them. It was as if they concentrated only on objects and people at a safe distance or no lower than eye level. Otherwise, it was doubtful they would choose to live in a city that, while the center of commerce and society, was so dangerously crowded and reeked of eternal soot and other, more noxious, odors. Yet Miriam Lattimore, Dowager Countess of Moncrief, was not the usual grande dame of fashion and arbiter of social mores. If she had been, she would not have spent an entire morning attempting to acquire a governess for a child born on the wrong side of the blanket. Nor would she be suffering such pangs of conscience now.

She turned to John with iron resolve, the look in her

eyes defying any protest. "John, you and Peter"—she indicated the footman, who still stood at the head of the horses—"fetch the child and place him in the coach. The least we can do is offer this woman and her child sanctuary until he heals."

"But, madam," Katherine attempted to interject, but her gesture was as futile as the carriage driver's had been.

"No, I insist," said the Countess of Moncrief, mother of two grown sons and a daughter not yet wed, patroness of numerous charities and benevolent societies, friend to three quarters of the ton, and gentle listener to the complaints of her elderly companions. She reasoned that it was foolish to spend so much time on worthy charities if she failed to extend a little Christian compassion so close to home.

"But, madam," Katherine began again, but this interruption proved as futile as the first.

"We will obtain medical care for your son and see that he's cared for. I cannot say how sorry I am about this. I would not willingly hurt a child, and this small gesture is the least I can do. Please allow me that."

"He is not my son," Katherine finally managed to interject.

"He is not?"

"Likely one of the beggars roamin' the streets, m'lady," John offered. Katherine glared at him. So did his mistress, with such a frosty glance from her ice-blue eyes that he shuffled his feet awkwardly and stared at the ground.

"Does his lack of money mean that he is less important than any other child?" Katherine asked him. There was an edge of anger to her voice. John did not look up, but his exposed neck reddened. "If that were so, then half this world is populated by such as he."

"No, of course not," the countess demurred, taking pity on her servant. It was quite evident that the young woman had taken it upon herself to champion the little boy. And from the looks of her own dress, brown as the dust beneath their feet and as threadbare as the victim's own clothing, it seemed as if she were not too far from sharing the penurious condition of the child. The only difference was in her speech. There was no cockney about her tone, no lower East End accent. She spoke, Miriam realized, in the same cultivated tone as her own daughter.

A daughter who was rendered mute by the scandalous actions of her parent. Miriam sat beside the unconscious child, grateful not only for her daughter's unusual silence, but that the young boy had not regained consciousness. Otherwise, she suspected, his pain would have been unbearable.

"We should begin to search for his parents," the countess said to Katherine, who sat opposite her, next to Melissa.

"I do not think they are worrying overly about his absence," Katherine contributed. "His face is badly bruised, but not from the accident. It looks as though he has been beaten."

Despite Melissa's frantic signaling—all waving eyebrows, widened eyes, and angled head, as if Miriam were not aware of Katherine's presence next to her—she gave directions for John to return home quickly and for Peter to summon their physician.

Katherine Anne Sanderson felt as though she had been tumbled end over end like dice in a cup. This last hour had been tumultuous, nothing like she had envisioned of her first visit to London. The trip from Sheffington had been interminable, taking days instead of the hours promised. The poor weather had delayed them for one whole afternoon while they waited for the muddy roads to dry. When she'd finally descended from the badly sprung coach, she'd nearly fallen from fatigue.

A few minutes later, tired of walking, she had set her valise down. Just for a moment. Only long enough to place both hands on the small of her back and bend backward, stretching her sore muscles. It had been enough time for an enterprising urchin to filch her case. Her valise, holding the last of her meager possessions, was flung into the mud and muck of London's streets. Her only good dress had spilled from the case, as had the two precious volumes of John Locke, but the eager young thief had quickly picked among her things and found the silver mirror that had been her mother's.

She had not behaved with any propriety. Fatigue had been buried beneath a very real rage, and she had sprinted after the youngster.

Only to have him dart in front of the team of aristocratic horses pulling a magnificent ebony lacquered carriage. Only to be trampled beneath their wicked looking hooves.

She could not help but think that it was all her fault.

Her benefactress had gently but firmly escorted her to the carriage, and she allowed herself to be scooped up into the other woman's generosity as though she lacked a will of her own. She sat, squeezed between the wall of the carriage and a haughty young lady with a supercilious stare, feeling as out of place as a frog in a drawing room, and about as ill dressed.

The interior of the carriage was luxuriously padded with soft blue velvet. The hangings on the windows were of silk, fringed with ball tassels. Two sconces sat on either side of the window opposite the door, their brass fixtures polished to a soft gleam. Even the floor was carpeted, with an intricately patterned rug of blue and rose. Only the sight of the two of them, the little boy so badly injured and herself clad in a rumpled traveling gown, marred the picture of understated elegance. It made her forget, for a moment, the sights outside the window.

She had been in London less than one afternoon and she loathed it. She hated the smells, and the mustard-colored sky, and the sounds of so many people pressed into such a small place. She hated the crowds, the feeling of being unable to move freely. Whatever made her think that London would be her salvation?

She clasped her hands on her lap, trying to will herself smaller so that her skirts would not brush those of the young woman next to her. It did not work. She could feel the girl shifting, pressing against the window so that she would not touch Katherine. It was such an obvious gesture that Katherine flushed.

The carriage finally stopped in front of a townhouse in a quiet square of prosperous homes.

Her companions were assisted from the carriage, the young woman muttering something dire about her mother's charity work as she flounced to the top of the steps, disappearing within.

Two servants were summoned from the house, and as they prepared to lift the small boy, still breathing stenoriously through parted, pale lips, Katherine turned to the older woman.

"You've been very kind," she said, pride stiffening her backbone and her resolve, "but I cannot impose any further, madam." They had arrived at their destination; the child would be looked after. Katherine, however, had no idea what she was going to do.

"Nonsense, child. You can keep me company while we wait upon the physician." There was a carefully assessing look in those ice-blue eyes, yet her gaze was neither cold nor was it unkind. Katherine had the strange notion that the other woman appeared aloof only because of her looks, not her nature.

"Am I right in assuming," the Countess said now, "that you are just come to London?"

At Katherine's nod of assent, she continued. "We shall discuss this after the poor boy has been treated." She firmly propelled Katherine up the steps behind the servants, who had constructed a makeshift litter for her patient.

Katherine wondered if the other woman ever failed at

anything she set her mind to. Or did the world simply crumble beneath her gentle purpose?

Katherine found herself installed in a small room on the top floor of the house, overlooking the formal gardens to the rear. It was a lovely room, part of the nursery suite and adjoining the room where the little boy lay still and silent beneath the doctor's examination. He'd not yet regained consciousness, which was not altogether a bad thing, as the setting of his legs would prove to be agonizing.

The countess—she now knew the identity of her benefactress thanks to the voluble nature of the maid—had sent a tray of tea and refreshments to her. She had nibbled on two sandwiches, and although she cautioned herself about appearing too greedy, she eyed the remaining food with longing. It had been two long days since she'd had much of anything but the meager contents of the hamper she'd thought to bring for the journey.

She turned as the doctor entered the room, followed by the countess. Both wore grim looks.

"Will he be all right?" Gone were memories of the urchin who had stolen her valise. It was odd, Katherine thought, that circumstance could so alter your perceptions. An hour ago she had been enraged by the child. Now, she worried about him.

"If he had not been half starved, perhaps he could have survived," the doctor said, his tone that of someone who had had, of necessity, too much practice dispensing bad news. It was a kind voice, without being steeped in compassion. A dispassionate tone, while conveying a certain degree of pity.

Katherine turned to Miriam in horror, tears choking her voice. "But it is all my fault. If I had not chased him, he would still be alive." And she had not even retrieved her mother's mirror. It was lost, somewhere, on London's streets.

"Nonsense, child. If blame is to be apportioned, it is mine to assume." Miriam sat on the nursery cot and turned to her friend.

"Thank you, Edward. I appreciate your promptness and your assistance. I am only sorry that we could not do more."

"I, too, your Ladyship," the old man said, bowing stiffly. "One day, perhaps, we'll be able to look inside the body without cutting it first. Now? We can only guess."

"Another medical miracle, my friend? What shall we do with cholera at an end, or measles no longer decimating a whole population? There will be no use for those of your profession." An imp of humor showed in her eyes for just a second.

"I'm sure that there will always be a place for those of my profession, my dear," he replied, the formality of the previous moment replaced by friendship. He nodded at Katherine and left the room to make arrangements for the child.

"I would wish that were not true," Miriam said, glancing at the door beyond which Edward had disappeared. "Would it not be a wonderful world if there were no disease, no grinding poverty?" For a moment, Katherine wondered if the other woman addressed her, or was merely voicing her thoughts aloud. "As it is, I fear that this child's death will forever remain on my conscience."

"You cannot blame yourself for the actions of your driver, ma'am."

"Thank you, child, but I feel my own share of guilt." She smiled wanly. "If nothing else, it was a series of coincidences that led to that poor child's death. I, too, played a part in it."

"My governess used to say that there was no such thing as coincidence. She said that what looked like happenstance was the hand of God acting to put a plan into motion." For a moment, Constance's face appeared brightly in her mind, her eyes sparkling with intelligence, her angular face earnest and eager.

The countess eyed her unwilling guest with interest. Perhaps the governess had been correct.

"Tell me a little about yourself, my dear," Miriam said, as she motioned to a straight backed chair opposite her.

Katherine sat and pondered how to respond. The older woman's regal appearance, immaculately coiffed white hair, and severely tailored gown spoke of wealth and privilege, yet her warm blue eyes glittered with curiosity, not malice. The chiseled lips softened in compassion, not disdain. As she was contemplating her answer, the countess spoke again.

"Perhaps I should put this on a more businesslike footing, child," she added, having noted Katherine's hesitation and wishing to put the girl at ease. "Have you, perhaps, come to London seeking employment?"

Katherine looked down at her hands, twisted nervously together, and made a conscious effort to unclench them. She smoothed down her ugly brown dress and wished she appeared more presentable. Money had been scarce to nonexistent in the past year; fripperies like pretty dresses were luxury items when weighed against food and shelter. She had wanted to look practical, hadn't she, and more importantly, older on this trip to London. An unwilling grin brushed across her face as she thought about the past two days sleeping upright in a jostling carriage. Her bone-deep fatigue added to her years as nothing else could.

"I had thought," she said in the silence, "to become a governess."

"Have you no family, my dear?" Miriam Lattimore could read the words that went unspoken. Genteel poverty screamed from the folds of the once-fashionable dress now dyed to hide wear and stains; it shouted from the demure repose of the figure of the young woman. Whoever she was, she had been raised well. Her nails were clean, and it was obvious that her shoes, now covered with the dust of London, had once been carefully polished.

But more importantly, she had cried for a little boy. A stranger who had stolen from her.

"No," Katherine said simply. The effort of explanation was too much. The influenza epidemic had taken her father, then her mother, then Constance. Only when there was no one but herself left at Donegan Castle did it dissipate.

It seemed too much to say. The grief that she had felt for the the past year, coupled with the difficult journey, then the trauma of the little boy's death, seemed to deplete what reserves she had left.

"And your servants?" Miriam asked with implacable gentleness.

"There were no servants left since last spring." There had been no funds to pay them, and Katherine would not ask for loyalty from people who had to make provisions for their own families.

"You do not mean to say you have been alone all this time?" Miriam's voice was horrified. Although her husband's demise had come as a surprise and a secret relief, she had never faced the possibility of being alone. First, there were the children, then the countless relatives who seemed to multiply each year, and finally, a score of friends.

"Have you no friends, no acquaintances to come to your aid?" If Katherine had known Miriam Lattimore, she would have recognized the gentle prompting for what it was—a masterful technique for discovering the most information in the least amount of time. It was a ploy that Miriam had perfected over the years, which had saved countless hours and aggravation in rearing three very headstrong children. However, as quickly as she ascertained information, she was also very reluctant to divulge it. People confided in her for the simple reason that she never betrayed their confidences.

"No, there is no one." Katherine stated the fact baldly, without emotion, but the loss of her family still shone in her eyes. It was grief and something else, which brought to mind another face and another pair of luminous eyes. Miriam almost exclaimed aloud when she realized where she had seen that look before.

"Tell me, dear," the countess asked abruptly, "do you like the country?"

Katherine smiled. The first unrestrained smile in months, but Miriam didn't know that. She only knew that the smile was incredibly lovely, and it illuminated the younger woman's face.

"After the last two hours, I am more sure than ever that I adore the country."

Miriam smiled warmly at Katherine, as if to dispel other, less pleasant memories.

"And why, my dear, have you chosen the role of governess?"

"I am afraid that my education is the only asset I have."

Miriam smiled. The child did not realize that her greatest asset was her beauty. Sunlight tinged her auburn tresses into flame. Russet eyes peeped out from beneath winged brows and long, fanlike lashes. Her full coral lips curved enchantingly over white, even teeth. Despite the dress, and the haphazard hairstyle, and the nervous tension, Katherine before her exuded a womanliness that would only ripen with time. Time, and a little sustenance. Her speech was refined, if tinged with the lilting accent of the border. Even the fatigue evident on her face did not detract from her allure.

"My child," the Dowager Countess of Moncrief said imperiously and impulsively, "I have a proposition for you."

* * *

Katherine was to discover that Miriam Lattimore rarely allowed much time to elapse between an idea and its execution, which is why she was bundled up into an immense traveling coach at sunrise the next day.

Within an hour, the countess was breakfasting with one of her favorite people.

Despite her genial air of friendliness, she was no fool. Survival in a family like hers would not have been possible unless one was as wily as a fox, as cute as a cuddly kitten, and about as threatening as a newborn puppy. Life had taught her to trust her instincts. Her long dead husband had taught her to trust no one. Therefore, she saw no paradox in hiring a young woman fresh from the country and then obtaining advice about her actions from her solicitor.

"Well, Duncan, what do you think?" the countess asked, having apprised him of the salient facts in the matter.

"Miriam," he said, one eyebrow wiggling upwards, "how I do wish you wouldn't rush pell-mell into these situations and then inform me. Why do you never call upon me first?"

The familiarity of long friendship—Duncan McCorkle had known the countess when she was simply Miriam, the neighbor with braids flying, impossibly horse mad, and the best tree climber in the district—warmed the edge of censure in his voice.

"Duncan, be serious. You know I don't need you to tell me what to do. I simply want you to tell me if I've done right. There is a difference, you know."

"You want absolution, old girl. Or forgiveness," he said wryly. "I always marvel at how you never ask permission. In this case, I cannot but believe that you haven't done right at all. After all, you don't know this young woman.

How do you know she won't abscond with all the silver and leave Mertonwood stripped bare?"

"She can have all the blasted silver, as long as she loves Julie," Miriam said, her look of irritation making her blue eyes appear almost cold. Duncan was not dismayed. He had seen that look before and conceded that it was highly effective. It did not, however, sway him in the slightest. "I don't know on paper, dear friend, but I know here, and here." She touched her chest, then her temple, with one slender finger. "That's what counts, after all."

Not really, he thought, but did not voice the words. He would investigate this latest find of Miriam's, and then if there was anything the earl should know, he would ensure he did. The long years of friendship not withstanding, there were times in which women should simply trust that men knew best.

Miriam eyed her friend with a knowing look. "Get that look of male superiority off your face, Duncan, or I'll toss this jar of marmalade at you."

There were times, she thought, in which it was more prudent to forget titles and simply be Miriam.

He glanced at her, saw the steely determination in her eyes, remembered too many times when he had been the object of her irritation, and sighed.

Chapter 2

The fifth Earl of Moncrief didn't give a tinker's damn that the front steps of Mertonwood had been washed down with lye or that the entrance drive had been newly raked. He hadn't cared when he led Monty into the stable that it was clean and smelled as fresh as a meadow. He really didn't even care that his greatcoat was splashed with mud, that his hair was slicked down with rain, or that his underclothing felt as if it had been worn for a week. There were only two things in life he cared about at this moment: a brandy four fingers high and to see Julie once and for all. Everything else, including all the discomforts he had suffered in the last three hours, paled in comparison.

He wondered what sort of missive would placate his mother. Something that would convince her he had performed his fatherly duty, that his illegitimate daughter was in good hands, that he had personally assayed her care and comfort. Something that would silence his mother and let him go about the business of living his life in relative peace. That duty would have to wait, however, until after the brandy.

He nodded at his stunned butler in some surprise. Good God, but Townsende should have been pensioned off years ago, he thought, as the old man took his greatcoat and almost dropped to the floor from the weight of it. He shrugged out of his form-fitting waistcoat and entered the drawing room, heading unerringly for the decanter of brandy on the sideboard. No valet, no attendants; only he and one sodden horse had made the breakneck journey from Moncrief.

He yanked on the bellpull and wondered what ancient servant would shuffle forth. He was pleasantly surprised when a pink cheeked buxom lass appeared.

"You have managed to impress me with your subservience," he said, in the middle of her third curtsy. "You can cease at any moment," he said when she bobbed again, the edge of her apron clutched between two beefy looking fists.

The Exeter was due in port in the next three days, and here he was, playing games with the parlormaid.

"Townsende," he yelled as he waved the maid away. She scuttled to the door in fright, turning wide eyes upon him as if he'd just grown a wicked set of horns upon his brow.

The elderly man entered the room with the gait of a crab.

"Yes, your lordship?" White eyebrows punctuated an otherwise expressionless face. Not so the eyes. They were faded blue, but held a spark of something that looked suspiciously like humor in their depths. Freddie was not amused, nor was he tolerant, at this particular moment, of his butler's sense of humor.

"Find someone in this mausoleum to draw my bath and fetch me something palatable to eat."

"Yes, your lordship."

"Someone who does not bob quite so much."

"Yes, your lordship."

"You," he intoned, extending one long arm with an equally extended finger pointing at the sunken chest of his ancient servant, "will not be the one. Do you understand?"

"Yes, your lordship."

"If all we have in residence are the stable boys, have one of them do it, do you understand?"

Townsende had the good sense to only nod.

It was his own fault, Freddie thought. Moncrief was his home when he was not forced to attend to business in London. He was responsible for seventeen parcels of land throughout England, five of which sported ancient houses such as Mertonwood. Granted, it was a profitable little jewel of an estate, prosperous farm land surrounding the house on three sides, the fourth occupied by a thick wood. But the damned place carried too many memories, too many ghosts that traversed its halls and cavorted in the stables. He hadn't been back here since his wife died, but it wasn't for the love of Monique that he had avoided the place. It was fury, plain and simple.

It hadn't seemed practical to maintain a full staff at a residence he never visited, which now accommodated a new nurse and one small baby.

Now, it looked as though he would have to pay the price for a little fiscal frugality.

"Have the master's suite prepared, Townsende," he said on a long sigh, and the elderly man nodded again and shuffled toward the kitchen.

Freddie glared at the half-witted, buck-toothed nursery-maid, who stared back at him with frightened eyes. So far, he had been nearly drowned in a downpour that rivaled Noah's flood, then greeted by the most pathetic of ancient creatures who made no secret of the fact that he enjoyed every jot of the Earl's discomfort and discomfiture. Then, he was nearly scalded to death in an oversized tub which his father had paid a fortune to have installed and which took too many buckets of water to adequately fill. Next, he had eaten a barely adequate luncheon of bread and cheese, with the explanation served on the side by a stammering cook that most of the staff had already eaten the leftovers of the main meal and would that "carry you over to dinner, m'lord?" When he had attempted to change into something warm and dry, he discovered that all of his old clothes, and his father's, had been given to the poor. Finally, clad in damp clothing that smelled suspiciously like horse, he had come to the nursery to find his daughter, only to be told that his daughter wasn't tucked away in her crib—she was with Miss Katherine.

And where the hell was Miss Katherine? Not anxiously awaiting his arrival. Certainly not standing in the foyer waiting to greet him with his daughter in her arms. Or had his mother not bothered to tell the elusive Miss Katherine that her employer would be paying a visit?

He heard the directions to Miss Katherine's room with a barely tolerant ear, skipping over the sibilant "*s*'s" that rolled from the nurserymaid's protruding lips like a tortured snake. By the time he was at the door, he was beyond courtesy, eons past decorum, and spoiling for a fight. The soft response to his knock did not diffuse his irritation, but the sight that met his eyes banished all trace of anger.

It stopped his heart.

Silhouetted against the afternoon's mist sat the most perfect picture of Madonna and child that he had ever seen. An auburn haired siren sat in an enveloping wing chair, its robin-blue upholstery a perfect backdrop for the tendrils of soft reddish curls that spread to her shoulders. She wore a yellow wrapper that had been pushed open by the blanket-shrouded fingers of a sleeping babe. The infant's cheek rested against a creamy bosom and her rosebud mouth lay open against a lace covered breast. The woman's lips grazed the golden curls of the child. At his entrance she froze, and attempted to cover herself without waking the baby.

"Who are you? What are you doing in my room?" It was difficult to sound irate while whispering, but somehow she managed. He only smiled at her autocracy.

"Who are you, and what are you doing in my house?" he whispered back, approaching the two in silent, measured steps. When he stopped, the fabric of his trousers brushed against her exposed knees. He looked down at her for a long moment, taking in the gentle swell of bosom, the creamy skin, the soft full lips, the angry, glittering eyes.

Her gaze widened. From the tips of his rain soaked boots to the top of his tousled hair, he was huge and wide.

In the lower hall between the dining room and the small sitting room, was a collection of family portraits, aligned so that space had been left for the portrait of the current earl. Perhaps if they had been of better quality, they would have been hung at his ancestral home, but they were amateurish in the kindest of statements, hideous in the most truthful. She knew each ancestral portrait, however, looking for signs of familial attachment in Julie's budding face. The first Earl of Moncrief, a rogue with coal-black hair, an ironic twist to his lips, and a pair of glittering green eyes, stared out at her from one of the oldest portraits.

Katherine gasped. There was no question of his identity. "You look just like the first earl."

"Quite," he said dryly, paying absolutely no attention to what she was saying. The sudden movement of the baby had created a diversion, capturing his attention as nothing else could. A tiny face wrinkled in dismay, and rooted close to warm, swelling flesh. The lace on Katherine's chemise sagged, leaving an ample glimpse of heaving breast and one coral-tipped nipple. He wondered if she knew that her lips and her nipples were exactly the same shade.

She glanced down at herself and flushed.

He grinned, noting that the blush of her cheek now joined the retinue.

"I presume you have come to see your daughter."

He did not speak, but bent forward from the waist and stroked the sleeping baby's cheek, trailing a finger down its plump expanse until he touched her tiny, pert nose. The fact that Julie's face was resting on a delicate spot did not occur to Katherine until she felt the unmistakable pressure of a much larger finger pressing against her nipple.

She flushed again, with anger.

He grinned again, unrepentantly.

She stood abruptly with Julie in her arms, a remarkable feat considering that she had to catch her gaping wrapper with one arm and hold onto Julie with the other. The baby was not happy at the interruption and began to fret with tiny snuffling sounds. Julie's father was still standing much too close. There was only one thing to be done. She handed Julie to her father, bending his reluctant arms into position to cradle the child. She smiled brightly at his look of discomfiture, while her freed hands allowed her to tie the belt of her wrapper securely.

"Your daughter, my lord," she said, and walked across the room to the open door. "Shall I call you when her dinnertime is near?"

"Good God, woman, what do I do with a baby?"

"May I suggest that now is a bit late to be considering that?" Katherine closed the door firmly behind him, the noise loud enough to wake Julie for good. She took umbrage at the cautious hands that held her, and squalled loud enough for Katherine to hear her from the other side of the door.

By the time Katherine opened the door fully dressed moments later, Julie was screaming.

"Here, let me take her," she said, as Julie squirmed in tense arms.

"I think she's wet me," he said in disgust. He handed the baby over to Katherine with his hands under her tiny arms, attempting to avoid contact with the portion of her anatomy that was undeniably soaked.

"I'm not surprised," Katherine said with a small smile, "It does happen, you know."

"Not to me. In fact, I think it's a first." Upon his damp shirt was another, wetter spot. His lip curled as he pulled it away from his skin with two fingers. The Earl of Moncrief was not in the best frame of mind. He stank, and he was hungry, tired, and irritated beyond measure by the fresh faced and poised young beauty standing serenely in front of him, his smock-draped daughter cooing into her neck.

It was not a condition he cared for.

"Did you not have younger brothers or sisters, my lord?" Katherine held the baby against her shoulder, absently patting her bottom, cradling her head in the crook of her neck.

"I do, but I was not summoned to the nursery whenever their nappies needed changing," he replied, curtly.

"Pity," Katherine called over her shoulder as she closed the door in his face. "I do so dislike incompetent men."

She heard him yelling for Townsende in a voice that thundered through the hallways and through her ears, reaching the tiny voice of reason squirming somewhere in the more rational part of her brain.

What on earth had she done?

She managed to avoid the earl for the rest of the evening by the simple expedient of staying cloistered in her room. It was the first time she hadn't put Julie down for the night and she missed the ritual of telling her a story, even though Julie was much too young to understand. The simple truth of the matter was that unless Katherine got her reactions to the earl under control, she could not trust herself in his company. He had touched her, intimately, and leered at her with his devil's grin, but she had never been so caustic to any person, let alone an employer.

Despite the countess's intervention, Katherine was very aware that it was the earl she needed to impress. It was he who paid her salary, and it was his decision, or whim, that could cause her trunk to be packed and herself summarily dismissed on the spot.

Then why, knowing all this, had she responded to the man the way she had? It was as though when he spoke, some bell went off in her head. Prudence was suffocated and stupidity marched in and sat down in the front row of her brain.

The next morning, when she was certain he had departed Mertonwood, Katherine went to the kitchen to fetch Julie's porridge. On the way past the gallery, she once again stopped in front of the picture of the first earl. Ignoring the heavy tray and its contents, she stared at the picture for the longest time.

"You are a handsome rogue, aren't you?" she said aloud to the portrait, a small smile curving the corners of her lips. "And you know it, too, don't you, you devil?"

"Thank you," a warm voice spoke just behind her ear. She almost dropped the tray, but steadier hands reached out from behind her and grasped it before it fell. It remained as a barricade in front of her, his wide chest a solid wall in the back, effectively trapping her against him.

"You startled me." It was more an accusation, he thought, than a statement. The top of her head reached only to his shoulders, but what was pressed against him was softly scented and all woman.

"Please let me go," she said quietly, determined not to say anything untoward. Determined, also, not to give in to the nervousness that his presence caused. She could feel the hard imprint of his body against hers. Twice now, he had bent the bonds of propriety. And twice, she had done nothing about it. "Please." Some hint of vulnerability in her tone made him bite back the teasing remark he'd been about to make.

"Certainly," he said calmly, stepping back and allowing her to pass. "You only had to ask." He grinned, a dazzling white grin that crinkled the lines around those magnificent green eyes, making him appear younger.

Only when she had reached the first landing did she allow herself to stop and gain her breath. She closed her eyes and balanced the tray, steadying herself against the sudden weakness in her knees.

"Are you all right?" No, she wasn't. Between Julie's teething and her own panicked thoughts, she had spent a nearly sleepless night. She opened her eyes to find him staring up at her, the grin still in place, his eyes strangely darkened to a deeper green. Was such a thing possible?

"I thought you were gone," she said baldly. She meant forever. He knew exactly what she meant.

He leaned against the banister and surveyed her. "I find that I have important duties to attend to here."

"Such as?" She stepped away from the wall.

"Do you always question your employers, Katherine? Is nothing sacrosanct with you? Is everything open to discussion, to debate? Do you not ever simply obey?"

"You know, my lord," she said, the acid of irritation eating away at any pretense of civility, "I have the distinct impression that you are playing with me, like a cat would a mouse."

He laughed outright. "No, Katherine, not a cat. A tiger, perhaps, but never just a cat."

"You do not dispute the analogy, however." The tray was getting heavier, and she wanted to escape. No, she must escape, before the charm he exuded found a toehold in her mind. Before she recognized that their repartee was strangely exciting.

Too late, Katherine.

"No, I do not dispute it," he replied, looking up at her, his grin faded to a small smile, the hunter-green of his eyes intent with some undefined emotion. Warning?

She left him then, leaning negligently against the banister, his eyes deepening with the light of battle, his lips curved in a smile of anticipation.

Julie was fretful all morning with teething pains. Katherine found that her mood echoed the baby's. She paced with the child, walking the length of the nursery and back so many times that she wagered the distance was halfway to London by the time Julie finally settled down. She laid her in her cradle and covered the tiny bottom that stuck straight up in the air, patting it gently before she turned away.

"If we have thome laudanum, Mitth Katherine, the wouldn't thuffer tho," Julie's wet nurse lisped.

"I won't give a baby laudanum, Sara. But maybe some whiskey would help. Just a little to rub on her gums."

Which was why she found herself tiptoeing down the stairs to the drawing room, entering the room with the caution of a sneak thief. Only when she was certain that the earl was not inside did she enter and approach the sideboard. She poured just a little whiskey into one of the cut glasses.

"Tippling so early, Katherine? I suppose somewhere in the Empire the sun has already set."

Was it her fate to be confronted by this man all day? Katherine sighed and turned. "It is not for me, my lord," she said. Somewhere, he had found clean clothing. The white linen shirt and black, form-fitting pants, accentuated his coloring. The man looked like a pirate. All he needed was a cutlass and a knife clenched between his teeth.

"Oh? Are you sneaking rations of grog for the servants, then?"

"I'm not sneaking, period."

"You gave a wonderful performance of mouselike steps,

then." He joined her at the sideboard and poured a small brandy for himself. "I hate to see a lady drink alone. Join me?" He tipped the brandy to his mouth.

She stared at the strong column of his neck, the corded muscles, and watched as he drank.

"It's not for me" she repeated, her voice strangely tight. "It's for Julie."

"Good God! Are you giving the baby spirits?" His eyes lightened as he looked at her in horror.

"No," she hastened to correct his impression. "She is teething and I was just going to rub a little on her gums. It deadens the pain, you see, and it's so much safer than laudanum."

"Have you tried oil of cloves? I hear that helps."

She glanced at him in surprise. "No, I didn't know that. I'll ask Cook if she has any."

"If she doesn't, try grinding up some cloves first. I know it's deucedly expensive, but try it first, before the whiskey. If it doesn't work, then you can resort to spirits."

She regarded him with suspicion. "How do you know about teething pain?"

"You do not have to be a baby, Katherine, to have suffered from toothache. Nor have I sprung full grown from my mother's brow." He smiled at her, and she turned away from the magnetism in it. The Earl of Moncrief was a charming rogue when he wanted to be. "Even as handsome as I am."

"You do know I wasn't referring to you, my lord, when I made that comment this morning. It was the first earl who had caught my attention."

"Of course, and the fact that he and I share a remarkable resemblance has nothing to do with it."

"Nothing at all." She grabbed the tumbler of whiskey—just in case—and turned to leave the room.

"I'd like some company at dinner this evening," he said, arresting her departure in mid-step. "Last night's desertion was acceptable. Tonight will not be. I'll expect you there."

"My lord, is it your policy to dine with your servants?"

If all my servants looked like you, possibly. It was a thought that went unvoiced by only a hairbreadth. He did not want to see her eyes widen in anger, and a flush pinken that delightfully smooth skin. He wanted a return of the Madonna, the heavenly peace she had exuded, the air of quiet benediction. It was a hunger that struck him as exceedingly dangerous. And almost irresistible.

"I'm afraid that I'll have to decline, my lord," she said in the face of his silence. "With regrets. You see, I fully anticipate that Julie will keep me up this evening, and I'll need to rest."

"You can rest later," he said, his tone almost brusque. "You will dine with me this evening. I need to ascertain what type of person I'm entrusting with the care of my daughter, you see. Call it an interview of sorts."

"An interview? Have you not decided that I am worthy of the position?" She was appalled.

Visions of creamy limbs entwined around his, coral-tipped nipples touching his lips, sighs of wonder and passion, clouded his thoughts for a moment. That was the only position the delightful Miss Sanderson should occupy.

"Just be there, Katherine. For once, don't argue with me."

It sounded so much like one of Constance's admonitions that she fell silent and walked out of the room.

Due to the countess's insistence that six months of her salary be advanced for incidentals, Katherine boasted two new dresses. Neither one of them was appropriate for formal occasions, but both were more than adequate for a country dinner. Abigail, one of the young maids imported from the village, insisted upon helping her dress, a function she had adequately performed for herself in the three months she had been at Mertonwood.

"I don't know what the fuss is about," she told the young maid crossly. Abigail had just informed her that the earl had ordered a sumptuous dinner with no less than five courses. The very last thing she wanted to do was to have a long, involved dinner with the Earl of Moncrief.

Abigail managed to coax her thick hair into curls, and piled it on top of her head. Only her adamant protests prevented the girl from powdering it, a fashion that had lost favor decades ago. As it was, her hair was swept up onto the sides of her head and fastened with her mother's tortoise shell combs—the only thing of sentimental value left to her, since they had been in her reticule and not in her valise the day she'd come to London. Tiny emerald chips adorned the flat edges of the combs, and she thought them too formal to wear, but Abigail oohed and aahed so fervently that she gave in, finally.

The green wool gown was simply constructed with a fitted bodice that flared at the hips. When she had the dress made, she had been thinner. Now, Katherine smoothed the fabric over her bodice, feeling overly snug there. Pulling and poking and having Abigail yank the dress from the hem didn't change anything. She looked down at herself. Each slight ridge was accentuated by the deep green material. Compounding the poor fit was the fact that the dress was also too long; she'd not the time nor the inclination to hem it.

"Abigail," she said, twisting around and pulling at the waist with a final jerk, "this dress is much too tight. I can't possibly wear it, and we certainly do not have time to alter it."

"Don't you worry, Miss Katherine. Just wear your shawl, and his lordship will never notice." Abigail had undergone a transformation where the earl was concerned. Nerves had given way to anticipation.

It wasn't his lordship Katherine was worried about. It was the knowledge that her breasts were outlined high and firm, and that her nipples poked into the soft material as if they were tiny sword points. How could she possibly maintain her composure while feeling this way?

She let Abigail tie the soft gold sash around her waist. Katherine fastened the tiny gold earbobs to her ears and glanced at herself in the mirror. With her shawl gripped tightly in front of her, she looked presentable. No, better than presentable, she thought with less modesty and more honesty. Perhaps the glow in her cheeks was due to the sudden warmth in the room, or perhaps it was caused by anticipation of the evening. Regardless of the cause, it brought a sparkle to her eyes.

Before descending to the dining room, she visited Sara in the nursery. Julie was still sleeping fitfully. With final instructions to Sara to call her if Julie awakened, she descended the three flights to the main floor. She was so conscious of her footing in the overly long skirt that she did not see the earl until she was nearly at the foot of the stairs. She stopped when they were eye to eye. His, a deepening green, narrowed and faintly calculating. Hers, a warm amber, widening with each moment that passed silently between them.

"Did you know," he asked, the timbre of his voice low and resonant, "that you are wearing Moncrief colors?" His eyes dropped to the tight bodice of her dress, visible now that the shawl had dropped to her elbows. Her nipples strained against the soft wool, lengthening as he stared. He looked up into her face again, and her color turned from rose to crimson.

"No, I didn't know." Why was her mouth so dry, and the words themselves seeming to stick in her throat?

"I suspected not," he said calmly, and held out his arm as if she were titled like he, and required such courtesies. "Green and gold does, however, suit you perfectly," he said, as she hesitated and then placed her hand upon his arm. They entered the dining room.

She muttered some grateful inanity, and allowed him to seat her to the right of him. She looked to the end of the long table, and wondered if her placement so close to him was exactly proper. Proper? From the moment she had met the earl nothing had been proper.

He pulled out the chair for her, and with a nod dismissed Townsende. As she sat, his fingers brushed her shoulders. It was a fleeting touch, and she should not have felt it through the thick wool, but somehow she did. As he moved to his own chair, his hand skimmed the nape of her neck. Another gentle touch, but devastating in its result.

It was the dress. The bodice was too tight, an open invitation. It was the dress that stifled her breathing and made the room too warm, too heated. It was difficult to catch her breath, or to still the trembling in her hands.

Townsende shuffled into the room bearing the first course, as the footman poured the wine.

"Are you accustomed to wine at meals, Katherine?" her host inquired with lazy charm, watching her over the edge of the goblet. She picked up her own and drank thirstily from it.

"Let us say that I am not unaccustomed to it, my lord."

"Since we are dining *en famille* so to speak, shall we dispense with formality? You may call me Freddie."

It was not the wine that caused her to giggle. It was the idea of addressing this imposing beast beside her by a name as inappropriate as Freddie. Freddie was the name of a beagle pup with outsized feet and ears that brushed the floor. Or a guffawing squire with a beet-red nose and a waistcoat to match, who pinched young ladies during recitals and reeked of rum. Freddie? No, never.

"No," she said truthfully, "I could not possibly call you Freddie."

"You object to my name, Katherine?" His eyes narrowed,

and his face flushed beneath his tan. If she didn't know better, she would have thought that the earl was disquieted.

She suspected it took more than candor to cause him embarrassment. After all, she thought, recalling the tales that circulated about him, this was the man who had seduced an innocent, and when she became pregnant, calmly announced to the world that he had no intention of compounding one mistake with another. And when the object of his seduction had died unexpectedly in childbirth, this was the rogue who calmly ignored the vicious rumors and set his infant daughter up in a house far away from the spying eyes and tattling tongues of society. Part of the story of the earl's outrageous conduct had been parlayed to her by the countess, but the remainder had been eagerly told by the chattering servants, none of whom seemed to hold any censure in their hearts for the man seated to her left.

"May I speak frankly, my lord?" she asked finally, toying with the tines of a fork, unaware of the smile that wreathed his mouth at her absentminded gesture.

"When have you not?" he asked wryly.

"Then here it is. I could envision a thousand names for you before my fevered brain would latch upon Freddie. It simply will not do."

"Oh? Pity my mother had not consulted you at my birth."

"Pish, you know I'm so much younger than you. Do not be absurd." She sipped at her wine. The room was growing warmer and the wool was cloying.

"We have not yet begun our dinner, and not only have you maligned my name, but I have been firmly placed in my dotage. Would you agree to abstain from attacking my character until dessert?"

"If I were you, my lord, I'd beg for a longer reprieve. From what I've learned of your character, it could not stand up to a drubbing."

His bark of laughter was surprising. Almost as unexpected as the shiver that trailed up her spine at the look in his eyes. They did not mirror anger; instead, they were filled with something strangely like admiration.

She must stop drinking this wine, Katherine thought, as she took one more sip.

"I was not maligning your name, my lord, and you know full well you aren't in your dotage." Her spoon created a figure eight pattern in the heavy cream soup. She concentrated on the bowl and did not see him motion for the footman to fill her glass again. "I merely commented on the inappropriateness of your name."

"Explain." He leaned back in his chair, folded his arms across his chest, and watched her intently.

"What is your middle name?"

"Allen. Froedrich Allen Lattimore." Until this moment, he'd never thought the whole lacking. Nor had he ever thought himself inappropriately labeled. Freddie had simply been a name.

He watched as she took another sip of the potent wine, and wondered if the flush on her face was mimicked elsewhere. Would she be as warm on every inch of her flesh?

"That is a little better, I suppose. It is a rather nondescript name, though, isn't it? Lattimore is the best of the three. Would you mind if I addressed you as Lattimore?"

"Very much. I would prefer you called me a pet name rather than my surname, Katherine. It reminds me of when I was in short pants. Or at school." At her look of incredulity, he laughed.

"You will have to admit it is rather difficult to envision, my lord," she said, studying his features carefully as if trying to discover the little boy he had once been. It was impossible.

"Call me anything you wish, just stop *my lord*'ing me. You are as bad as that insipid maid who greeted me yesterday.

I am not such an ogre that I wish to be reminded of my consequence at every waking moment."

He did not need to, did he, being as large and as overpowering as he was. Anyone in the same room as the Earl of Moncrief could not fail to notice his consequence. Right now, it was playing havoc with her sense of survival, a trait honed to sharpened steel these past six months.

"A myriad of possibilities come to mind. Rabbits are very nice, but you do not seem very bunny–like. Hawk would be more appropriate, but hawks are such noble-looking birds."

"You do not think me noble, Katherine?" His eyes narrowed, and he wondered what tales she had been told.

"I think you too noble, my lord," she replied, smiling, then took another sip of wine. She was reassured by the fact that the level in the glass had barely moved.

She teased him with a smile. "If we were to give you a name that echoed your nobility, then think how pompous you could become. No, we need to think of some sobriquet that would not denigrate your character and, at the same time, would give you something to aspire toward, like humility." She steepled her fingers in front of her, the second course forgotten as she closed her eyes and thought. The earl motioned to the footman who filled her empty glass once again, before leaving the bottle beside the earl and slipping from the room.

"I have never thought of humility as a goal." The sliver of lamb, drenched in curry sauce, reached his mouth without his eyes leaving Katherine's. He ate with the same economy of movement that he did everything, she thought. Lean, graceful movements, like a cat.

"I have it, my lord," she said, smiling brightly as if startled by a revelation. "The perfect name. It suits you like a tailored waistcoat."

His fork stopped in midair as he watched her warily.

"Tabby. Don't you think it's perfect?" Some imp of

mischief prompted her to lean toward him and softly mimic, "Meow."

His full lips curved upwards as he stared at her pursed mouth.

"Same family, perhaps, but I choose another."

"Oh, and what would your choice be?"

"A tiger. As I recall, I mentioned it to you before."

Katherine squinted at him, concentrating on those green eyes and that strange, lopsided grin of his. Yes, he was tigerlike. Strong, predatory, and infinitely dangerous to whatever quarry he pursued. And she had the most absurd feeling that she was being stalked.

Constance had periodically warned her about the impulsive side of her nature. It was a personality defect she had struggled against all her life, and one that she had not exhibited in the last six months. She had been responsible. She had been mature. She had adhered to each rule, whether written or implied. Yet this man, this handsome, virile employer of hers, was driving her beyond prudence.

She stood, offering no explanation for her actions, and left the room. He began to stand, to follow her, when she turned and motioned him back to his chair.

"I will return shortly," she said, but gave no other explanation.

In the kitchen, the cook looked at her as though she had lost her mind, but gave her what she wanted. She marched back into the dining room with her burden.

"Cats like cream, my lord." Katherine plunked down the saucer of cream before him, its contents sloshing against the rim. "Even tigers." His laughter echoed in the room as she returned to her chair.

"You are an outrageous young woman," he said, his eyes alight with mischief and that other emotion she still could not name. "I'll bet you gave your governess fits."

"Constance frequently threatened to quit," Katherine admitted, looking down at the tablecloth and feeling about three feet tall. His smile made her feel as young as Julie, and once again she mentally kicked herself for giving in to whatever impulse he seemed to prompt within her. He did it so easily, push her beyond the boundaries of being a well-bred young woman, straight into being a hoyden again. She could easily imagine succumbing to his charm, and wondered, for the first time, if tales of his victim were altogether true. He might lure, but she doubted if the victim went unwillingly to the sacrifice.

"Do you know what I wish, Katherine?" He dipped one large, long finger in the cream and brought it to his mouth, gently sucking the tip. She could not ignore the gesture, the drop of thick cream rolling so slowly down the expanse of his fingers. She licked suddenly dry lips, a gesture that increased his smile.

She shook her head and finally focused on the full plate before her. She realized that she had not as yet eaten. Good God, was she getting tipsy?

"I wish you nursed Julie," he said, his voice low and stirring the hairs on the back of her neck. "I wish that your breasts gave her suckle." There was not a sound in the room as she turned and met his eyes in shock. She could not look away, even though she knew she should. Even though her breasts, the object of his discussion and his look, felt as though they were blossoming beneath his interest.

"I could place my lips upon your nipple and, with the touch of my tongue, coax the milk from your lovely breasts. That's the kind of cream that tigers really prefer."

She stood abruptly, almost causing the chair to overturn. "You are the one who is being outrageous, my lord," she said in a loud voice. Too loud.

She left the room before he could speak, but not before she saw the smile hovering about his lips.

Chapter 3

The next afternoon, a windblown, exhausted young man arrived at Mertonwood on a fresh and fiery-looking horse. It was Jeremy Lattimore's contention that all his brother's horses had been sired in the pits of Hell, and each one of them should be shot at dawn. Of course, the fact that he hated the beasts and much preferred a stately carriage to being atop one had no bearing in the matter. As his father's son, Jeremy had been prepared to judge horseflesh since he had been in knee pants. The problem was, he genuinely hated horses, and his brother's in particular. It was a secret loathing that was evident each time he was forced onto one of the huge, mean-tempered sons of Satan.

His companion on this mission, a tall and lithe man of indeterminate age, looked on in genuine amusement as Jeremy attempted to dismount with the dubious assistance of the aging Townsende. The elderly butler had grasped the reins of the horse and was trying, without much success, to convince him to remain still. The horse, whose name was Thunder but whom Jeremy had renamed Boswick in honor of a childhood bully whom he had also hated, shifted his head, bared his teeth, and sidled in one direction each time Jeremy had a leg free and was sliding to the ground.

"Good God, man!" Jeremy finally shouted, exasperated, furious with the damn horse and his own ineptitude, and thoroughly routed by the stares of his brother's valet, who sat atop his own horse with all the aplomb of a born horseman. "Don't you have any grooms around here?"

Townsende drew himself up with wounded dignity. "The staff is somewhat limited, sir. I believe they are occupied at the moment." Dropping the reins to the ground, he mounted the steps to the white double doors and disappeared inside without a backward glance.

Jack finally slid from his horse with ease and stood at Boswick's head, stilling the horse until Jeremy could dismount. Valet and gentleman looked steadily at each other before whoops of mirth escaped Jeremy's lips and a quirk of amusement appeared on the solemn older face.

"Good God, I thought he died years ago!" Jeremy turned to the steps and watched the door slam with all the force the old man could muster. Jack only shrugged Gallic shoulders, and handed the reins of both horses to a groom who had suddenly appeared from the other side of the stables.

"Pardon sirs," he said, brushing his cap from his head and bobbing as he took the reins from Jack's hand. He looked, awestruck, at Boswick, soon to be renamed Thunder, and a gasp of admiration escaped white flecked lips. In fact, the man was covered in white paint, as if a blinding snowstorm had struck. "The earl's gots us whitewashing the fences for the paddock, he does," he said in answer to their curious stares. "Never seens a body for paintin' things." With a bow and a scrape, he led the horses away, talking to Thunder in the low, respectful tone appropriate for one of the earl's magnificent thoroughbreds.

Townsende was absent from the foyer; the only person

who met them was Abigail, whose habit of bobbing had been curtailed somewhat due to severe lectures from the housekeeper.

The two men who met her in the entranceway were normal-looking, if a little tired and travel-weary. She smiled at young Jeremy, but it was the older man who intrigued her. He had a look in his eyes that spoke of hidden pain, as if he bore a burden he had carried for a long, long time. She smiled at him, too, hoping that the dimple in her cheeks would coax an answering smile. It did not, and she was strangely miffed when he simply nodded at her and asked in a voice not unlike the earl's if she knew her master's whereabouts.

Only Jack knocked on the library door. Jeremy mounted the stairs to a room he hoped had a real bed with a real fire and the promise of some hot water and some whiskey, not necessarily in that order.

When the earl bade him enter, Jack opened the door, slipped inside the room with practiced ease, and met the handclasp of the man who rose to greet him with the warmth of his own.

"Jack!" the earl said in genuine pleasure. "God, I'm glad to see a friendly face."

"Being in the outlands doesn't seem to have diminished your flair for working, I see," the other man said in a fluid and cultured voice. The desk behind which the earl sat was strewn with papers.

"I think I'm working in desperation, my friend, instead of love for it. It's either the isolation or the incessant cry of a teething baby or that damnable witch who's driving me to accomplish miracles."

"Miss Katherine, I presume?" the other man asked wryly.

"My mother evidently has talked too much. Again."

The nod of the other man brought a quick, rueful smile to the earl's face.

"She should do what other mothers do, retire to the

country,'' he said, and the other man smiled in response. Both knew that, with respect to her children, Miriam Lattimore had her own set of rules. Her son might have acquired the title and trebled their fortune, but he was still her son, and that would never change. One of these days, he often thought, she might treat him as if he were thirty-four instead of still in short pants, but he didn't hold out much hope that that particular behavior would come about soon.

''I know she didn't drop that little gem of wisdom in your ear just to hear herself talk. What did my mother wish to accomplish?''

His friend grinned and, at the earl's gesture, accepted the chair in front of the desk. Alone with the earl, Jack Rabelais let down the almost automatic guard that surrounded him with others. He was more than a secretary, having a working knowledge of most of the earl's businesses. Since the earl prized his privacy, he sometimes doubled as valet. But his most important position in the earl's life was that of friend. He most probably was the only genuine friend the Earl of Moncrief possessed. He neither coveted the earl's wealth or position, nor envied him.

The émigré had once borne the title of count in his native France, the noble equivalent of an earl in England. Years had separated him from his title, the estates in the Loire valley, and the fortune that had gone with them. Years, Bonaparte, and a decimated nobility. He no longer grieved over what he could not have, but he sometimes wept for what might have been. One of those long dead memories was of a young, sweet wife and two infant boys.

''I think she worries about you,'' Jack said, speaking honestly. ''Have you seen the child?''

The earl's face was wreathed in a smile. ''Not only have I seen my daughter, but she has christened me, I'm afraid. But for the last two nights, she had done nothing but scream, poor mite. I have chosen the masculine prerogative and banished myself from the nursery."

"And the nurse?" An eyebrow winged upwards, and the blue eyes twinkled with irreverent humor. Jack Rabelais knew his friend too well. The Earl of Moncrief was obsessive about two things—working and playing. He had devoted sixteen hour days to acquiring a fortune and then expanding it, but he rewarded himself with fine horses, excellent whiskey, and women whose beauty rivaled any Original of the ton. It was that very trait that had brought him to this trouble today. Celeste Cavanaugh had been a beauty all right, and too easily drawn by Freddie's charms. Enough, in fact, to ignore all edicts sternly impressed upon her from the nursery. Jack knew his friend, and he also knew that the earl was not as much to blame as the gossips would have it. Young women tasting passion for the first time, and feeling a tendre for a man gifted with the Earl of Moncrief's looks, sometimes throw caution to the winds and indulge in a little game of seduction themselves. However, the earl had never divulged any details of the lovely Celeste's downfall. And he hadn't asked.

"Well, have you met with Barnen yet?" The earl blessedly changed the subject to business. The less Jack knew of Katherine, the better. He knew his old friend would not approve of his behavior. Hell, he wasn't sure *he* did.

"No, he is still in New Lanark. I understand that he will be visiting London soon. I left word that you'd like to meet with him."

Harold Barnen was a Manchester cotton spinner who had begun a community in New Lanark, Scotland, in 1799. It was an historic undertaking, a model of what factory life could be like if owners showed care and compassion for their employees. Barnen, who had gone to work in his family's cotton mills when he was nine years old, had strong beliefs about what could be accomplished by cooperative ventures. Now a very wealthy man in his early fifties, he was attempting to reform the law itself. The earl had modeled most of his factory villages from these experiments. Although children of the poor had always had to work at whatever undertaking would support them, and add coins to the family's coffers, the new factories blossoming on the English landscape provided a devastating future for the youngest child. Barnen, and the influential men he'd gathered about him, wanted Parliament to enact the first factory laws that would provide guidelines for the more unscrupulous factory owners. Children under the age of nine would not be permitted to work, and no child under the age of twelve would be permitted to work more than twelve hours per shift. At the present time, children barely older than toddlers toiled in the dark, cavernous, fiber-laden air of England's cotton mills.

"We'll probably miss each other again, then," the earl said wearily. If that's the case, I'll just go to New Lanark."

"You've picked the wrong season for it, Moncrief. Better wait until spring." Jack was the only one who had ever addressed him by his titular name. He'd first met the intense young émigré after Jack had enlisted in the English army to fight against Napoleon. They had introduced themselves as they had waited side by side at Waterloo, not long before the gun batteries destroyed what was left of their cavalry regiment.

It was not for his survival skills that Freddie appreciated Jack, but rather for his ability to doggedly pursue his course of action, a single-minded approach he himself emulated. For the first few years after the Reign of Terror had begun in France, Jack's intent had been to protect his family. When that had failed, his goal became more distilled, finite. Jack wanted to single-handedly destroy Napoleon, eliciting a measure of revenge from a world gone mad. That objective had finally been realized. Whatever Jack's personal goals, they remained his secret. Freddie was simply grateful for Jack's companionship and dedication to the Moncrief enterprises.

Katherine was deeply involved in explaining the necessity of scything the grass near the home woods to three of the young grooms, who stood in front of her spotted with whitewash and scowling with an expression not too unlike that of her employer. Julie sat near her in her basket, feet firmly entrenched in her mouth, arms waving with the sheer exuberance of babyhood. She suffered no ill effects from exchanging her days for nights, but the same could not be said for Katherine and Sara, who felt as though they were approximately a week shy of the sleep they needed.

The deprivation might account for the look of irritation she shot the grooms and the edge of her voice as she set them to chopping down the waist-high weeds. It was no wonder that all three were wishing fervently that the baby would either begin crying immediately or fall asleep, so that the interminable lecture would cease. Of course, their actual thoughts were more bluntly phrased.

With a frustrated sigh and the feeling that not one word of what she had said to them made an impression, Katherine waved them away and scooped the precious basket up in her arms, cooing softly to Julie. She was halfway to the rose garden, where she spent most afternoons, when she realized that someone was standing on the steps of the house, staring at her. She could either walk up to him, which seemed rather forward, or remain where she was, which seemed rather backward, or pursue her original plan and continue on to the garden. She decided on the last, reasoning that if whoever it was wanted to converse with her, it was up to him to seek her out.

He did. A young man a few inches shorter than the earl plopped down beside them on the bench, glancing around him at the denuded bushes, and maintained a very polite but bizarre silence. He leaned over the basket and extended a finger to Julie, who grasped it without a pause. Katherine watched him as he made cooing noises to the baby, pursing his lips and plumping out his cheeks in a gesture that made him look almost cherubic. His brown hair slid over a too high forehead, and hazel eyes widened with the effort to charm the baby. He looked up to find Katherine staring at him. He flushed, which only accentuated the impression of youth. He squirmed on the seat for a moment, pulled his collar out from a suddenly perspiring neck, and grinned.

The grin was so unexpected that Katherine smiled back.

"Hello," he said.

"Hello," Katherine answered.

"I'm Jeremy, Freddie's younger brother. Oh, damn, I hate it when I do that. Oh, I beg your pardon," he said, shocked at his lapse of language.

"It's quite all right," Katherine replied with amusement. She could not imagine two less likely brothers.

"I'm forever introducing myself as someone else's something or other." At Katherine's look of confusion, he continued. "Oh, you know. Hello, I'm Freddie's younger brother, or Melissa's older brother, or the countess's younger son, that sort of thing."

"I see." Katherine's smile was warm and welcoming.

"You don't really. You're just being kind. People always seem to be kind around me. Impressed with my consequence. No. Devastated by my charm. Not likely. Thrilled by my manly bearing? Never. But nice? Always, forever, endlessly nice."

Katherine was laughing, as thoroughly charmed by the young man as Julie had been. Her laughter coaxed an answering smile on Jeremy's face. A smile that was soon transformed into echoing laughter.

When Katherine finally recovered her composure, she

leaned across the basket and put her hand on Jeremy's arm.

"I'm Katherine Sanderson," she said, "and I think it's quite wonderful to have people always be nice to you. It must be because they sense you are a nice person."

"Oh, I already know who you are," he said, with more honesty than tact. "Freddie told me to find you. Oh, I say, I didn't mean to sound rude. You see? I'm not even sure I'm nice at all."

Katherine appeared to be genuinely kind, which was fortunate, considering that he had spoken as if his brain were jelly. At least her laughter had not been mocking.

In an effort to excuse his lapse of manners, he continued. A wiser man would have ceased his nervous explanations, but Jeremy Lattimore was too young to have experienced the setdowns that would make him more reserved, and too naive not to speak what was on his mind. "There are things about me I don't like very much," he admitted.

"Oh, I think that's true of everyone, don't you?"

"No. I think some people are quite enamored of themselves. They act as though they're quite pleased with each little thing. I, myself, have many bad habits."

"Come, I don't believe that. You seem a very upstanding young man."

"Aha, you don't know the awful secrets I carry around, then," he said with a mock leer. At least, he intended it to be a leer; it emerged as a combination scowl/smile. Katherine bit her lip to keep from smiling.

"Pray, sir, divulge all." Katherine entered into the spirit of his game.

"Well, for one thing, I swear. You, yourself, can attest to that."

"I can," she nodded, "and it is a detestable habit. Go on."

"Well, I'm not very patient sometimes."

"Excusable. Patience is a virtue, but if all virtues were

attained so easily, then they would cease to be virtues, wouldn't they?"

"All right, I'll concede patience, then. How about this? I hate horses. Loathe,detest, hate the stupid beasts."

"Well . . ." Katherine tipped her finger beneath her chin and cocked her head as if weighing the matter seriously. "I can see how that might cause difficulties, being a gentleman, but I truly don't see it as a bad habit. Perhaps a matter of disposition."

"Mine or theirs?"

Katherine finally allowed herself to smile. "Why, theirs, of course. You, yourself, are a model of rectitude, a veritable paragon in all that is good and pure and manly."

"Do you really think so?" he asked seriously, sitting up straighter on the bench, his gesture of twirling a leaf in front of Julie's gurgling face forgotten at her words.

"Is my opinion so important, then?" she asked, just as seriously.

"As a member of the female species, yes. You see, maybe I can be categorized as nice, after all, but that's hardly the sort of man a woman dreams about. I'm not at all dashing or rakish."

"Like the earl?"

"Exactly," he said, nodding. "It's deuced difficult being younger. Especially with someone like Freddie as your older brother. He seems to do things so effortlessly. Nothing is ever difficult for him. He rides well, he dances well, and the women. . . . Well, some of them have even ruined themselves over him," he said looking down at Julie.

Katherine leaned over the basket and a suddenly quiet baby, and placed her hand on Jeremy's arm. "There are many kinds of men. But the best kind, I think, are the quiet ones. They are the ones with constancy, with devotion. I think any woman would be thrilled to find a nice man who was more than dashing and more than rakish."

"Do you really think so?" His look was hopeful.

"I know so," she said gently. "Is there someone in particular you are hoping to impress?"

"Yes," he said, smiling and looking off into the distance as if the home woods had been transformed into a face. "Am I that transparent?"

"No, not at all," Katherine lied.

"You're a very nice person yourself, Katherine," he said, standing and looking down at the sleeping baby. "It makes what Freddie said even stranger."

"Oh, and what was that?"

"Well, first he told me to invite you to dinner and to say that it would be the four of us, in case you said no. Then he told me to guard my loins, my limbs and my lineage should I tangle with you." He watched with confusion as Katherine tipped her head back into the sun and laughed with no restraint.

Katherine was a delightful dinner companion, Jeremy thought, quite forgetting that in London they would not dine together at all. Here, at Mertonwood, social boundaries seemed to have blurred, and it no longer seemed important that she was just a servant. He watched her across the dinner table with puppylike adoration, well aware that the feelings he had for her did not interfere with what he felt for Beth. He was also well aware that each time he smiled at her, his brother frowned. The kindness of her personality shone through her occasional answering smile. After the way he had behaved like a fool in the garden, she had even allowed him to lead her to dinner and had listened to him as if he had something to say. He felt a tinge of pride at the irritated look on his brother's face. It was about time Freddie realized that he was grown, too. Jeremy was tired of the patient look of wearied resignation on his older brother's face each time he talked to him about something important. After dinner, he was going to broach the subject of Beth, and it was imperative that Freddie take him seriously.

Jeremy wondered idly if his mother had *sent* him to Mertonwood. Instead of allowing his ardor to cool, as she had said, and Beth's to flourish, he mused that it was quite possible he had been manipulated into spending a few days at the old estate. It was rare for the countess to entrust any kind of secret to her younger son, not because she didn't trust him, but because he had the unfortunate ability to see friends in unlikely places. This ability also led him to divulge everything of interest happening presently in his life. As a secret keeper, he was detestable. Yet, as a teller of tales, he was beyond par. Jeremy had the unique talent of being able to soak up atmosphere. He could describe personalities, clothing, moods, and recall dinner conversation with pinpoint precision. Which made him the darling of his sister Melissa, who made him recount each moment of a dinner party, ball, or soiree until she could close her eyes and imagine herself there, too. He imagined that Mama would very much like to hear about this evening, with two of the guests acting politely antagonistic and refusing to look at each other.

Jack thought it very odd, also, but not for the same reason. It had taken exactly five minutes in the company of those two to realize why sparks were flying. The tension in the room could be felt with an outstretched hand, even though young Jeremy valiantly tried to keep the conversation going. Which was difficult, considering that Katherine was quite obviously attempting to ignore the earl.

He watched her with an assessing look. If she thought it strange that the earl's valet sat at table with them, she neither mentioned it nor seemed taken aback. It took him a moment to realize that he had not often dined with governess either. Yet, the young woman seated to the right of the earl was the least likely servant he'd ever seen.

She wore the same green dress that had caused her such

embarrassment the previous night. However, Abigail had worked diligently this morning to alter the bodice with tiny, almost invisible stitches, and it no longer hugged each curve. The earl's first glance had been filled with chiding disappointment, and a tiny smile. Her face was slightly chapped from being in the wind all day and that was the only reason for her color. She was fatigued from having worked steadily all afternoon, and that was certainly the only explanation for the weakness in her lower limbs, and the slight trembling of her hands as she delicately cut her glazed mushrooms. It had nothing to do with the gazes of all three men. One open and boyish, filled with honest delight. The second, studying her surreptitiously beneath lowered lids. The third, glaring at the other two with the unmistakable air of ownership. Jeremy's look was the only one she could countenance, thus, most of her remarks were addressed to him.

"How is your mother, Jeremy?" Since they had started on a first name basis, she saw no reason not to continue in that vein. From the look on his face, the earl evidently disagreed, but before he could object to their familiarity, Jeremy answered with a twinkle in his eye.

"Fine, Katherine," he said, emphasizing her name, "but she had just found Melissa out, I'm afraid. The chit was embarking on a nefarious plot to accompany her friend Priscilla to a ball, I believe."

"Oh, no. She wouldn't be so foolish." Katherine's voice was genuinely concerned. From what she had seen of the countess, she was not a woman to cross.

"Unfortunately, yes. Unfortunately for her, I mean. Now, Mama has delayed her debut. Melissa had only to wait a week or so, but Mama has it in her head to visit Moncrief for the duration. Or at least until the beginning of the regular Season. Melissa hates the country."

"She should have thought of the consequences of her actions beforehand," his older brother stated curtly.

"Yes, but Melissa is young," Katherine interjected, not looking up from the table. "Sometimes the young do foolish things."

Jeremy watched the expression on his brother's face with interest. Freddie was oblivious to the curious looks directed his way as he stared at Katherine's bent head. It was not anger, Jeremy decided, that darkened his eyes and made the frown between his brows appear somehow dangerous. It was not quite passion either, because he'd seen his brother enraptured—albeit temporarily—by one of his newest conquests. If anything, the expression on Freddie's face was of reluctant compulsion. As if Katherine Sanderson held some sort of irresistible lure to the inveterate pursuer. Who was chasing whom, Jeremy wondered.

Jack had no trouble deciphering the look but was concerned about its implications. Katherine was out of her league. If she meant to entice Moncrief, the best way was to ignore him. Despite his very real work habits, the countless hours he devoted to enlarging his fortune, the fact of the matter was that Froedrich Allen Lattimore had never really been denied anything he wanted. He had not been tested by life. Of a certainty, there was the odd little inconvenience, the incident that stirred his conscience, but for the most part, his life had been one without deprivation. If he hungered, he was fed. If he lusted, he was appeased. If he craved, be it woman, mount, estate, or factory, sooner or later, that plum dropped into his lap.

He didn't know the meaning of denial.

Jack could only conclude that Katherine was simply unworldly. He hoped she wasn't that stupid.

"Gather, gather your youth," he quoted obliquely into the tense silence. "Just like this flower, old age your beauty will wither."

"De Ronsard!" Katherine exclaimed, delighted to discover someone else familiar with Pierre de Ronsard's poetry. "Do not forget, *'Vivez, si m'en croyez, n'attendez à demain, cueillez dès aujourd'hui les roses de la vie.*" Her accent was the French of France. Jack looked surprised, then pleased. They exchanged a conspiratorial smile.

"Well, since I don't speak French," Jeremy said petulantly, "would someone please translate?"

Jack complied with a nod, smiling at Katherine as he did so. "Live now, believe me, wait not until tomorrow, gather the roses of life today."

"An adequate philosophy," the earl amended, "but I prefer Publilius Syrus: 'Let a fool hold his tongue, and he will pass for a sage.'" He stared at Jack until the other man's smile changed character. It did not dim, but it grew wiser as he recognized the expression in his friend's eyes. All during the tumultuous relationship with the headstrong Celeste, Moncrief had never been jealous. Even after some of her more celebrated and public assignations, designed to spark some possessive emotion in the earl, he had not acquiesced to her wishes. He had maintained an aloofness during that liaison and others. Jack was worried. This did not augur well, especially not for Katherine.

The Earl thought that his dinner companions were as diverse a group as any professional hostess could assemble. Jeremy, his younger brother, whose innocence still clung to him like an unshed cloak, confused eyes darting among them as if to understand the subtle thrust and parry of unsaid words. His friend Jack, perhaps the most complex person he'd ever known—aristocratic and yet publican, a man whose lineage could be traced back seven generations, but who could tie a cravat with the ease of inbred servitude. Jack was a learned man, but most importantly, he had the ability to grasp salient facts with uncannily quick precision. Which was the reason Jack was the only other person beside himself to know all facets of his business. Which was why Jack should not be seated at this table, watching the byplay between Katherine and himself with knowing and too wise eyes. Katherine, the seductive female who was impulsive and caring, womanly and childish. And lastly himself, one of the five richest men in the British Empire, presiding over a dinner being consumed by two servants and one untried boy, and enjoying every moment of it. Passion and anger were heady lures, and even a fool could recognize those two emotions at this table.

At the end of the meal, Katherine tried to escape from her dinner companions. The gentlemen, however, in deference to her solitary state, eschewed the smoking of cigars and the drinking of port in private. She sighed, wishing they had acceded to custom. It would have made her departure so much less obvious and, of course, easier. Not only was she tired from two nights of being up with Julie, but the imp of mischief had been replaced by a singularly wise voice that urged caution around the Earl of Moncrief. His behavior the night before had managed to shock her, true, but it was her own that humiliated her. At supper with her parents, she had drunk only watered wine. Never had she imbibed quite as many glasses of rich bordeaux, nor had she ever embarrassed herself as thoroughly as she had last night. Her penance had been to be awakened by Julie's screams of discomfort and to be unable to banish the blinding headache accentuated by the baby's cries of pain. What had made her challenge him the way she had? Was it the way his eyes lit up, as if he were world-weary and desirous of some worthwhile occupation? Or was it simply to make him smile? Whatever idiotic reason, she could barely look him in the face now.

To her great relief, the Earl and Jeremy immediately left the room for the library.

Jack entered the room behind her, standing until she sat in one of the two chairs closest to the fireplace. He joined her after pouring himself a small glass of port. "May I get you anything?"

Katherine shook her head, watching him as he sat with fluid grace. He cradled the glass in one hand as he stared into the fire. He turned suddenly, catching her look, and smiled. It was a strange smile, half tinged with sadness, as if the previous gestures had summoned painful memories.

"Tell me about yourself, mademoiselle," he urged, shifting slightly so that he faced her. "How does a young English lady acquire such a delightful French accent? It is not schoolroom French."

"It is if the young English lady is half French," she said, and smiled at his surprised look.

"Then I am pleased. Which of your parents hailed from that most noble of races?" His glance was wry and half mocking.

"My mother. Her family was from Verdun, but she left France in 1798."

"It was a good time to leave," he agreed solemnly. "But you say Verdun? What was her name?"

"Lizette de Bourlange. Why do you ask?"

"Verdun is not that populated, mademoiselle. And I have had friends there. But surely you are incorrect. The de Bourlange family is extensive. To the best of my perhaps faulty recollection, they have managed to retain most of their wealth even after Napoleon. Is it possible that you are mistaken?"

"About my mother's name? Hardly." Her smile was kind.

"Yet, with the force of the de Bourlange family behind you, there would be no necessity for this." He waved his hand around the room as if to encompass Mertonwood, the earl, and her present situation.

"Mr. Rabelais, my mother never spoke of her family. Perhaps she was from the poorer branch. Perhaps their wealth meant nothing to her. When my mother severed her ties to France, she made a new life for herself. As I must. There is no reason to try to find a family which cared so little for one of its own that they would ignore her for twenty years."

"Your pride is important to you, isn't it?" he asked kindly. "There are things that happen in war, mademoiselle, which make the sane act crazy and the crazy to take on an appearance of sanity. Who is to say who should reach out the first hand?"

"I do not wish to reach out a hand, Mr. Rabelais. It is not necessary. I am doing quite well on my own."

"Yes, but perhaps there comes a day when you cannot, as you say, do well on your own. Promise me that you will consider appealing to them. It could not hurt you, and it could benefit you well." She would have been annoyed but for the intent look on her companion's face. Something flickered in his dark eyes, a look of warning, a caution about the future. She nodded only once, a curt nod, but it was enough. The look disappeared, and he relaxed against the back of the wing chair, crossed one leg over the other, and sipped from his glass.

"What about yourself, Mr. Rabelais? How come you to work for the earl?"

"He offers me freedom, noble purpose, and a schedule that promotes forgetfulness. He also gifts me with his friendship. It is a daunting inducement for employment."

"You are a strange man, Mr. Rabelais," Katherine said with great honesty and unconscious cruelty.

"How so?" A man did not wish to be called strange in the presence of young beauty, he thought wryly.

"You are obviously educated and well read. You have the manners of an aristocrat, yet you work as a servant."

"As I might say the same for you," he chided with a warm smile.

She flushed.

"I am a Frenchman, mademoiselle, in a country whose memory is still impregnated with the horrors of a war with the French. Am I too good to dig ditches? Shall I muck stalls? Am I too elevated, or not elevated enough?" He did not allow her to respond. "Besides, there are all types of servitude. There is that of the drinker to the wine, the gambler to a deck of cards, the glutton to a well laden table. Honest work should not denigrate a man. It is when he attempts to gain something for nothing that he should be censured both by himself and by the world."

"And yet, you would have me find a family I do not know in order to escape honest work." Her tone was mildly chiding.

For the first time that night, his eyes mirrored his smile. "Touché, mademoiselle," he said, half bowing from the waist.

She laughed, generous in defeat.

They sat in companionable silence for long moments, until the silence was punctuated by the sound of uncontrolled yelling coming from the direction of the library. Katherine glanced at Jack with a worried frown. It was difficult to tell who was shouting the loudest, Jeremy or the Earl. Although the exact words were difficult to decipher, the tone was not. Both men were livid.

She stood and extended her hand to the Frenchman. As was proper, he did not kiss an unmarried woman's hand, but as was vastly improper, he held it tightly in his own.

"I think that it's best I make a hasty retreat, Mr. Rabelais," she said, attempting to draw her hand away.

"Not until you call me Jack."

"Very well, Jack, now let me go," she chided gently, "before the earl comes barreling out of the library and we both must bear the brunt of his anger."

"I did not counsel you to contact your family for money alone, mademoiselle," he said earnestly, "but for protection should you need it. Will you promise to do so if necessary?"

"What is it you think will happen to me?"

"A thousand things that a young woman like yourself is ill equipped to handle, mademoiselle."

"I have managed to survive quite well without them this long, Jack. I doubt that I should ever come to that pass."

"Ah, that inflexible pride. In that, you and the earl are alike."

"That's not fair, Jack. To let me leave with such an insult . . ." She laughed gently. His last glimpse of her was a daunting smile, a swift salute with one hand, and the trailing strand of silken auburn hair.

"Be careful, Katherine," he whispered after her. "You may be in more danger than you know."

Katherine was disappointed the next morning to learn that Jack Rabelais had departed early. "Riding with the dawn about the earl's business," one of the stable boys had said quickly, before he found an urgent reason to leave. Pretty little thing, he thought as he took long, striding steps to separate himself from Katherine, more chores, and more lectures. But bossy she was. Very, very bossy.

Katherine shifted Julie to her other hip, tried to disentangle her bonnet from the baby's searching fingers, and strode down the road and across Mertonwood's vast lawns. Thanks to the grooms, it had been cut to a manageable height. Ten minutes later, she halted on a small rise overlooking the curving road. She put Julie down gratefully on her well-padded bottom, and spread the blanket that she had kept tucked under one arm. She sat on the corner of the blanket, skirt spread around her and pulled Julie into the security of her arms. The baby squirmed, and with newly discovered talent, crawled to the edge of the blanket once more. She discovered something interesting in the grass, and Katherine reached over and plucked the rock from tenacious fingers before Julie could put it into her mouth.

"You cannot eat everything, Julie," she said tenderly, reaching into her pockets for a piece of sugared toast. She unwrapped it from a clean handkerchief and plopped the baby on her bottom again, bribing her with the toast.

"This is a lot better than rocks, love," she crooned, and Julie leaned against her, drooling with moist glee as she gummed the hard bread. Katherine sat beside her, knees drawn up and face pointed toward Mertonwood Forest.

"You look as though you would like to escape into the wood," Jeremy said, from behind her. She glanced up at him and smiled in welcome.

She motioned to the opposite corner of the blanket, and he eased himself down beside her.

"No, I was just thinking that the home woods should be culled," she said. Saplings and brush were normally removed from the first five or six feet of encroaching woods, not just for an aesthetic look, but to prevent the trees from expanding across the landscape. Mertonwood Forest had been allowed to return to a natural look, with its once well-laid paths overgrown, and its borders flowing onto green lawns.

A pleased squeal from Julie attracted her attention. Jeremy followed her gaze to where a chubby hand rested on the immaculate fabric of his trousers. A chubby hand filled with wet chunks of gummed toast. Jeremy winced, Julie smiled, Katherine laughed.

"I am sorry. To be around Julie is to be armed with either chain mail or an apron seven feet high and four feet wide." Katherine brushed aside the tiny hand and cleaned it with the handkerchief. She offered another piece of toast to the baby, while smilingly warning Jeremy.

"You do like my little niece, don't you?" Jeremy asked, watching her nestle the baby closer to her, out of his way.

"I love her," Katherine answered, putting her lips against the silken head, kissing the baby softness.

"She's very lucky, you know. One wouldn't think that, what with the circumstances of her birth . . ." He halted at the look in Katherine's eyes. It did not bode well for continuation of that sentence. "Well, you know . . ." He began to try to explain such churlishness.

"Yes, I know, Jeremy," she said, irritation rasping her voice, "and so will Julie, when the time comes. Why everyone is so concerned about it, I don't know. God forbid that the pure lines of the Lattimore family should be diluted by *bastard* blood." She said the word with cruel glee. Jeremy flinched at her cool look.

"I am sorry, Katherine," he said in apology. He reached out for the baby's hand and took it without attention to its condition.

"Apology accepted," Katherine said curtly, wanting to snatch Julie's hand from Jeremy's tender grasp.

"But I meant what I said, about her being lucky," he continued, studying the tiny hand. He didn't tell her Julie's life had not begun well. Celeste's family had dumped the baby unceremoniously upon Freddie's London townhouse steps one night. Celeste's father hadn't even stayed to talk with Freddie, only left terse instructions that the earl was never to contact them again, that Celeste had died in childbirth and that they couldn't be bothered to raise his brat. Freddie had not turned his back on his child, a gesture that had shocked the ton, secretly pleased his mother, and only confused his siblings.

"She has you, and that evens out any liability," Jeremy concluded. He watched the cool look transform into something warmer.

"Thank you, Jeremy. That was very sweet." The young man flushed and Katherine looked away to spare him further embarrassment.

"I came to say goodbye," he said abruptly.

"Goodbye? But you just arrived."

"I know," he said glumly, "but after last night, the greater distance I can put between myself and Freddie, the better."

"I did hear your quarrel," Katherine admitted.

"Quarrel? It was a bloody rout. Oh, pardon, Katherine." He flushed again.

"That's all right, Jeremy. We've already decided that swearing is one of your bad habits, remember?"

"Swearing and fighting with my brother. I forgot to mention that, didn't I?"

She nodded, smiling. "But what did you fight about? I mean, if you want to tell me."

"I don't mind. It's just so complicated." He ran his fingers through unruly brown hair. "My father left me those estates not entailed to Freddie, you see. He left the estates, but no money to go along with them."

"It's a condition a lot of people find themselves in," Katherine agreed gently.

"Unfortunately, those people don't have Freddie for a brother."

"He won't help you with their upkeep?" The idea did not conflict with Katherine's impression of the earl.

"Just the opposite. He wants to declare me his heir, settle a sum of money upon me now, and help me make them pay," he moaned.

"That sounds like a very generous thing to do, Jeremy. Where is the problem?"

"If it were anyone but Freddie," he tried to explain. "Freddie has this absolute compulsion to control everything within his domain. I don't want to be Freddie's heir. I don't want Freddie to question each expenditure, each farthing. I don't want to have to constantly explain each separate action. Call it pride, call it independence; it doesn't matter. Katherine," he said, imploring her with a look to understand, "I have to live my own life, free of Freddie. If he had not made so much money in the past ten years, there wouldn't have been anything to share from the original estate. It's been Freddie who's supported us all this time."

"Yet you would be quite willing to marry an heiress and

let her money support you," Katherine said reasonably, grabbing Julie when she would have scooted into the grass.

"That's different."

"How is it different, Jeremy? You spurn the wealth of your own kin to marry for someone else's. It doesn't seem very different, actually."

"I suppose, if you put it that way, it isn't," he said, his eyes fastened on a blade of grass his restless hand had plucked from the ground, "But I'm afraid it's a moot point anyway."

"Why?"

"Because I've already found my heiress, and it frankly doesn't matter anymore. But it matters to her family that I'm land rich and coin poor."

"And you feel something more for her than acquisitive glee, is that it?"

"Katherine," he began earnestly, "I wouldn't care if Beth had no money in the world. I would willingly make my own inheritance pay, even if it meant working all day and half the night like Freddie does. I know I could do it, with Beth at my side. Freddie is furious that I want to marry now. Says I'm not old enough, can you believe it? He wants me to wait, at least five years. I don't want to wait, Katherine. If her father cuts Beth off without a penny, I'll still want her for my wife."

"Does Beth feel the same?"

"So much so that she suggested we elope," he admitted with a small smile.

"It sounds as if the young lady may have a good idea." She grabbed one plump little ankle and tickled Julie's foot. Katherine's next words were so at odds with Julie's laughter that Jeremy glanced at her. She would not meet his eyes. "Too many times, Jeremy, plans are made and the world intrudes. Take your happiness where you will and when you will."

"Yes, and if we do, it won't be Freddie who heaps scandal on the family, it will be me."

"Tell me, just what is so scandalous about your brother? Other than Julie, I mean." The last words were whispered above the baby's head.

He smiled. "Freddie is a law onto himself. It's what makes people so livid. He doesn't care that most of the members of polite society have never forgiven him for becoming fantastically rich. If he had made his money at the gaming table or at the 'change, it would have been acceptable, but Freddie entered trade. He owns factories, and he is not just an absentee owner. He spends most of his time directly involved with them. Nor does he give a fig about the other rules of society. He wouldn't marry Celeste, even when her father challenged him to a duel. He openly criticized England's handling of Napoleon, said we deserved Waterloo because it was 'criminally imbecilic to have left the man alive.' "

"I get the idea," she said, laughing.

"One thing about Freddie is that he isn't a hypocrite. If he doesn't like something about you, he'll tell you. He isn't two-faced, but like Mama says, he doesn't suffer fools gladly."

Katherine was glad that she wasn't the only one to feel conflicting emotions about the Earl of Moncrief. She found herself warming slightly toward the man. It was not pity; one did not pity the earl. Yet, it was a compassion of sorts. He was a man at odds with the very same society that had bred him. The fact that the Earl of Moncrief genuinely did not give a flying farthing what anyone thought of him was something she should not have forgotten.

In fact, she was still disposed to think kindly of him when she entered the kitchen, smiled at the cook, and thanked her for the toast.

"Julie thought it a wonderful treat, Nora."

"Well, my little ones thought so too, miss. Glad she approved." She turned and retrieved a pan of tartlets from the oven, effectively dismissing Katherine. It was strange, but Nora always acted oddly around the baby. Even though she had a heart of gold, she treated the child with a certain constraint. The reason for her antipathy was not difficult to discover. Yet, why would anyone blame a baby for her parents' marriage, or lack of it? The question of Julie's legitimacy simply didn't matter.

The earl stood in the foyer, removing his riding gloves when Katherine appeared and stepped toward the staircase. She intended to bathe Julie before the night chill began. When she and the earl almost collided at the foot of the stairs, it was Katherine who smiled and apologized. Freddie started, both at the blooming picture of health she presented and at the first truly civil words she had spoken to him.

"I beg your pardon, sir," she said, smiling, "I certainly did not mean to molest you on your own stairs." She looked down at the baby, squirming in her grasp. Bits of sugary toast dotted her face, and her hands, despite Katherine's attempt at cleaning them, still bore traces of her snack. Katherine covered them with her own and smiled up at the Earl. "Your daughter is not as refined as her father," she said, glancing at his immaculate clothing with an approving look. He had evidently been riding but still looked as fresh as if he had been standing still all morning. Only his hair gave an appearance of activity, as it curled around his nape and fell forward over his brow.

"I have been exercising Thunder," he explained, looking at her curiously. "I'm afraid that Jeremy has nearly ruined my horse."

They mounted the steps together. "Oh, because he now shies at every sound and shows signs of nervousness?"

"How did you know?"

"My father kept quite a large stable. He loaned one of our bays to the parson one day, a man not well suited to riding. It took Father two weeks to reassure Epicitus that a rider could again be trusted."

"Epicitus?"

"Father did have a way of naming things, you see. Our sheep—at least before the flock became so large—used to have pet names. I especially liked the names of the rams."

"Oh, and what did he name them?"

Surely that wasn't a blush on the indomitable Katherine's face? "Oh, it was a silly thing, really."

"Come, Katherine, I detest people who begin a story but never have the nerve to finish it. What were their names?"

"Diogenes, Zeus, Morpheus and, uh, Priapus," she said weakly, trying to restrain her smile.

The earl's shout of mirth could be heard in the kitchen. "A ram looking for an honest sheep, the superior ram, the sleepy ram, and the, uh, manly ram?"

"Yes, I'm afraid so," she said, her grin wide.

They stood on the third-floor landing. The earl was surprised to discover that he hadn't remembered climbing the steps, so enchanted was he by this new face of Katherine.

In fact—and not for the first time—he found himself wondering about Katherine. Who was she really? She had the social graces of the landed class, the speech of gentry, yet she was evidently forced to work for a living. What was her background that she spoke of horses with such fondness and Greek mythology with such ease? She'd admitted to having had a governess, but he'd never heard her assume any airs. She treated the cook with the same graciousness that she treated Jeremy. Her reaction to the earl was never very far from outrageous, however, except for now, with her sudden display of amiability.

But with each passing moment, Katherine was feeling less congenial and more nervous. How could she have forgotten the earl's intense vitality? He was standing much too close, his presence mocking her earlier compassion. How could she have possibly imagined that this arrogant man should be treated with empathy, sensitivity? It was like trying to pet a tiger.

"Katherine . . ." His voice was low, soft, infinitely menacing. She could feel its effect down her spine, as though he had played a chord upon her bones.

"Yes?" She swallowed, a miracle unto itself, and wished he would move so that she could pass. Julie, drat her, was lolling heavily against her neck, asleep from the sun and the play. Not at all a deterrent for her father.

"Nothing," he said. "Just Katherine." He bent and, before she could stop him, kissed the spot on her throat where a pulse beat strongly. She had opened one button of her dress and it was here that his lips strayed. She told herself later that it was because Julie was in her arms that she did not move away. She explained to herself that she did not make that mute sound of surrender deep in her throat, that her head had not arched back, that she had not wished for more, much more, as he gently sucked, then tenderly brushed that spot with a hot, wet tongue. She pretended that she wasn't bemused and silent as the earl laughed softly, stroked a tender finger down Julie's cheek, and descended the staircase with that centaur grace of his.

She was getting very proficient at lying to herself.

Chapter 4

Jeremy left that afternoon, on a tamer mount than he had arrived upon, and with his departure, the house suddenly became too small. Katherine was very conscious of the fact that only a few servants stood between her and the earl, and they were employed by him.

Other thoughts, equally as disturbing, intruded.

In desperation finally, seeking an escape from herself as much as from the presence of others, she left the house, heading for the stables.

She had ridden ever since she was a little girl, horsemanship being as important to her parents as the ability to embroider or to conjugate Latin verbs. The latter occurred mostly because she was an only child, and as her Papa had said too many times to count, "No sense wasting your mind, puss, just because you're a female." He'd always wink at Mama while making that pronouncement, and her mock frown would dissolve into a smile, a shake of her head, and a long suffering sigh.

Riding, however, was one of those occupations that had

been pushed into the background. She enjoyed it as much as she loved reading, but both pursuits had given ground beneath her recent duties. In the case of riding, there hadn't been a mount to use since her parents had died and their bloodstock had been sold to help pay outstanding debts. Nor did Mertonwood boast an extensive library; by the end of the first month, she had exhausted its meager fare.

But now the earl's stable was occupied by two horses, the infamous Thunder and an oversized stallion that must be, by his very size if not his noble disposition, the earl's own mount. She spared a commiserating glance at the nervous Thunder, but it was Monty who drew her attention. Both horses looked to be out of the same sire, what with their markings, the strength of their withers and the hand span they reached. They were not horses meant for park-like strolls; it was quite evident they had been bred for stamina and endurance.

She would have given the last of her small hoard of wages to sit astride Monty's back.

Katherine stood and watched the magnificent horse for a while, appreciating the beauty of form and grace which disclosed his thoroughbred paternity. The white star upon his fetlock was the only splash of color in the unremitting ebony satin of his coat. He didn't seem upset by her undisguised admiration; except for one warm snort blown through distended nostrils, he seemed to think she was beneath his concern. He was much more attentive to the mash specially mixed for his delectation.

One cautious boot edged up the bottom board of his stall. With a push, she stood, surveying him even closer, her arms crossed upon the top boards. One hand dug into the pocket of her skirt and she withdrew the apple she'd obtained from the cook, luring the animal closer by dangling a piece over the side of the stall.

"Oh, you beauty," she praised him, as he turned his

head effortlessly and nipped at the apple held out between outstretched fingers. He was as fastidious as a duke, as gracious as a prince, as she continued to feed him the treat one quarter at a time.

"And what will you do, my fine lad," she chided him, smiling, when he plucked the last piece from her fingers, "when there is nothing left? Will you be fickle then?"

"Have you been taking lessons from Jeremy, then, that you would ruin my horse?"

She should have been surprised at the sound of his voice or, turning, to see him standing so close. But she wasn't. Nor had she sought his presence. Julie was napping, the house was too confining, and the day too intoxicating to resist.

"No one could ruin this gorgeous creature. More like he is king over his own domain," she said dismissively, turning back to Monty. The horse had stopped butting against her hand and now looked at them inquisitively, speculation almost humanlike in his wide brown eyes.

The earl hiked himself up next to her and folded his arms in the identical position. It was the only similarity between them. He towered over her, even draped against the stall as he was. His nonchalance was practiced, hers desperately hard-won. His clothing was rich, the country look casually obtained. Hers was of the country masquerading as stylish. Yet, both their gazes were fixed upon the stall's inhabitant, and their silence was rife with unspoken questions and even more mute responses. He wanted to ask where she'd learned to be easy around horses, especially a stallion like Monty. She wished she could tell him about her father and his love for animals. He felt an intense curiosity about her upbringing—it had been the only thing left gray and amorphous in his mother's letter about her. She wanted to ask him if all his horses were like Monty. He found himself wondering at his curiosity about this girl-woman; not the first in his experience, but sufficiently rare to be noticed.

The moment passed in which two people of disparate backgrounds could have discovered that their pasts were not that dissimilar. Nor were their hopes and dreams. Yet, years of blithe remarks and self-protective armor separated the essential man from his position of Earl. And too many youthful mistakes and a perceptible fear of the future prudently suggested of Katherine a shield of civility.

Nature, however, always capricious, forever mutating, constantly shifting identities, created in two healthy humans a knowledge of the other. It was as if having been set aside by logical thought, it pulled them jealously back into awareness once more. The shift of his cuff upon his wrist, exposing its tanned surface, seemed to her to be of infinite import. The subtle musk of her scent seemed out of place and thicker in this air filled with the usual smells of hay and horse. The whorl of hair upon his nape lured her eyes, the white-boned grip of her fingers upon the weathered gray of the slatted boards seemed to him too arresting.

She lowered herself from the stall, brushed her palms over the coarse cotton of her skirt.

She studied the ground, strewn with threads of hay, pounded hard by generations of horses being cooled, walked, and led to waiting stalls. Her lashes were too thick, too long, he thought. As if her eyes could take flight under the weight of them.

Her breath came hard; he wondered why his blood was pounding like a callow boy's. Nature stepped aside, pleased with the outcome of her plotting.

"You court danger, Katherine," he said, his voice without rancor. Simply stated, it was the truth. Around him, she was not safe, and it was time she knew it. It was not that he was overcome with lust; it was not that he had lived months of denial. It was, quite simply, something he could not define. And what could not be understood defied control.

He wanted her, he admitted that. He wanted to hold her now, and under the interested gaze of his stallion, ached to plunge into her with the power of it. He wanted to pinion her by the hips, and savage her until her neck arched back and she screamed with the pleasure/pain of it. He wanted her to call his name, and scratch him with her nails, and bite his shoulder with those pearly white teeth.

And she wanted him gone.

If he would only leave first, then she wouldn't have to brush by him with her full skirt, tasting the edge of danger. She wouldn't need to nearly touch him to leave, and feel the warmth emanating from him. As much as she felt something between them now. Something dark and forbidden and so delicious it was like the taste of bittersweet chocolate melting on her tongue.

"It is dangerous, this," he said, and the words should have sounded ominous in the near dark. They did not. Instead, they promised pleasure, hot drugging bliss.

Disaster waited for her in his look.

She did not move as he took one step toward her. It was her last bit of conscience strained and rejected. She let her hands fall to her side and watched him.

Her blood was hot and sluggish; a thrumming beat maintained an eerie tattoo somewhere low in her belly. Her breath was painful, anticipatory, even her fingertips were full, torpid, swollen. She wanted to suckle him, offer herself up in small bites for his delectation; needed him to be satiated by her, to feed upon her.

Dear God, what was she doing?

Her lips throbbed, and he had yet to kiss her. She bit the inside of her lower lip, tasting the swell of her own flesh, feeling the heartbeat trapped between her teeth, racing, pounding. He was only a second away; a scant inch separated their bodies. A lifetime of rules divided them still.

"Come to me, Katherine," he said softly, both hands on her upper arms. Not forcing her back, not bringing her forward, just remaining where they were, each of them separate, unique, but bound by his hands, a bridge across reality.

"No," she said, disputing his lure, the almost magical pull of him. Her eyes were wide, he thought, the eyes of a trapped young fawn. He could not look at them for long. He looked down at her mouth instead, pink and slightly open, and wanted to suck the breath from her.

"It would be so much easier if you would only say yes."

She smiled, ducking her head so he would not see her amusement. How autocratic of him. To want seduction, but not the effort of it.

One finger tilted up her chin. Another stroked the edge of her smile.

"You would show levity now?" His own smile made a mockery of the accusation.

"I feel less like smiling, my lord, than running as if all the demons of hell are at my heels."

Yet all thought of running dissolved at the touch of his mouth on hers. A coaxing whisper was all he needed to breech the cavern of her mouth, a teasing tongue all the invitation needed to convert a tender kiss into more. He inhaled her breath, nipped her bottom lip, then licked the wound with the tip of a tender tongue. Broad hands palmed her cheeks; intrusive fingers wound through her hair and pressed hard against her skull as if to bind her to him more closely. Her hand clasped around his neck, hung on as he deepened the kiss, marking her, branding her with passion.

Long moments later, he lifted his head, his breath hot and panting in the sweet forest of her hair. His arousal beat hard, engorged with blood and painful in its intensity.

He'd never felt this way in his life, so aching, so pained, without restraint. At this moment, he could thrust himself within her and think the world well lost. Standing in a stable with the sound of harness and horse, with the possibility of intrusion at any moment. It was too late to think with reason. Too damned late.

He bent his head and found her mouth again with the same unerring accuracy a babe finds a straining breast. He stroked his tongue against hers, tasting her, relishing the soft, muttered sounds she made, as if unable to bear the sensation beneath the fragile framework of skin.

"Come to me," he said, as he had before, and reason was mute.

For only a second.

Katherine jerked free, slamming against the boards of Monty's stall with the force of it. An animal whinny of protest punctuated the sudden tense silence.

"No," she said, that one word forced from a throat constricted with panic. He read the answer in her amber eyes, and something else even stronger. It prevented him from going after her as she ran from the stable.

Fear.

There was irony in the fact that Julie slept peacefully and still Katherine could not sleep. She was almost grateful to be summoned by Abigail at midnight. When she entered the nursery, Sara was nervously trying to quiet a red-faced and squalling Julie. Katherine rubbed oil of cloves on the baby's swollen gums and, motioning Sara back to her cot, took Julie down to her room.

She walked with her long after the baby had fallen into an exhausted slumber. The sight of that small open mouth so close to her breasts recalled words it would be wiser not to remember. Images it would be safer not to envision. His head of coal-black hair with that one lock that continually fell across his forehead. His head cradled on her breasts, not unlike his child. Her nipples puckered, elongating, stretching as if to fill his mouth.

The demon.

He'd taunted her with words, and now those words would always haunt her. He'd thrown her own impulsiveness back in her face, daring to shock her. She had no one to blame but herself, didn't she? Once again, her governess's voice resounded in her mind. "If you'd remained the lady I raised you to be, none of this would have happened." Katherine did not doubt it.

The earl might relish his position as a pariah, but he would be welcomed back into society should he wish it. And herself? She could not change history, never alter her past. She would never be welcomed in that exclusive enclave. Her past was too shameful, her actions too shocking.

Yet, it had been exciting to verbally spar with the earl. Exciting and dangerous.

And how well she knew the price of danger and the payment for it.

She had brought it on herself. A man had offered his arms and she had been coaxed inside a warm embrace. She had forgotten the warnings of her upbringing, the caution of years of teaching, willing to pay whatever price society demanded for the feeling of being comforted, for being loved.

She had been so lonely.

His name was David and for a while, she'd been in love. No, not in love. She'd been grateful for the attention, flattered by the fulsome praise, mollified by promises of marriage, a future secure and not frightening.

To want so much and be given so little, that was only pitiful. To be willing to accept so little and call it love, that was the meaning of shame.

In the end, she'd only felt shame. Not the warm emotion

poets called love, not even passion. Yet, David's kisses had never tasted like those stolen in a stable.

The need she'd thought expunged flared up with jeering ease.

The Earl of Moncrief was dangerous, wicked, and charming, delighting in both his wickedness and the spoils effortlessly rendered his.

And she was not the creature of practicality she pretended to be. She was impulsive and rash, willful. David had taught her that. Taught her, too, what she would be willing to do for a kind touch, a warm embrace, a promise of affection. She was not a being adhering to the rules, but one ruled by her emotions.

And staked out for the kill.

She walked to the nursery carefully, so as not to wake Julie. Sara was sleeping noisily on the pallet near the crib. By the light of the nursery candle, she tucked the blankets around the baby and stood watching her for a moment with tender eyes.

When she turned, he was there. Dressed in black trousers and a crimson dressing gown, he loomed in the doorway like a colorful bird of prey. His hair was tousled, as if he, too, had sought sleep but had been unable to find it.

"You stalk like a tiger," she accused softly, and in the gloom of the nursery, his eyes gleamed.

"How many tigers have stalked you, dear Katherine?" His lips quirked in humor.

She faced him, clenched hands balled on her hips. "One for certain, my lord. But that one should have his claws removed and his fangs pulled."

"Is that so?" He moved closer, until there were only inches between them. She could smell his scent, and her fancy made it dark passion laced with brandy, tinged with the thin cigarillo he smoked after dinner. His breath fanned her face as he extended one long finger and tilted her chin up so that he met her eyes. The crib was at her back; there was no room to move. It was an adequate sop to her conscience. Her feet stayed locked into place, prisoner of that one finger placed gently beneath her chin and of the green gaze of her jailer.

"Tigers can be made to purr, sweet Katherine. Like a tame and contented kitten. Would you like to make me purr?" Part of her wanted to open up beneath his coaxing, to stroke his hair back from his forehead, to feel his lips beneath the tips of her fingers, to feel the hardness of his chest beneath her own. To continue their loveplay of this afternoon. To finish what he had so effortlessly begun. The other, more rational, more Constance-like part, jerked away from his touch and turned away, before he could interpret the flaming color on her cheeks for something it was not.

"I do not want to tame you, my lord. I wish only to be left alone." Her voice was strangled. She kept her hands clasped tightly in front of her, even when he bent and brushed his lips against the exposed flesh of her throat. Tigerlike, going for the kill.

"What do you want of me? Do you have every female within scenting distance heaving themselves on the ground for you? I care for your daughter, my lord, or have you forgotten?" The angry color on her cheeks and the furious glitter in her eyes made him pause, but not for the reasons that Katherine would have wished. It was not her impassioned words that halted him, but rather the vision that she appeared in her anger. The soft candlelight touched her curls to reddish flame. Her eyes were wide, the pupils dilated. Her mouth was loose, the lips parting as if coaxed by another's, her breath quick. This is how she would look after loving, he thought, all warm and open, flash and fire receding, passion-weary.

He smiled, a devastating smile, and Katherine could only stare at him. He bent down and touched her lips with his own. The softness of silk warmed to fire. Silk draped over steel, as he pulled her firmly into his arms. His lips skimmed the surface of her own, the tip of his tongue traced their contours, delineated their outline. That same insidious tongue darted insistently to the seam of her lips and demanded entrance. Minutes stretched into hours, days, years until he finished exploring her lips, the tender flesh inside her mouth, the edges of her teeth. She was the cavern, he the explorer bent on exposing every secret. Their breaths mingled, their tongues dueled. When he finally released her, she lay her forehead against his chest, too dazed to push away from him.

"That is part of what I want, Katherine," he said, his voice a ribbon of dark whisper. "I want you to tame the tiger."

It was the sound of the chambermaid moving down the hallway which had roused Katherine from the lethargy of the earl's embrace. That, and the sudden, horrifying knowledge of what she was doing. It was not seduction; she'd made it too easy for him. She pushed at him until he finally released her, seeking the locked comfort of her own room.

Constance would, no doubt, have been able to handle the Earl of Moncrief. Nor did Katherine doubt that her governess would have had stringent advice as to her own wayward nature. But Constance had never been faced with such an unsettling presence, nor forced to hide in the nursery like a child escaping punishment. Upon reflection, Katherine decided that her governess would undoubtedly have been able to handle the situation, but she herself was at a loss at where to begin.

She did not see him leave until afternoon. Only when she was certain that his massive stallion had passed through the stone gates at the bottom of the hill did she emerge from the third floor and gratefully escape the confines of the house.

Michael was kneeling beside a bed, mulching the dormant bushes against a winter that was fast approaching. He had been a friend from her first days at Mertonwood. Her own home had been perched upon a rocky hill unsuited for growing anything, designed as it was for defense. But lack of experience did not prevent her appreciation of the beauty of Mertonwood, especially its rose garden.

She knelt beside Michael, who smiled in greeting, and she began patting the mulch around the base of the bushes, duplicating his gestures automatically, feeling comfort in his presence and his wordless companionship.

They worked silently for almost an hour. Except for his occasional sidelong glance, Michael did not indicate that he thought her behavior strange.

Only when they were finished and the small barrow of mulch was empty did he speak.

"It takes a mighty lot of problems to do that much mulchin'," he said with a smile. His face was so wrinkled that it was the only horizontal line on his face.

She straightened, relieving cramped muscles, and smiled back. Work sometimes was the only deterrent to worry.

"A few," she agreed.

"Well, feel free to work out your problems any time. I could use the help."

She laughed. "You have a promise, Michael." The time spent had crystallized her worries, although she'd come to no conclusions.

What was she going to do about the earl?

A wiser woman would simply leave.

Yet, she had lost her parents, her home, and her friends. Could she bear to lose Julie, too? She had walked away from Donegan with the knowledge that the only future left to her was employment of some sort. Her devotion to

Julie stemmed not from any gratitude to the countess for employing her. She had taken one look at Julie's pixie face, at the pointed little chin that jutted out at the world, and felt her heart lurch. When the baby was placed in her arms, and Julie snuffled and whimpered only once and then was quiet, it was as if a great stone had been placed on Katherine's chest. But it was when she nuzzled her, smelling softness and sweet baby's breath, that a fierce protectiveness began to well up inside her.

When Julie smiled for the first time it was Katherine's heart that stopped at the sheer beauty of it. When Julie cried, it echoed an ache somewhere deep inside her. When Julie was ill, it was Katherine who anxiously kept vigil beside her cradle. She was alone in the world, without family and without friends, and on some level it was as if the two motherless children recognized each other. Need and love were born at the same moment. Julie was the only one who would notice if she were not here, and until now, she had been the only one here for Julie.

Could she really just walk away?

Julie had brought love back into her life. Total, uncomplaining, all encompassing, unconditional love. She could not lose that.

But neither was she a fool.

The need for comfort, for the closeness of a human being, had been so desperate in her for such a long time, it was probably the reason she loved holding Julie so. It seemed as though every inch of her skin longed to be touched, calmed, cooled.

By the earl?

What would he have done if he'd known her thoughts in the stable or in the nursery? She had come within a breath of wanting to satisfy her curiosity, of wanting to know if surrender would be as glorious as he promised. She'd wanted to feel his bare skin against hers, to have an end to the frustrating feelings his touch evoked and his kiss enhanced. She'd wanted to know if ruin was as pleasurable and as passionate as he pledged with a stroke of tongue and a smoothing palm.

It was only a matter of time.

He had shown her that by the ease with which she fell into his arms. The earl had coaxed with a teasing finger, and like a bemused schoolgirl, she'd followed eagerly. It was not so much a question of nationality as of basic temperament. Although it would have been easier to blame the French half of her, Katherine suspected that such would have been the case had she been Russian or Scots.

There was something wayward, something perverse about her nature. Some indefinable something that made her want to feel all she could feel, experience everything his touch hinted at, his smile promised, his eyes divulged. She had, after all, nothing left to lose. Why did she keep fighting it, him?

Society be damned.

Yes, it was only a matter of time.

Not until he beckoned, but until she did.

The home woods lured her and she walked toward them, oblivious to the slight chill in the air. The oaks of the forest were still laden with the morning's rain, and large, plump drops dangled from skeletal branches. She closed her eyes and listened to the sounds around her, breathing deeply, inhaling the aromas of the forest, moss and bark, wet leaves and the tang of wild onion.

"You are a true sensualist, Katherine." He spoke from behind her and she turned, unsurprised. He was forever doing that, appearing just when the air grew quiet, as though magically transformed from serenity itself. Yet he had been in her thoughts all day; it was no surprise to conjure him here now. He was leaning negligently against a gigantic oak, his back braced against its gnarled surface, his legs and arms crossed as he surveyed her calmly.

"I am not a sensualist, my lord, simply an observer of nature."

"To observe nature is to let one's senses become unchained from that which is expected, Katherine. You must give freedom to the eyes, ears, to the sense of smell and touch. It is the essence of sensuality."

"Why am I not surprised that you turn each setting into an arena for seduction?" She smiled, and he wondered if she knew his restraint. She had been uppermost in his mind all day, and it was a rare occasion indeed that business was supplanted by a lovely face.

"Am I seducing you? Please let me know; I was unaware." He uncrossed his long legs and moved toward her. She remained where she was, watching him advance. He walked like the tiger he wished to emulate, making barely a sound on the leaf-strewn forest floor.

"Do you know what I wish?" she asked, turning away from the sight of him, so dominant in a setting that should have overpowered most mortal men. Towering oaks and green shadows were no match for the Earl of Moncrief.

"For me to go away?" His voice was laced with humor.

"You would do no such thing," she said, her own smile less certain. "No, I wish you would attempt to see me as more than a conquest."

"What makes you think I do?"

She laughed then, and he thought the sound appropriate in this setting of green earth and nature. She was a nymph of russet shadows and fertility. Nature come to life in coral and auburn and gold.

"I am not as naive as you would have me be, my lord. Whether it is because there is a lack of other acceptable females or because you are simply bored, it is quite evident that I have been chosen your latest target. Nor has my position as your servant, subject to your whims, escaped my notice."

"You think I would use one to secure the other?"

She clasped her hands before her. If she felt nervous, it would be unwise to let him see. If she did not, it was one thing she did not wish to admit; it would make her ruin so much more calculated.

She turned to face him finally, and almost stopped breathing. He was quiet, as still as the forest around him. Silent in waiting, an implacable patience against which she had no defense. A shaft of sunlight crowned his head; Lucifer before the fall. It wasn't simply that his features were arranged in proportion to one another, it wasn't simply that each individually was strong and unblemished. His nose as arrogant as any Caesar's, his high cheekbones reminiscent of Mongol warriors, his emerald eyes taken from Ireland's valleys. It was the aura that surrounded him, self-crafted, a sense of power, of determination, of laughter and promise, of passion sweet and heady. He lured and he beckoned, but he offered the world according to Moncrief. A world alien and strangely known. A world she occupied in her most flagrant dreams. Luxury and plenitude. Satin nights and velvet days.

"I know nothing about you." As a reason, it was weak. As a defense, it was futile.

"Tell me what you want to know. I'll divulge as much as you desire and keep hidden what you choose not to discover."

"How accommodating you are."

"You will never know," he said, his wolfish grin strumming something secret and once dormant.

"I am not prepared to be your mistress, my lord."

"A strong word, that."

"What would you call it, then?"

He would call it stupidity. As crass and as idiotic as anything he'd ever done. Since Celeste, he had been wiser than this. Celeste had been the almost perfect mistress, except for her nobility. She'd been innocent and trusting, and fresh from the schoolroom. While her parents were initially thrilled that their daughter had captured the eye of the infamous earl, horror soon overcame their greed when it became apparent to what lengths their only child had gone. The Earl attempted to convey to Celeste and, later, to her parents, one salient thought. It did not matter to what extent Celeste had gone; he would never marry her.

Once was quite enough, thank you.

Since then, he took no young things to bed, he did not fornicate with nymphs. He only drained his lust with experienced women who knew the players and the playbill before the curtain opened. Not amber eyed beauties with skin as fresh and as smooth as the inside of a rose petal.

Not virgin Madonnas.

Yet, reason did not control his baser impulses on this occasion, or any occasion peopled with Katherine Sanderson. He had this odd feeling when he was around her, as if her smile was tied to his loins somehow.

"You'll never lack from your association with me," he said. Calm words belying turbulent appetite.

"I'll want that in writing," his erstwhile nymph said, shocking him to the core. He had the oddest feeling that the tables had just been turned, that the hunter was now the hunted, that the prey had cornered him.

"You're not above bargaining, then?" Strange, he'd thought more of her than that. Or less, perhaps, not to know her own worth. Strangely, it did not diffuse his anticipation.

"I have little to bargain with, my lord," she said, and the wry grin touched him in a way no coquettish smile would have. He wanted to tell her all she possessed. Beauty, certainly. Humor, rare in one so young. A clear and guileless gaze, and a heart that showed love so easily and without restraint. Modesty was too much icing on her cake. She did not need it. Yet, he was astute and experienced in negotiations, and he knew his best course lay not in illuminating her, but in silence.

He smiled and she looked away, thinking it too tender a smile.

"I will grant you thirty days of me, in return for a contract of sorts."

The silence was total. She should have heard the sound of birds, the rustling of squirrels pawing through the fallen leaves searching for nuts, the soughing of the wind through the trees. Instead, she heard nothing but the beat of her heart as she waited for him to speak.

His voice, when it finally came, was soft and laced with humor. "Why only thirty days, my dear? Why not a hundred? A year? Ten years? Will I be sated in thirty days? Will you wear me out before then?"

He craved only that which was denied him, wanted only something he could not easily have. It was part of her appeal for him, she thought, and also part of the reason their bargain would last only a month.

"You intrigue me with your time limit," he said, when she didn't speak. "I've never yet taken a mistress with such a requirement. They normally want undying devotion and promises of fidelity unto death. And what would you claim for the ravishment of your flesh, Katherine?"

She glanced at him, amusement flashing in her smile. She relished, then, his discomfiture. It was knowledge he tucked away for later.

"Thirty days, and then freedom."

"Not jewels, nor carriages. You surprise me." His voice was indolent, his gaze sharp-eyed.

"I want Julie in my care for as long as I wish it."

"You must have gold between your thighs, my dear, to think I'd trade my daughter for simple lust."

Nothing was simple around the earl.

"No, my lord, I do not wish to take your daughter from

you. I only wish employment as her governess until she no longer needs me."

"You could have that without submitting, shall we say, to my baser instincts."

"No, my lord, I would not. I would always be waiting for the day when you tired of this hunt, or I displeased you or said something that you took amiss. This way, I am at least protected."

"Protected?"

"You would have to agree to leave me alone after that time. I would want to remain at Mertonwood, but you would never visit here."

"And my daughter?" he asked, his eyes narrowing. "Am I never to see her?"

"She is six months old, my lord, and this is the first time you've chosen to occupy yourself with her welfare. I doubt that her presence in the world will alter your future plans."

"You judge me harshly."

Celeste's legacy to him had been a blanket-draped basket upon his doorstep and a reputation hanging in shreds. The reputation did not concern him overly much; the basket's occupant did. That one small scrap of humanity was presumably meant to resemble him, but instead had the marked appearance of a shriveled strawberry. He'd thought to have her raised somewhere out of sight, and then, when the time came, marry her off to the best husband money could buy. It was a generous plan, one that went far beyond those of some of his peers who, faced with the inconvenience of illegitimate offspring, farmed them off to live with couples in the country. Neither their survival nor their ultimate welfare was ever considered again.

He was not such a monster. Yet, he was now being chastised by a slip of a girl for doing more than he should have done. Despite his fulsome irritation with Katherine Sanderson at this particular moment, the earl smiled.

She thought it was a grin a tiger might make.

"If you wish to see Julie, my lord," she said, her fingers pleating the wool of her skirt, "then I'm certain I can arrange to be absent during that time."

"This is a conversation I'd never thought to have," he said, his grin fading. "Nor is this a bargain I'd ever thought to strike." What was so odd was that he could be so irritated and so filled with desire at the same time. They were not emotions he'd ever felt in tandem.

"Thirty days, Katherine? It is either too little or too much; I've not decided." His eyes narrowed as he looked at her.

"If I have learned nothing in the past year, I have learned to protect myself," she said, an unwitting partial answer to his unspoken question.

"And has your life been so onerous, then, that you would sell yourself for a little security?" It was not the first time he'd wondered about her, but the first time he'd asked the question. She turned away, her gaze fixed on a point in the distance.

"My past is not part of this bargain between us, my lord. That must be one of the conditions."

He studied her for a long moment, as if he could discern her secrets through careful examination.

"What happens if you wish this agreement between us to continue beyond thirty days? Would you then wish for a diamond a day, a ruby per week?"

"It will not continue beyond the specified time, my lord."

"You have such little faith in my charm," he said, and smiled his most charming smile.

She did not tell him what she suspected, that thirty days would be almost too long with him. She wanted to touch him, to have him hug her, to cuddle against him and let the world go away. She wanted to bask in his smiles and hear his laughter. Most of all, she wanted to discover if the excitement she felt in his arms would be magnified in his bed. Thirty days would be a touch of magic in her life. Sunlight after rain. Yet, not long enough for him to burrow deeply into her heart. Not too long, after all.

And afterwards?

Would she be able to walk away from him? It was either that, or surrender herself completely to him, become another possession the Earl of Moncrief barely noticed.

"Then we have no bargain to discuss," she said, stepping away from him. He held out one hand as if to stop her and brushed her sleeve. She shivered at his touch, a small gesture, but one that indicated, at least to him, how tenu ous was her composure.

"It is a good thing I've not pinned my consequence upon your surrender," he said softly.

"And have I surrendered?" The look she gave him was sharp enough to cut, he thought. No, she hadn't surrendered. She'd bargained the way a good fishwife would, selling her wares in a hay-filled barrow. And all the while, she'd trembled. What a study in contradictions she was.

"No," he said, allowing her a victory. It was a shallow one at best, because he knew, from her widening pupils and the flush on her face, and the breaths that emerged too fast from her chest, that the final victory would be his.

"Who has harmed you so greatly that you would bargain yourself so cheaply? As my mistress, you could have a life in London, a secure and comfortable future, a promise of my fidelity for a period of time."

"If you honor this contract then I have a future, my lord. And someone to love who will love me in return. I'll have a warm home and enough to eat. It seems like a reasonable bargain, and not one so cheap."

"Yet, you would still remain a servant. It seems a waste."

"Where love goes, my lord, it knows no servitude."

"You speak of Julie, and not myself, I imagine."

Her laughter bubbled freely. "My lord, it truly would

be a disaster to love you. Your child, yes, because she has not yet learned to manipulate, to overwhelm, to conquer. You? No, my lord, I am not that foolish."

"Yet, you have managed to learn your own brand of manipulation."

"My mother was French, my lord. They are eminently practical people."

"But even your mother would caution you to trade your virginity for something more substantial than a promise of employment and a month of satisfaction."

She stared at him with amber directness. Either she had become expert at hiding her emotions, or there was truly nothing there—no fear, no anticipation. She smiled then, and he would have almost believed it tender but for the wry edge to it.

"Who said, my lord, that I was a virgin?"

Chapter 5

It took one hundred and thirty-two hours for the earl's solicitor to be summoned from London. One hundred, thirty-two hours and seventeen minutes. She knew the exact moment because of the earl's penchant for informing her curtly of it. She was also aware of the passing moments because of two things: the earl's constant and annoying presence; and her own doubts about her future course. The second would not have existed but for the first.

He seemed to take her announcement of her nonvirginal state as some sort of red flag waved in front of his face. She'd never seen a man change so quickly. He went from gently teasing, that lambent glow of desire firing his green eyes, to smoldering rage. Possessive anger. Which was patently idiotic, of course.

Now, he seemed to amuse himself by making inroads on his campaign of seduction by being where she was every moment of the day. Wherever she was he appeared, be it larder, pantry, or sewing room. He was underfoot in the nursery, knocked on her door in the dawn hours to ensure she had awakened, demanded her presence at dinner. Afterwards, when she would have liked to escape to the relative sanctuary of her room, he insisted that she remain in the library as he devoured the contents of the daily courier's bag. It was as if he wanted to absorb her, immerse himself in her daily life, study her, perhaps watch her like an animal who toyed with its food just before wearying of the game and devouring it.

He seemed to delight in penetrating that calm shell she erected around herself. He would say the most outlandish things, like the time he entered the laundry room and picked up one of her chemises, glancing from the lace-trimmed bodice to her chest, as if measuring the dimensions. "We'll see if you grow bigger after a month," he said, and tossed the garment back into the washtub, leaving her blushing and furious.

She did not understand him. On the surface, he was a simple man, if one wandered no farther than his words. A rake, a despoiler of the innocent, and the not so innocent. Ruthless, without conscience. Yet, it was his order that spared Townsende of the heaviest duties, yet left the old man's dignity intact. It was to him that the youngest maid came when accused of thievery by an older servant. After listening to all the facts, stonily declared by Mrs. Roberts and tearfully denied by the maid, he'd settled the matter by having the young girl sent to another of his estates. From the look he conveyed on Mrs. Roberts, it was clear he had not believed her charges, but at the same time had no proof with which to refute them. The old hunting dogs, still kept in the kennel behind the stable, loped tiredly to him, and he would spare a moment to gently scratch their flopping ears.

On those rare occasions when business kept him bent over papers strewn across his desk in the library, she felt his presence as if he were in the room. She could almost feel the slight brush of his linen shirt against her bare wrist, see the tanned face with its tiger eyes and their hint of mockery, smell the scent of him even though she stood alone with Julie in the nursery.

Even in her bed at night, visions of him readily appeared before her, a nighttime vision guaranteed to keep her from sleep.

He had not touched her. Except for being where she was, smiling softly or grinning wide, he made no demands upon her. She would sometimes catch his eyes upon her, watching her steadily, and his finger would stroke the fullness of his lower lip. It was as if having won the war, he was content to avoid another skirmish.

He decided, he said, to call her Kat. "If I'm a tiger, dear Katherine, then you must be a member of the feline family also. Why else would we share such an affinity? Besides, it suits you. Sleek Kat, purring Kat," he murmured, tracing a finger near the line of her jaw. It did not touch her, but that almost-caress caused her to shiver as though ice had been brushed across her skin.

What female would not arch into his hands, and stroke the length of every limb? What woman wouldn't purr under his touch? It was a thought that, oddly enough, irritated her beyond measure. Consequently, she lived those hours with overstretched nerves, listening for the rolling thunder of carriage wheels, waiting for the gleam of sunlight on silver at the gates.

In her bed at night, she could almost feel him next to her. She could imagine the arch of one foot as it slipped seductively up her bare leg, the band of muscle in his arm as he pulled her closer, the coarse belt of hair that tickled her breasts. She could envision his lips on hers, his warm breath slipping from between salted lips, a tongue teasing, darting, flicking. The rasp of a new beard was almost real, as she could feel it skating across her throat, down her shoulders, and over taut, budded nipples.

It was danger, it was magic, it was passion, and he had yet to touch her.

Katherine Sanderson, newly named Kat, was his. Firmly, completely, and unequivocally, for as long as he wanted her. Despite what she said about that damned agreement, she would purr as long as he sought to stroke. He wanted her. God, how he wanted her. Sometimes, looking at her with Julie, the need to thrust inside her was almost more than he could bear. For countless hours, until that idiot Williams showed up, he would be in pain, acute physical pain.

She was ready. Ready and more than willing. In the morning she would be soft, rumpled, with the pinkness of warmth still on her cheeks, lips ripe, open and swollen from being kissed awake. He wondered if her breasts awoke in that same state, those proud nipples thrust upward in the air, sensitized by the feel of his breath. Would her legs entwine with his, slipping softly upwards until they felt him grow at her touch? Would she be softly reticent, demurely innocent in the morning and in need of coaxing, or would she meet him like his mate, aggressive, needing, wanting?

Kat. Freddie smiled with pleased anticipation. He had not felt such excitement since he was a boy. She had piqued his interest with her practical assessment of her situation and her demand for legal protection. These long hours of self-denial had been the price to pay for her easy capitulation. She had almost made it too easy. He had punished them both by withholding the touch she had grown to expect. He had stroked her with his eyes, followed her until she knew the feel of his presence, his smell, his size alongside her. She had grown to anticipate turning and finding him near. It was an act of gentling, used when taming skittish horses, gaining the trust of children and softening women.

She could have won a house in London, and support for life, but all she wanted was to serve him. Was this not the most tantalizing irony of all?

It made it simpler that she was not a virgin, even though her calm announcement had infuriated him at first. A strange reaction, that. It didn't matter if she'd had other lovers, as long as she maintained fidelity while she was in his bed. Fastidious by nature, the earl disliked crawling into sheets warmed by another man.

He would have no other infidelities in his life.

Katherine had erased Monique's memory with her innocent charm, her devilish mind that prompted witty answers to even the most mundane questions. Yet, his mind cautioned wariness, to be distrusting of the most banal of lures: charm. It was a tribute to Katherine's allure that Freddie had managed to confine himself at Mertonwood for days and was even contemplating remaining here for over a month. At no time since his honeymoon had he been able to bear Mertonwood with such equanimity. Yet now, he no longer stared down at the stables with visions of his wife and another entwined within his mind; he no longer gazed at the home woods and knew that somewhere within these stately oaks and leaf-padded grounds his wife and another man would be engaged in passionate and immoral lovemaking. Nor did he spend much time concerned about the sport that had occurred on the bed he slept in at night, the same bed in which his wife had curled up in sleepy and adulterous repose next to another. She had fortunately died with her lover, thereby sparing him the necessity of exposing a scandal. There had been whispers, true, but he had faced them down. He smiled, mirthlessly. No, he had supplanted them with Celeste's downfall into ruin. That tale had easily offset the first, and for his mother's sake, he was glad.

Monique and her lover had carried part of him to their separate graves. He disliked admitting that they had destroyed his ability to trust. His was a nature well able to acknowledge its own responsibility, and he would not grant either of them that much power. Yet, marriage was not, and would never be, among the ceremonies at which he was an active participant. He had tasted the joys of connubial bliss, and he'd just as soon hire any future mates. As long as Jeremy lived, he had his heir.

In his adult life, Freddie had given his trust to only one person: Jack Rabelais. Jack had earned that trust by nearly dying at his side. He doubted that he would ever willingly give it to another, especially a woman.

He entered the library where his nervous solicitor sat, perched upon a chair as if to take flight any moment. The man looked rumpled and sleepless, which is the way any man would look if he were summoned across the length of England, he thought sardonically. He waved the man down into his chair while he rang for refreshments. It would not do for the solicitor to faint from hunger.

"Relax, Williams, you're not being discharged. Nor are any of the contracts you've drawn up in danger. I simply have a matter of a personal nature I wish you to handle." He pushed his notes across the desk to Williams, who scanned them, looked at the earl in disbelief, then read the page more carefully. He lay the sheet down on the desk in front of him as if it were infected.

"My lord?" he asked in an incredulous whisper.

"Quite so," the earl said, with humor, understanding his solicitor's shock. The document Katherine had insisted upon was novel in the extreme. Instead of being couched in flowery language, she had insisted that the words be baldly stated. "There is more shame in dark corners and slithering fears, my lord, then in the simple words of truth," she had said.

"But doesn't the young lady understand?" Williams was still pale, and Freddie motioned for Townsende to pour him a stiff drink. While the solicitor finished it, the earl leaned back and crossed his arms, sipping his own in silence. He waited until the shuffling servant left the room before he motioned to Williams to continue.

"Even if you were not to honor the terms of the contract, my lord, she would have no power to enforce it. A male member of her family would have to sign for her to empower the contract, but I cannot countenance how any member of a young lady's family would sign this." He pointed at the offending document in scorn.

"I know that, Williams. You know that. But the lady in question does not know that. And," he added, casting a stern eye on the squirming solicitor, "I wish to keep it that way."

"But, my lord," said the stammering man, "to take advantage in such a way seems . . ." He did not finish his thought. Instead, the earl's look brought to mind the tremendous expansion of his growing firm—thanks in large part to Moncrief's business concerns—the new house in Mayfair, his wife's penchant for dressing from Worth, the new carriage, and the pretty young thing who was waiting for him to return from a trip his wife believed would take over two weeks. He swallowed, and considered his options.

"I will witness it, my lord," he said, any temporary concerns of his conscience buried by worries about his purse.

"You do that, Williams," the earl said calmly, and smiled.

It was done.

Signed, sealed, and formally delivered into Katherine's hands with an unctuous bow by the fawning Williams. A month of her life for the promise of a secure future. Two errant thoughts struck her as she stood in a beam of fading sunlight: Was the bargain worth it? And what would her mother say?

It was strange that she did not summon Constance to

her mind, but perhaps not so strange after all. Constance, like the maiden aunt she often appeared to be, had never married. Passion for her governess was wrapped up in words or shrouded in thoughts of long-dead philosophers. It was not lusty and real, in the guise of the Earl of Moncrief. It was not images of damp sheets and wet skin.

Her mother would have understood. With her slight smile and twinkling eyes, she betrayed her knowledge of life each day. Words like "Remember, my little love, when there is a rainbow overhead, there must have been rain," or "Life is like soup, dearling, having substance or barely edible," she indicated her pragmatic approach to living. Her mother would have understood. Perhaps not condoned, nor approved, but Lizette would have known why.

The earl could burn her to cinders.

Which led to the second thought. Was any alliance with him worth it? She sat in the comfortable chair in her sitting room and looked toward the home woods.

Ever since she was a child, she had sought solitude when faced with a problem. Until her parents' death, her most urgent concerns had been the color of her new sash or the location of her new calfskin shoes. Childhood worries had changed overnight, as her thoughts became occupied with fighting for survival—how to eke out an existence for herself and her small staff, and how to save the manor house that had been her family's home for generations.

She hadn't done so well at survival, it seemed. She was back in the same position she had been before, only now, it was complicated by her love for Julie. She had lost Donegan, her family of servants had scattered for paying positions, and her maidenhead had been sacrificed for a future that only existed in dreams.

It was the supreme irony that the one thing that was so highly touted about a female was the one thing she'd barely noticed losing. Oh, yes, there was a pinch, and a spot of blood at the end, but it was the discomfort about the whole act that she noted most. It hadn't been worth losing her marriageability, really. In fact, until the incursion of the Earl of Moncrief into her life, she had wondered what the poets and the bards had sung about. It wasn't that it felt bad; it had been mostly boring. The second son of the Duke of Westerland had been less interested in her opinion than he had been his own pleasure, groaning and breathless, pushing on top of her and into her with less technique than enthusiasm. David had not been a very nice young man, but his promises of undying fidelity had been more palatable than the shouts of creditors mounted on Donegan's steps. Still, she really should have been wiser.

Constance had died the month before, and her parents had been gone for nearly four months. The influenza epidemic which had decimated her family and the village near their home had finally spared the rest of them. Katherine knew that she would have succumbed to anyone's blandishments, as long as they held her and let her cry. She had, quite willingly, bent the bonds of propriety herself until they snapped.

A much wiser woman had discovered that the map of life has a way of changing just when you set the last compass point down on paper and brushed off your hands, sighing in relief.

The young heir to the heir to the dukedom, it seemed, could not align himself with a lowly baron's daughter, penurious as she was. Nor was she a virgin anymore, and the moment when he condemned her loose ways—idiot that he was—was truly the moment the last drop of her innocence bled away.

Her habit of solitude had not helped her then, and it didn't look as though it was going to help now. What she needed now was the same thing she had desperately needed six months ago: money and security.

And love?

Love was one of those pleasures she had given up, like riding and reading.

There was a time in which she could have easily escaped the consequences of her actions. Today, the moment she signed her name in flowing script upon the imposing looking parchment, Katherine had taken the step to banish any shred of innocence.

Was the bargain worth it? Only time would tell.

If she were isolated from society in the future, it had been her own conscious decision. The earl had lost nothing. Indeed, his reputation might well be enhanced by the sheer effrontery of his deed. After all, everyone secretly loved a rake. They might condemn him aloud as morally bankrupt, but he made their hearts pound.

Like hers?

Yes, like hers.

As long as she sat by the window, intently watching the shadows lengthen among the trees, she could hold back the night. The sun would ease into the horizon more slowly, the evening chores would be delayed, dinner would be set back, and her world would soften easily into twilight instead of rushing to darkness.

That was what she pretended. She was wrong.

An hour later, Abigail knocked on the door. Two maids followed her inside the room, bearing a hip bath and buckets of hot water. So much for a discreet alliance, Katherine thought, a wry smile contorting her lips.

She bathed under the ministrations of the three who, despite her protests, remained in the room. Abigail dumped a vial of rose-scented perfume in the water, and sprinkled it around Katherine's nude body until the entire room was redolent of a spring rose garden.

Too soon they left her. Clad in a soft yellow wrapper over a matching nightgown, she stood at the window. Night had slipped in like a black cloth, shielding the scenery from prying eyes. She knew the stables only by the flickering lantern hung on a hook outside the broad door. The path to the garden was illuminated only by its paved white rock. The sweep of mown grass was gray, barely moon-touched, a landscape of eerie beauty.

Her hands twisted nervously on the belt of her robe, fingers whitening under the pressure. It was one thing to objectively view her future, dispassionately counsel herself in the most practical path. Quite another to wait placidly for her own surrender.

It was as if the smothering darkness had also suffocated any thoughts of passion. Desire was only a word, replaced by another, stronger emotion.

Panic.

With that intuitive knowledge of him which she simply accepted, she sensed his presence before he spoke. Although she had not heard the door open, Katherine knew when he entered the room, as if the air subtly changed, or the space they shared was narrowed and compressed. He moved, as always, with the grace of a predatory animal, lithe, sliding. She didn't flinch as large hands encompassed her shoulders and pulled her against his chest. She was waiting until the bubble of fear percolating inside of her exploded and she lost what composure she had left. Strangely, disconcertingly, it seemed to dissipate with his touch. He put his arms around her until they folded over her own, trapping her within the hard, warm cocoon of his embrace. She leaned her head back until it touched his chest and sighed. Not an expression of surrender, she told herself, but of recognition. She grew warmer as they stood there staring out at the darkness, her fingers no longer cold and stiff, nor her legs shaking and weak.

She looked up at him as he gently turned her in his arms. He lifted one aristocratic finger and drew it up her throat until he reached the tip of her chin. With gentle strength, he forced her face up until her eyes met his.

"Second thoughts?" His voice was deep and melodious, echoing with the dark sensuality that defined him.

Her smile was fragile, a gift of light, unshaded, however, by fear. What she had done she had done with no thought to its undoing. It had not been an impulsive gesture.

"Would it do any good?" she challenged.

"No," he said simply. She allowed him to cradle her against him, inhaling his scent. He, too, had bathed in preparation, and the dampness of his shirt she attributed to his lack of patience. How like him. The odor of linen, brandy, and the unique scent of his own skin was as much an aphrodisiac as any devised by man.

But truly, would she need any? To be around him was to recognize the depth of his appeal and the futility of her resistance.

"Come," he said, that damnable command, and this time she went with him. The knock on the door shattered her reverie. He allowed her to hide in the bedroom as the servants, preceded by a sternly disapproving Mrs. Roberts, entered.

After they had left, she entered the room again to find him lighting the beeswax candles arrayed over the small damask-covered table. Silver serving pieces were placed beside both settings, their gleaming lids echoing the glittering light. Nestled among the softly shining silver and the sparkling etched crystal were three white roses, tiny buds that had been plucked from the last blooming rosebush. It was an intimate setting, totally seductive, and very, very practiced.

"Lovely," she said, and the edge to her voice alerted him. His green eyed gaze took in the flush upon her cheeks, the glitter in her eyes.

"Am I being chided because of my preparation, Kat? It would seem to be more onerous than lack of forethought."

"I do not honestly see how one could ever accuse you of lack of forethought, my lord. It appears that you have a surfeit of it. I applaud your scene of seduction, my lord." She lifted the lid of one of the serving dishes and peered within. Tender baked chicken was arranged upon a bed of wild rice. She could smell curry and other spices not familiar to her.

She sat, his attention strangely unnerving, and calmly buttered a dinner roll that was one of Nora's specialties. She would not look at him; she knew what she would see. He would be silent, unmoving, a statue hewn from bronze anger. He would not intimidate her. She would not allow him that.

He sat down opposite her and reached for a roll, duplicating her movements. They sat silent at the intimate table for long moments, neither speaking, neither trusting simple words. As a scene of seduction, it was perfect. The only thing lacking was the participation of the seducer and the seduced.

"Tell me about your home, Kat," he finally said, breaking the silence like a hammer will shatter glass. It was a voice devoid of irritation, and when she looked at him he was smiling softly, those perfect lips curled sweetly at the ends.

So like his daughter.

"There is not much to tell, my lord." One finger swirled the crumbs on her plate, pushing them over to one side with delicate precision.

"There must be something about it that would pique the interest of a casual observer. Tell me, is it like Mertonwood?"

"Donegan is small," she said, grateful that he steered the conversation to something more palatable. "It is nestled among an outcropping of rock, overlooking green, rolling hills. It is an old place, steeped in history. The roof leaked and the flagstones were chipped, but I loved it. It is unpretentious, I think, like myself."

"Kat, there is not one unpretentious bone in your body." The humor in his voice was unmistakable. "You may loudly disclaim a fact, but that does not make it true."

How well she knew that. She thought of the many times she had arrogantly stated she could save Donegan. Creditors, servants, steward, and even Constance had looked doubtful, but her faith had never faltered. Until, of course, the end, when she had seen that her bluster would never make reality out of wishful dreaming.

"What is it that causes such a look?" He was genuinely surprised to find her mood softening, not to passion but to sorrow. "Had I known to cause you pain, I'd never have asked," he said gently. "It is all in the past."

Tender words from a man not given to them, for a reason even he would denounce.

What he said was true. Her memories of the past could only haunt her present and spoil her future. Katherine glanced at the man opposite her and wondered who he truly was. She had seen the concerned landowner, the careful steward, the businessman, the unwilling father. She had spied the arrogance of command, the lover who teased, but she did not know the substance of the earl. Who was this man who was to shortly merge his body with hers? Was he kind or cruel, careful or improvident? Was he a gambler or a planner? What did he want from life; what were his goals, his dreams? He sat beside her with the insouciance of a born noble, proud, determined, coached in the pleasures of the flesh and more than willing to share and demonstrate his prowess. But who was he? She knew she was likely never to know. He would divulge only as much of himself as he was comfortable to reveal, expose only that which he consciously allowed. She doubted he would ever willingly show pain or anxiety or fear. His demeanor was of strength, of body, will, and purpose. His was not the personality to bend to another's. Nor did he willingly entrust himself, or parts of himself, to others.

Katherine did not know how closely she came to defining the earl by his own terms.

He served her the roasted chicken, wild rice, and vegetables himself, mounding her plate high with food as though she had been a serf toiling in the fields all day.

"Were you an only child?" he asked unexpectedly, in the act of pouring wine from the chill-misted bottle.

"How did you know?"

"A lucky guess, perhaps. But children who have been raised singly have a certain independence in their manner. Not unlike yours. They seek their own counsel rather than depend upon the dictates of others."

"That sounds remarkably like you, my lord."

He grinned. "It is a trait that oldest children also share, I'll admit. But I spoke of your rather startling announcement, my dear. Your lack of virginity, Kat."

"I do wish you would refrain from calling me by that silly name," she said, annoyed.

"As I wish that you would begin calling me by mine."

"It is a subject we have already discussed, my lord. I cannot call you Freddie. It simply does not suit." It was her turn to grin at him, and he stopped in the act of sipping his wine to stare at her over the rim of his glass. By God, she was lovely, with her hair unbound and swirling over her shoulders. The flush of embarrassment had receded somewhat, leaving her cheeks only faintly touched with color. Her lips were deep coral, full and parted slightly. And those eyes. They could cut with malice or heal with compassion. They sparked and raged and softened with equal fervor. He shifted in his chair. The rest of her, a vision he had studiously avoided lest this evening come to an abrupt conclusion, now lay unveiled for his pleasure. The soft yellow wrapper had parted, allowing him a glimpse of creamy flesh silkily covered by sheer, taut fabric. He envied her nightgown.

"It does not matter what you call me, Kat. Only that my name is on your lips, and often."

"Then shall I call you despoiler, ravager of innocents, unprincipled? Rake?"

"I spoil nothing, Kat," he said with a wicked smile. "Some would say that I leave it enhanced by my presence. If I've ravaged an innocent, it was at her request. I have a myriad of principles, most of which dictate my life but which I have no desire to enforce in others. I do not care to be an arbiter of morality, you see. Rake? Perhaps. I have no adequate defense for what others think of me. I simply do not care, most times. But we digress. I believe the subject was your virginity. Or," he said, one eyebrow winging upwards, "the lack of it."

She looked at him for a full minute without speaking, ignoring the chicken cooling on her plate, the wine warming in her glass. It was a testament to his self-mastery that he suffered her intense scrutiny without batting an eyelash. Two adversaries measuring the strength of the other. The thought that he was about to bed this nemesis lent a curious sparkle to the moment.

"Is it important to you?" Faint words spoken just as tremulously. Perhaps they encouraged honesty. He would wonder, later, why he had told the truth with such ease.

"Yes." Simple, uncomplicated. Yet infinitely complex.

"I thought myself in love."

He would have preferred other words. The quest for veracity was suddenly a journey he didn't want to continue. Why, was not difficult to determine. He simply didn't want to hear the trace of betrayal in that slightly husky voice. Nor did he welcome a mist of sentimental tears or painful regret stamped upon her features.

Tonight was his.

"And now?" He heard his own words with something

akin to disbelief. His conscience, unplagued as it was at any other time with any burden of note, had asserted itself with a vengeance.

She smiled but said nothing, which infuriated him at the same time it garnered his admiration. She was too well versed in tactics of war, this girl-woman, with her gift of retreat and advance. She was as brilliant a strategist as Hannibal encircling the Romans.

"Do you still fancy yourself in love, Kat?" His insatiable curiosity about her required a few answers. By God, he'd left her with her secrets, but this one, this solitary riddle, would be solved.

"No." She gave him what he wanted, but not the spirit of it. She did not flesh in the details as he'd expected, brought nothing to the confession but the simplicity of it. No. That was all?

"Do you come to Mertonwood often?" She was like the most talented of London hostesses now, turning the conversation to something banal and boring. He allowed her the pretense of believing his curiosity appeased. The subject was artfully closed, but not forgotten.

"You chastised me for my lack of parental concern, Kat. You know how little I visit the place."

Mertonwood had been the fourth earl's playground, a site for a few parties whose scandalous activities were still regaled. She had not been at Mertonwood for very long before the entire history of the Moncrief family had been divulged to her. Her sources should have forgotten the long-dead earls and concentrated on the living one—the information would have been so much more useful.

"My grandfather was born here, and although he lived at Moncrief, this was the place he always considered home. He was an old man by the time I was born, but two more kindred souls never existed. He taught me to ride. I was three years old at the time, and almost too far past the age of learning without fear, he said." His face was changed by the memory, softened. The edges of his mouth curled upwards, the faint line on his forehead disappeared.

"Why, then, do you not visit more often?" She was disturbed by the humor lurking in his eyes, the soft look of memory diffusing their power. He was approachable, suddenly, and it frightened her. For the first time, it was possible to imagine him as a young boy, laughing with glee. Climbing trees, mastering his first horse, fishing from the banks of the stream that flowed into Merton Forest. She did not want him more approachable, softer.

She did not want to *like* the Earl of Moncrief.

"It was my father's retreat," he said simply. The words divulged little, but the look on his face fleshed in an explanation. A derisive twist of his lips indicated his feelings for his father, emerald shards of green hardened still further.

"I wonder, my lord," she murmured. Gone was the boyish charm; in its wake was something infinitely more disturbing, a hardness, deliberate and ruthless, divulging more of his innate character than that revealed by his effortless appeal. "I suspect that it is more that you miss your grandfather when you are here. It is the same reason I would not choose to return to my home. The loss of my loved ones are so much more poignant in their rightful setting."

"Perhaps," he said curtly, dismissing her empathy and cursing himself for waxing poetic over the old man. The third earl had not been a gentle curmudgeon, but a stern and demanding taskmaster, made bitter through the years by the wildness of his only son. It was only with his grandson that he had allowed himself to relinquish, even a little, the bonds of autocracy and soften somewhat. Even so, his grandfather's kindness had an edge to it. The soft bundle of femininity beside him could not understand his past, and he was a fool to bring it up. He was also a fool to skirt so closely to less palatable memories, bitter chunks of thought that swelled in his gut like an ingested sponge. Why the hell had he? He shook his head as if to clear it.

Katherine saw the gesture, the retreat, and told herself it was for the best. It was safer, seeing no more than he wanted her to see.

"I'm sorry, Kat. Memories are best served for solitary times."

Too well she remembered the pain of doing just that. She wondered what secrets the Earl kept so closely guarded. Did she really want to know?

She ate little, but drank even less. That first dinner with him had taught her well.

He watched her nibble at the edge of the tart Nora had prepared for dessert, a timid tongue darting out to whisk away the crumbs from the corner of her lip. He had been in a semi-aroused state for over a week, he reasoned, an hour or so longer would not kill him. At least, he hoped not.

She grew aware of his scrutiny finally, and she blushed. Then cursed herself for allowing him to fluster her.

He sat motionless, fascinated by her darting eyes; she looked everywhere but at him.

"Kat," he murmured, his eyes never leaving her face, "you have a crumb on the corner of your mouth." Startled, she brushed her fingers across her lips. "Pity," he said, "I wanted to lick it off for you."

At her quick, admonishing look, he smiled. "Do you delay the inevitable, Kat? My tongue knows your mouth even now. Each line, each soft curve, each swelling measure of lip. Is it that you're afraid?"

"My anxiety, I believe, is superfluous." Katherine sought control and did not find it. She clasped her hands beneath the table and stared at the congealing food on her plate. She anticipated the scrape of his chair, the touch of his large hands. Surprised, she looked up to find him still seated, his eyes fixed upon an index finger tracing the curve of a crystal goblet. He licked the tip of his finger, then traced the rim until a barely audible hum broke the silence. The low and resonant sound followed the circular motion of his finger, not unlike the way she chased the gesture with her eyes. He glanced at her.

"This is what I want you to feel, Kat. A strumming, as if all your senses were concentrated in one place and one finger was playing you like an instrument." As exposure, it was intense, a confession of intent. To render her without will, without regard. A being of sensation, but not sentient.

The knowledge did not stop the throbbing in a dark and secret place only he seemed capable of unlocking.

"I have often envied women," he said, leaning back in the chair and folding his arms across his chest. Comfortable, yet not relaxed. That would come later. Much later, if the near pain in his loins could wait. "They are capable of feeling so much. But it has been my experience that, except for a fortunate few, they have never been taught to feel at all." His gaze was intent, retribution for her earlier regard. "Did your lover teach you much, Kat?"

Not as much as you. The words were left unsaid, but she wondered if he knew anyway. A spark leapt in the green pool of his eyes.

"They have a spot," he continued, "that is the height of pleasure. Little more than a tiny bud which flowers, under the right conditions, of course." He smiled and watched her face. "But we must not forget those luscious breasts, however. Did you know that your breasts are quite large for your frame, Kat? I had not realized until now."

She could not meet his eyes. If his aim were to embarrass her, he was doing quite nicely. If he meant to quell her anxiety, that had faded beneath the strange and not unwelcome feeling his words evoked.

She was quite magnificent, he thought, sitting there looking wounded and confused by the force of her own emotions. One touch and he would burn in a conflagration powerful enough to torch the whole of England.

He wanted the flames.

She had never seen anyone move so fast.

He carried her to the bed and removed her wrapper, his gestures not that of a man totally in control. She lay abandoned where he lay her, not caring, not feeling anything other than those sensations incited by him. A flush bathed her body and intensified as she looked into his strong face. She was warmth and swelling flesh that could not, somehow, exist without his touch upon her. She watched as he stripped his dressing gown with hurried fingers, and then stood, bare chested and glorious, before her. His midnight-hued hair was tousled, one lock slipping over a frowning forehead. She ached to smooth it away and banish the sudden frown with a kiss. He had summoned passion and something more with his words, a wild type of needing that encompassed nurturing, tenderness, longing.

"You are so beautiful, Kat," His voice was harsh. Gone was the soft, melodic tone; in its place was appetite, impatient and exacting. As eager as the flesh he suddenly bared. She stared at that part of him that jutted proudly from a nest of black curls, not chiding herself for wanton thoughts when she ached to touch him there, too. He was masculine perfection, forged iron and warm skin.

The soft yellow nightgown was ripped from her body, but she did not shudder in revulsion. Nor did she whisper words of contrition or condemnation when he knelt beside her, naked, studying her as though she were a subject for a painting, and he meant to capture her for all time on the canvas of his memories. She lay exposed, not by her flesh, he thought, but by the wonder in her eyes. It told him what he needed to know, that if she were not virgin in body, she was in mind. The lover who had initiated her had done nothing but find his own release, a stupidity that caused the earl to smile. She wondered at it, seconds before he kissed her.

"Sweet Kat," he murmured across her lips, before his tongue stroked their outline and darted between them, licking, delicately touching. She smoothed one hand through black hair and pulled his head toward hers, but he wouldn't move, wouldn't deepen the kiss.

"No, Kat. Not yet," he scolded, and wet one finger with his tongue. Wide eyes watched as he placed that finger against her breast, circling the nipple but never quite touching it. The seductive tableau ended in a smile from him, and an unwilling sound from her. He lay beside her and gently placed her head in the crook of his arm, keeping his face only inches from hers.

She had never felt so feverish, so demented in her life.

"Shall I kiss you here, Kat?" he asked as his finger finally, achingly, touched her nipple, pressed lightly against flesh rendered hot by words and gentle teasing. He waited until she nodded, her face pressed against his chest. "You must say the words, Kat," he said, smiling.

"Please," was all that she could master, and that one word was all the permission or urging he needed. His mouth, molten heat and flicking tongue, kissed her breast, avoiding the one spot that desperately sought solace. She placed her hand below the curve of breast and lifted it to his mouth. He glanced at her, a quick, knowing glance, and took the offering she presented. He sucked the elongated nipple deep into his mouth, then bit gently as she arched up from the bed. Gentle mastery, as he suckled her in apology. The straining nipple grew longer in his mouth, a tender autocrat, demanding surcease.

She was soft everywhere, he thought, before thought was a thing of the past and only feeling remained. He licked her under both breasts, soft, tender flesh, while he prayed desperately for restraint. The pain was excruciating, the torture unimaginable, the heat of her overwhelming.

If passion were wine, it would be burgundy, a deep bordeaux as heady in scent as it was in taste. Languid on the tongue, bitter and lulling until the blood boiled deep. His mouth was wine, all the subtle flavors of the vineyard. Sweet and promising that flicking tongue, full bodied those lips plucking kisses from her. He sighed in deep satisfaction when her mouth opened beneath his and she met his plundering tongue with hers, just as restless.

Impatient fingers strayed to her thighs, all thoughts of teasing forgotten as he fought against a need so powerful it almost robbed him of breath. He found her wetness in acute relief and boundless gratitude, and moaned against the taste of her.

"Oh God, Kat," he mumbled against her throat, offering up indebtedness to an understanding God that his patience would not be strained any further. "You are so wet. So hot." He spread her open for him, praying that he could last the next few moments, and that lusting after this woman would not ultimately kill him.

He felt as though he were dying.

He tipped up her chin with fingers wet with her own passion, forcing her to look at him. His eyes were pools of reckless abandon, shards of green light through which deviltry, self-deprecating humor, and barely leashed restraint shone through.

She blinked and he shut his eyes for a moment, weak in the face of her innocence. Again, he stroked his hand through her intimate curls, this time barely touching her. He watched her eyes as she struggled to hide her feelings, to mask the totality of her need. She wanted to throw her legs wide open and demand that he end this. Fill me, she could say, if her experience had been more, or her innocence less. As it was, she was inarticulate with wanting.

"Please," she murmured, eager lips against his suddenly reticent mouth.

"Please what?" Please make her beg, or I will, he thought. He could not take much more.

She looked into his eyes with a directness that was at odds with her surrender. "Please," she said, "make me purr," and pulled his head down for a spiraling kiss.

He spoke for both of them when he murmured against her eager mouth, "Gladly."

He entered her in one swift, hard movement, barely noting that there was no obstruction to his possession. She reached up and licked his lips with a suddenly talented tongue. He moaned, his need an entity of its own, and it was difficult to concentrate on anything but sensation after that. She met his downward movements with an upward push of her body, meeting him stroke for stroke, need for need. She didn't know that to be truly ladylike she should have lain beneath him unmoving. Nor did she know that to be truly a whore, she should have feigned the response he coaxed easily from her. He shuddered in surprise and something like fear when her passion exploded around him, sucking him into a vortex unlike anything he'd known.

Who was the seducer and who the seduced, he wondered as she lay beside him, replete with satiated passion and sleeping the sleep of the just. She turned, curling into him, and he automatically nestled her closer, then questioned his own actions. He studied her as she slept, unknowing that his face mirrored his confusion, and that the color of his eyes were a deeper green than they had ever been.

Chapter 6

He seemed younger as he slept, Katherine thought, but not childlike. No boy would have that strong chin, those full lips, those sweeping lashes that rivaled a courtesan's in length and fullness. Nor would a boy have a chest that wide and muscled and boasting a pelt of black hair. He was turned on his side, an arm outstretched to cradle his head, a large hand hidden beneath her pillow. His other hand stretched across her hip as she lay facing him.

He branded her as his even in sleep.

Memories of their lovemaking flushed her already-tinged cheeks, yet she had no thoughts of regret. If she had set into motion forces for her own destruction, then she was honest enough to admit that she had done so willingly. Yet, if she had to embark upon the road to ruin, at least she had the good sense to choose a talented seducer.

The innocence of her body had been denied him, but not the purity of her mind. Forever after, a gesture, a word, might remind her of abandon and seduction, splendor and unquestioned surrender. She would never be the same, but then, she had suspected that before their bargain was struck. If she had fled from Mertonwood without entering into this unholy alliance, she would have always wondered. Now she no longer wondered, but she would always remember.

He eyed her between slitted lids warily.

What would it be, tears or anger?

Mornings after could be messy scenes, either sprinkled with regret or fury, neither emotion designed to be shared with a party unwilling to partake of them. He was well aware that he had occasionally been chosen as an antidote to boredom, an act of vengeance against a straying mate, bait for a jealous but lukewarm lover, or simply as a challenge. Regardless of the motivation that lured or propelled a woman into his bed, he had come to expect reprisals in the morning.

The pouting face betraying remorse needed to be kissed into submission, the raging virago demanded coaxing humor. The willing woman of the evening before almost always clutched her honor around her like a well-worn robe, able to bear self-scrutiny only by claiming seduction. He never understood how these women could blithely overlook their own willing participation in the act of love and then decry it in the morning.

During the last few years, those messy little scenes had made seduction less a lure than a bother. In a moment of candor, Freddie would have admitted to seriously contemplating a liaison with a member of the demimonde. Not only would such a long-term arrangement prevent entanglements like the one that resided in the upstairs nursery, but it would also mean that he would not have to endure waking and, in those first few moments of drowsy contemplation, wondering what kind of hell he would face.

He awaited Katherine's first words with caution.

"Hello," she said softly, not turning away when she realized he was watching her.

"Hello," he responded, just as softly, still not certain of her mood. She was as lovely this morning as he had known she would be, flushed and warm from his loving and from a deep sleep. He rolled closer to her, testing, but she didn't move away.

Neither tears nor anger. Good, that answered that question.

She eyed his frown curiously. Perhaps the earl was used to London hours and detested mornings. She had learned to wake with the dawn and Julie. The sky was still pink outside, the winter sun hiding behind gray clouds. Evidently, he would be better served to sleep until noon, or at least until his mood improved. Katherine turned on her back and stretched, preparatory to leaving the bed, when he moved.

He rolled toward her with animal grace and caution, but she breached the distance between them first, surprising him by kissing his forehead as if he were Julie's age, and then smoothing his hair back with one slender hand. It was both a nurturing gesture and a tender one, and it disconcerted him so much that his next words were not those he whispered on mornings after—words of praise rehearsed for years and summoned to even a hazy mind. His mind stumbled on the truth, recognized it, and blurted it out before he could restrain himself.

"I've never known anything like last night," he said, honesty providing an edge to his voice, a hesitation that even he recognized.

She flushed, and it was a reaction he'd half expected.

"Are you real?" he asked against the flesh of her neck. She giggled when he bit gently and then caressed the spot with his lips and tongue. He looked into her laughing eyes and thought that there were worse ways to awaken.

"I'm very real," she said, looking at his serious face. He was the one made more than human. Last night had been so different. So much more than she'd ever experienced before. The duke's second son did not compare favorably at all.

She smiled, and he grinned, and for a moment, they lay there side by side, in perfect accord, too happy to worry about the fact that society would have it otherwise.

He pulled her toward him, rolling over, the result being that she found herself resting on top of him. It was a strange position, but no less novel than the exploring hands that trailed up her sides and around to her back. She wiggled when he found a particularly sensitive area and giggled when he deliberately began to tickle her.

"No fair," she accused, but he didn't relinquish his hold.

She straddled him, her knees grinding into the mattress on either side of his waist, her nakedness tinged pink by the dawn light. She attempted to pin his hands down, but he escaped her grasp easily, his aim to find more places where she was unbelievably ticklish.

When he only laughed at her squirms, she bent and ran her tongue over a nipple half hidden by swirling black hair. He gasped in surprise, but she didn't pause, only turned to the other and tongued it, too. For good measure, she nipped at him gently with her teeth, then straightened. Her smile was as fresh as the new day and as winsome as a young child's. He ignored the challenge she issued with her saucy grin and delighted in watching her. For this moment in time, she was unfettered by restrictive society or rules, playing with passion as though it had been a gift granted only to her and to him. She was naked the way a child is naked, with freedom and delight and the uncalculated joy of it.

There was a mark on the top of her breast, a long red scratch, and he traced it with a gentle finger.

"Did I do that?"

She wanted to tell him he had done that and more. He had branded her with his touch; even now there were places on her body that moved more stiffly than before, warm, secret nooks she had believed insensate, but that he had taught her were ripe with feeling. But she didn't, she only nodded, her smile dusted with tenderness.

"I'm sorry," he said, a lover's morning apology. She blinked rapidly, unwilling to admit the emotion peppering her eyes. Instead, she bent and nipped at him again, summoning his yelp of surprise, banishing her tears equally as fast.

"You'll have to do penance," she said, her lower lip caught between her teeth. "A small penance," she amended, then laughed when the great earl would not cease his frown. "A kiss," she said, leaning over him.

Surprise and unwelcome introspection was nudged aside to kiss her. A kiss flavored with wonder, elation, and a deep sense of rightness so foreign it was frightening. He kissed her with tenderness, then with potency, and finally, with a full and heavy dose of morning passion. He kissed her with lips and tongue, and words.

"Kat, sweet Kat, lovely Kat," he murmured between kisses. He held her face still, his lips exploring her face across the bridge of her nose to her forehead, down a silky cheek to her chin, up again to the closed lids with their fluttering lashes, and then back to a smiling mouth. He reached up and pulled her down to him more completely, nuzzling her neck, then moving down to sweet, creamy breasts. She cupped herself for him, and he lay beneath her, sucking gently, then harder, as she arched her neck and closed her eyes at the feeling. It was what he had promised he would do and she aided him in suckling her. She wanted, in a strange and unsettling way, to feed him all the unique and new feelings she was experiencing right at this moment.

He reared, tossed her effortlessly onto her back, and entered her with a force he had not used the night before. Castigating himself for his haste, he realized he had slipped fully, if tightly, inside of her liquid warmth with ease. He reached a hand between them to feel her, and she was hot and slick for him. Again, her quick climax precipitated his own, as he felt the silken walls clamping tight around him.

It was, he would think later, a dangerous delirium.

He fell back into a languor that quickly led to sleep, oblivious to the tender kiss she placed upon his lips, or the fact that she left the bed soon afterwards.

It was a bitterly cold morning, and although snow had not yet touched the ground this season, it was promised in the low-hanging gray clouds and the scent of frosty moisture in the air. Outside, errands were performed with the greatest of speed, warm flesh battling against the encroaching cold. The windows throughout the house were fogged as the fireplaces were refueled with carefully dried logs. It was a drab day, a cheerless day, and the earl felt better than he had in months.

He stood at the doorway of the cozy nursery and watched Katherine feed his squirming daughter. Julie's flannel-covered arms were flailing in the air, either in excitement or revulsion for her breakfast of thin, gray oatmeal.

It was odd, he thought, that he even visited these third-floor rooms. Most of his titled contemporaries sired their heirs, then studiously ignored them until they had outgrown nappies and colic. Children were conceived in duty and reared on sufferance. It was foolish to become too attached to one until it had survived infancy, and even then life expectancy was not guaranteed but for the most hardy. The children of the ton were carefully isolated until their manners were established and their education begun. In other words, until they were civilized. This was accomplished by the simple expedient of paying for it. Wet nurses, nurses, governesses, tutors, and companions earned a living by training and teaching the sons and daughters of the nobility. Society established the final building blocks of character, namely a set of rigid strictures to obey and a system of sanctions for those who would refute them. Parents were superfluous in the nobility, and one who involved himself in the day-to-day life of his child was considered eccentric.

The earl did not doubt that the lure of the nursery was the auburn-haired figure who was now cleaning a small, messy, but cherubic face. Strange, he had difficulty remembering Celeste's face, even though her child had the same coloring. He remembered small gestures, a softly pouting mouth, a pert, tipped nose. Celeste had been doll-like, almost fragile looking, as though life were always a little too much to bear. She had engendered in him an overwhelming sense of protectiveness, a feeling that was lacking in his relationship with Katherine. She was not one to be coddled, feted, wrapped in bunting and sheltered from the world. No, he suspected that the world should be warned about Katherine.

"Now that the imp is fed, what about me?" he asked teasingly, moving from the door.

Katherine turned in the act of coaxing a stubborn Julie into a clean smock. Her lips curved into a shy, happy smile totally at odds with the ruination of her reputation. Julie touched her mouth and mimicked the gesture.

"You're not an imp, are you, pet?" she asked the child, nuzzling the tiny nose with her own. Julie gurgled and gripped handfuls of curls. Katherine spent a moment trying to free herself from the tenacious grasp of the child. His own large, tanned hand intercepted Katherine's as he reached for his daughter.

His smile widened as he worked and remembered his mother's admonition. He wondered what she would say if she knew he'd followed her advice to the letter. She had warned him not to let too much time elapse before he got to know his child. "Time," she had said earnestly, her blue eyes imploring him to listen, "has a way of slipping between your fingers, Freddie."

Between your fingers.

"She's as stubborn as you, my lord," Katherine teased. She glanced up and froze. A moment ago, his smile had been almost tender, his face relaxed and sated, those green eyes unbelievably clear. Now, his face was etched with strain, the long groove of a frown sharply delineated. His lips were only thin horizontal lines. He was intently studying the tiny fingers nestled in his own large palm. Abruptly he flung the hand away and strode through the room with long, measured strides. The door to the nursery slammed hard enough to rattle the panes of glass in the window.

She found him in his library, standing by the frost-etched window, idly watching the first flakes of snow waft from the sky. In his hand was a snifter of brandy, and judging from the level in his glass, he had already consumed a major portion of it. It was evidently to be his breakfast. He was motionless, his shoulders straight, his back rigid. The hand that gripped the glass was white knuckled, and his jaw was clenched, the muscle on the side of his face warning her that his peaceful pose was deceptive.

If she touched him, would she set that tension into motion, like a tightly wound spring suddenly uncoiled? Katherine stood, quietly, until he acknowledged her presence. He had known from the moment she walked into the room, but he was not ready to speak. Not yet.

"Do you know, I can't quite decide about you," he said finally. She wondered if the silence had been as onerous for him as it had been for her. She ached to touch him, to stroke those rigid shoulders, lay her face against that unyielding back. But she did nothing, restrained by his barely leashed rage. "I think your protectiveness admirable, Katherine. It's almost as if you bore the child and not Celeste."

"I do not know what you mean, my lord."

He spun, and she flinched at the look on his face. If fury were ever brought to life, it existed in his expression at that moment. "Dear God," he spat, not trusting himself to close the distance between them, "surely you can summon up something more friendly than that! If not after last night, then at least this morning!" The words were bitten off, the contempt in his voice real and solid and incredibly painful.

"Freddie," she said tentatively, one arm extended as if to breach the sudden chasm between them, "what is wrong?"

"Freddie. Dear God," he said, addressing the plastered ceiling as if the Almighty rested there, "she has finally deigned to call me by my name. Why now, Katherine?"

"You have asked it of me," she stammered, hating her nervousness, despising the face of rage that had turned against her, loathing even more her ignorance of the cause of it. She took one tiny step backward and he noticed the gesture, a sardonic twist of his mouth the only response.

"Why did you not tell me she is deformed?"

The absence of sound in the room was a noise in itself, a white silence as though they were cushioned, enveloped in the snow that slowly piled upon the windowsill. She could swear she could hear the sound of each snowflake striking the windowpane. The clock beside the door whirred and ticked, too loud. Even her breathing sounded painfully strident.

"It is such a little thing." Her eyes focused on the patterned carpet.

Her answer enraged him. "It is not such a little thing, Katherine," he said, his voice as brittle as cracking ice. "Her hands are webbed!"

"It is not her fault."

He rolled his eyes to the ceiling.

"It does not matter who is at fault. . . ."

"I will not have you saying it's because she's a bastard."

The moment was not ideal for interruptions, but she insisted upon championing the child. "I've never heard anything so idiotic. Nora won't look at her because she says she carries the devil's curse. Mrs. Roberts says that she wears the mark of God's disfavor. I will not," she nearly stamped her foot, "have you utter any such nonsense."

He faced the window and studied the sky as if it would grant him some answers. All it gave was snow, wet, white, plump snowflakes that covered the lawn, and promised impassable roads.

"Next you will tell me that rumor has it even the Plantagenets were equally cursed," he said. "I do not give a flying farthing if that is so. I do care that the child occupying the nursery upstairs is a peculiar."

"She is not a freak." The words were soft, the condemnation in her tone as harsh as the winter beauty outside the window. "You are the oddity. She is your daughter. What does that make you, who would denounce a child simply because her fingers are not perfect?" She stared at his back.

Of course, Katherine had known that Julie's hands were different; it was why she was bundled in smocks most of the time; the sleeves fell below her hands and were buttoned back. The webbing between her fingers was barely visible, and although the difference might cause her some anguish when she became a young woman, there was always the option of lace gloves. It was certainly not a reason to condemn her as a freak.

"You will have made a bad bargain," he said, running impatient fingers through his thick midnight hair. "You have shared my bed for no good purpose. I would have given the child to you with my eternal blessings. Now, as far as I'm concerned, you may have her call you Mama and set yourself up in your own establishment. I will, of course, settle a small amount of money upon you, but once that is exhausted, do not think to come to me. Pity, Katherine, that Williams was so punctual."

"That is the most insane thing I've ever heard," she said fiercely, her anger rising as swiftly as his. She balled her fists at her sides and clenched her teeth tightly over words she would have loved to shout at him.

"Insanity is not a trait that runs in my family," he said with implacable calm. "But it certainly runs in Celeste's if they thought they could foist her little misfit upon me." His laugh was dry and utterly without humor.

The drone of his words blanketed her thoughts just as the falling snow swiftly blanketed the ground.

"Everything must be perfect for the lordly earl, is that it, Freddie? You must only have the most thoroughbred of horses, the most unblemished child, the most virtuous mistress? How lucky you are to have only the best in your life. How utterly without compassion. I am surprised you wished to bed me, not being a virgin. Should I thank you for your charity?"

She turned and left the room before he could speak, desperate to put some distance between them. She was a fool. Who else but a fool would ache to touch him, would yearn to speak some calming words? Where was the tender lover, the smiling, gentle man of the morning just passed? This man with stiffened shoulders and patronizing tone had lost all of his reason.

Katherine's rage matched his measure for measure as she flew up the stairs to the nursery. She swept Julie up from Sara and returned to her room and remained there exactly thirty seconds. Long enough to notice the rumpled sheets, the remains of the dinner dishes still on the table, the scraps of yellow silk. She uttered a particularly vile Anglo-Saxon curse, learned surreptitiously from one of the stable lads. Looking down into Julie's sweet, smiling face, she excused herself in loud tones. Julie didn't mind; she thought the trip down the stairs in such a huff a grand adventure.

There was not one room in this mausoleum to which she could escape with a six-month-old child. She didn't want to see him at this moment, could not abide his presence, but other than the nursery or her bedroom, there were few places to go. Most of the other rooms were closed off, unheated, and she would not subject Julie to the cold. Katherine returned to the nursery, dismissed a curious Sara, and sat in the rocker with Julie, angrily propelling herself forward with both feet.

"Your father is an idiot," she told the gurgling baby. The earl would recant his stupidity, if only he had half a brain and a more generous heart. It didn't matter that the sweet little fingers were linked by a delicate film of skin. It was not a punishment from God for her bastardy. Julie was just a good-natured baby, promising beauty and a loving heart. Nor was there any dispute as to her parentage. Her eye color was changing every day and, after a few months, would deepen to the green of her father's. The little nose was a perfect mimic of the larger one; the chin was identical. The evidence was right before his eyes, but the earl only saw the fact that she was less than perfect. He was willing to deny his own daughter because she was different.

Fool.

Katherine didn't know if she cursed him or herself.

She had the better part of six months' salary remaining in her reticule. It would not last long, but if she were careful, it would be enough to get home to Donegan and last the winter. Granted, the house was no longer hers, but the people in the village still knew her, and there were plenty who would open their homes to her.

And in the spring?

No one hired a governess with a child.

The only area in which she had shown a talent, if one

discounted playing the pianoforte and the harp, dancing, French, and card games, was passion. She demonstrated a decided vocation for passion. Perhaps she should become a member of the demimonde, she thought, with the first flash of humor since the scene in the library. Katherine Anne Sanderson, destitute daughter of Sir Robert Arthur Sanderson and Lizette de Bourlange Sanderson, of Donegan Castle, would like to announce to all and sundry her new vocation—courtesan extraordinaire. Available for parties, routs, masques, and balls. Fluent in French, musically adept, artistically incompetent, yet can offer conversation, compassion, and superior ability in bed sport.

She was still smiling at the thought when she looked up to find him standing in the doorway. He moved like a ghost, she thought, frowning. The look in his eyes demanded attention and she acquiesced, returning his gaze with her own, somber and direct. Had he spoken any words but those he spoke, she would have gone to him and tried to cozen him from his anger. Had he smiled, or had the hardness of his eyes been muted by any emotion other than rage, she would have re-thought her own alternatives. But the moment passed, and anger still boiled in him, mixed with a volatile emotion over which he had no control. Betrayal. She sat, maternal and nurturing, the baby batting at her face and trying to eat her hair, and the look she gave her was one of tenderness and love. Sweet understanding and caring.

"If you want the brat," he said, the words scraped against the constriction in his throat, "you'll pay for her, Katherine. I still have twenty-nine days left."

Dinner, if not a disaster, was at the very least uncomfortable. Katherine wore her blue serge, the second of her new dresses. Before she forced herself down the steps and into the dining room, she tucked Julie in for the night. In the process, the baby drooled upon her shoulder and, of course, the earl noticed.

"If that is the extent of your wardrobe, Katherine, at least allow me to have you clothed properly." She smiled, a polite, disinterested smile which managed, by its very civility, to irk him.

Since his arrival in the nursery and his crude announcement, she had shot from rage to despair to fear and back to rage again. All her emotions were now distilled into determination. Until she made a decision, the great Earl of Moncrief would not have the power to affect her. She would not cower in the face of his anger. He might be enraged, but she would manage to be serene. Let him be petulant, she would be placid. The remainder of the dinner, therefore, was spent with the earl going out of his way to be as acerbic and as vile as possible, while Katherine tolerated his moods with exceptional good grace. When he returned the ornate server to the kitchen with a command to strain the gravy of its lumps, she ignored him and complimented Nora on the succulent beef.

Only once did she say something, and that was when he swore at the footman and demanded that Townsende pour out all the bottles of the vintage he had just decanted. She smiled, and addressed the footman. "It is not your fault," she told him, ignoring his sudden, confused look. "The earl is a perfectionist, you see. Everything must be just so for him."

"Katherine," he began, but her bright smile was suddenly wobbly, so she would not look at him.

She spoke idly of the beauty of the snow touched by the rays of the setting sun, while the remainder of his dinner conversation deteriorated to grunts and monosyllabic snorts.

He consumed a bottle of wine (freshly decanted by Townsende, of course) with dinner, and a goodly number of servings of port following it. She refrained from commenting on his obvious love for the bottle and he refused to tell her that he rarely touched spirits, but that this visit to Mertonwood demanded something of an alcoholic nature. Often, and in great amounts.

Katherine sat calmly in the drawing room while he worked in the library. After a while, she amused herself by letting her fingers dance over the keys of the pianoforte. She drifted into playing a country ballad, which began on a lilting note and ended in a crescendo of keys.

"Evidently, there's much that I don't know about you," he said. She had grown accustomed to his silent entrances, accustomed, also, to the feeling that announced his arrival. As if the very air were heavier, somehow still, waiting for his words. It was a pity she was growing so attuned to the mocking earl.

"I do not play perfectly," she said, her tone calm, polite, and utterly infuriating.

"You play very well," he said, irritated. She had been oddly acquiescent this night, a ploy that did not suit her well. She was not demure, he thought; even as a child, she would have challenged any adult's rule. She was a hoyden, a trial, an irritation. A ruby among diamonds.

Katherine only nodded, his compliment neutralized by the obvious disdain with which he addressed her. He was spoiling for a fight, and she was not going to accommodate him. She smiled as she stood, drawing her skirts away from the bench.

"Go to your room, Katherine," he said bluntly, clenching his hands at his back. "There is one activity in which you excel. I'll join you shortly."

Her flush was not caused by passion, nor by the anticipation of it. It was the crudeness of his command, the anger that still sparked brittle from green eyes.

She left the room with all the dignity she had never mastered under Constance's care, the lessons of ladylike decorum once easing into giggles and wry comments.

Tonight, she needed such lessons, required the hard-won grace, as she held herself tightly, her chin thrust up to prevent the sudden, surprising tears from falling, from betraying her hurt. They pooled in her eyes instead, adding dimension and depth to a look already fathoms deep with wounded dignity.

He should not have felt her pain so acutely.

Any moment, he would step through that doorway, and she must choose which role to play before he did so. Should she pose as the reluctant innocent, afraid of the power of the passion he had unleashed, or should she welcome him in her bed?

The feelings he evoked by being in the same room were as filled with promise as those when he touched her. Her insatiable curiosity impelled her to come closer to the flame; something more powerful than simple inquisitiveness made her stand so close to the heat. A fascination unlike anything she'd ever felt made her want to touch him, brush her fingers across his shoulders, press her palm against his neck, tuck a wisp of hair behind an ear. A warmth pooled in her stomach at his look, when she watched his hands pick up a glass or his fingers tap impatiently upon a table top. Even his neck intrigued her, that strong, tanned column.

Yet, she was infuriated by his autocracy, his condemnation of a child simply because she was not flawless.

He had the power to bring her to tears, she who had not even cried at her parents' funeral, standing dry-eyed as they were laid to rest together. He, the arrogant, aloof earl summoned her tears with a caustic look and cruelty cloaked in words.

She wished she could be a statue beneath him, a cold marble edifice he would simply enter and leave quickly because of the chill. She wished she would not enjoy it, but the futility of that thought brought a small smile to her lips.

She was a daunting sight, he thought, enough to quell his irritation. The tracks of her tears anointed a soft smile.

Did she mean to unman him, then? An empowered conscience had given him a damnable quarter hour already. Did she mean to finish the job?

"You constantly surprise me," he said softly, his gaze not focused on that flushed face with its slightly reddened nose and lips that looked to have been kissed numb already, but to the sight of her propped up in her bed like a little girl prepared to be read a bedtime story. Except that no little girl had ivory shoulders that rounded so delectably, or smooth, soft breasts that plumped up the thin sheet that covered them, or the long line of limbs outlined by the comforter spread across the bed to ward off the chill.

He smiled, a particularly wolfish grin.

"Honor is not exclusively the province of men, my lord," she said softly. "I have made a contract with you."

It was a silly pretense, but one he allowed her. And she knew it by the quick shuttering of his eyes, and the soft smile that replaced the grin.

"I suffer no martyrs in my bed, Kat. Nor will I accept piety in passion's stead." He sat on the edge of the bed, his hand resting on the other side of those long legs.

"You, perhaps, could benefit from a few prayers uttered for you," she declared, with honest charm. He loomed closer, his breath brandy-laden, coming just an inch from her lips, his eyes focused downward on the sheet slipping with each heavy breath she took. It was not fear that caused her blood to beat, hot and thick. He raised his head slightly so that she could see his eyes, bright with need.

"Do not think, Katherine, that I mean to force you." It was strange, she thought, that he used her full name only when he was angry. "Passion that uses force," he continued, "is only violence renamed. I seek a willing partner for my games, not a fearful one. Do you join me, or do you fight us both?"

She had already fought that battle with herself, and she knew the answer well enough, but it did not mean that she surrendered with such ease. "And if I win peace of mind as the prize for the latter, my lord, what do I garner for the former?"

"Comfort during cold winter nights?"

"It is quite cold at nights, my lord. But I have adequate shelter against the chill." She pulled the comforter up to her chin.

"Perhaps," he said with a smile. He shifted so that his chest lay heavily against her own, one hand palming an eager breast. "But no blanket can cover you as warmly as I can."

He was insufferable, egotistical, empirical, and maddening, but she had to admit he'd won that point.

Chapter 7

The dim morning light entered the small, frosted window with reluctance, revealing a world already encrusted with the first winter white. Snow was heavily laden on pathways, piled high upon dormered roofs, spread thickly on the green mat of Mertonwood's lawn. Drifts barricaded the stable and kitchen doors, imprisoning and insulating both animal and human occupants. Beyond, in the forest, ice ornaments hung from heavy branches bent deep under the weight of snow. What had not been transformed into a silent snow ballet was now a living mirror of silver white, as if nature had become weary of green and sought to mask it.

It was quiet in the cold blue bedroom. Only one of the occupants of the bed slept, occasionally moving restlessly. The other had been awake for a long time.

Sounds began to drift upwards from the heart of the house. The grumble of a maid as she bent under the load of wood destined for the fireplaces; the querulous voice of Townsende, whose arthritic bones suffered in winter's unrelenting cold; the faint clank and clatter of kitchen pots; Mrs. Roberts key weighted belt. From outside came the shuffling, booted crunch of Michael, as the gardener and one of the footmen began to clear a pathway from the kitchen to the stables. Every sound seemed magnified and muffled at the same time.

Activities were as they had been on decades of winter mornings. The stalls were still mucked in the stables, the cook still warned of dire punishments if her newly cleaned floor was tracked through, the maids still complained as they lifted heavy kettles of boiling water for the morning wash, fires were laid, curtains drawn, front steps swept.

It should have been just the same.

Yet, nothing was the same.

A fragile tendril of smoke found its way to the cold room. One of the fireplaces had become blocked by the heavy snow and the smoke billowed back into the house. There was an odor of frying rashers, the bite of the crisp cold, the aromatic tang of tobacco, the faint hint of violets and herbs used to scent the sheets, and the musky odor of sex.

The feel of the roughened sheet seemed oddly harsh, as did the brush of hair against her sensitized skin. The rasp of one long muscled leg against her slender one, the soft sinking suction of the mattress, the plump resilience of a feather pillow—all of these were sensations that seemed as new and as fresh as the morning. Fingertips seemed to feel without touching, as if they were capable of retaining memory. Katherine felt the sweeping sworl of eyelashes against her own flushed cheek, the fullness of her lips as if they swelled outside their borders.

She should have hated him.

She was strangely reminded of her home, of Donegan Castle perched upon chalky cliffs, impervious to the boiling sea below. But the cliffs were not immune to the sea's power, and each wave that crashed against them carried away part of Donegan's foundation.

Each time he touched her, he took something of her with him.

She wanted to love, but never this man. To love the Earl of Moncrief was to gift him with something he would never treasure, nor acknowledge. The greatest danger lay not in his character, but in her own.

She had always been loved. For simply existing, and then for being herself. For being charming, or mutinous, or a challenge to her parents' patience and then, later, to Constance's. Loving had come just as easily to her. The love for her parents, for Constance, for love itself. Then for Julie. And now?

She would be the greatest fool on earth to love this man. He had never lied to her, never professed affection or deep emotion. The only thing he'd wanted from her was something she'd granted easily.

The only thing she wanted from him was something he would never relinquish.

She could honor their contract, and at the end of it take his largesse and his daughter and make a new life for herself.

She would lie with him night after night until the feel of his large frame next to hers was familiar, until the feel of his body cuddling hers in sleep was so necessary that rest was impossible without it. She would kiss him until every type of kiss was known and appreciated; every way of mating learned and lavishly experimented with; every inch of skin touched and tasted.

Yet with each touch, she would leave something of herself behind. With each hug, he would leave a memory she'd never be able to banish; with each kiss, he'd brand her so well and so ably that no other man's touch would ever be as welcome or as skilled.

It was something she'd known before the bargain was ever struck.

He promised passion and delivered obsession. He

demanded participation and accepted surrender. And when this unholy bargain was over, he'd pay the price with ease, his conscience salved, his future unchanged, his lust satiated.

And her?

Could she forget him?

In the next few days, Katherine learned how to arouse the earl with softly whispered words, with skillful, silken movements. He learned that the days passed quicker in winter. She learned that passion was not a substitute for affection. He learned that his wanton of the night became a silent prude by day. She learned what men wanted from their mistresses. He learned that men wanted more from their mistresses than ardor that disappeared with the dawn. She learned that she could guard her feelings with the care she had not given her own virginity. He learned that he needed to erect a wall of reserve around himself. She learned that it was possible to feel rapture, even if she also felt rage. He learned that she was not childlike at all; at times, he could not discern her moods or her emotions.

If their nights were heaven, their days were hell.

Around the ever-watchful and curious servants, they were studiously polite. Without their presence, they were simply silent. Katherine had attempted to converse with the earl, but every intelligent comment was ignored. When she asked about his shipping line, having overheard an instruction given to a courier, he had smiled and asked if she were pleased with her new wardrobe. When she inquired as to his other properties, he commented on the dessert. A remark about the king's interest in architecture prompted another about how pretty she looked. When she asked about the new machine being tested in the barn, he had simply smiled and refused to comment. She was never asked for an opinion, never treated as though there were anything north of her neck but a pretty face.

On the one hand, it infuriated her; on the other, it made planning for her departure that much easier. She did not want him to change, to soften. She did not want him to be anything but insufferable.

For the earl's part, he treated Katherine with the same benevolent neglect he had treated all the women in his life. His money and his power isolated both his mother and his sister from poverty, pretty clothes occupied their attention, and there were enough duties to keep them from being bored. What women truly wanted, it was his contention, was flattery, a little attention, and a goodly purse. It never occurred to him to talk to Katherine. Men talked of business, of politics, of nations and kings. Women talked of fashion and, depending upon their age, a husband, their children, or the servant problem. Men were interesting. Women filled a void. Yet the idea that he ignored Katherine was laughable.

He never grew tired of watching her. Her gestures were fluid, womanly. Her speech carefully modulated, and never screeching. Her passion was remarkable, but more than that, she did not cling. She was not helpless, and although feminine, she did not flutter like an overly dainty woman. She was, in fact, so involved in her own life at Mertonwood that he rarely saw her during the day. She was either nose-deep in the linen press or in the kitchen helping a less taciturn and more resigned Nora. He would occasionally spy her bundling up and traipsing between the stable and the barn, involved in God knew what business.

They did not discuss Julie.

He had not realized how much he missed having a woman in his life. The long months between Celeste's death and Katherine had been filled with frenetic activity but little else. He liked having the constancy of one woman available to him. He knew that when he walked upstairs to her room, she would be waiting, a warm and welcoming goddess of loveliness, awaiting only his arrival.

He must simply talk her into coming to London with him. He did not relish the idea of soliciting a companion from the available courtesans. No, Katherine was his. Tutored by him, trained by him, available. It would undoubtedly mean additional conditions, he supposed, to that silly contract of hers.

Perhaps he could persuade her to board Julie somewhere.

Or perhaps he should just have the child taken to a foster home, so that Katherine would have no option but to accept it.

He resolutely returned to his desk, his mind not on the contract with the Lincolnshire mills, but rather on another solution.

He was beautifully dressed this evening, Katherine thought, in tailored black, which made him look like a prince of some exotic realm. The black evening dress did nothing to mask his physique; instead, it enhanced the muscled torso, the long legs, the broad shoulders of the body she knew so intimately. It was not proper, she supposed, to call a man beautiful, but he was. As darkly luscious as Satan himself and possessed, no doubt, of the same disposition. Which was probably unkind, but not by more than a hairbreadth.

The truth was, she hated him at that moment, and mixed into the hate was a pain so close to her heart that a razor's edge could not separate the two.

It had been Michael who told her of the coach summoned from London. The same that now resided in the stable, its driver sleeping on the third floor, all fed and warm and replete with a tumbler of brandy. The coach was to take Julie to some unknown destination, as though she were no more important than a puppy or a stallion who would not obey a trainer.

Hatred was not enough, Katherine thought, her mouth fixed into a perfectly inane smile. She wanted to tell him that she knew of his nefarious plot, but that would be the height of stupidity.

Julie would be banished, all right, but the great Earl of Moncrief would lose his mistress at the same time.

She wondered if he'd notice.

"I have a proposition for you, Kat," he said, charm oozing from his unctuous smile.

She sat in her customary place on the small brocade loveseat, her skirts arranged in the proper position around her, her ankles crossed, shoes at the proper angle. Her hands were folded in her lap, shoulders perfectly straight. The dress was one of many that he had had made for her from the store of material imported from London. Fortunately, one of the young maids had once been apprenticed to a seamstress and had worked diligently during the past few days to prepare an adequate wardrobe for the Earl of Moncrief's mistress. Katherine had wanted to tell him not to bother, that she would not occupy that position long enough to justify the effort, but in the end, she'd remained silent.

This particular dress, in a rose-hued and richly patterned fabric, brought out the soft shine of her eyes and the thin wash of color on her cheeks. Freddie watched for a moment in pleased appreciation as she bit her lips and tried not to show how much she loathed him.

He leaned against the sideboard, a magnificent male animal in his prime, a contradictory man who was as complex as a puzzle and as convoluted as a curling snake. He rarely showed emotion, unless it was anger, or impatience. He surrounded himself with reserve, a sort of noblesse oblige against which she had no adequate defense. The only way to survive around the Earl of Moncrief, Katherine knew now, was to cloak herself in the same style of reticence. In darkness, she was free to touch him in tenderness and call it passion, to lace her fingers through his hair and call it lust, to kiss his face gently or allow him to hold her close.

And to whisper words of love in her heart.

But not now.

And never again.

"What is your proposition, my lord?"

He laughed, a sound that seemed to bounce around the room. "Am I never to get a name from you, Kat?"

She remembered the one time she'd called him by name and he had tossed it back in her face.

Her smile was fixed and just a shade less than frozen. "I have many names for you, my lord. Which one would you care to hear?" Despite her resolve to seem civil, anger demanded expression.

His winged brow arched and one corner of his lip curled slightly. "Have I been so terrible a taskmaster, then?"

"You stated you have a proposition, my lord. I would hear it now, if you don't mind."

"Very well," he said curtly, irritated beyond measure that she had spoiled the mood. "Very simply, it is this: You bargained and lost. I would arrange it so that the bargain is more to your benefit."

She did not speak, but watched him with eyes curiously bereft of emotion, he thought, as if she wore a painted mask behind which the real Katherine hid. It was an observation that made him strangely uneasy.

"I would like to provide for your future. I would prefer that we make other arrangements for Julie, but of course, if you insist, I could establish a household that would accommodate her."

"Of course," she said dryly.

"You would be amply rewarded, of course. My position is such that you would want for nothing." Except honesty.

Except respectability. Except compassion. Katherine smiled, which increased his feeling that this was not going as he'd planned. Reaching beside him on the sideboard, he drew a small, tufted box forward. He placed the box on her lap and returned to his original stance.

"This is only one of many small tokens you will receive," he said, watching carefully as she opened the box. Inside, nestled on a tiny pillow of satin, was the most beautiful ring she'd ever seen. A brilliant green, almost translucent, oval-shaped emerald was surrounded by diamonds. She lifted the ring, turned the filigree band and almost laughed aloud at the words inscribed inside. *In asperta veritas.* In hardship, there is truth. It seemed an unlikely motto for the present earl.

"Tell me, Freddie," she said, not looking up, "did you wrench this from Celeste's finger as she lay dying?"

"It belonged to my wife," he said shortly.

"Strange, I hadn't known you were married," she said, not at all surprised at the admission. There were too many things she did not know about him.

"What is your favorite color?" she suddenly asked.

"Blue, but then, it's a recent choice."

"Oh? I would have thought it to be one of your ancestral colors, green or gold." She matched the charm of his smile.

"I seem to have fond memories of blue lately." His cat eyes gleamed with mischief as she remembered the color scheme of her suite. Even in this, he could not be honest. The lump in her chest swelled.

"The ring is worth a fortune," he ground out, more irritated by the moment. She twirled it on one finger as if it were a bangle won at a country fair.

"You have always been generous," she murmured. Except with your thoughts, your hopes and dreams, the truth itself.

"Let me know your decision in the morning," he said abruptly, then turned and left the room.

During the next hour she sat, still and silent in the drawing room, holding the ring like a child who refuses to give up a candy. He offered up a future, a future that would twist her into something she was not, deny who she was now, and banish a past whose memories were part of her.

And he had done it so easily.

He didn't know her, or he could not have insulted her so deeply and with such facile words. He had offered her his wife's ring, and would never ask her to marry him. He denied his own daughter because she was less than perfect. He promised a future for her, yet made arrangements even now to hide her away somewhere.

The tender sharing lover, the sweet, teasing rake, the domineering arrogant male, the bemused and sleepy noble. All of these guises poured into her mind with a hot, sweet warmth.

She said goodbye to all of them.

How little he'd known her, how little he'd cared to know. She was frightened and already lonely. To escape from him would be the easiest act she would ever perform and the hardest thing she had ever done. She would never again feel the strength of his arms around her, or see the slanting grin that pleased her so much. She would not feel his presence in a room or detect his bay rum cologne in the hall. Nor would she see his knowing look across the dinner table, or hear his laughter boom.

But she would never feel this pain again, this knife slice through her heart and her soul, as he cut her to ribbons with a few deft words and even more adroit untruths.

She stood, stretching cramped muscles, retrieved the box from the cushion, and placed the emerald inside. She closed the lid carefully and walked down the hall to his library. Inside, she placed the box with its priceless ring in the exact middle of his desk. Unaccompanied by a note, it simply sat there, mute testimony that certain things could not be purchased, some things she would never sell.

In her room, she did not turn toward the pier glass. She knew that her solemn mood would not be mirrored in her face. She would look as serene as before, with no hint of the rage or sorrow or disgust that bubbled up inside her. She sat in the wing chair and stared out at the dark, frosty world. How apt that the countryside was frozen, immobilized by an icy touch. She, too, was chilled, as though her heart beat slowly, crystals forming on it even now. How long she sat there she didn't know, but it was long enough for the house to settle down, its servants departing for their own quarters. It was long enough for the fire in the grate to turn to glowing embers. Long enough for her to hear the door close gently down the hall.

It was, finally, enough time for truth to surface from the pain and the sadness. She would go to him one more time. Not for honor, not because of words written on a contract. But because she wanted to pretend, one last time.

That he wasn't who he was, arrogant and unprincipled and ruthless. Or that she was smarter and wiser and cared less.

She wanted, one last time, to feel his arms around her, to feel his lips on her, to feel him inside her—not for him, but for her. Not to protect Julie, or because she owed him anything. But only to pretend that she didn't hate him. Or perhaps to pretend that she didn't love him.

She stood and reached behind to unhook the rose dress. She draped it over a chair, removed the rest of her underclothing and began to wash herself with the icy water remaining in the ewer. Despite the fact that her flesh was chilled, it only echoed the feeling somewhere deep inside her. She didn't shiver as she wrapped the soft flannel robe over her nakedness. Nor did she react when she opened the door and a small draft blew the wrapper away from her body. The flooring was cold against her bare feet, but it was only a thought. She was numb, unfeeling, mindlessly seeking only the type of warmth she had become accustomed to in the past weeks.

She did not knock on the heavily carved door, but pushed it in, uncertain of her welcome.

He lay on his back, arms crossed beneath his head, eyes staring at the heavily brocaded crimson canopy. She stepped into the room, closing the door behind her, the noise causing him to calmly turn his head and watch her approach. She stood at the foot of the bed, one hand braced against the heavily carved post.

She unbelted her robe, letting it hang from her shoulders for a moment before it slid to the floor. She let his eyes drink their fill of her silhouetted against the glowing fire, and then she spoke.

"Make love to me, Freddie," she said winsomely. It was all she had time to say before he reached for her and pulled her into his arms.

Chapter 8

When the sun finally scattered its feeble rays across a snow swept horizon, Katherine was in the stable, saddling a restive Monty. Julie lay in a basket on the worktable, already muffled by layers of warm wool, her pert nose peering up between more blankets.

"I've a sister near Mertonwood Village," came a rusty voice from one of the large, open doors. "She'd be a sight easier to reach than that castle of yours."

Katherine turned, startled, but did not stop tightening the saddle's girth.

"Michael, I'll not endanger you or yours."

He closed the door quietly and came closer, each step crunching upon the icy ground. He rubbed his bristly chin with one wrinkled hand. "Gets mighty lonely in the winter, what with her man gone and all."

"Thank you, Michael, but it would be safer if I reached Donegan." The manor house had long been sold, but she still had friends there. Village girls gone to matrons now, who would shelter a friend and a baby through the winter months.

"The weather be bad, miss, what with another storm coming. 'Tis'na right to take the little one out in this. Besides, Bertha would love to have her to dote on, never having a babe of her own."

"Would he find us?"

He didn't try to soften the condemnation in his look. "I'm thinkin' you should have thought of that afore you bedded the man." Katherine did not look away from his eyes, narrowed as they were by wrinkles and sun lines. She accepted his honest statement for what it was. Truth. Unpalatable, uncoated by tact or prevarication. Constance would have said the same thing. "But I don't think he will. Most likely, he'd think to come to your home first."

There was that, of course, if the earl even bestirred himself enough to look for them. But the earl had money and power, two things she'd never possessed, and the prerogative of them frightened her. Not enough to stay, but enough to be wary of him. When she said as much, the old man frowned at her.

Michael, whose family had been farmers for generations, understood the soil and the wind and the power of God Almighty in His most elemental form. He understood power, but only as it related to bending to the will of God, the rains, and the failure of crops or their thriving.

"You go on to Bertha; I've told her about you. Don't you mind about the Earl finding you. Get on your way before the babe gets chilled, and stay on the south road until it forks to the left." He proceeded to give her the rest of the directions, which he had her repeat twice, before he stood at the stable door and motioned that the way was clear.

With Julie's basket tied in front of her and a blanket Michael had insisted she throw over her own traveling cloak—her newest and most timely gift from the earl—

Katherine tapped the reins lightly and Monty raced from the stable as if the hounds of hell were after him.

And maybe they were.

Perhaps one day he would come to his senses. But Julie was not going to pay the price for her father's stupidity. Not as long as Katherine was able to protect the baby. It was a vow she had made during the never-ending night, as he took her again and again.

The roads were barely passable, the fact that they had made it this far a tribute to Monty's tenacity and her own determination.

She was surprised at the ease of her departure. She had crept from the earl's bed, committing his sleeping form to a memory that would be unearthed later—when the time had come to think of him and not her compelling need to escape—and eased from the master suite quietly, fearing that the soft sound of the closing door would have wakened him. But, he slept as one exhausted. He had reason to be fatigued, she thought, a blush warming her cold features. She had not had time to say goodbye to Sara when she'd spirited Julie from the nursery, or any of the other staff that populated Mertonwood. Farewells were better left unsaid, anyway. If he could, Michael would send her trunks on to her, after the earl had returned to London and there was no further threat. Each mile, each step, drew them farther from Mertonwood, and farther from the earl. It was a separation she could feel with her flesh.

She regretted the necessity of stealing the earl's horse, and reasoned that it was little enough to take. She'd left the emerald ring and not touched the strongbox located in his library. Perhaps one day, when the weather grew warmer, she'd have Michael return the horse to Mertonwood. There were a great many things to regret about the past weeks. Some were of her making, others were foisted upon her. She did not regret her surreptitious departure.

But she bitterly regretted the night before.

It was as if all the nights they'd shared had never been. As if he had distilled every nuance of talent and skill into those few hours, and attempted to brand her with his knowledge. Tiny abrasions marked her flesh from his rough cheeks, his impatient lips. In a few days, the marks of their mating would fade. In time, the memory of her surrender would fade also. If she were fortunate; if she were blessed.

His reaction to Katherine's departure was not out of character.

He didn't betray by even the flick of an eyelash any discomfiture with her act. Nor did he betray to his curious housekeeper the rage he felt. His eyes were focused but clear, his mouth firm and straight, his bearing lance stiff. His unclenched hands rested upon his hips. His voice, when it came, was moderate, unhurried, without inflection.

"The child is gone, too, I expect." It was not a question.

"Yes, sir," she answered, a ghostly smile of righteous vindication shaping her thin lips.

"That will be all, Mrs. Roberts," he said, motioning to the door with one quick nod. She was not basking in triumph to such a degree that she did not catch his meaning.

He stood still in the middle of her room, noting the evidence of Katherine's hasty departure, silent and unmoving. He bent down finally and picked up the yellow nightgown she had discarded, folding it carefully and holding it as if it were a precious remnant, an icon of cloth.

He pressed it against his face, inhaling her scent. Violets and musk. The face that emerged from the fold of silk was ravaged. No one would have had difficulty deciphering the emotion glowing in those eyes. It was the look of a man who studiously avoided softer feelings yet suddenly found himself in the grip of them. It was the look of someone who was forced to recall pain even as more anguish was heaped upon his memory. It was the steely, cold look of a man who, in that moment, became more implacable, more unyielding.

It was hatred, supremely distilled and poisonous by the drop.

It was well past noon before Katherine had found all the landmarks Michael had indicated, covered as they were by the heavy snow. At one point, she thought she had been traveling in circles, but it was only the sameness of the landscape. She credited their arrival at Bertha's cottage to the intrepid Monty's intelligence and spirit.

During fair weather, the trip could easily be made on horseback and would have only taken an hour or two, but with the winter storm, each foot became a triumph, each yard a boast.

She felt like a frozen statue of frost. She climbed down from the saddle stiffly, brushing off the snow and ice crystals that clung to Monty's mane. Every part of her felt cramped and frozen; she had stopped shivering a long time ago. The tendrils of hair that had escaped her bonnet and scarf were icy and stiff. She praised the horse as she led him down the path to the cottage. There was nothing to be seen. Drifts of snow obscured her vision of the landscape; only wisps of dark smoke indicated where the cottages sat huddled under the ferocity of the storm. Not for the first time, she blessed Michael. She would not have been able to reach Donegan in one day, and she doubted they could have traveled much further.

Slowly, with stiff and cramped fingers, she untied the basket from the saddle.

"The little mite don't suffer none, I hope," said a voice beside her.

Constance had often warned her about believing too

quickly in first impressions. Yet, as she wearily stood, holding the heavy bundle that was the loudly protesting Julie, Katherine thought that she had never seen a more wonderful sight than Bertha Tanner's smiling face. Perhaps it was the flight from Mertonwood, the difficult journey, the fact she had not eaten since dinner the night before; perhaps it was more, but all she knew was that when she saw the round, red-cheeked face of the woman who offered sanctuary to a stranger, a burden was lifted from her shoulders.

Bertha wordlessly took Julie, stepped aside, and grabbed Monty's reins. Toward the rear of the cottage was a small, snug structure not much bigger than his stall at Mertonwood. Inside, an irate-looking nanny goat was tied to one of the ceiling poles. Katherine wondered what kind of companions the two animals would make, before removing Monty's heavy saddle and sodden blanket. Bertha hefted Julie onto one hip and opened a pail and poured a measure of oats into a makeshift trough. Other than Julie's occasional gurgles, the silence remained unbroken. Neither woman spoke, Katherine too tired to do much more than care for the horse, Bertha reserving judgment until creature comforts had been attended to.

With Monty warm and fed, and eyeing his new stall mate with some curiosity, Bertha led the way inside the rear door and motioned Katherine into the warm snugness of the cottage. She put the baby down in her basket near the hearth and turned to Katherine, subjecting her to an intense scrutiny in which not an inch of her person was spared. Bertha's tiny black eyes swept past the nondescript bonnet tied firmly by a woolen scarf, down past the layers of blanket and cloaks to mittened hands, and still farther to the old, scuffed boots that had been hers since Donegan. The two looked at each other steadily, a world of questions and answers brimming in each pair of eyes.

In the one, a knowledge of the world and human nature, for all that she'd rarely left Mertonwood Village. In the other, a plea for sanctuary, for some form of absolution, for a badly needed oasis of peace and serenity and acceptance.

Finally, after what seemed like hours under Bertha's intense assessment, the older woman nodded, having made a decision. Without a word, Bertha placed her arms around Katherine and hugged her, patting her back through the layers of clothes. Katherine lay her head down on the older woman's shoulder, and for the first time in a very long time, cried.

When finally the tears were done, she sighed heavily, incredibly weary. She barely realized that her cloak was being stripped from her or that she was being bundled into a warm bed piled high with soft woolen blankets. For once, she didn't think of Julie's welfare.

She didn't think at all.

Chapter 9

When Katherine awoke, it was to the same tuneless melody she'd heard in her sleep. She looked around the room with some surprise, not remembering much after collapsing against Bertha. Everything was neat and orderly, without ostentation, solid and sturdy. The home of generations of farmers.

The fatigue she still felt was one of the spirit, not of the body. She pulled on a pair of slippers that were sitting on the floor near the bed and a shawl that was draped over the one chair in the room. She followed the sound of singing and entered the main room of the cottage.

Bertha was seated in front of the fire on a rocker that had comforted generations of Tanners, softly crooning to a fascinated Julie. The baby was dressed in a long flannel garment that covered her feet and then looped around to form its own blanket. Droplets of milk sheened her smile, the bottle with its improvised teat placed on the table before them. It was the one worry Katherine had had, separating Julie from her wet nurse so soon, but even that concern had been dispensed with in light of Bertha's common sense. That, and the nanny goat. She smiled.

When she heard Katherine enter the room, Bertha half-turned, but didn't stop her singing, or her rocking.

"I've always wanted a baby," she explained when the song was done. She held Julie with ease, having had plenty of practice with Michael's brood.

"You may not think that in the wee hours of the morning," Katherine said with a smile, sitting on a stool near the fire and pulling the shawl tightly around her. She felt as though she would never get warm.

"You aren't one of those who let a child cry for the good of it, are you?" Bertha asked cautiously. Katherine was amused by the way the woman hoisted Julie up and cradled the baby against her shoulder. She looked the epitome of a mother bird, ready to protect her young. Perhaps not a bird after all. Bertha was built solidly and compactly, without her brother Michael's muscles. Her hair was pulled up into a starched cap, and what showed was not a nondescript gray, but a pure white. Katherine wondered if her hair had been fair when she was young.

"No," Katherine answered, "When a child cries, it's for a reason. I doubt that if I were without speech, I would like it much if everyone ignored me." The two women smiled at each other in perfect accord.

"Bertha," Katherine began, anxious to broach the subject before her nerve failed her, "What did Michael tell you of me?"

"Enough for me to get the meanin' of it. Plenty to read between the lines."

"I don't want any hardship to come to you." That was the overriding thought in her mind, not to bring danger to these good people. Katherine had no doubt that the earl would retaliate when he'd realized she had left. Not that he had any feelings for her, not that he really cared about his daughter, but because he was like a spoiled child who threw a tantrum when deprived of one of his toys. And she was, like it or not, one of his newest playthings.

"Nothin' he can do to me," Bertha said calmly, as if reading her unspoken thoughts. "This house has been in the family since my father's father. We're not tied to the earl's estate like some here. My needs are supplied. If I want for anythin', 'tis not for somethin' the earl could take away from me. But I wouldn't spare too much thought on it. I 'spect he doesn't care much one way or 'nother for this little one, and there are plenty of pretty women left with no sense."

Katherine didn't flinch from the censure meted out in the unblinking gaze of the other woman.

"I suspect you are right on both counts, Bertha," she replied, resolutely forcing away the thought of the earl with another woman. He could bed the entire northern half of England for all she cared. As long as he stayed away.

Was he barricaded by the same storm that had made travel so difficult? He would have discovered her absence by now. Would he stand at the window and curse the snow, or would he occupy his day with work and barely notice her departure? Would he remember her at all?

She would never know.

It was just as well she was gone, the earl thought as he stood at the window of the nursery and looked out at the snow-covered landscape. Sara had been moved to the servants' quarters, prior to returning home. Without Julie, there was no job for her to perform. The fire had been banked and the grate swept clean. Frost clung to the inside of the window. The crib was bare, the rocker stilled and empty, the room cold. It was just as well.

He must be in London soon for the opening of the House of Lords. He must be there to support the movement for the Factory Act. It had been a driving ambition, a goal that had been in the forefront of his life for years. Then why, damnit, could his legs not move and his hand not shut this door?

He stared down at the home woods, the path through the rose garden, the snow-swept grounds. Monique's ghost had finally been exorcised. Instead, another took her place. Possessed of a lilting laugh, eyes that sparkled with intelligence, a smile that challenged, a wit that sliced the unwary even in defeat. This ghost of his would not be laid to rest. It swept, instead, into the corner of his vision, a trick of the wind, a limb that brushed against another, showering the ground with even more snow. It was only the darkness of the hall pooled in shadow that made him think a shape stood there, watching him.

He was a man of iron will, dedicated to a lifetime of bondage to an empire he had constructed with bare hands and fertile mind. He was fastidious by nature, orderly by necessity, goal-oriented by choice. His character was not one to be beset by doubts, by worries, by a postmortem of every deed.

Then why was he doing it now?

Why, then, did he have the feeling that the ghost that haunted him was fueled by the power of his conscience? Where was she? Was she well?

What the hell had she been thinking of, to run away in the worst storm in years?

One of the reasons the Earl of Moncrief had amassed such incredible wealth was that he never ceased to ask questions.

His peers, he'd often thought, were mottled with a uniformity of dress, speech, and actions. They left the prestigious universities of their fathers, having no idea how to exercise that most unused of organs—their brains. He had often thought that if the underclass ever realized the majority of the nobility were so incredibly stupid, they would wage an overnight revolt. All it would take to win a bloodless coup would be a few men who had learned to question, instead of blindly accepting all the ignorance and foolishness handed down from generation to generation.

He was well aware that he was an enigma to his peers, in that he spent his days working. He shuffled papers, dreamed dreams, and inspected, poked, prodded, and questioned not for a living—there was now plenty in the Moncrief coffers to supply his and a few future generations with an extravagant lifestyle—but for the sheer enjoyment of it. Excitement was a new modification to an existing design, a different and better way to do something old and trusted, an idea that had never occurred to another. He dealt in commerce with men who had made commerce their lives, not caring that there were those among the nobility, ignorant and without purpose, who would condemn him for "getting his hands dirty."

While his peers were gambling away their inheritances, Freddie had transformed what funds his father hadn't managed to spend on his mistress and his lavish lifestyle into an empire of interconnected businesses. The coal mine supplied coke to the iron smelter, which provided rolled bars and sheet iron to the shipworks, which transformed the metal into cargo ships, which in turn transported excess coal and coke abroad. On return voyages, they carried raw material from the southern states of America to his rapacious cotton mills. His woolen mills were supplied with the long-haired wool from his Leicester sheep farms, and cargo ships exported the resultant woolen products throughout the British Empire.

He soon gained the reputation of being innovative. If it was new, he would try it. If it was recently invented, the earl would test it. If it could double production, he would purchase a hundred.

Freddie surrounded himself with men of original thought, men who possessed an artist's knowledge of the new technology and could shape the very metals from the earth. He was a member of the British Royal Society, he craved answers as another might crave wine.

He spent money lavishly, on his stables, his family's comfort, his many homes. Yet, more funds still went into the factories that dotted the landscapes of his holdings. More currency went into the small villages which adjoined the huge buildings. He disliked the idea of having slaves; consequently, the houses of his workers were larger and rented fairly in his factory towns. The stores were run independently and competed fairly for the purses of well-paid workers. A new invention of sorts was the school in each small village. Sometimes there were only two or three students; near the larger factories there were upwards of thirty to a class. It was not enough for people to know how to read and write. They must understand the machinery, the technology, with which the future would be shaped. He needed trained, educated workers who could make intelligent decisions. It never entered his mind that he was hated and feared by a few of his fellow industrialists for those advancements. It would have made no difference if he had known.

Few people knew of his diverse interests. Only Jack knew that to protect the inventors and the new men of science, the earl supported them secretly. He funneled funds to support their families, purchased homes away from the sprawling mass that was London, provided serenity in order to relieve any worries that might have hampered their brilliant minds.

Freddie prized those qualities about himself that set him apart as different, his curiosity and lack of fear of the novel, the unusual, and the unique and the fact that he greatly appreciated free thinking.

Yet, he had denied his child because she was different and was enraged by Katherine's independent actions. It was the first time he'd ever held the mirror of self-knowledge up to himself, and he found himself disliking the man facing him.

It was impossible to banish either of them from his mind.

He'd never had such musings about Celeste. She had had no goals but to become his countess, by any route necessary, no passion but the procurement of wealth. She was prepared to be exactly what he wanted, as if he'd sculptured her from his needs to the exclusion of hers. He couldn't remember ever hearing her discuss an idea, a thought, a wish with him. It was as if, out of bed, she was the most vacuous woman he'd ever known.

Katherine had never been boring. He'd known that even as he had chosen not to investigate the personality behind the charming smile. He'd seen that flash of anger when he'd consciously dismissed her questions as worthless, her curiosity as an intrusion. It had been protection at its most basic, a truth barely uttered even to himself. He didn't want to be impressed by her intellect or discuss his business concerns with her. He had grown too close to her as it was; witness these idiotic musings in an empty nursery.

He knew too little about her.

What had she been like as a little girl? Who had loved her as a baby, that she would have known, instinctively, how to handle Julie? What did she dream about? It occurred to the earl, with the briefest flash of pain, that he knew more about Lucy, the belowstairs maid, than he knew about the woman who had shared his bed for two weeks.

It had been safer to keep her at a distance. Then why in hell couldn't she stay there now?

She'd stolen his horse, damn her. He hoped that Monty was cared for but more importantly, that his fierce stallion had led them somewhere safe and warm.

Where was she? Had she been so desperate to escape him that she had chanced a bitter storm? And Julie? She would never have harmed the child. He stood in the nursery that he had avoided for over a week, suddenly eager for the sight of that friendly little face.

He was no longer enraged; he felt strangely empty and incredibly weary, as if drained of will and energy.

Where was she?

Where was his daughter?

He might never know.

Chapter 10

Katherine's days flew by in a pattern of routine, bound by the snows that blanketed the landscape, measured by the warm, wintry cocoon of Bertha Tanner's cottage.

Except for Michael, there were no visitors to the cottage, a fact for which she found herself grateful, since even Michael's presence made her strangely uncomfortable. His first visit was the worst, coming three weeks after her departure from Mertonwood. She ached to ask if the earl was still in residence there. Did the weather keep him snowed in? Was he well? Did he miss Julie? Did he miss her?

The fact that she asked nothing was more telling than if she had plagued him with questions. She didn't notice the intent look that passed between brother and sister on Michael's departure.

Christmas came and went with the speed that marked the winter. She was enfolded in the warmth of Michael's family, his wife Meg and the three younger children still at home. It was a quiet time, with the villagers meeting in the square Christmas night to light a huge bonfire, a tradition dating back to pagan times. She and Bertha chose not to exchange gifts, deciding instead to purchase small wooden toys for Julie from the peddler. Katherine tried not to recall the bustling exuberance of Christmas at Donegan Castle, when all the servants and the residents of the castle met in a festive party on Boxing night, dancing and singing, and growing tipsy from her mother's potent wassail. She tried not to remember, but it was hard not to think of those days of love and celebration. Especially lately, when all the emotions in the whole world seemed to rest upon her shoulders. She wanted to cry and to laugh, to scream and to shout. But mostly to cry.

The cottage was small, but instead of feeling confined, she felt secure in the snug rooms. Her days were spent caring for Julie—at least when that duty was not usurped by a doting Bertha. No grandmother could have loved the child more. When Julie did not occupy her, she found little things around the cottage to keep her busy, anything but assist in the sewing that seemed to occupy most of Bertha's time. Her mother and Constance could have explained, laughing, that it was no use to try to convince Katherine to wield a needle. It was simply one of those things she did not do well, and like most people, Katherine tended to avoid those chores that she could not master.

Bertha transformed some of Katherine's dresses into miniature dresses for Julie, as tailored as the originals had been. Katherine saved the garments made of the finest fabric for a secondhand apparel market. She could trade them for either money or cheaper clothing. She had made no plans yet, but Katherine was certain that whatever her future would bring, she would no longer require a wardrobe suitable for the mistress of the Earl of Moncrief.

He should not have been in her mind so much. She should not be able to recall him with such ease. At night, in the small bedroom she shared with Julie, she would lie awake sometimes until dawn, thinking of him.

When she had left Donegan, she had been able to put her old life behind her. Except for errant wisps of memory, she did not grieve overmuch for the past. Her parents were dead, Constance was dead, and Donegan Castle would never belong to a Sanderson again. She had closed the door in her soul that led to that life and resolutely walked into her future. It had not been easy, but it had been done.

Why could she not do that now?

He refused to stay where she put him. When she unearthed the washboard from its perch beside the cottage wall, a shoot of brave grass was unveiled. Green and lustrous, it reminded her of his eyes. When she shoveled out the ashes from the fireplace, the charred and black remnants of the fire called to mind the hue of his hair. When she closed her eyes and breathed in the crisp smell of ice and snow, she was reminded of his scent, something clean and uniquely his. And when she stretched, cold and shivering in her lonely bed at night, she remembered a time when warm flesh had comforted her, when his heat had warmed her as brightly as any fire.

She did not want to remember him, and she did not want to cry at odd moments when there was nothing to cry about.

He probably didn't even remember her.

Freddie thrust inside her and she moaned. She clutched him with lethal nails, making triangular gouges on his back. He didn't protest; it was an apt physical counterpart to the pain in his head. He'd had enough whiskey to give him a blinding buzz, but not enough to feign passion. The lust that he'd thought enough suddenly wasn't, and for the first time in his life, he wasn't sure he could finish. He thrust again, willing himself to complete the act, to think of anything, anyone, other than the woman who lay panting beneath him.

And anyone but *her.*

He shuddered, feeling himself explode, more grateful that it was over than anything else. It wasn't good enough, but then, it hadn't been good enough for a long time.

He rolled away from her sweaty body, from her too-small breasts and her too-wide hips. She stroked his back playfully, tickling his ribs, and he stood rather than have her touch him. He had to get away before the anger inside him broke free, before he said something or did something totally inappropriate and out of character for the Earl of Moncrief. It was barely caged, this rage, and he never felt it more acutely than he did at times like this.

He dressed hurriedly, elegance sacrificed for speed, not bothering to explain to his partner that it was better he left. The woman in the bed was a baronet's wife. If he tried, he could probably manage to remember her name. She was not at all exclusive; she had been rumored to have bedded half the ton, and although their numbers were small, that still amounted to a fair number.

Thank God she wouldn't be able to supply the gossip mills with information that the illustrious Earl of Moncrief hadn't been able to perform.

But it had been a close thing. Too damn close.

It was as if Katherine had cursed him that last night, foretold what his future was to be, and all without a word spoken.

He remembered the night too well. On some level, she had been what he wanted her to be, a willing body bereft of will, thought, or speech.

At the finish, when passion was spent and Katherine lay gasping beneath him, her heartbeat echoing the frenetic pace of his own, he'd known somehow that this was not the way he'd wanted it to be.

He wanted the passion, the sweat sheening on her flesh. Craved the hot, molten warmth that surrounded him. But he wanted more from her. He was spent, but feeling cheated somehow, as though she'd kept something of herself from him. She'd given him her body, but it was something more he desired. Something he could not define. Or perhaps he could. He missed her easy wit, her teasing charm, her words uncoaxed, unrehearsed. Herself.

When he would have drawn Katherine into his arms, she moved. An infinitesimal gesture, but one he noted. As attuned as he was to her, he knew she withdrew not only physically, but in another, deeper, sense. Without a word spoken, she'd held herself tight against the edge of the bed. They'd both pretended that the shadows did not hold words too painful to speak.

Now, whenever passion reached its peak, when he should have been mindless with heat, he was at his emptiest. Dead, hollow. There weren't enough women in the world to fill up the hole inside him. There wasn't enough whiskey, either. Or brandy, or port, or wine, or a thousand other spirits whose sole reason for being drunk was forgetfulness.

Damn her.

He wished fervently that she was writhing in pain, then knew that he didn't. He wanted her to be hurting, he prayed for her safety. He pleaded with a vengeful god to make her ill, then begged for her health. He wanted her out of his life and he desperately wished her into his bed. He wanted her out of his thoughts, and he wanted her in his heart.

He didn't know what the hell he wanted.

And then he did.

He wanted Katherine.

When the snow began to melt, it was as if part of her, long dormant like the tender plants beneath the snow, also began to dissolve. Katherine threw herself into a whirlwind of cleaning, calling back a time at Donegan when there had been no one to help and the maintenance of the house had been left to her. She shook the rugs until years of dust were coaxed from their fibers, polished the old wooden floor until it gleamed, scrubbed the tin ornaments on the shelves, gingerly washed cherished family dishes until they sparkled on the sideboard. She helped make soap from the tallow stored in the small building next to the cottage—the same building which still housed her stolen horse—added lime and white ash and cooked it down until the noxious smell permeated the air.

She washed, and she cleaned, and when the weather cleared, she took Monty out to exercise him, treading a path around the cottage until they unwittingly had walked a perfect circle.

Part of her exertion was designed to keep at bay the thoughts and the memories, uncertain as to her future on the one hand, too certain about her past on the other. But mostly she wanted to repay Bertha, not just for her hospitality, but for the way in which she'd refused to judge or scold or condemn her when it would have been easy to do so. There would come a time, very shortly, when Katherine knew she would impose even more on the other woman's generous spirit.

Julie had spent the winter learning to walk, and it was a chore to keep after her all the time. She'd learned to smile with that daunting, toothy grin and Katherine was hard-pressed to scold her for misbehaving. Together, she and Bertha were all the family that any little girl needed.

With the thaw, Katherine began to take Julie on her morning exercise circles with Monty. Although at first the giant horse whinnied nervously—not certain what this tiny, dictatorial creature wanted—he learned to be as docile as a lamb with Julie sitting on his back, pulling at his mane with two chubby fists and trying to say something like "giddyup, horsey," words that did not translate well into northern England's speech.

Other changes were appearing that spring. Changes

Katherine pretended not to notice. Nature, however, has a way of being stubborn. She didn't have an appetite, despite Bertha's scolding. Food was plentiful in the small cottage, neatly stored in barrels in the pantry or in the springhouse. At dinner, Katherine made a pretense of eating, mainly to avoid Bertha's sharp eyed looks. Smudges appeared beneath her eyes, and her cheekbones seemed more pronounced.

She knew she wasn't ill.

Her breasts were fuller, almost painfully tender at times. Her waistline was thicker, despite her lack of appetite. When she began to awake with nausea, Bertha's suspicions were aroused. When she fainted one cold morning, they were confirmed, and Katherine's worst nightmare came true.

"It be the earl's child, I 'spect," Bertha said gently. She was worried about her young guest. Although she had been prepared to love the baby, no one had told her that she might come to love the woman, too, like the daughter she'd never had. Katherine was not a slack-mouthed jade, looking for pity where none was warranted. No, she had never asked for favors; instead, she had occupied herself about the cottage doing what a true daughter would have done. Now she sat at the scarred oak table that had seen generations of Tanners, staring down at her red, raw hands as if surprised to see them still firmly attached to her wrists.

"What you be doin', Katherine? Have you made any plans?"

She absently patted Katherine on the shoulder, anxious that she move or speak, or make any sign that she was still alive. Katherine wasn't the first girl to get herself into trouble and Bertha would bet she wouldn't be the last, so instead of offering advice about men and babies, well after the fact, the best thing to do was to help her make some decisions.

"There's a woman lives up on Baxton way," Bertha

began hesitantly. "I hear tell she's helped a few rid themselves of burden." She hoped that the horror did not show in her voice. Bertha had wanted a baby since she was a little girl, helping raise her own brothers and sisters. It seemed a shame that there were ones who would do anything to rid themselves of a child. Yet, she offered the alternative to Katherine with a generous heart, hoping and praying that she would not take advantage of it.

Katherine's expression reflected her own internal revulsion. "No," she said firmly, finally shocked from the numb shell which encased her. "Dear God, Bertha, I couldn't do that. Even if it is the earl's child, it's mine, too." What she didn't say was that she couldn't believe it was true, and wasn't that an idiotic statement to make? However stupid, it was the truth. It was the one thing she hadn't thought of. And the one thing which should have always remained uppermost in her mind, what with Julie's illegitimate birth.

And *he* certainly should have recalled it.

It was something else to lay at the feet of the pompous earl. Except, of course, that the earl did not have to bear this child, or rear it.

Dear God, what would she do?

She had most of her wages still, but she was not so stupid as to believe that she could live for long on them.

It struck her then, as she sat at the table and tried not to notice the worried look on Bertha's face, that the past year had been spent running from one catastrophe to another. She had left Donegan to find her future, only to find the earl. She'd escaped the earl encumbered by a child she loved, yet now she was contemplating running again, this time not only with his daughter, but pregnant with his child!

When could she ever run far enough or fast enough?

And when would she ever stop running?

"I suppose I could leave," she said tentatively, testing the waters of Bertha's kindness.

"Leave?" Bertha was genuinely shocked. Of all the choices she wished she could offer Katherine, leaving was not one of them. Besides, where would she go?

During the long winter nights, the women had kept each other company by talking, and in the way of fire-lit conversations, whispered so as not to disturb Julie, pasts had been unearthed and exposed. Katherine's story had not engendered pity in the other woman. Pity was reserved for the blind and the lame and the war veterans without work, not for an able-bodied young woman with looks, breeding, and intelligence. Nor had Katherine asked for compassion. Tales of Donegan were told with humor, some tinge of regret, on occasion misty eyes: Her father's bear-like voice raised in mock ire, her mother's equally strong tone teasing him from his playacting, and Constance's smile as she whisked a young Katherine away, so that the adults could play at adult games. The day she had walked away from Donegan was spoken of without tears, without regret, being as it had been, without alternative. She told Bertha of London and of meeting the countess.

Of the earl, she spoke very little, but her longing was there in her voice. Bertha wondered if Katherine thought she didn't know, or couldn't suspect. The small cottage that cradled them had been the scene of passion of its own. The stone slab in the graveyard perched upon the hill marked the death of her love, not her memories or her knowledge.

It was the determination in the younger woman that stirred Bertha. A resolve that, unless halted, would carry Katherine out into the world among strangers.

"You'll do no such stupid thing. I won't hear of it. To leave me alone with only my bones for company, when shortly I'll have another sweet baby to cuddle? No," she said firmly.

"I can't do this to you, Bertha," Katherine protested, laying a hand on the other woman's arm. The winter had kept them safe, the roads having been treacherous this year, but along with the spring came a threat. She didn't think to escape the earl forever. Despite his departure for London weeks before, he loomed as a power of which to be wary.

The earl would savor revenge.

She shivered, a presentiment of danger. Because he would ask for only one thing in his quest for personal justice; that much she knew about Freddie, Earl of Moncrief.

He would demand total annihilation.

Is it in the nature of those less strong to envy those seemingly without weakness? She knew the Earl of Moncrief, and with that knowledge had come a grudging respect. She felt the power of his will; knew the ruthlessness of his determination; had spied, only fleetingly, the awesome enormity of his personal power. Freddie was omnipotent in his world. Had he been born a tailor's son or a blacksmith's boy, she did not doubt that he would have still achieved any goal he desired. What Freddie wanted, Freddie obtained, be it the new railroad or a ship capable of steaming across vast oceans.

What chance had she against such resolve?

And yet there was her own determination, newly fueled and kept alive by the slight rounding of her belly. Her child. Hers, not his. Not ever his. Not subject to whims of his paternity, not dominated by the force of his will.

It would be more than a clash of wills, this battle, and battle she was sure it would be. Perhaps not now, but one day, they would wage war. To the death.

She could not lose.

"I'll tell the earl, if you go," Bertha said, a stubborn glint in her eye. She would have said anything to prevent Katherine's precipitate departure. She had no idea that her ploy so acutely mimicked Katherine's own thoughts.

"Bertha, you would not," Katherine answered calmly,

knowing full well that the other woman would die before harming her or Julie.

"I would not wish to, Katherine, but if it meant savin' you from yourself, then indeed I would. You will stay here, have your babe in comfort and security, and then we'll worry what will be next. You can't be movin' willy-nilly about the world right now." Bertha's mouth was pursed into a mulish line, the same expression Constance would have worn.

Katherine wondered if she were doomed to be protected by the ghost of Constance for the rest of her life, or sheltered by the wisdom of morc pragmatic fcmales. Yet, she had once attempted to be practical, and look what it had garnered her. A child to be born out of wedlock. So much for pragmatism.

Bertha watched the play of emotions across Katherine's face and wondered if she had pushed the point too much.

"Take one day at a time, dear," she said, the quick hug she gave Katherine one a mother might share. "Leave the rest for the angels to sort out."

Katherine only hoped her particular guardian angel was up to the task.

Chapter 11

"America?" the earl asked, surprised. "Why the hell America?" He stared at the older man in disbelief.

Harold Barnen calmly regarded his partner. The earl had never been known for his patience, or his political prudence. Lately, however, he was even more apt to lose his temper.

"I am purchasing a town there," he answered, without raising his voice. The earl abruptly sat down opposite him, near the roaring fire that blazed almost as uncontrollably as his temper right at this moment.

"You are purchasing a town," he repeated, attempting by redundancy to give credence to this surprising revelation. It didn't work.

"It is presently called Harmonie, but I have a vision, you see, of turning it into the greatest living experiment of social reform," Harold said, smiling. "I have it in my mind to change the name to New Harmony. What do you think?"

"I think you've lost your mind."

"No, just my patience with Parliament," the older man

said, geniality bending to irritation. He stood and began to pace, a habit he had when pontificating, something he did very well lately. It was, Freddie thought as he leaned back in the chair and prayed for patience, something that was irritating in the extreme. But then, he had little tolerance for anything these days.

"The king is more interested in commissioning buildings than in social reform. The Corn Law has done more to undermine British civilization than any single act. In a few years, we face revolt. Already, people are beginning to starve in the streets. How can I promulgate reform in a country that is so determined to force farmers from their homes and starve their own people? What great dreams were had before the war with France. Where are they now? Now, I have not lost my mind, only my hope."

"You speak of dreams, yet you turn your back on your own."

"I leave New Lanark in capable hands. What is a supposed self-governing community worth if they require a strong figurehead? No, the people of New Lanark are equipped to choose their own destiny. I am a father only, and a parent must sometimes let go of his child."

"Yet, what about your reform in Parliament? Surely you don't intend to lose that impetus? If nothing else, what about the time everyone on the side of your cause has spent? Damn it, Harold, what about my time? Isn't that worth a farthing?"

"Of course, my friend, of course." Harold smiled benevolently at the younger man. The earl had instigated reforms of his own, a decade before they would become law. The fact that he was a peer of the realm was doubly exciting. The earl had the power of his title and the not-insubstantial power of his fortune to back it up. Harold had a fortune and a dream. Yet, he was willing to risk it all. He wondered if the earl ever gambled on anything.

"I cannot empower Parliament to act with a conscience.

You can. In fact, I expect you to. One day I might return, but not before I try. You see, I must try. What is a goal unless it is attempted? What is a dream if the dreamer is so frightened that he never gives it a chance? New Harmony will be a community of like-minded souls, the power of the one for the all. No more will there be individual pursuits. The good of the whole will be uppermost in each mind."

It was a pursuit of thought that the earl instantly discounted. If Harold Barnen wanted to embrace socialism, he was welcome to it, but not if he tried to force the concept down his throat. The funds that employed thousands of people were garnered because of the abilities of one man—him. In an effort to feed the countless numbers of unemployed men who streamed into his villages hoping for work, he had poured more and more money into his factories in the last months. Prices were soaring, people were starving. Coupled with the diminished demand for cotton goods, because clothing took second place to food, the factories were working at half capacity. The earl was financially secure, however, being as diversified as he was. He did not look to one single industry for his fiscal well-being. A damn good thing, he thought.

But when Harold went off on a tangent about the whole being greater than the parts, he instantly dismissed his verbal perambulations. It was the hope of attaining more, of giving their children more than they had, that empowered some of his best and brightest employees. People needed less socialism and more opportunity. But because of long-standing friendship, he did not illuminate to his old mentor how radically their viewpoints differed.

"Come with me," Harold said impulsively. "See what we can do together."

The Earl smiled. "I cannot at this time, Harold. However, if your community is still alive a few years from now, I'll be among your most ardent visitors."

"How little faith you show in me, my friend," Harold said, his glance filled with less rancor than his words indicated.

"Do we part company because I share no faith in your ideas?"

"Or trust in me, perhaps?"

"You're one of a precious few who have my trust." Freddie's smile was tinged with mockery. He stood, preparing to depart. He'd stopped to see his old friend after news of his journey had reached him. Now, he wanted out of London. He wanted to go home, to Moncrief.

"Have you given it so unwisely, then? I seem to recall a young man determined to change the world, believing in good and truth and mankind, all without equivocation."

Freddie pulled on his gloves, concentrating more on the act than on the knowing face of his friend. "Young men grow up, Harold, and face the world."

"And lose their faith?"

"More likely, their trust," Freddie replied.

"You'll find that it is as like to humankind as the wish for love. We all crave the ability to find both emotions. Like food and water, they are necessary for survival. Be like a seed casing, my friend. With the spring, the casing melts away and allows new roots to form. You are in the winter of your life. Spring will come soon enough."

"When did you begin to wax eloquent about horticulture, Harold?" the earl asked with a small smile.

"Oh, did I not tell you? We've a few scientists in our group. In fact, we've sent some Chinese seeds to Harmonie. Can you imagine the community we will form?" He was off on new raptures about his colony in America, leaving Freddie listening with half an ear, part of his mind occupied with thoughts of spring.

* * *

Winter vanished as suddenly as it had arrived. One day, the snow clung heavily to tree branches, mounded on the ground, filtered the air in a white shower; the next, the drifts melted into the soggy soil, nourishment for a spring that thrust itself arrogantly into the world. Everywhere Katherine looked, the signs of a new season appeared. The rolling hills were transformed from barren white to a verdant green, the bravest spring flowers shot up into the sunlight, the earth smelled sweet and fresh. Sparrows paired and mated; in snug, warm burrows nature renewed itself—foxes and rabbit, squirrel and ferret, hedgehog and mouse.

Her own body ripened with promise, and her skin stretched taut beneath the concealing folds of her dress. As spring rolled into summer, she grew heavier, waddling from one chore to another with more determination than grace. Bertha chuckled and called her a mother duck. Julie thought she'd swallowed a ball, and many times patted the hard firmness of her abdomen as though there were a ball there in truth.

The time at Bertha's cottage had been good for both of them, Katherine thought, as she stood watching Julie running from one flower to the next like a frenzied bee. She delighted in her as if Julie were her own child, watched with maternal pride her first halting steps, shared each accomplishment with Bertha, a proud and doting grandmother of the spirit. She had shared the progress of her pregnancy with Bertha, too, as each new symptom was discussed and the pride in her active son grew with each lurching movement beneath her skin.

Katherine had no doubt that she carried a boy. The knowledge seemed to have been part of her since the awareness of his existence. Would her son be like his father, ruthless, demanding, autocratic? Would he be mischievous, a daring masculine version of herself? Would he love books and music, or sports and horses? What would he be like?

The closer to her delivery, the more she wondered. And the less she feared.

She had attributed emotions to the earl he had not, evidently, possessed. He hadn't cared, after all, and the revenge she'd believed him capable of was only in her mind. The need to run from him had been mitigated by her safety over the spring, her condition, and another, more onerous, worry.

The seasons had not been kind to Bertha. Each day it seemed as if more and more life was drained from that once cheery, plump face. She'd turned to Michael for advice, but his troubled face had echoed her own fears. Every morning it took longer for Bertha to emerge from her bed, the painful arthritis making each move a separate agony. The cough that had not been present in the winter was growing worse, until Katherine had seen the red splotches on a handkerchief that Bertha tried to conceal. Yet, as ill as she became, she refused to speak of it, or of Katherine's future.

As if Katherine would leave Bertha unattended. She had grown to love her like a surrogate mother. It was Bertha who scolded her when she did not eat enough, who coaxed her into smiling when the occasional moodiness overcame her, who defended Julie when Katherine would have disciplined the child.

The love between the two blossomed. Julie would bounce into Bertha's bed in the morning, face brightly wreathed in a smile. The answering smile on Bertha's face was a delight to behold. Katherine didn't have the heart to scold Julie, even when the child would fly in from the meadow with a grimy fist clutching a handful of wildflowers and burrow into Bertha's arms.

Julie was a year and a half of radiant life and bustling energy. As she grew, her face more closely mirrored her father's. Her eyes were the same sparkling green, her chin bore the same stubborn bluntness. She had some of the same mannerisms—the way she held her cup, four fingers straightly aligned along the edge; the sometimes startling grace of her childish movements. Katherine would catch her watching something with the intent, predatory look of her father, and memories would flood into her mind.

She placed her hand against the small of her back and rubbed it absently. The pains had been coming since before dawn. She and Bertha had compared their knowledge, which was relatively little, since neither had given birth. It had been Michael who had provided the solution. His wife sat in the cottage below, systematically arranging what would be needed, calming an almost hysterical Bertha who insisted upon walking to the door periodically to ensure that Katherine had not given birth on a hillside. It was Meg who suggested that she walk until the pains became more frequent.

"Not good for her to lay down betimes," she said in the tone of one who had done this six times before. Bertha was rapidly changing her mind about her sister-in-law's expertise however, as Meg remained placid and unworried despite the amount of time passing.

Katherine was oblivious to Bertha's worry. She stood on the crest of the hill and felt the soft breeze upon her cheek, the tendrils of hair blown free of the bun at her nape. With one hand, she absently brushed it back and stared in the direction of Mertonwood.

It was too far to see, and a lifetime away.

Only a few short months, but a world separated them. It had been long enough for his babe to grow, to mature, to demand, finally to be born. Long enough to create a life, but not long enough to erase his memory.

Was there enough time in the world to banish him from her mind?

The wind soughed heavily and Katherine blinked back tears.

In a perfect world, they would have awaited the next cycle of life together. He would have been with her, holding her hand or bracing her against him, his presence blocking out the hotly shining sun as she stood in his shadow and leaned against his strength.

She didn't live in that world. That world existed only in the long, white ether between sleeping and waking, when fairy tales coated them both in personas easily manipulated by a willing mind and an eager soul. He would be a prince of regal bearing and noble purpose, believing in honor and justice and the far off, faint echoes of chivalry. She would be a princess, in a dress shimmering with cobweb silk and clad in virtue, an example of beauty and chaste love.

She didn't live in that world.

Her world was filled with sleepless nights and the sound of his voice, deep and resonant, or the figure of him ghost-like beside her in the bed, only to vanish with the dawn.

Even after her shape had been distorted by the heavy, active body of their child, she still wanted him. She winced at the admission but forced it from her, as she stood staring in the direction of the scene of her capitulation. For that was what it was, wasn't it? Surrender, Katherine, he'd said, and she had. Will, body, and, lastly, mind.

What was it, if not surrender, to think about him so often? Her breasts, now laden with milk, tingled with the memory of his fingertips and the once-promised threat of a suckling mouth. Her ears heard words long silent, her lips still felt his kiss. Her cheek felt the brush of his breath.

She placed her hand above her eyes, shading them from the sun. There was nothing to see but the rolling hills obscuring her view of Mertonwood and its tall chimneys. If she were a bird, she could fly the distance easily, soaring over the trees of Mertonwood Forest, dipping low beneath the gates, circling the green lawns and spying, with a beady eye, the room on the third floor that had been the nursery, the suite on the second that had been hers, the earl's dominion occupying a full corner of the second floor.

How long had she known him? A few weeks, that was all, and yet she felt as though he would remain in her mind for all time. Would any other man be as commanding, yet walk with inbred stealth? Tiger, he'd called himself, and she smiled, an infinitely wiser smile than she would have worn a year ago. He was power and magnificence and as carnivorous as any tiger. And yet he had bowed his head before her, supplicant in passion, sensuous in abandon, demanding her touch as eagerly condescending as any cat. Arrogance and grace. Words to conjure him up, summon him.

Would any other man have that ease of outrageousness, be able to strip the veneer of politeness from her and call forth the irrepressible child she'd been? They were partners in their crime, were they not? And she, petty thief that she was, had stolen a child from their union, and he, consummate burglar, had stolen something almost as precious—her innocence and her peace of mind, and a future without fear. Because she would always wonder at his tenacity and his motives. Did he stalk her, like a tiger, rapacious and lean, or did he play with her fears? Did he care enough to find her, or did he banish her from his thoughts as easily as he had disavowed Julie's existence as his daughter?

And this child? She held both palms pressed against the still mound of belly, hurting now with the promise of birth. Would he leave this child to her, or would he steal him as easily as he'd stolen so much else from her?

Had this child been conceived that last night? Her heart rebelled at the memory. The moment she'd really looked at him, stretched upon the brocade cover like a pasha, she'd known that somehow, this night would be different.

She felt too exposed, too vulnerable, and it was not just because of her nakedness, but the tremulous moment itself. He had come to her then, naked as she, and met her standing at the end of his bed, she still gripping the twining leaves and heavily embossed wooden flowers of the post as if to be saved somehow. He stood a breath away, chilled yet impervious to the cold. Too far from the fire, yet colored by the flames, casting orange and red upon the superb sensuousness of his body.

"Are you afraid?" he asked, a teasing question voiced with gravity. She shook her head and reached for him, but he stepped away. A tiny motion that proved to her that it was not just her body he craved but her total exposure. Naked in form, and rendered naked in action.

"You are so beautiful," he said then, and there was anger in his tone. That she'd rejected his offer of bonding by harlotry? That she was not ugly? It was a fact of life to her, nothing more important than the fact that Donegan's walls had been gray. Usual, normal, unimportant.

He thought otherwise. "Do you know," he said absently, the tip of one finger tracing a line from her shoulder to the inside of her elbow, "I sometimes think you are the most beautiful woman I've ever known. When you smile, or when your eyes are crinkled with some insult you're ready to level at me. And then the mists fade, and you're no more lovely than a hundred other whores I've fucked."

She flinched, and then smiled, paradoxical reactions he'd begun to expect from her. "I've never claimed to be a great beauty," she said, and a sound that was not quite a laugh emerged from him.

"No, you haven't," he admitted, "and you eschew new clothes. You accuse me of robbing corpses to give you jewels, and you demand justice for babes and tolerance for all."

"I am just myself," she said helplessly, inarticulate in self-defense, having had no practice in it. Nor did she have protection against that look in his eyes, that sudden wanting look that recalled the bitter face of a child pressed against a doorway, hungry and feral. Craving a full meal, a bed, and perhaps even love, but most certainly what other people had. She'd been robbed by this child, and he'd died for it.

What would this man take from her, and what would be the price they'd both pay?

"Did you love him well?" She blinked several times, the intent as well as the meaning of his question confusing her.

She smiled, which maddened him, thinking that her tender wisp of gesture was meant for the idiot who'd taken her virginity. In truth, it was a sadder smile than he realized, because she could not envision the second son of the duke. Somehow, his appearance was muted by the man who stood arrogantly, nakedly in front of her.

"You've asked me that before," she said, which was not the answer he sought. She'd answered him before, but that answer had been short, unrevealing. For some reason, he wanted her disclosure now. Instead, he demanded another truth from her.

"What are you willing to do for love, Kat?" His fingers widened to encompass a full breast, to hold, to encapsulate with a touch. A cage of flesh for flesh.

She shivered, not solely at his touch, but at the question. It was to be exposure then, fully. To render her naked in spirit.

"Anything," she answered bravely, and it was his turn to flinch. She looked down at the floor and then up into his eyes, and said it again, so there was no mistake. "Anything." And in the saying of it, there was more than bravado in her eyes, there was resolve. The full breadth of her willingness was there, the full scope of her devotion, the full measure of her sacrifice.

But not for him.

Never for him.

He pulled her forward by the touch of his hand upon her breast. She was a woman, that was all. Not a muse or a ghost or a phantom of his mind. She was assembled parts and pieces similar to other women, no more, no less than a thousand like her. She was a smile, and a glint of dark eyes, and auburn hair that swirled like a forest of autumn leaves. She was magic and forbidden allure, she was nurturing tenderness.

She was his.

For this night, and a hundred other nights, and a thousand thousand, if he deemed it necessary and wanted it, she was his.

He bent and tasted the skin of her shoulder, holding her immobile by the threat of his teeth. It was a gesture of submission and conquest. Sparkling and falling from her lashes, a tear was wept for innocence and for herself, forever standing outside society's strictures. And one for him, lean grace and masculine perfection, with the hard glitter of bitterness showing in his eyes, effectively chasing away other, softer emotions. She did not move but let him nip at her, her eyes going to the tousled lock of hair that fell over his brow. Two fingers gently smoothed it back, and she half turned and laid a soft kiss upon that tanned skin.

A tear fell upon his face, and he cursed her for it; in the long, dark echoes of his soul, he cursed her for mastering him without a word spoken.

"The only tears I want from you, Kat," he said viciously, honestly, "are the ones you'll weep between your legs."

It was not a gentle lover who pulled her to the mattress, who stood over her and worked her with his fingers and then his lips until she nearly crested with the pleasure of needing him inside her and the pain of being denied it. He would stop, his self-torture as evident as hers, face pressed against the softness of her belly, his breath a white puff in the cold room, his body resting heavily between her outflung knees. He clung to her as though she were the tormentor. She shook with the need he evoked by lips and tongue and touch, and he grabbed her at her hips and covered her so close that not a bead of sweat could have divided them. In moments such as this, he would wait until the rhythm of her wanting had subsided, until her blood beat normally, and then begin again, raising up to suckle at a turgid nipple, sliding down to feast at other swollen flesh.

Only when his own control was ebbing was there a chance of salvation. The air was filled with soft, mewling sounds and low-voiced encouragement. The scent of him and her and sex was so heavy in the air that it, too, was an arousal. He entered her, finally, his back arching with the need to touch her womb, so full did he make himself. A battering ram, demanding the final surrender, exposing the final need.

Of the rest, Katherine couldn't recall. Other than feeling as if she were dying, of his arms there at the last, holding her, sheltering her as she fell from heaven again. She was a thousand sparks of spirit, her body resting heavily below somewhere. She knew, somehow, that it was imperative she draw up the scattered bits of herself. She could not allow him to touch her, knowing that if he did, with his warmth and his hint of tenderness and his threat of ownership, she would never want to leave.

But she had left, and within hours the child conceived in passion and carried in sadness would be born. Katherine swallowed heavily, past the lump of unshed tears.

Finally, Bertha breathed a heavy sigh of relief as Katherine caught Julie's hand and together, the two people she had grown to love like the children she'd never had descended from the hillside.

Later, Michael would take Julie on a long, circuitous

ride on Monty. There was no longer the need for secrecy; the earl had long since departed for London. He would never know that he had sired a child shortly to be born in a cottage only a few short miles from Mertonwood.

Chapter 12

"What the hell is it now?" he growled, as Jack slid through the doorway after a perfunctory knock. The earl half turned from his position near the window, where he had spent the morning staring at the view. It was an occupation that had involved his vision, but unfortunately allowed his mind free rein in other, less pleasurable pursuits. But then, he was seldom occupied in any pursuit that could be called pleasurable lately.

Damn her.

Jack regarded his set face for a moment, before he dropped the sheaf of papers onto the desk.

"I think you need to review these instructions once more, Moncrief, before they go any further."

"I don't need to review a damn thing. Just get the dispatch to Henderson. Have the masonry work begun as soon as the foundation is excavated. I want it done within the week." He didn't bother to turn but remained standing in front of the window, as if the plants bordering the path to the garden were fascinating objects of study.

"Then you've just committed a few thousand pounds to building a cotton mill in sheep country and a woolen mill in a swamp in Wales." The tone was faintly mocking, but combined with another emotion.

It was the compassion, faintly veiled, that finally prompted the earl to stride to his desk and investigate his previously executed orders. He stared at the paper as though an idiot had forged his name. He glanced at Jack, a self-deprecating smile twisting his lips. He crossed out several sentences, inserted a few more, and handed the missive to the other man. Jack had once again proven his friendship. Or his courage. No other person would have dared done what he'd just done.

"Thank you" was all he said, and both men knew that the gratitude was for more than the error he'd illuminated a few minutes ago.

"Any news?"

"Nothing," the earl replied, idly twirling the quill within his fingers. "Not a damn thing."

"You are planning to look yourself, then." It was not a question. Jack Rabelais knew his friend. Half his problem rested in sitting here waiting for information. Moncrief was a man of action, as he himself was. When his wife and children had disappeared, he had ruined three good horses racing through Napoleon's France looking for them, only to find, too late, that they had been victims of the revolution's latest killing machine, the guillotine.

"Is it any better than sitting here and single handedly destroying my own enterprises?" Again, that wry smile. He had waited, albeit not patiently, for months. As it was, five men had been hired and fired for their lack of information, if not for their lack of trying.

"At least, if you exhaust yourself, my friend, you might be able to sleep at night. That, if nothing else, would be an improvement." If it were possible to age ten years in the months since Katherine had disappeared, Moncrief had done so. His green eyes, once so lively, were shadowed by lids that were swollen and red. Lines of fatigue were etched across his brow and scored vertically between his nose and his thinly etched lips.

"I kept thinking," he said softly, concentrating on the quill rolled between his fingers, "that the spring thaws would bring word. That they would have found her body and Julie's huddled together for warmth. I wondered if I could live with myself if that happened. And, when it didn't happen, when there was no sign, I asked myself if I could live with myself anyway." The chance of her survival was greater with each passing day, yet his investigators had been unable to find anyone who remembered seeing a woman and a child boarding a coach. Nor did he think she had enough money to have hired a private vehicle. She'd left the ring behind with no note, a message as implicit as her departure. There was always the chance she'd sold Monty, of course, but even the horse auctions had borne no fruit. There had not been a stallion matching his appearance reported anywhere.

In other words, Katherine had disappeared from the face of England.

"You must remember, Moncrief," Jack said kindly, "that it was her decision to leave."

"Now, that is a comforting thought," Freddie muttered, his eyes sharp and penetrating. "Anything to escape a fate worse than death, right, Jack? Even fleeing into the worst blizzard to strike England in years."

Guilt had been his companion for so long, he didn't begrudge it nudging reason aside and plopping down in the middle of his soul. Some way, she must have discovered his plans for Julie, and he shook his head as he thought of that. It would be better for his peace of mind if he didn't think about it right now.

Damn her. She'd chosen risking death to him.

And if that wasn't rejection, he didn't know what was.

Jack did not bother to answer. The guilt that was ravaging his friend was not easily dismissed, nor would a kind word dispel his sense of self-loathing. Only time and distance would do that. Or finding Katherine. He gathered the papers and turned to leave the room.

"I honest to God never thought she'd turn me down." Freddie laughed, a humorless bark of mockery. "And now, the only woman who ever rejected me is the only one I can see when I close my eyes." He turned back to the window as the door shut soundlessly.

He thanked God that Jack had left so precipitately. What else would he have confessed if his friend had remained? The fact that if he were blinded tomorrow, he would not forget her face, the shape of her lips when she smiled, the dimple that formed when she laughed, the storm of her eyes when she was angry. He could be paraded in front of a thousand women, and he would know her scent. His hands could be severed at the wrists, and he would never be able to forget the rounded suppleness of her shoulders cradled in his palms, the feel of her skin beneath his fingers.

He would never forget the saucy way she tilted her head, her graceful hands that made arcs in the air as she talked. Her softness, her way of cooing to Julie, the perfect picture of motherhood that she created when she was with the baby. Her generosity, her openhanded friendship with the servants at Mertonwood. Her air of vulnerability when caught off-guard, the truant child of her spirit. Above all, her talent for dispensing love with such ease.

He had cut a wide swath through London, only to find that satiation did not come as easily as it had before his conscience lay scarred and in ruins. And physical ease really didn't mean that much when he paid with guilt.

He had sought willing partners from the lists of the ton, auburn-haired women with sultry mouths and firm, soft fleshiness. At first, he was incensed that they did not, even in the darkness, assuage that yearning deep inside. Then, he was simply unable to perform, as if his brain were firmly tied to his loins, and logic ruled. His reputation for moodiness increased, and with his shunning of available women and his aversion to society, so did his allure. He became an increasing challenge because of his apathy, but the more they threw themselves at him, the starker the contrast between Katherine and the noble women who found nothing incorrect about their own immorality, but who would have castigated Katherine for it.

He was chaste, and it was laughable.

His mind had made a paragon of virtue out of Katherine, as though she'd died a martyr, saintly, blameless. He needed to see her, to make her human again. He had spent too much time praying. Fervent, soul-deep prayers that she lived and prospered and had not been made the less for those few weeks at Mertonwood. He needed to exorcise her from his brain, his body.

Or maybe he just needed her.

"Now, Katherine! Now!" Bertha didn't want to scream at her, but Katherine's strength was waning, and it was clear that this birth was outside of Meg's experience. Bertha reasoned that it couldn't be much different from birthing a calf, and she had seen what could happen when a calf was turned wrong.

She propped Katherine up and yelled in her ear. Katherine mutely turned away, away from the relentless voice that would not let her rest. Bertha hauled her up again, pulling her by the arms, and shouted, "Now, or as God is my witness, Katherine, I will pull this babe from your body."

Nineteen hours of labor had taken their toll. Katherine's hair hung lankily to her shoulders, where it met the sodden garment she had been wearing since the birthing began in earnest. How many days had it been? She pushed against

Bertha, using her as a brace, and with the last of her strength, pushed the child from her body. She felt herself tear, but the flesh had long since been numbed by the force of the birth. She slumped down into Bertha's arms, turned her face away into the pillow, and slipped into a sleep so deep it mimicked unconsciousness.

The water was not cold enough, Bertha thought with a trace of fear. It was either not cold enough, or the fever that was raging through Katherine was enough to torch the sheets upon which she lay. Despite Meg's protests, she insisted upon changing the bedding again, until there was not a trace of the birthing blood.

Bertha Tanner was angry, and it was an anger born of decades of being without a child and coming to love this woman as if she were her own. In the cradle beside the bed lay a wizened, red-faced infant, but she was not about to gain one to lose the other. While she prayed, she cursed, if not at God, then His system of justice that would allow this to happen.

Katherine had fallen into a deep sleep after the baby was born, a sleep that took on an unnatural aspect even to Bertha's untrained eye. Her breath was too loud, her skin too flushed. Within hours, Meg had begun to whisper childbed fever.

Bertha changed Katherine into a new gown, discarded Meg's birth canal packing made of cloths that had seen too many birthings and too few washings, and laid Katherine in a clean bed again. She dismissed Meg, sending her to her own home to care for Julie, the best favor she could do at this time. She ignored the relieved way in which her sister-in-law took her leave, and sat beside the still form until night became morning and morning turned once again into another day. The second night, the baby fretted, and she gave him a sugar teat and extended her prayers for the infant son of the earl, hoping that the stern God of her ancestors would unbend to forgive sin occasionally.

Katherine only dreamed.

Of the seas crashing against the cliffs near Donegan and boiling between her bare toes, of the tall marsh grasses bending in the wind. Of the pungent scent of ginger from the kitchen, and baking bread with her mother. Of the herb garden in all its summer profusion, lemon verbena and basil and sage. Of the smell of camphor from her mother's sick bed, and the coughing, gasping sobs of a man not used to tears, weeping for a love too soon lost.

And she dreamed of him.

Striding toward Mertonwood's stables, mounting his large horse with centaur grace, laughing in the forest, the dapple shadows of brown and green camouflaging his face, green shadows of emerald eyes filled with laughter, gentle purpose, yet always misted with mystery. Hiding hurt or pain or something she could not explain. The beauty of him, fire-lit and strong. The calculating earl, easily bestowing a ring costing a fortune and jealously retaining words that cost him little. Tender lips, and even more gentle fingers, and a voice that demanded attention and obeisance.

Once, she dreamed he was beside her, his lean and long hand stroking back the dampness of her hair, bathing her forehead with cooling water, raising her body from sheets too damp and clinging. There was an aura of light around them, which intensified as long as she touched him, a glowing brilliance darting from their fingers as if sparks met where they touched. She smiled, and could feel the answering smile on his lips as if they were her own. She moved toward him but the light separated them both, so she was content to stand and stare at him as if never getting her fill. How tall he was, how strong. She ached to feel his arms around her, to feel the comfort of his strength, but it was enough that their fingers touched and arched and touched again. Somewhere a breeze blew, and it lifted the tendrils of hair from her cheek and brushed against his.

She was filled with peace, because he was here. Somehow, he'd known she needed him. Somehow, he'd come. She gripped his arms hard, and begged him not to leave her, and he agreed in a voice strangely like Bertha's to stay as long as she needed him.

He started at the northern end of England and worked south, stopping at hamlets no larger than a bend in the road and consisting of a thatched hut, spending a long time in the major cities, where he hired runners and young boys to act as criers. In London, he had an army working for him, from the youngest enterprising pickpocket eager to earn some legal coin to the barristers attached to the King's Court. He met with ships' captains from the Americas to the China trade. He investigated white slavers with a sinking heart, bondwomen matching her description with an anger he could no longer control; he traced routes into Scotland and Wales by coach. He utilized his own staff, and information was brought to him about servants with children newly employed at the great houses of England. He offered an obscene amount of money for any news concerning her whereabouts. He began to believe that if anything had happened of consequence in those months between October and July, he had information about it.

Except, of course, where Katherine Sanderson was.

When he returned to Moncrief, it was with resignation, not triumph. His search had been fruitless and without merit. The sight of his home did not make him pause, as it usually did. Nor did he care that the summer day was a perfect backdrop for his home. The tall spires of each of the four turrets stretched into the blue sky, but he didn't notice; nor did the mellow brick illuminated by the sun to a stark white cause him to smile with pride of ownership.

He had learned over the years, to trust in his instincts

and they were screaming at him. There was something he was missing, something he should have done, something he had overlooked. Despite its nebulous nature the feeling persisted, and it was a troubled man who entered the gates of his home, followed by men who had come to know a great deal about their employer in the past months. Namely, that one rode hard and furious with the earl, and it was not wise to complain either about the mission or its inconveniences.

He began to have the strangest dreams. Dreams in which he could see Katherine as though she were no more than a handsbreadth away. These dreams, poignant and filled with regret, were all alike in one regard.

They always ended with the sound of a baby crying.

Chapter 13

Her son was born with black hair and bright blue eyes. A large and long baby, his hands and feet appeared huge to Katherine, out of proportion to the rest of him. When she asked Bertha if she thought that was true, the older woman had only laughed and said that he would grow into them.

Her long illness had dried up her milk, but the young girl who had been summoned from the village sat close to Katherine as she nursed her son, sharing in the experience with her as she grew stronger each day.

" 'Tis a miracle!" Meg gushed every morning when she visited, but Bertha only snorted and rolled her eyes to the ceiling.

"More like good nursin'," she would say cuttingly, but Meg would not take the hint, nor had she ever explained her precipitate departure that day.

Katherine only smiled faintly. Each day she grew stronger, and she was only grateful for the chance to live, to see both her children grow and flourish.

Robert showed early signs of being his father's son. He insisted upon being fed every two hours, despite the fact that Katherine knew the wet nurse had adequate milk. On those rare occasions when he didn't require sustenance, he demanded attention and would fuss when he was placed in the cradle Julie had outgrown.

She thrived on his demands.

Whatever feelings she had once had for the earl were oddly projected onto her child. Admiration for the earl's looks became maternal pride at the black tufts of hair on the small head, at the eyes that would gradually change hue like his sister's. Appreciation for the earl's quick mind became doting fondness as her son became fascinated with the shape of his hands, began following her face with alert eyes, and cried unless she was the one who cradled him. Even the physical had its counterpart, as she would hold her son close and feel his sturdy softness, rub her cheek against his downy head, press the hand with his already-long fingers to her mouth. His skin was plump and smooth, his hair soft as silk.

She loved everything about this child whom she had conceived in abandon and birthed in secret. Love was sitting quietly in the darkness with him sleeping against her, his tiny head nestled in the spot between her neck and shoulder. His lips would breathe softly against the spot his father loved to kiss. Love was bathing his tiny body, dressing him, talking to him as though he could understand every word. In a very strange and inexplicable way, love was also granted, in absentia, to the earl, who had transformed her life. First with passion, then with the miracle of his son.

She had worried that Julie would feel usurped by this tiny stranger, but the little girl was acutely possessive of her brother; the only time she was still for a moment was when she tenderly played with him, helping him learn to roll over and then to sit. Robert was enamored of his older sister, yelling loudly whenever Julie's energies pulled her from his circle to something else that had caught her attention.

Katherine no longer thought of leaving. Bertha's careful nursing had resulted in her regaining her health, but it was evident that there was nothing she could do for Bertha. Each day she gained strength, the older woman seemed to lose a little more of hers. Katherine's remaining at the cottage became a labor of love. She cared for Bertha in small repayment for all that the older woman had given her, and she cared for her children without concentrating on their uncertain future. She found that she was tired a great deal, but sleep never came as swiftly as she wished. Sometimes, in the deep darkness of a country night, when all was quiet, she would watch her son and daughter sleeping and allow herself a few moments to think about their father. If she longed for something in those quiet moments, no one knew, and there was no shame in dreams.

The Dowager Countess of Moncrief sat with pursed lips for most of her journey. Her maid, Jenny, was hungry and tired of the incessant traveling but she knew better than to say a word to her furious mistress. It was plain that the countess had a regular bee in her bonnet, and part of her troubles was the earl. Jenny sighed, but was careful to keep her exasperation from reaching the ears of the countess.

Mertonwood had been deserted, except for the skeletal staff that still remained in residence. The countess had spent the better part of the afternoon closeted with the head gardener, and Jenny could bet they weren't discussing roses. She wondered what the earl had done now. Surely something fierce for his mother to get that tight look around her mouth and that glint in her eye. Why, just a few years ago, the rascal had ruined a girl fresh from the schoolroom.

Jenny was certain they were on a fool's errand, probably to correct some mistake the earl had made and that his mother would handle. It was true the man had a wizard's way of making money, but he sure had problems dealing with people. Jenny sighed again. She had been with the countess for over twenty-five years. Long enough to know Freddie inside and out, to have suffered with the woman who was his mother, to have witnessed enough scandal to fill the pages of the *Spectator.* Not that the earl was responsible for all of it, mind you, but trouble did seem to follow him like a favorite puppy.

When Freddie was twelve, for example, there was that incident with the chambermaid. It had never occurred to the countess, or to anyone else, that Freddie would have taken such an interest in the opposite sex at that young age. If it had, the countess would have ensured that her staff was comprised of homely young women with less buxom looks, such as those who occupied each house Freddie lived in since the age of thirteen. As it was, his hobby—so to speak—was taken to school with him, where frantic headmasters wrote glowing words about his intellect and horrified tomes about his conquests. The countess had spent too many holidays trying to reconcile proper behavior in her son and being conciliatory to his headmasters, most of whom were bribed with promises of Lattimore bequests if Freddie was allowed to remain in school.

Then there was Monique. Jenny shivered, and the countess glanced at her in irritation. She smiled weakly, turned to the window, and tried not to think of those dark days when scandal had covered the Lattimore name like a low lying fog, ever present and clinging.

Monique, the young wife who was the object of Freddie's adoration. Monique, who collected admiring looks like other women collected hats, who beckoned every man into her web like a dainty, poisonous spider. She'd viewed the countess not with the love of a daughter for a mother-in-law, but as a woman might view a rival. And a rival she'd been in truth, had she not? She'd died the same day and in the same carriage as her husband's father, and it didn't take an Oxford don to know what they were doing together. Or had been doing for weeks at a time hidden away at Mertonwood. Yet, neither the countess nor her son had ever spoken of it within another's hearing. It was a secret they shared, and perhaps part of the reason the Dowager Countess of Moncrief was a little more understanding about her son's escapades than anyone else, as if she alone knew what devils drove the earl. God knew she had been willing to get him out of one scrape or another since then.

The countess had changed. She was no longer the slightly flighty woman concerned with her own existence. No, she had begun to take an interest in the world outside her own palatial estates. But while the tragedy of her husband's death had made a better woman out of her, it had made a more ruthless man of Freddie.

Which is why their journey, begun in London with Duncan arriving near dawn, had been filled with hours of tense and worried silence. Jenny reasoned that if the countess had wanted her to know, she would have told her. It did not stop her curiosity, however, nor her certainty that Freddie, Earl of Moncrief, was at the bottom of it.

Miriam Lattimore was well aware of Jenny's curiosity. She also knew that Jenny tended to view Freddie with disapproval, which at the current moment in her life, she did too. Words did not seem adequate to describe her emotional pendulum. She quite frankly did not know whether she was enraged with her son, or simply despairing. Freddie had always been kind, even if that kindness was occasionally cloaked in self-interest and hidden by anonymous deeds. He had never before, at least in her experience, been a despot.

It was Duncan who had brought word of Freddie's search, of the incredible amounts of money expended looking for one woman, of the monstrous reward offered as an incentive and a lure. Coupled with the description and the mention of a baby, she'd not had to look long to put two and two together.

It was probably all her fault.

She had badgered Freddie into visiting his daughter. Miriam did not want Freddie to act with the same callous regard his father had had for family ties. Illegitimate or not, Julie deserved to know her father. And yet, for almost a year, Miriam had not bothered to inquire after the child or the young woman for whom Freddie now searched with such desperation.

She'd brought them together, hadn't she?

The lovely young woman from the country, unsophisticated and unspoiled, championing the young thief who'd stolen from her, weeping tears of anguish for a life too quickly taken. And Freddie, jaundiced and betrayed by people he'd loved, colored by an existence that offered wealth and privilege, but not trust and never compassion.

A union destined to occur. A disaster waiting to happen.

Dear God, what had he done? It was Michael who had filled in the gaps, an uncertain man who'd taken one look at the countess's determination and something else he'd seen in her eyes, and divulged as much as he'd known of their story.

John slowed the carriage before a small cottage. There was no sign of life except for one small girl, perched on the single step before the oak door. Miriam stepped gingerly from the carriage, avoiding a slight incline in the ground, and onto a path formed by flat, rounded rocks. She stopped just in front of the child, who eyed her both with the suspicion of someone not used to seeing strangers and the bright inquisitiveness of youth. She was clad in a clean oatmeal-colored smock with a yellow ribbon neatly tied around her waist. Her hair was long, dark and swirled around her shoulders like a dark halo. Her round face was like Celeste's, but her features bore Freddie's stamp of paternity, his eyes, alert and curious, daunting in a child's face. She stood when Miriam reached her, as if wishing to dart away. She kept looking behind the countess to the horses, which stood restlessly under John's command. Between the horses and Miriam, it was difficult to decide which held the child's attention more.

"Hello," Miriam said softly, remembering how toddlers are apt to be torn between a budding independence and a terrifying fear of strangers. "Are you Julie?"

The child nodded, for the moment her attention diverted from the horses. Miriam wanted desperately to reach out to the girl, but prudence and wisdom held her back. This was her granddaughter, but she didn't quite know what to do, when suddenly the child took any further decision out of her hands.

"Mama!" Julie called in a loud voice, running inside the cottage. For a moment, Miriam was nonplussed, but then relieved at the sight of an older and more beautiful Katherine as she stood at the doorway to the small cottage, calmly drying her hands on an enveloping apron.

Katherine remained in the doorway, not speaking. A tiny frisson of fear raced down her spine, but it was not mirrored in her face. She had known this day would come. The reckoning. That he had sent the countess was both a surprise and a relief.

"He has developed some sense, after all," she said wryly. "Are you his champion, then?"

"If you're speaking of my son," Miriam said, "he doesn't know I'm here."

That was a shock.

Behind her, Jenny stood waiting for this drama to unfold. Before it did, however, she was banished summarily to the coach. In a huff, she drew her full skirts around her and marched back down the path, forgetting twenty-five years of training as lady's maid and sometime confidante to a member of the nobility.

The countess paid no attention to Jenny's petulant departure. She was still entranced with the sight of the little girl, now half hidden behind Katherine's full skirts. Occasionally, she would peep out from behind them, finger in mouth, staring at the stranger who was her grandmother.

"She looks like a small female version of Freddie," the countess said, still aching to reach out and embrace the little one. She would have to wait until she'd gained her trust.

"Your son doesn't think so," Katherine said, stepping aside and grudingly allowing the countess to enter the cottage.

The look of curiosity on Miriam Lattimore's face demanded appeasement. Katherine wasn't sure she was in the mood to explain.

"I don't understand."

"Your son does not seem to think she is worthy to be his daughter," Katherine said tersely. "Far be it from me to attempt to change his mind, countess."

"Since you are the mother of my grandson, do you think we could possibly arrive at a first name basis? Please, call me Miriam." She laid one hand on Katherine's arm and felt the shiver that raced through her at her words.

"You know?" The words were pressed past the weight upon her chest.

"Freddie is no more aware of his son, Katherine, then he is your whereabouts."

"Thank God," she said, sinking weakly onto the small chair next to the fireplace. Although it was too warm for a fire, everything lay in readiness for the next time it would be needed, a sure sign of proper housekeeping. In fact, everything about the small cottage glowed with care. There was not a speck of dust anywhere, and everything shone.

"If he did not send you, then why are you here?" Only the look in her eyes softened the question. It was uncertainty, fueled with the remnants of fear.

"To see my grandchildren, to see you. To offer my assistance." The countess sat on a small frayed chair opposite the fire,

"You will not tell him?"

"At the present moment, I do not feel that it would be wise for me to speak to my son," Miriam replied. "I am not certain I could keep a civil tongue in my head. In a way, I feel as though I've failed him if he's turned out to be such a monster."

"It takes two people to create a child, Miriam. Do not discount my own participation." Katherine smiled at the novel experience of defending the Earl of Moncrief.

"Yes, but you were young and foolish. That is to be expected of one of your age and experience. Freddie's behavior was not. He took advantage."

Katherine only blinked at the countess, stymied for a moment for a rejoinder. It was true, she was younger than the earl, but she doubted she was quite as foolish as the other woman charitably made her out to be. However, she was not so idiotic as to insist that the countess comprehend her own active participation in the seduction, especially since that would label her a whore. Therefore, the only recourse was silence, a silence curiously laced with genuine humor.

"Tell me," Miriam asked, leaning toward Katherine, "why did you never say that your father was a baron?"

"Would it have made a difference?"

"In my hiring of you, you mean?" At Katherine's nod, she answered truthfully. "No, it was quite evident you needed employment. But it might have made a difference in the way Freddie treated you."

"That makes him sound more of a monster than ever,

madam. I prefer to think of him as simply a randy goat and not a pompous, class-conscious randy goat."

Miriam laughed, a surprised snort of laughter that evolved into almost hysterical glee. Oh, Freddie, she thought, what have you done? The young woman sitting across from her was more than a match for her son. She was not only intelligent but a true beauty.

After Robbie's birth, Katherine's beauty had blossomed into lushness. Her face had matured, the cheekbones becoming more pronounced, the hollows deeper. Her lips were fuller, the curving dimple on one side of her mouth accentuated by her smile. Her breasts were full and her waist had returned to its original curving lithesomeness. Her way of viewing the world had changed, too, becoming more direct, as though seeing the fallacy of most of it through the uncompromising honesty of her own vision. She had borne shame but no longer felt shameful. She had almost died and, in doing so, had found those things worth living for. They were not endless longings, and dreams too steeped in fairy-tale imaginings to ever come true. She had been stupid, but stupidity was only a sin if it was endlessly repeated. And Katherine had no intention of doing that.

Julie peeped out from behind the chair, took several tiny, tentative steps in Miriam's direction, seemed more secure when the woman barely glanced at her, then retreated slowly to her safety behind Katherine. When she repeated the gesture only moments later, Miriam calmly reached into her reticule and retrieved a small, gaily wrapped package. She laid it on the arm of the chair beside her, ostensibly ignoring the child. Katherine smiled at Miriam's wisdom. Julie would come to her when, and if, she chose.

Katherine stood, looking at Miriam, making a decision that had been unsolicited. She left the room for a moment, entering her small bedroom. She returned bearing a sleepy baby, four months old. He was firm, solid, warm from sleep and incredibly wonderful. Miriam looked at him in delight as Katherine handed her the baby.

Miriam cradled the firm little body next to her own and felt tears well from eyes that had not wept in so long. Within moments, the baby decided he wasn't ready to be awakened yet and settled down into relaxed slumber against his grandmother's chest.

If Katherine had thought that the look on the Dowager Countess's face when she had seen Julie was something to behold, it was nothing compared to her expression as she sat holding Robert close to her. In that moment, barriers of age, societal standing, background, wealth and prestige were forgotten. In her arms, Miriam held the child of her child, proof that life would go on. Countless years were swept away, with all their attendant memories, and the child who rooted against her could have been Freddie. Hair as black as a raven's wing or the deep darkness of a country midnight. Soft, firm body with incredibly big hands and feet, long, chubby legs, and sweet curving arms that ended in hands that grasped fitfully at everything in sight, as if to say "mine!"

Miriam held the little boy against her, swept back the black hair with a tender hand, and thanked God that she had lived to see this day. Julie seemed to have lost fear of her the moment Robbie was put into her lap, or perhaps it was childish jealousy that prompted her to emerge from her protected spot near her mother and venture close to her grandmother. When she stood before her, then wedged close to the chair beside her, leaning into her, Miriam thought that all the most beautiful experiences of her life were as nothing compared to this moment. She would do anything in her power to see Katherine happy and content, as long as her grandchildren remained an integral part of her life. It did not matter that Freddie had less than a jackass's sense and had not married either of their mothers. These children were as much a part of her family as if they had been nobly born and raised.

Their father, however, had a debt to pay and a lesson to learn.

"Tell me, Miriam, how did you find us? As to that, how did you learn about my father?"

"Duncan, my dear. My solicitor. He had investigators the length and breadth of England. I suspect Duncan of being involved in secret work for the government. It would suit him, the rogue. However, he does do well. Look at how he outsmarted Freddie's men."

"Freddie?"

"Did you not know, my dear? It is the one thing about my son that I applaud. He's been looking for you ever since you left. I must commend you upon your canny logic. Who would think to look for you here?"

"It was less logic than circumstance, Miriam," she said, thinking of the storm that had brought her here.

"You know, of course, that since you have no legal ties to Julie, he could take the child from you." She whispered the question, concerned not for the sleeping baby, but for the little girl who stood staring at the package still resting on the arm of the chair.

"But that's not true," Katherine said, standing. She disappeared into the other room, searched through the valise that had carried her belongings on that snowy day so long ago, and found the much-folded document. Returning to the main room, she handed it wordlessly to the countess. Katherine removed Robbie from her arms and returned the baby to his cradle, while the countess scanned the document. When the younger woman returned, Miriam folded the paper, again condemning her son for his stupidity, and wondered how she would say the next words.

Tact was sacrificed for bluntness, and she said, "This is not worth the time or the paper used to execute it. You were, quite frankly, duped. There is no other way to put it. My darling son used his not-inconsiderable powers of persuasion and, no doubt, a suitable bribe to his solicitor. But this paper, this contract"—the Countess flushed, remembering the exact phrasing—"has no validity and would not have any credence should Freddie choose not to honor the terms of the contract."

"Why?" Katherine's eyes were narrow slits.

"Because, my dear, you are a woman. At the time, you were a woman below the age of your majority, plus you were unmarried. If, however, you had been married, you would still not have been able to execute any such document without your husband's signature. You simply have no legal rights."

"That's unconscionable."

"That's the law. Perhaps one day it will change, but not as long as men control power in the world. Even I cannot, as a matron, as a countess, execute documents without Freddie's consent or approval. My wealth, such as it was, was dependent upon my husband. Now it is subject to my son's whims."

"But how do you stand it?"

"There are ways, my dear. There are ways." Miriam smiled.

Julie edged closer to her grandmother. Miriam turned to the child and held out the brightly wrapped package. Julie allowed one finger to spring free of her mouth, smiled impishly at Miriam, grabbed the present, and darted behind Katherine to open it.

"I cannot think why he would still concern himself with us," Katherine said, her anger growing each moment. "Especially since he considers Julie deformed, a freak."

Miriam was struggling between loyalty and curiosity. Finally, curiosity won. "Tell me," she said, glancing at her granddaughter. There was nothing readily apparent about the child that was different from any other normal child.

"Look at her fingers," Katherine bid, a small-voiced directive that Miriam obeyed instantly.

"Freddie's a fool," Miriam Lattimore said firmly, the one and only time she had ever broken ranks and spoken of her son in less than glowing terms.

Katherine smiled. "I have begun to think so."

Miriam sighed. "I apologize for birthing a man so devoid of sense, my dear. I can only accredit his father's side of the family for some of it."

Katherine smiled, and the older woman met it with one of her own.

"What are your plans, my dear? Freddie will discover your whereabouts only too soon." She had no qualms about protecting Katherine from her son. Freddie deserved to reap the consequences of his own stupidity.

"Duncan," she explained at Katherine's questioning look. "He will tell him," she said in a frosty voice. The frost was reserved for Duncan.

"But what has he to do with me, with all of this?" Katherine was one step away from total exasperation.

"Duncan has a highly developed and misplaced sense of chivalry, my dear. He feels it is Freddie's right to know. Blame me if you will. I let the boor travel with me to Mertonwood, and he left again this morning for London. I made him promise not to do anything until after I've spoken with you. Beyond that, all of our years of friendship, I'm afraid, will not dissuade him from his purpose."

"I cannot leave now, though, Miriam. There is Bertha, you see."

At Miriam's look, she explained. "She is very ill. I fear she has not long to live. I could not leave now when she needs me."

"But does she not have family?"

"Yes, she does. But she has also been family to me," Katherine said firmly. "She took me in when no one else would, and she's not condemned me for what I've done," she added.

"And have I done so, my dear?"

"No," she answered softly, "you have not."

Katherine stood, and looked down at the older woman, a member of the nobility, true, but more importantly, a woman of courage and compassion. A woman she'd liked from the moment she'd met her. At the time, she'd wondered if anyone could sway Miriam Lattimore from her gentle purpose, and now she knew how difficult it would be.

"I can't help but wonder, though, if my life is to be spent fleeing from your son. I won't do that, Miriam. If it's confrontation he wants, then I won't deny him. If it's war, then I'll battle him if necessary. I won't run anymore. I'm tired of running."

"And Robert? He is the lure, Katherine, if not Julie. Freddie has no heir," she said softly. "He would want his son."

"My son, not his."

"Was it not you who stated that it took the two of you to create him?" Miriam's chiding look was softened by a slight smile.

"I will not fault him for his duplicity, Countess," Katherine said, the force of her tone startling Julie. The child edged closer to her mother and gripped the edge of her skirt with one hand, the other clutching the half-unwrapped present. "I was a fool, and I've learned well how not to be one. I will not fault him, either, for his arrogance, his autocracy, his way of looking at the world as though it were created for his amusement alone. I will not even blame him for repudiating a child whose only sin was to be born out of wedlock, and whose only crime is a slight imperfection. But, madam, make no mistake about my feelings for your son. He may have whatever in the whole wide world he wants, but he will never have my children. Never."

There was a look in her eyes that did not bode well for her son, Miriam thought.

The countess left a short time later, promising to return when she could. Bertha and Miriam had spent some long moments eyeing each other, before launching into a conversation that castigated Freddie and lauded Katherine and the children. If Miriam was horrified by the skeletal thinness of the older woman, she didn't indicate it by word or deed. If the cough that was Bertha's only sign of energy frightened her, she did not mention it either. Toward the end of the visit, she leaned over the bed and, clasping both frail hands in hers, she looked into Bertha's lined and flushed face, meeting the look in her eyes.

"Thank you" was all she said, but they both knew what she meant. It was genuine appreciation for love given unstintingly, for care and concern and shelter from the storm. For a nest of peace and safety for Katherine.

"She's welcome," Bertha replied, a humorous glint in her eye, a frail smile wreathing her lips.

Katherine walked Miriam to the coach, where Jenny sat, fuming. John looked none too happy, either, and despite Katherine's nod of recognition, he turned aside. Where trouble is, that one follows, he thought with a grimace, unconsciously duplicating Jenny's earlier thoughts about the earl.

"How is Jeremy?" Katherine asked.

The older woman turned to her in surprise. "Oh, yes, you would have no way of knowing, would you? Jeremy has added his own layer of scandal, I'm afraid." Her eyes were filled with humor rather than censure. "He and Beth Thompson eloped last year. Her father, the Duke of Granbury, threatened to disown the chit, until, of course, he discovered that he was about to be made a grandfather. Now, all is love and kisses. Jeremy is the son he's never had, Beth is cosseted and again his beloved only child. By the time the babe is born, he will have purchased the remainder of England for him. He already owns half of it."

Unlike her first two grandchildren, Katherine thought, then chided herself. It was the difference between legitimacy and being born on the wrong side of the blanket, pure and simple. And the protective impulses she felt for her children, while understandable, would not make them less illegitimate.

"I'm so glad for Jeremy," Katherine said with genuine fondness, recalling the young man so at odds with his brother. "He is happy, then?"

"He is ecstatic. The only fly in the ointment seems to be his and Freddie's continuing antipathy."

"Your older son does have that effect on people," Katherine observed.

"There are times, my dear," Miriam Lattimore said, her eyes twinkling, "when I believe that my children are conspiring to place me in an early grave. Melissa has the same stubbornness as her brothers. She is the reason I must return to London. She's in the midst of her first season and fancies herself in love with a young marquis. If I had my way," she continued with a heartfelt sigh, "they would marry within the week, and she would become a staid matron overnight. Unfortunately, her whims seem to change with the dawn, and by the time I return, she will undoubtedly have fallen in love with another."

Katherine smiled, the thought crossing her mind that she was indeed fortunate in Miriam. Freddie's mother could have been a termagant or, worse, someone like Mrs. Roberts, who judged people by her own beliefs, and when they could not hope to match up, dispensed not Christian charity, but stern contempt.

It had been, all in all, a pleasant visit. Only once before she left did they come close to disagreeing. Miriam pressed a small bag of coins into her hand before entering the carriage. Katherine demurred, attempting to give it back.

"You don't understand, Katherine," the countess said firmly. "This is for Bertha. Use it to buy what comfort you can for her now. Use it later for a fitting service. What you have left will be adequate to send for me when the time is right." The few moments spent in the rear bedroom had shown her that Katherine was right: the older woman was very close to death. In those few moments, she had seen the awareness in Bertha's eyes, and something else: a love as strong as familial ties for Katherine and the children.

Without a further word, Katherine took the bag.

"Let me know, Katherine, when it's time, and together we will make plans. I do not want to lose my grandchildren. Promise me that you will not disappear again."

It was a decision Katherine had made in her heart long before Miriam Lattimore appeared on the doorstep. She was tired of running.

Katherine smiled at the older woman and placed her cheek next to hers. It struck her then that they were not so far apart, she and the countess. Both had children they loved and wanted to protect. Both would be willing to do what they had to do in order to protect them.

"I won't," she said, stepping back, and in that moment, a bond was formed. A promise was given.

Duncan McCorkle was not in awe of the Earl of Moncrief. He had seen the boy in his nappies, for God's sake, had seen him grow to a young man, assisted his mother in extricating him from countless difficulties, know all his foibles, and treated him with the understanding and the fondness of a father, which he had often wished he had been. Yet, the same lack of title that had prevented his suit from being accepted by Miriam's parents had allowed

Duncan to achieve what few men realized: a power base that was at least equal to, if not greater than, the Earl of Moncrief's.

The fourth earl would have been very jealous of his son, Duncan realized. Not only for the fortune he had amassed, but because of the man he had become. Freddie was not blind to the plight of the poor, but he did not seek recognition for his acts of charity. He did not follow society's whims with sheeplike devotion, as did most of the peerage. He questioned rather than accepted. Nor did he seek to change the world by personal anarchy, but rather by altering it from within, witness the amounts of money and energy spent with that goal in mind. He was an impassioned speaker in the House of Lords, well-respected, if not a little feared. He truly did not seem to care if others approved of him or not. He was autonomous, this man. It was his greatest virtue and his worst fault.

Because he was emotionally independent, the earl expected other people to be the same. He was not connected, Duncan thought, and this isolation Freddie maintained was his most foremost weakness. The Earl of Moncrief was a little too dispassionate, a little too detached from the world of people. He expected people to react in predictable ways, as though they were the machines that fascinated him; as though they would follow a prescribed plan of action.

One of the joys of living, Duncan had long ago decided, was the simple mystery of people. It was the uncertain nature of mankind that made life so exciting.

Nor was the earl performing as expected. Duncan had anticipated anger, but instead he was carefully composed, addressing most of his remarks with his back to the room, staring out the enormous window of his office that overlooked the structured gardens below. It was a gesture saved from being rude only by Duncan's perception of the man he addressed. Duncan's training in observation took note of the tightly clenched hands, the soft voice that carried its own edge, the stiff stance of the man before him.

Strange, when he pictured the earl, it was never in this townhouse that so obviously bore Miriam's touch. It was always at Moncrief, commanding his not-insubstantial kingdom from that towering edifice of white brick and rock.

"Is she well?" The voice was oddly muffled, another clue.

"From what I can gather, yes." Duncan wondered if he had made a calculated error. Recriminations, however, were a bit late at this point, he realized. The words had already been spoken, the deed had already been done. He wondered if Miriam would ever talk to him again.

"And the children? They are fit?" A rasp in the tone, something Freddie wished to keep restrained, but which hinted at rage. Or grief.

"Yes, very healthy, as I understand."

"His name. What is his name?" Not an odd question, was it? Duncan reasoned, unaware that Freddie was having difficulty concentrating on any coherent thought at the moment.

"Robert." Duncan shifted some papers in his lap, found one, and read from it. "Robert Arthur. Named for her father, I believe."

"A baron, you said." That explained the education. A voice, familiar due to its presence in his thoughts of late, echoed. Her father's horses. Hell, her father had kept a stable worthy of his own.

The earl turned. Between his hands a quill had been snapped in two. His eyes were shadowed, his face gaunt, as if he had not slept well for too long a time. It was a thought with roots in truth. Yet, the emotion that suffused his looks now was not fatigue, or simple displeasure, but a more complex one. His eyes were slitted, his lips clenched tightly.

Duncan wondered, again, if he had made the right decision.

"Thank you, Duncan. I appreciate the information; I will not forget it."

"I did not come here because I expected compensation, Freddie," he said, just as stonily.

"I know that, too. I am only grateful for whatever impulse prompted your frankness. I take it my mother is aware of your visitation?" Their friendship was no secret.

"Not yet," Duncan admitted, thinking that the explosion would come soon enough.

"Then let's not tell her for a while, all right?" The earl's smile was not at all humorous.

"In this matter, I shall not intervene further, Freddie," was all the concession Duncan would make. He had done enough.

"Good," Froedrich Allen Lattimore said. "It's my turn now." He smiled grimly and looked down at the snapped quill in his hands with something like surprise. Duncan believed, at that moment, that the earl would have given anything to have had something, or someone, else beneath his fingers.

Chapter 14

They looked like crows standing silently on a hilltop, Katherine thought. The inhabitants of Mertonwood Village, clad in their mourning garb, watched as the wooden coffin bearing the earthly remains of Bertha Tanner was lowered into the grave beside her husband. They paid their last respects to the woman each of them had known since birth. Each person had a story to tell about Bertha's kindness. The women wept; each man seemed to have something blown into their eyes. The older inhabitants of the village remembered a bouncing country lass, the younger ones a kindly woman of middle years. The matrons remembered a softly maternal woman for all that she had never borne a child of her own.

Her own memories were something to savor, Katherine thought, as she stood beside Michael and watched as the coffin dropped inch by inch into the open pit in the earth. Bertha, laughing at Julie's antics. Bertha, scolding her for doing so much work. Bertha's warm companionship in the cold winter evenings. Her kindness and compassion when

Katherine had been filled with so much self-doubt and fear. She owed a fortune to this woman, one that could never be repaid in love or sacrifice.

She followed Michael and his family to the edge of the grave, let spill the dirt clenched in one hand, listened to the droning voice of the parson with half an ear. She had performed this ritual so many times in the past, it was almost second nature to her now. She stepped back as Michael accepted the condolences of the villagers. Meg was in the cottage below, preparing the food that would be offered to the mourners and minding the children. Katherine had argued with her about village customs and had won this skirmish. She didn't feel it right that they should be present at the funeral, preferring Julie's memories of Bertha to be only pleasant ones. And Robbie was much too young to know what was happening.

The end had come peacefully, in her sleep, the way Bertha must have wanted it. Katherine had been roused, not by Julie's excited laughter, but by the silence in the cottage.

Soon it would be time to contact Miriam. Within a week, Michael's son and his family would occupy the small cottage. Although he had said that she and the children could stay as long as necessary, Michael's eyes would not quite meet hers. It was time to go.

"Hello, Katherine." It was a voice she had heard in her dreams.

She whirled to face him.

He stood in the early morning mist like a specter from her past. A ghost, complete with chiseled face, narrowed eyes, and drawn mouth. He had aged, this phantom, as if he'd lived a decade in the year since she'd seen him. She stepped back, a futile gesture, but he did not move, remaining still and silent, watching her with a cool and calculating gaze.

Cat's eyes.

She had not profited from their parting, he thought. Her mourning dress was so old that not only was the style out of date, but the black had faded to rusty brown. It was rare that dark-haired women could wear black. She looked beautiful, damn her. The stark hue emphasized her creamy complexion and brought out the hint of color on her cheeks.

Despite the hideous dress, the solemnity of the occasion, and the drab, pigeon-colored morning, he'd never seen her more beautiful. She stood in the cool wind that swept across the hillside like a druid princess ready and willing to do battle. Her auburn hair was wound in a coronet; her eyes, which had been misted with tears when he'd first seen her, now glinted with anger.

His mouth twisted suddenly, in a grin or a grimace, she didn't know.

Katherine grasped the folds of the skirt in her hands and turned again, marching past the suddenly interested faces of the mourners and following the path down the hillside. She kept walking, knowing that he followed her with steady, silent footsteps. She halted at the fork in the path. One well-trod trail led directly to Mertonwood Village, the other to Bertha's small cottage. She turned, planted both hands on her hips, and blocked his descent.

"What do you want?" she hissed. As a civil greeting, it was somewhat lacking. Yet what she was feeling was somehow greater than mere words could express.

If she had a pistol, she would have shot him.

How dare he come here, on this particular morning, with his air of dominion and his shadowed eyes? The first words he spoke should have been an apology. He should have been tentative. He should not have stood on a hilltop with the wind blowing his hair over his forehead, and looked as tired as he had, so that something shifted inside her and ached to give him comfort.

Damn him!

"My children," he said calmly. He watched as her face changed. Good. He wanted her to fear him. He wanted some indication that she had gone through the same hell as he. There was nothing changed about her, nothing frowsy or frayed or weary. He glanced down at her trim waistline, then up to the curve of her swelling bodice. If anything, she was riper and more womanly than before. Nor did her face show any signs of the passing months. There was only a hint of fatigue around her eyes, no deep grooves etched around those full lips, nothing to suggest that she, too, had wondered and worried, or been attacked by a conscience fueled daily by regret.

Her beauty, paradoxically, made him angrier.

"Oh? Since when have you decided that you have children, my lord?" Katherine drew herself up and forced herself to challenge his green-eyed glare.

"Since I was informed of it," he said, treasuring the tiny blossom of fear that shone in her warm brown eyes, "and not by you, I might add. Was it knowledge you intended to keep hidden from me forever?" He did not doubt the paternity of this child. There was nothing covert about Katherine; she was direct to the point of bluntness, or simply unschooled in deceit.

His faith in her nature did not mitigate his wish for retribution. He wanted payment for nights of sleepless pacing, for hours of soul-searching, for days of wondering what kind of fool he had been. He had stared at the snowdrifts, picturing her lost and frightened. He had castigated himself for being a fool, for giving her so little choice that she would flee from him. A defenseless woman thrust into the world with little to protect herself. Hah! He wanted restitution for the times he had sought physical release in the arms of another woman, only to be unable to perform because she had neither the winsome seductiveness nor the innocent passion of one auburn-haired beauty.

It didn't matter that most of his thoughts were illogical,

if not irrational. He wanted compensation, by God, and he was going to get it.

"Have you decided that Julie is perfect enough for you now?" she asked, unknowingly tiptoeing too close to the raw edge of his temper and his conscience. "Your seed may bear fruit," she bit out, "but even an idiot can sire a child. It takes a true man to be a father. In your case, my lord, you have no children."

Why had he thought she'd be like other women? Why had he believed that tears or pleading would be her greeting? She'd never done anything he'd expected; why should now be any different? Most women would have knocked on his door, babe in arms, and demanded hush money, if not complete support for their child. Katherine wanted him to roast in hell if the snapping look she gave him was any indication. Why, on God's green earth, had he thought she might possibly be happy to see him?

"You will never have my children, Freddie." His name was a curse on her tongue, and it pushed the flame of his temper one notch higher. "I was the one who bore one and nurtured the other. I have sat with them at night when fevers made them ill, rocked them when they cried from colic or teething, prayed over them when nothing else seemed to work. And you think I'd surrender them easily to you? You have all the paternity of a fish, Freddie. Not bloody likely!"

She stalked down the path, ignoring his swift footfalls behind her.

He reached for her, goaded beyond reason, nudged one step past the boundary of civilized action. She pulled away but he swung her around, his grip as punishing as the accusation in his eyes.

"You gave birth to my child," he said, his tone softened by the look of her so close to peril in his arms. Flushed cheeks and flashing eyes, full lips parted for breath. "Mine. I will always be a part of you because of that. You will always have something of me. Don't you understand? You can't walk away from me so easily."

"Watch me," she said, seething with anger and something else, something that made her want to run from him right this moment, to a secure burrow where she would be alone and safe.

He ignored the swift compulsion to kiss her, ignored, too, the sudden wish that anger was not the powerful emotion seething between them.

"You are the fool, Katherine, if you think to challenge me," he said softly. "Those far wiser have learned, to their disfavor, that I do not retreat from a battle."

"Would you wage war over children, my lord? Even a child you've repudiated? Do you not care that there would be no winners here? The only victims would be the children you profess to want so ardently."

"No, if we wage war, Kat, you will be the vanquished."

It was a threat, in all its polished and silver tone. A few words issued civilly in a voice cultured and benign. Promising with a smile what all the power of the Moncrief money and name could bestow upon someone so unwise as to provoke him.

If hatred were a color, she thought errantly, it would be blue. Like the glint of toledo steel. And it would taste like pure ice, a shard chopped from a frozen well.

At this moment, she hated him with such ease. He had had everything he ever wanted from the minute he'd drawn breath. Looks that lured, intelligence that questioned why and reasoned the answers, and a position in the world, secure and inviolate. He was possessed of a family who loved him even though they did not understand him, a fortune with which to be frugal or profligate, an easy charm that beguiled the unwary. He had it all, this man with his sea-green eyes, now storm tossed, and the mobile mouth, which now threatened.

He had never been bested, this earl with the idiotic

name. Never been challenged, never defeated. Never conquered. And he demanded to be a winner in the battle fully joined between the two of them. More than he wanted two little children whose only sin in life was to have been sired by him. Katherine had no qualms about assigning to him such nefarious motives; she'd had plenty of time in the past year to dissect his character at leisure. He did not want to attempt the role of father. He didn't want to concern himself with his children's future. He didn't want to teach them to ride, or laugh at their stories, or worry about them.

He wanted to win.

Perhaps she hated him most because he elicited compassion from her so effortlessly, concern that was so starkly not reciprocated. She noticed the circles beneath his eyes, but he didn't seem to care that he leveled accusations at her bare moments after someone she'd loved had been buried. She noticed his hair, too long, almost unkempt, but he'd not seen that her hands were red and chapped. She was concerned about his thinness, but had he thought of her laboring to bring his son into the world? Where had he been on snowy nights, when she had lain in her solitary bed, thinking of him and wondering about him? Had he done the same? She smiled, and it was such a cold and impersonal grimace that he frowned at it.

If it were war, as he so blithely warned, she would come to it well prepared. She would bring courage and self-reliance to their battles. Courage she'd not shown before, and self-reliance hard won through cold winter nights and endless summer evenings. She would engage in war with the illustrious Earl of Moncrief, but this time her weapons would be honed from experience and tempered with knowledge.

She was no longer the insipid child who had loved the thought of love so well that she had bequeathed her maidenhead and her future to a noble young man devoid of noble intent. Nor was she the slightly wiser young woman who had entered into an unholy bargain of her own making with a dissolute rake.

Because, when all was said and done, and all their chips were laid side by side upon the sideboard, she could not fault him for her own stupidity. That idiotic contract they'd signed had been a sop to her own morality, not his. Curiosity, danger, and passion had empowered her descent into immorality. That, and the dark allure he promised. He had not pushed her into his bed as much as he had stood aside and allowed her to leap into it.

If she were ruined by sharing his bed for too many days and by bearing him a son without benefit of clergy, law, or any other of society's restrictive covenants, then the guilt was as much hers as his. Hers, for believing she had no other choice; and his, for covering up the alternatives with a smile and a cozening charm.

They were equally matched in their sinning.

They would be equally matched in their battles.

"Bring out your cannons, my lord," she said, with a thin smile. "I am ready for them."

"I have it within my power to have you arrested, dear Katherine. Are you willing to be imprisoned to protect my children from me?"

He smiled at the look of confusion on her face. "Do you not remember stealing my horse?"

She rolled her eyes to the heavens. "Feel free to do what you will, my lord. I will not hesitate to divulge all of the details of our sordid little encounter. Including that scrap of nonsense called a contract between us."

"Do you think I care?" His smile was pure mockery, the glint in his eyes true daring. "It matters little to me what you tell the world, Katherine."

"Perhaps to you, Freddie. But not to your mother." It was almost worth bantering Miriam's name to see the florid look that appeared on his face.

It was not a truce, nor was it a draw. It was, instead, a period of study, in which each learned from the other. What lines were to be drawn—none. What subjects off limits—again, none. What scars to be left scabbed and untouched—none. What quarter to be given—finally, none.

It would be a rout, with one of them left bleeding in the sand. For a moment, the promise of open warfare was almost a relief, and then again, it seemed a terrible waste of energy and emotion from two people who had already demonstrated that they could use both to better purpose.

"Why?" Perhaps it was the question she should have asked at the beginning. "Why do you want them? For spite? For revenge? Why can't you just leave me alone? I've never asked anything of you, but I am asking now. Leave me with one good memory of you." Katherine did not look at him.

"And was it so bad, what we had?" He stroked the curve of her cheek with one gloved finger. She stepped away to avoid the lure of his touch. It would be so easy . . . too easy.

"No, my lord," she said, and smiled. It was a difficult smile to retain, being as brittle and as cold as it was. She was not used to sophisticated games of ennui. "It was instructive. So much so that I contemplated a life as a prostitute." For about thirty seconds, but he didn't need to know that. "Yes, Freddie, I consider the time well spent." For a moment, she thought she had gone too far. Never had she seen such a look of blind rage on another person's face. And for a second, there was another emotion there as well. A hint of something almost too impossible to believe. Nor did she give it any credence. It was a trick of the light, a shadow flickering over his face, before it assumed its austere lines. It could not have been pain she saw.

"Then you won't mind when the children leave your company." His smile was equally chilled. "You'll have more time to seek out a new protector."

She conceded that round to him. She couldn't think of anything more vile.

"Then it is war," she declared, all pretense forgotten in this stark meeting between adversaries, the last chance for armistice gone in the flick of a downward lash. She lost her smile as she stared up at him, too many memories flashing between them, adding a bittersweet tinge to the taste of anger.

"If you wish it, Kat." The pet name made her flinch, and for a moment, she thought he'd reach out to touch her again, so she stepped back to avoid the brush of his fingers. It was a strange tableau she would always remember: his outstretched hand frozen between them, and the look they shared in that cool, silent morning.

Regret too deep for speech.

Chapter 15

Miriam was weary, and her cheeks ached from the insipid smile she'd worn all night. She was frankly very glad the evening was drawing to an end. Soon, very soon, she earnestly prayed, she would be reclining amidst her pillows and the weariness would slip into well-deserved sleep.

Melissa's betrothal dinner had been a grand success and the ball following it had been amply attended. Her daughter was radiant with youthful bliss, her betrothed happy and proud, his parents fondly appreciative of the marital prize their son had won. Miriam was just tired. She knew that the young marquis would be run a pretty race before a month had passed. She wished him luck, but more importantly, a hasty wedding.

Two out of three married off, she congratulated herself, wishing her eldest son would heed the object lessons of his younger siblings. Freddie, however, was quite another story. She suspected the effort to convince Freddie to attempt matrimony again would take more time and energy than had both of her other children combined.

Yet, Miriam Lattimore was not dissuaded. She was, in her way, just as stubborn as he, just as autocratic when needed. And certainly as devious.

Peterson slid behind her, years of silent practice making his gesture almost imperceptible as he bent and whispered in her ear. "M'lady, there is a young person here, a Miss Katherine Sanderson, who wishes to see you."

The social smile was instantly transformed into a genuine expression of pleasure. How wonderful! And the children! The smile broadened, and if the betrothed couple thought the look on her face contained more happiness than it had all night, neither spoke of it.

Katherine stood in the foyer of the townhouse, wrapped in a rich red woolen traveling cloak, which contrasted sharply with her black mourning attire. Her face was etched with strain, her eyes haggard. As Miriam approached, she reached out with both hands, gripping the other woman's tightly, as if she might leave.

"Are they here, Miriam? Are the children here?"

"What are you talking about, my dear?" Katherine looked as if she were about to faint.

"He's taken them." The look the younger woman wore was one of hysteria barely leashed. She allowed Miriam to place an arm around her shoulders and lead her into the sitting room, waiting numbly as Miriam closed the sliding doors and poured a measure of brandy at the sideboard. She forced it into Katherine's hand, and then guided the hand to her mouth. As Katherine gasped and choked, Miriam sat beside her, trying to chafe some warmth back into cold hands.

"Now, my dear, suppose you tell me what you mean. Where are the children? Are they not with you?" Years of being married to the fourth earl had imbued Miriam with the ability to mask her emotions tightly behind a facade of gentle sweetness. Her brain, an organ quite able to sift through facts with startling ease—Freddie had inherited more than his good looks from his mother—was already beginning to piece the story together.

"Begin at the beginning, my dear," she coaxed. "I've found it's always a logical place to start." Miriam pressed more brandy upon her, and Katherine wondered if the other woman's aim was to make her roaring drunk as she told the tale.

"I don't believe it," Miriam said finally when Katherine was done. Brandy had the strange and novel effect of loosening her tongue and flavoring her speech with a few unflattering truths. She had told of Bertha's death and her grief, but most of all of the confrontation between the two of them. It was not simply brandy truth which betrayed her own bitterness, but a long and difficult journey to London on Monty, who had found himself once again bearing her toward safety and comfort in weather conditions less than ideal. The young footman who had grasped the reins had seemed surprised to find himself leading the earl's favorite and long-lost mount toward the stable, but no less surprised than the butler, who had opened the door to be confronted by a distraught young woman with the light of battle in her eyes.

"I don't believe it," Miriam said again, but Katherine took no offense. Because there was no truth greater than the knowledge that strummed through her veins right at this moment: Freddie Lattimore had her children. And she was going to kill him. The choice of weapons could be his.

"And you're certain that it was Freddie?" It could only have been Duncan who told him, that fiend. Miriam set aside thoughts of retribution for later.

Katherine's head nodded violently, discharging the haphazard knot on the back of her head, sprinkling the yellow damask sofa with raindrops. "When I returned to the cottage, Meg was still there and the children were fine. Later, when the mourners arrived, I put them both down for naps. Everything was fine. Even later, after everyone left and we'd had dinner, nothing was wrong. It was only when I woke up the next morning that they were missing. He said he wanted his children, but I never thought he would do anything this awful." It was true. Somehow, she had ascribed certain behavior to Freddie, none of which would lead him to do something this sinister. She'd envisioned a war of words, a campaign of resolve against resolve. At the very worst, she had thought he might use the courts to win his children. But she'd never thought he would steal them.

"Have you sent word to Mertonwood?"

It was the first place she'd thought of, but no one had seen the Earl. Michael had gone himself, his grief at burying his sister supplanted by his very real concern over the children's disappearance. She had to, on some level, believe that they had been taken by their father. At least, Freddie would keep them safe and free from harm. She hoped.

Miriam frowned. This was not like Freddie at all. He was very seldom empowered by anything other than logic, cold, ruthless, well-planned. But this action was one a man under a great deal of emotion might have perpetrated. It was not like Freddie at all. No, he'd not always thought before he acted. One only had to look as far as Celeste to see that. Yet, his motives could almost always be reasoned out, and his behavior did not border on the bizarre. At least, not until Katherine's incursion into his life.

Freddie had definitely changed this past year. He'd grown leaner and more dangerous-looking around the eyes. He had snapped at servants whom he had never before addressed in a surly manner, he had been moody and unpredictable most of the time. And now he'd absconded with two children; the presence of the first had never troubled him before, and the existence of the second must have come as a shock.

But how very odd for Freddie to be acting this way.

Froedrich Allen Lattimore, fifth Earl of Moncrief, feared by many and respected by those who understood his vast business empire, his dedication to the pursuit of science and to the building of a new dawn of technology, capable of quelling a room of his peers with one frosty glance, had spent most of the day being brutally assaulted by his almost two-year-old daughter.

She would not stop screaming, which she did with the full force of her not-incapable lungs. Her face turned scarlet and hot, her eyes bulged, her lips paled, and her little body became rigid with impotent fury. Everyone within hearing distance—by his reckoning, at least two miles—turned to stare at the mean tempered brute who would abuse such a lovely child.

She also seemed to delight in hitting him, with tightly clenched fists. He was not being pummeled by delicate baby punches. No, her fists were formed with thumbs outward, and whoever had taught her to box had done a damn good job of it. As if that were not enough, she had turned her not inconsiderable jaws upon him, clamping sharpened teeth onto any portion of his anatomy exposed to her rapacious fangs. Both of his hands were temporarily bandaged with pieces of his neckcloth. She seemed to delight in the taste of his flesh as a normal child would crave a sweetmeat. She didn't, this child of Satan, want anything like a sweetmeat, or an iced cake, or a new dolly, or a pony, or a shiny penny, or a windup toy that made a funny sound—he knew because in the course of the morning he found himself attempting to bribe her with each and every one of them. No, this imp of the devil wanted only one thing: her mother.

Neither his stern looks nor his shouted commands made any impression on her at all. She seemed not to notice when his own face grew pale in anger and his brows swept together in a sure sign of his own rage. Nor did she seem the least concerned by the stentorian tone that echoed throughout the carriage with the peal of a thunderclap. It was doubtful if she could hear him over her own shrieks. Short of bodily picking her up and attempting to quiet her by the simple expedient of putting his hand over her mouth—which is how he had been bitten in the first place—there didn't seem to be anything he could do to establish order in the situation.

His consequence—and his hands—were suffering as a result.

His son was as quiet as his sister was obnoxiously loud. Yet, while Julie occasionally quelled her rage long enough to partake of food—fuel for more rages, he suspected—her brother had stoically refused to eat during their entire journey. The damned wet nurse he'd hired didn't know what to do about it, either, even though he had lost his patience long ago and had begun to shout at the idiot. What was one more sound in a carriage that rolled through the countryside with all the subtlety of a cageful of howling animals?

"Why isn't he eating?" he demanded, when it was quite evident that his son refused to partake of the proffered breast. The wet nurse had only shrugged her shoulders and turned back to the baby, prompting a look his father could have sworn was revulsion to flash across his tiny face.

Freddie could not blame his son. He'd thought the girl was clean enough, but a clean smock did not necessarily indicate a clean body. The smells in the coach, unwashed flesh, soiled nappies, and the rusty scent of his own blood were enough for him to have lost his own appetite.

He was not a happy man.

The elation that had swept through him at his successful venture of the night before had been almost a sensual feeling. It had been absurdly easy. If his financial empire ever collapsed, he reasoned, he could take up burglary for a living. However, he would think long and hard before engaging in the act of kidnapping again.

Especially of his own children.

The small window of the cottage had opened with a twist, allowing him to breach the sill, enter the small room where his children slept, and hand each one out to the waiting driver standing in the hedges. Neither child had awakened sufficiently to make more than a token protest, not enough of a noise to awaken Katherine sleeping in the adjoining room.

The first hour of the journey had been incredibly easy. Both children slept, and he had a chance to study the daughter he had not seen in over a year, and his son, a stranger to him still. He admitted, in that quiet time before the dawn, that his motivation for bringing Julie was neither noble nor particularly admirable, fueled more by guilt than it was by paternity.

The rosy mist of dawn pushed long fingers of light into the carriage, a clarion call to the day and his own stupidity.

Julie was no longer the tiny baby she'd been, but a toddler half a step away from childhood. The country air had done her good; there was radiant health in her firm little body. Her black hair was plaited in a long braid that hung over one shoulder. Her smock covered dimpled knees, and one tiny finger was lodged in the corner of her mouth. Winged brows covered green eyes; he had seen them when she'd awakened briefly in the lantern light of the interior of the coach. Her face was a strange mixture of his and Celeste's features, his chin and nose, Celeste's cheekbones and shape of face.

The moment Freddie saw his child in the light of dawn,

shame such as he'd never known swept through him. She could not have been more his child than if his name were stamped across her forehead, yet he'd denied her both his acceptance and his compassion. The faint webbing between her fingers was still visible and perhaps a few narrow-minded people would call her names, but he vowed, in that moment, that she would never learn them from him. The discovery of his possessive paternity left him feeling curiously saddened, that odd emotion immediately followed by a rage so intense that he nearly swore aloud. She was his child, by God, and Katherine had taken her. In that moment, he managed to forget that he had once wanted her banished from his life.

His daughter used dawn as an alarm clock. She had been savage ever since. When she wasn't calling him "bad man!" at the top of her voice, she was calling for "Mama." How dare Katherine ingratiate herself with his daughter so strongly, ignoring that niggling bit of sanity that questioned his own irritation, and if not that, his logic.

When sunlight reached into the carriage windows, Freddie had a second shock. There, residing in the wet nurse's arms was a perfect duplicate of himself. Again, green eyes, black hair, an aristocratic sneer that looked absurdly out of place mounted on a cherubic face. His son gazed at him with the same penetrating assessment that the earl had used on numerous occasions to intimidate his opponents. It was as successful in reverse. He smiled with parental pride. How dare Katherine hide this child's existence from him! It was one more thing to hold against her.

And he knew that whatever surly temperament they possessed must have come from living with Katherine for so long.

If the earl had not seen the stamp of paternity on both faces, by noon he would have turned the carriage around posthaste, returned to the small cottage in Mertonwood Village, dropped his children in Katherine's lap, bowed abjectly to her, with apologies, and left as quickly as the tired horses would allow. But these were his children, especially the termagant who insisted upon punctuating every hour with another blow to his midsection. He let her hit him—it was easier to suffer a bruise than another bite. He would have had a sneaking admiration for his daughter if only she'd chosen someone else to punish; as it was, he didn't relish being beaten into submission by his own flesh and blood.

The children had so intimidated the wet nurse that she spent the remainder of the long day curled up in the corner of the coach, sniffing audibly. She cringed whenever Julie made her semi-hourly parade around the coach seats. Sniveling coward. One of the advantages of her cowardice was that she no longer held his son, and as long as Robbie rested in his arms, Julie wouldn't hit him. Or bite. As her throat grew too sore to continue to scream, she concentrated, instead, on murderous looks.

He had to remind himself often that Celeste was her biological mother; the baleful look his daughter shot him was identical to one of Katherine's.

Freddie had expected some resistance from his children. After all, he was a stranger. Yet, he had been prepared to gratify their every whim, to placate their childish desires until thoughts of Katherine were as insubstantial as smoke in the wind. What he had not expected nor anticipated was out-and-out rebellion. Nor had he envisioned a loyalty and a love so strong that it would convert an otherwise acceptable child into a monster. He was damned tired of hearing the word "Mama" screeched from his daughter's lips like a prayer to heaven itself.

He had been a model child. (Miriam Lattimore would have howled with laughter.) He never behaved badly around his father. In fact, he would not have dared to misbehave in the fourth earl's presence. His memory failed to supply the detail that he had rarely been in his father's presence until he was seven years old and ready to be shipped away to school. Nor did he remember that what times he shared with his father consisted of blocks of five minutes—no less and, certainly, no more.

He would have to alter his plans, he decided. The ailing wife of the manager of one of his factories had seemed delighted at the prospect of caring for the children for a few weeks, at least until he'd settled things with Katherine. Now that plan seemed overly optimistic. Both of them had been thinking of a two-year-old with an angelic smile, a sunny disposition, a child's wonder and enthusiasm for new experiences. Robert had been perceived as a sweet young baby with a matching personality. Neither of them had envisioned a two-year-old imp from hell and a small, stubborn version of himself.

Damn Katherine! She'd done this on purpose.

The farther north they traveled, the more he wished he were headed for London. It was painfully obvious to him that he knew nothing about children and even less about his own. The few times he'd visited the nursery when Julie was a baby had not prepared him for either her intransigent behavior or for an infant whose sole activity was to peer sternly at him from beneath a prematurely wrinkled brow. His pride battled with his reason, and thankfully, common sense won. He gave the signal to the driver for the coach to halt at the next inn.

He paid the wet nurse what he had promised her for two weeks' work, summoned the landlord from the inn and had him prepare a traveling dinner. He would die in a lonely pauper's grave before he would venture inside a public place with the howling witch that was his daughter. She did, however, have to make a trip to the necessary, and although he offered the wet nurse extra coin, she took one fearful look at his daughter and backed away, shaking her head. He sighed heavily in resignation, an emotion somewhat alien to him, and led the squirming child to the building behind the inn. He was infinitely grateful that the demands of nature managed to momentarily silence her.

He spoke to the driver, paced outside until their food was prepared, and finally entered the carriage with a noticeable lack of eagerness. Swinging himself inside, he sat opposite his daughter who, although she still glared at him, held a protective arm around the sleeping bundle that was his son. He hoped the respite meant she would refrain from biting him for a while.

He sighed again.

Two minutes later, the driver turned the coach around and headed for London, his mother, and blessed sanity.

Jack Rabelais had been in the earl's service since Waterloo. In that time, he had admired the other man's tenacity, his open and exploring mind that searched for new and better answers to old problems, the financial wizardry with which he had built an empire. Being French and frugal by nature, he had secretly been impressed by Moncrief's generosity; he respected the man, felt a brotherly affection for him, had occasionally laughed at his human weaknesses; but he had never believed that Freddie Lattimore was devoid of common sense or basic human intelligence. Until now.

Now, he was beyond speech.

He'd been told the story by a pacing countess, who traveled the length of the yellow sitting room, slowing her relentless path only to navigate around one of the numerous silk footstools.

"Madam," he said softly, answering her before she gave voice to the question, "I do not know his plans, nor do I know where the children are. I would, of course, tell you if I did."

"Would you?" she asked, skewering him with a look.

"Would your loyalty to Freddie not prevent your speaking freely?"

It was a fair question.

"It seems that you have two parts of a problem here," he answered diplomatically, his lips twisted into an expression that might be construed as a wry grin and then again, not.

Katherine spoke for the first time. She had been sitting quietly in the corner, incredibly weary, almost numb from the brandy the countess had insisted she drink. Not numb enough, however, to miss the warning barely veiled in Jack's voice.

"Other than the fact that the earl has stolen my children, what other problem is there?" she asked. "I do not think it possible for the man to be more despicable," she announced firmly, uncaring that she spoke in the presence of the earl's mother and his closest friend.

Jack smiled, a thin-lipped gesture less of humor than of weary resignation. He had barely returned from business in Scotland before being drawn into this contretemps, but he would not allow his fatigue to prompt him to words better left unsaid. His comments, therefore, were those of a man navigating a particularly treacherous bog—slow and careful.

"Do you never wonder why you and the earl seem to strike such sparks against each other? Why is it that you have the power to disturb him far beyond the boundaries of any other relationship?" He spoke to her as though the bonds of propriety had slipped between them. He, once a count, but no more than a servant now, spoke to a baron's daughter with familiarity. Yet she, a baron's daughter, had given birth, illegitimately, to an earl's son. The entire situation was no stranger, he thought with a genuine smile, than his own relationship with Moncrief.

"Stupidity, Jack? His, not mine."

"Could it be," he asked, ignoring her sarcasm, "that it is because you two are so much alike? Both strong-willed people, both attempting to direct the other, when you would be more successful at bending."

"Do you suggest I do the bending, Jack?" The corner of her mouth turned down.

"The earl will not relent, Katherine. I know the man well enough to say that." He turned to look at the countess, who silently nodded. She, too, knew her son. "If we were successful in returning the children today, what would prevent him from acting tomorrow? That seems to be the second part of your problem."

"Why will he not leave me alone?" It was a question addressed to the room at large, and neither Jack nor the countess answered her. The look they exchanged, however, spoke volumes. It was a look filled with disquiet, with a knowledge of one of the personalities involved and a suspicion about the nature of the other. It was a look filled with resolve and an innate wisdom shared by two disparate people. Problems normally did not get better on their own; they required a somewhat dispassionate viewpoint, which it was quite evident neither Freddie nor Katherine possessed. Therefore, it was deduced, in a long, wordless look that required neither translation nor explanation, that these two needed a little assistance.

"You are not in the mood to hear my answer, Katherine," he finally said cryptically. He smiled at her, a soft knowing smile that was unseen by the object of it. Katherine had leaned back against the pillowy softness of the loveseat and closed her eyes.

"I will not just sit by and let him have his way," she said wearily. Fear had carried her forward into the night, past long stretches of deeply shadowed wood, from Mertonwood Village to London, to a place she'd barely tolerated when she'd first visited. Monty's speed had protected her from being robbed this time; his stamina had enabled her to reach London in record time. She'd stopped and asked directions three times, confused and frustrated by the twisting roads and crowded thoroughfares; it was the strength of her own will and Monty's endurance, rather than any Londoner's sense of bearing, that had carried her to the earl's door.

"Perhaps the best way to trap an animal is to know your prey," Jack said enigmatically.

Katherine looked at him as if he'd lost his mind, any ability to sift through his words departing with the weariness that suffused her. The same strength of will that had brought her to London was depleted now. In the comfort of the sitting room, with a glass of brandy burning through her empty stomach, surrounded by two compassionate, empathetic people, anger finally had a chance to surface. An anger whose strength she'd only felt twice before—on that long-ago day when she'd left Mertonwood, and two days ago when she'd seen the Earl of Moncrief again.

Miriam studied her surreptitiously, the answer to their dilemma perhaps not so impossible after all. In fact, it had been in her mind for days now, ever since she'd learned of Robert's existence. Of course, it would not be possible if Katherine was anyone other than who she was, a young woman of great appeal and even greater strength. Since the moment she'd first seen her, Katherine Sanderson had impressed her with her championing of the poor, of her subsequent love for a motherless child. She was intelligent, charming, beautiful enough to keep Freddie interested. More to the point, she had a strength of will to match her son's and—if she were not mistaken by the look on her face—an anger deep enough to combat Freddie's most intransigent moods.

It would be a match made, if not in heaven, at least in the bedroom. If Freddie hadn't wanted himself caught, he should not have baited his own trap.

Miriam hadn't realized that she'd spoken aloud until she saw the twinkle in Jack's eyes and the confused look on Katherine's face.

"Exactly," Jack said, his smile betraying only genuine humor and a relaxed ease that had not been present before. He stood and took his leave saying that he would seek out what information might be available concerning the earl's plans. He didn't fool her for a moment, Miriam thought. He did not want to stay and see the explosion that was sure to come once she'd mentioned the solution to Katherine. But what her son's fascinating French friend did not know was that Miriam Lattimore had not survived in this household by being foolish, nor by spiking her guns. There was a time to bait the bear and a time to furnish it with honey.

Right now, she thought, jerking on the bellpull and ordering tea, it was time to pull out the honey jar.

"What does he expect me to do?" Katherine asked after Jack had left.

"Perhaps make peace with Freddie," Miriam said calmly, not missing the look of derision on Katherine's face.

"I'd sooner pet a snake," Katherine snarled. "How can I make peace with him, Miriam, after what's he done?"

"There are many kinds of victories, Katherine," she said, sitting finally. She reached out a hand and captured one of Katherine's colder ones. Sandwiching it between her own, warmer, palms, she chafed it gently to warm it. "There is the overt victory, in which the army returns with flags waving and trumpets sounding. Then there is the quieter victory, of the spy with valued information. What does it matter how one wins, as long as the victory remains the same?" A small smile played around her mouth as she noted Katherine's stubborn look. They were too much alike, this young woman with her open heart and her son with a heart closed for too many years. A short time ago, she had longed for her bed, but at this moment, she felt alive and exhilarated as she hadn't for years.

"I will not simply retreat, Miriam," Katherine said.

"No one has asked you to, dear," she replied. "I know

my son, Katherine, and I know his propensity for stubbornness. He will not give up any more than I expect you to."

"No," Katherine said, in weary recognition of the truth, "he won't, will he?" And what did that mean to her? Would she spend the rest of her life attempting to escape the Earl of Moncrief? Would she have to emigrate, in order to finally best him? Part of her recognized the idea as a possible solution, another part recoiled at it. She loved her country; she didn't want to turn her back on everything she had once loved, didn't want to finally admit that she would never again see Donegan Castle, never raise her children as English subjects.

One more thing to lay at the Earl of Moncrief's feet.

"He won't give up, but neither will we," Miriam said, hugging her impulsively. "We have not begun to use the weapons available to us," she said with a broad smile.

"What weapons?" Katherine eyed the countess with a wary look.

"Why, Katherine, I'm surprised that you should ask. You brought my son to heel once. You can do it again."

"I have no intention whatsoever of bringing your son to heel, Miriam," Katherine said, emotion carrying an edge to her voice.

It was a wisp of memory that had chosen that moment to unleash itself, like an errant puffball blowing in the wind. A night of thunder and rain, a bristling fire, and the warmth of a naked male body.

She cleared her throat and glared at the woman who smiled at her with such inappropriate glee.

"Why not?" Miriam asked.

"Because I dislike him intensely!" And was that not a study in prevarication, that remark? Couched in truth, covered with layers of illusion.

She did not truly trust the Earl of Moncrief; there were too many sins to be laid at his doorstep. He had hurt her feelings, and her pride, and now he had stooped to performing the most despicable act.

But dislike him?

It was too mild a word for the cornucopia of emotions she felt about the earl. Too sweet a word for the monstrous rage that made her want to search for the nearest pistol and plant a bullet square within his heart.

It did not escape her attention that Miriam Lattimore was studying her with interest. Nor did she neglect to note that her feelings about the earl were just a little too emotional to be entirely lucid. But to accede to the countess's wishes and attempt to win Freddie over seemed a bit much to ask of her now.

"Perhaps," Miriam said, fascinated at the play of emotions on the younger woman's face, "but you are attracted to him. The fact that he is Robert's father is another point in his favor."

"Exactly what are you hinting at, Miriam? That I seduce your son in order to have him behave more civilly toward me? That plan seems a little cold-blooded."

Miriam looked at Katherine with fond tenderness. She chuckled, a throaty sound not unlike her son's. "Katherine, my dear, cold blooded is not a term I would ascribe to Freddie. Insensitive, perhaps. Irrational when it comes to dealing with you, certainly. Possibly even incomprehensible. But never cold-blooded."

"I could not see myself willingly enter into that kind of arrangement again."

"You did so once."

"Yes, but I do learn from my mistakes." The glance she slanted at the countess was filled with wry, unwilling, humor. "Besides, I had that stupid contract."

It was not the moment for Miriam to propose her intriguing idea. "We'll talk about it some other time," she said, patting the hand nearest her. "Right now, it is very late, and you've had a terrible day. We will find the children, but in the meantime, you should rest."

Katherine didn't tell the older woman that she didn't think she could rest as long as the children were missing. It would not be simple worry that prompted her sleeplessness, but a combination of fear and guilt. She had known, from the moment she'd left Freddie standing on the path, that he posed a threat. She should have taken steps to protect the children. As long as he was nearby, she should have done something. She had slept, instead. The gravity of the day and the confrontation with the earl had exhausted her. And while she'd slept, her children had been taken.

Only the information obtained by Michael had prevented her from a full-scale panic, and that was the news that a wet nurse had been hired near Baxton. The informant had only been able to supply a description of the coach, a long black-lacquered well-sprung carriage with no emblem or coat of arms. It so fit the description of the coach still kept at Mertonwood that Michael had verified its absence before returning to the cottage. Which meant only one thing, damnable proof that it was. That her children had been taken, not by a stranger, but by their father.

Not a thought to promise sleep.

Chapter 16

The problem, thought the earl, was that he wanted his children.

The five-hour journey in the dark had been relatively peaceful, with Julie snuggling up in the seat across from him in blessed slumber. Occasionally, she would twitch and turn, and he would cover her with the lap robe that had once again found its way to the floor.

He sat with Robert across his lap, the baby curled against him gently in sleep, his chin jutting firmly into his chest, as if he wished for a softer and more bosomy physique against which to lie. The earl shifted in small, smooth movements so as not to jar his son, and he was eventually able to prop his feet against the opposite seat, inches from where his daughter's shoes peeped out from under the blanket.

The moonlight entered the carriage windows, filtered by the trees bordering the rutted road, casting long shadows on the forms of his sleeping children. Robert was a monochrome study, his pale cheeks glaring whitely, his eyes and rosebud mouth dark with shadows. The earl was fascinated by the faces of his children—Julie's sweet and demure in sleep, with the promise of great beauty, Robert's sober even in rest. He picked up his son's hand, fascinated at the shape of it, the diminutive size. It was inconceivable to him that one day it might dwarf his own.

He was responsible now, in a way he had not been with Julie, for teaching his son what it meant to be a man. It was to him that Robert would look, as he had looked to his own father, for guidance, for advice, for a model upon which to pattern himself. He would not fail his child as his father had failed him.

It was incumbent upon him now to mold both of these thoroughly absorbing minute individuals into people who bore the weight of their responsibilities proudly, who grew to adulthood armed with security and values and, most of all, a feeling of being loved.

It was a daunting task he'd assumed, and the most odious part of it all was that he had done nothing but enjoy himself to have been granted it. He'd not known of their existences until they'd been born, had not been present at either of their births. He'd not worried about them, and until now, he had given their ultimate destiny little thought. He remembered, with not a little guilt, that he'd pushed Julie out of his life twice. And his motivation for plucking them from the woman they both called mother? Less paternal pride than a feeling of retribution.

Stark, unrelenting honesty was a poor traveling companion.

Why hadn't she told him? He would have given her a king's ransom for his son. When he remembered the sparse furnishings of the tiny cottage, his mind recoiled. It had not even been her home. What did she want that he could not provide? He would have given her a lifetime of riches, of comfort, of security. He wanted these children, and if he had to, he would fight for them. Yet, as an adversary, he was truly powerless. He told himself, with a rush of optimism, that it was not too late to win a battle or two, even if the war had already been lost. And yet, what would he have traded for these few precious hours? Would he have bargained anything for the delight of being humbled by a child who could strike terror in the heart of any man? Or the simple, quiet joy of holding his son's hand in the darkness? The answer struck him as solidly as a blow to his chest, and with it came the realization that he would never have traded anything for the ability to be with them.

It brought him too close to understanding Katherine.

A strange, unexpected feeling of shame traveled with the Earl of Moncrief that night, in a coach cloaked in darkness followed only by a hunter's moon as it traveled south to London.

Katherine had been unable to sleep all night, despite the weariness, the volume of brandy the countess had fed to her, and the stern admonition of the older woman to rest. Instead, she paced her room, across the expanse of carpet until it felt as though she were wearing a path in the deep pile. All she could think of were the children. Where were they? How were they?

What was she going to do?

Miriam's suggestion rolled around in her mind like a stone in a pail. Entice Freddie, charm him, seduce him. She shuddered, not in revulsion, but in very real fear. What Miriam did not know, and what she would never divulge to her, was that if the idea had merit, it also carried its own potential danger. She would not have to seduce Freddie. All she would have to do is fold down that barrier she maintained between them with studied anger and pointed indifference and allow the attraction between them to ignite once again. It had been there from the beginning. From the first moment she'd seen him and he'd put his finger upon the skin of her breast, she'd felt the flames of something blaze between them. A fire that consumed all things learned or intuited. Morals and mores, etiquette and decorum burned to ash beneath it. All that was left was some emotion more primeval than she had ever experienced or known was possible. A feeling far more sinister than danger and infinitely more powerful than seduction.

It would burn her alive.

Part of her frantic departure from Mertonwood had been because of her love for Julie and her desire to protect the child. Yet, she had spent too many winter nights coming to terms with the truth to deny it now: An equal part of the reason she had left was because of fear for herself.

What would loving him do to her?

She had been tempted, once, to tell him he could set her up as his whore or call her his slattern. It did not matter if he dressed her up in finery or keep her chained to a bed with only a chemise to cover her nakedness. As long as he loved her, let her be beside him, allowed her to share a little of his life, she would do whatever he asked of her.

Begging him would not have been too much.

And because his touch was becoming more than simply delicious, and his smile was almost a necessary component to brighten her day, she left. Before she told him that she derived the greatest comfort, not in jewels or in wealth, but in smoothing his hair back from his brow, or commiserating with him as he grumbled about the courier's delay or Mrs. Roberts's eternal carping. That a smile would wreathe her face as she sat and read and listened to the drum of his fingers upon the desktop, and that the sound of him whistling outside made her rush to the window to see what he was doing.

Foolish woman.

Foolish man.

He could not see beneath the anger, however; it was too

impenetrable. And she intended to keep it that way, in order to protect the heart beneath, the fragile emotions too vibrant and too real. If he'd thought, he would have realized that if she truly did not care about him, her response would have been apathy, not rage.

But thought was the last thing to surface between them, wasn't it?

A point that led her back to her original question. How could he have taken her children? What was he thinking of?

He wouldn't know that Robbie shouldn't eat grains of any sort, or else he would break out in those horrible hives, or that he had already been weaned from breast milk. Nor would he know that Julie needed activity, lots of it, before she could sleep the night, as if her body demanded an outlet for her vast energy.

The moonlight streaming through the windows mounted on both sides above the front door was the only illumination in the foyer, but it was enough. Katherine moved unerringly down the hallway across the landing, down the flight of stairs, into the sitting room, across to the area in front of the stairs. Like a caged animal, she walked back and forth, unwilling or unable to remain still. Peterson emerged from his room only once, candle in hand, alerted by the soft footfalls against the marble floor. When he saw her in the warm robe the countess had insisted she wear, he retreated quietly.

Would the night never end? How could the world be so silent, so still, so deceptively peaceful, when her children were missing? Make peace with Freddie? Hah! She would like to garrote the man. Or drop him from a cliff and watch him turn end over end before crashing to his death on sharp boulders. Death, at this moment, was too good for Froedrich Allen Lattimore. Make peace with Freddie? Hah!

"You won't do the children any good, Katherine, if you

are a wreck by the time we find them." The soft voice startled her and she turned, gripping the robe as if it would protect her.

"Yes, I know," she agreed, watching as Miriam descended the rest of the steps, one hand aloft, bearing a small bronze taper holder, the other wisely holding her long wrapper away from the stair treads. "I am so worried that to sleep seems almost obscene."

"Nonsense. I know my son, Katherine, and although he's been incredibly stupid, almost embarrassingly so in this instance, he would never do anything to harm the children. Freddie is a model of compassion, dear child; be reassured that he would never willingly hurt anyone."

"We are talking about the same person, aren't we?" Katherine asked without a touch of humor. "It is the earl we are discussing, isn't it?"

"My dear, I see we must have a long talk, as soon as you have had some rest. There are things you must know, you see, before you judge Freddie too unfairly. But for now, you must sleep."

"You sound as obstinate as Freddie," Katherine said.

"He is his mother's child, too, Katherine."

Miriam left finally, unable to coax Katherine to her room. She, too, could be as obdurate as any of the Lattimores. Miriam had, however, insisted upon lighting a few candles in the sitting room. Since Katherine was prepared to lose a small battle, she allowed her to do that, and also to place a small shawl over her shoulders so she wouldn't become chilled. She didn't tell the mother of her nemesis that she warmed herself with her anger. Katherine resumed her pacing, marching into the foyer, counting the marble tiles once more, then retreating back into the sitting room.

It was hours later that she heard the unmistakable clatter of hooves against the pavement.

It was only when she heard that voice, the same voice that had haunted her thoughts for far too long, that she raced to the door and yanked it open. The square was quiet, sounds that were inaudible in the daylight echoed loudly in the night—the scratch of match against palm, the hushed whisper of words, the scrape of boots as they descended from the coach.

Katherine ran down the steps as if escaping the devil himself, catapulting herself into the earl's arms. Except it wasn't the earl she longed to embrace, but the sleeping figure of her baby son.

"Oh, Robbie, Robbie," she crooned, as tears dropped from her face onto the baby's cheeks. She scooped him from Freddie's arms and held him pressed against her chest. The baby only snuffled a little, then, feeling the warm, reassuring presence of his mother around him, fell back asleep.

At Katherine's questioning look, the earl only inclined his head, indicating the coach. She peered into the shadowy interior, saw the bemused, sleepy gaze of her daughter and put an arm out for the child. Julie descended the steps, reached her mother, and grabbed one leg firmly, staring up at the earl with a triumphant glare.

Thus it was that the countess, roused from her bed for the second time that night, saw the unmistakable signs of war before anyone recognized that peace was no longer possible.

Katherine stood clutching her children, with the most unholy look of rage on her face. The look was mirrored by Freddie, who stood motionless, except for one hand outstretched over Robert's tiny figure. Julie stood between them, glaring at her father, hugging the one woman she'd known as mother all her life but who had no legal right to the title.

It was, thought Miriam, a tableau created by a God with a supreme sense of humor.

Or one who thoroughly enjoyed testing her.

She quickly stepped between her son and Katherine.

Miriam wondered what Freddie would say if he knew her sympathies were on Katherine's side. If she were in the younger woman's position, she might be tempted to take a butcher's knife to him. She managed, however, to separate them before blood was drawn, and turned to her son.

"Freddie, really. How could you?"

He bristled, an understandable reaction, he told himself, since his mother's tone was one he hadn't heard since he'd been in short pants. "Madam," he said curtly, "I will talk to you later. Why is she here?" he demanded, extending one bandaged finger toward Katherine, who stood clutching her children to her like an outraged madonna.

"Julie," Katherine asked, fascinated by the sight of the earl reduced to quivering fury, and equally caught by the shredded neckcloth used to wrap several fingers, "did you bite him?" Only once before had her daughter used that tactic of defense—against one of the village boys who'd followed his mother to the cottage for wash day.

Julie ducked her head sleepily, hiding behind Katherine's skirts. At the lisped acknowledgment of the deed, Katherine began to smile. "Good!" she said, and swept up the steps with Julie in tow, the little girl darting a superior look at her father, who was restrained from following them only by the fact that his mother had gripped his arm and was holding on like a bulldog.

Miriam thought it might have been easier to negotiate between Wellington and Napoleon than between these two. She sighed heavily, relaxed her grip somewhat, and preceded her tired son up the steps of the townhouse. At the landing he passed her.

"Freddie, leave her alone," she called after him as he continued up the stairs.

"I will leave the witch to herself, Mother," he said tightly. "I merely wish to see that my children are adequately cared for."

He guessed they must be installed in the larger guest suite, and he was rewarded when he swung open the door and found his ex-mistress and his children standing sleepily in the middle of the room. Julie was trying, without much success, to extricate herself from the folds of her long smock. Katherine glared at him as he covered the expanse of plush carpet and bent down to help his daughter. Julie pulled away, but he merely grabbed the hem of her smock and in one motion pulled it over her head. He undid the tight buttons on her little shoes and hefted her up into the canopy bed with a giant swing. She giggled, then remedied that lapse by glaring at her father once again.

Katherine placed Robbie on the loveseat in front of the fire, propping him firmly between the cushions so that he could not roll over.

"Don't you think they'd be more comfortable in the nursery?" he said, speaking the first words since he'd entered the room.

"First of all, the nursery hasn't been aired in years, and secondly, no one is going to separate me from my children. It may be acceptable in your world to ignore your offspring, but I won't do it." Her scowl was identical to the one Julie had given him only moments before.

He glanced over at his daughter, who had allowed sleep to claim her effortlessly. "She's quite a handful, that one," he said with a fond smile.

"Is she?" Katherine said, her voice just as chilled as before. She would not allow herself to be charmed by the winsomeness of the earl's expression or by the sudden tenderness apparent in his eyes when he looked at his children. "She is much like you, I suspect."

"And here I thought she got her temper from you." One side of his mouth curled upwards.

"I am, as you pointed out to me recently, not her mother. Yet, she could easily inherit your faults, my lord. You are not known for your easy temperament."

"Strange, everyone else thinks I'm the soul of amiability," he said, returning to the doorway.

"Then they do not know you as I do," Katherine responded, suddenly exhausted. She did not want to parry words with the earl anymore, she only wanted to rest for a few short hours before the children would awaken.

"Few people do, Katherine," he said shortly, before leaving the room.

She lay down on the bed beside Julie, slipped one arm around the warm, cuddly figure of her daughter, glanced over at Robbie, and knew that her rest would be short. Robert had probably starved in the day he had been away from her and could be counted upon to be up in a matter of hours. He was as Julie had been, waking with the dawn. She sighed, and allowed sleep to claim her like flowing water, washing away the tension, the worry, the anger, and the earl's parting words.

She did not know that, only moments later, a tall figure stood staring down at her and his daughter, or that he gently rearranged the blanket covering his son. Nor did she know that a look of pain entered his eyes, pain that was quickly masked but for all its brevity, was very, very real.

"How did she get here?" he demanded of his night-attired mother, who remained at the foot of the stairs waiting for him.

"She surmised—correctly I might add—that you might bring the children to me. About how she managed that feat, I believe Monty has finally been returned to your possession." The countess's voice was laced with anger. Despite what she had said to Katherine about Freddie's capacity for compassion, his actions of the day before had been unconscionable. No, most of his actions regarding to Katherine had been unbelievable.

"She rode Monty? To London?"

She lost what patience she possessed; the look of incredulity on her son's face banished the remnants of it. Civility was forgotten as she nearly pushed him into the sitting room and closed the sliding doors behind him.

"Sit!" she said in a voice that brooked no argument. "We will talk, you and I. Now."

Although it had been years since he'd heard that tone of voice from his mother, it brought back instant memories of riding one of his father's prized hunters at dawn, when he was ten and convinced of his horsemanship, or swimming naked in the creek with the gardener's equally naked daughter, or stealing one of his father's guns in order to go rabbit hunting when he was five. Perhaps his daughter did come by her temperament naturally, he thought with a smile.

All that Miriam saw was the smile, and it only made her angrier.

"Sit down!" She pointed to a footstool and her son obediently sat.

"I suppose you want to know all about Katherine," he began when his mother interrupted.

"I know all about Katherine," she said in a gritty voice. "You're the one who needs to learn some truths."

"What did she tell you?" His eyes narrowed as he stared at his mother. God, he was tired. He wished she would at least let him get some sleep before this harangue, but perhaps it was better to get it out in the open. This way, she wouldn't fume all night and come up with even more sins for him to justify. What he didn't know was that Miriam *had* fumed all night, and the list of his faults had grown with each hour.

"It was not what she told me, Freddie, it was what she did not say."

"Oh?"

"I have seen your infamous contract."

She let that sink in before she went on. "I know of women's rights or lack thereof, Freddie. So do you. Yet,

Katherine was too young or too ignorant to know what was going on. What you did was grossly unfair. It is one thing to set someone up as a mistress, quite another to take a gently reared young woman and act as though she were a member of the demimonde." Evidently Duncan had not spared any details of Katherine's past from his mother, the earl thought with dark humor. A baron's daughter. It was Celeste all over again.

He threaded his fingers through dust-ridden hair. "You like her, don't you?" He looked, thought his mother, as he had as a young boy, unable to come up with a good enough answer to mitigate her anger.

"Very much, Freddie. You must have liked her, too, once." Her smile was too knowing, he thought. *Like* was too simple a word to describe Katherine. Fascination, perhaps. Allure? It was impossible to put into one single word what he felt for her. She enraged him and entranced him, drew him like a siren's song. He liked to hear her speak, that sultry contralto of her voice altering words in an odd and fascinating way. He had been captivated by the easy, natural way she held his son, by the gentle nurturing of her sleeping hug around Julie. Yet, he had never been infuriated so fully by anyone in his life. She dismissed him with a regal and queenly air as if he were a supplicant somehow lacking.

Miriam smiled at her incredibly stupid son and wondered when it would dawn on him. Freddie was a genius when it came to new inventions, money, and technology, but he was acting like a dolt where Katherine was concerned.

If anyone could teach him about love, it would be Katherine.

If they could stop fighting long enough to realize it.

Chapter 17

The first person Katherine saw in the morning was not the bright and eager Julie, ready to face the day. It was the Earl, bending tenderly over his son.

Robbie waved energetic arms toward his father, grasped his nose within an intrusive fist, and attempted to pull it from his face. The earl laughed softly as Robbie smiled in triumph. He sat, dropped the bundle of nappies next to his son, and gently removed Robbie's sodden garments. Katherine stirred, propped herself up on one arm and watched them. This should be interesting. The great earl changing his son.

Was it something between males, she wondered, as the earl deftly untied the diaper and exposed his son to the cool morning air. Robbie did not, as he would were she changing him, point his little manhood straight up in the air in glorious male supremacy and attempt to douse his father.

The earl inspected his son as he lay quietly on the sofa, seemingly awed by the sight of the tiny body that would grow in strength and stature to match his own. Nor had she ever seen Robbie so fascinated with anything as he seemed to be by his father's face.

The earl had a strange look on his face when he scooped his son from the cushion and balanced him in his arms. It was, she thought, blinking rapidly, a combination of consternation, resolve, and tenderness. As if this puzzle that was a baby had just been revealed to be of infinite importance to him. Something to be cared for, cherished, and yet to be treated with caution and great respect.

He had problems toward the end tying the nappie into place, but after two attempts managed to secure it well enough so that it no longer fell off right away. With clumsy hands, he turned Robbie over, patted him gently on the bottom, while he dropped the soiled diaper into the chamber pot, his nose wrinkling at the smell.

When Robbie began squirming impatiently in his father's arms, she emerged from the bed and donned the borrowed wrapper.

"He's hungry," she said, reaching for her son.

"Can you make him eat?" the earl asked with a worried frown.

"Can I make him eat? It's more like can I make him stop. Robbie's never had a problem with appetite, have you, darling?" She nuzzled her son, delighting in the soft, baby smell of him.

"That's another thing, Katherine," Freddie said with resolve, following her. "Robbie's not an adequate name. Robert is more dignified, I suppose, but not Robbie." He shot a cautious look at his sleeping daughter and left the room.

"It is a sight better than Freddie, my lord," she said, prior to descending the stairs, "a fact I considered when naming my child."

"*My* child, Katherine."

"No, my lord." She stopped at the landing and turned

to him. "My son. You were never a part of it, except at the beginning. Did you decide he was your responsibility simply because he was a boy? What if he were less than perfect? Would you have ignored him as you did Julie? No, my lord," she hissed, "Robbie is *my* son."

She marched down the rest of the stairs.

"I am willing to admit that I may have been mistaken in regard to Julie, Katherine."

"How utterly gracious of you," she said as she entered the dining room and then beyond, to the kitchen. She moved with unerring instinct through the part of the house she had seen only shrouded in darkness. "Shall I petition for your sainthood, Freddie? Have you taken a look at Julie? She is as much your child as this little boy. Yet I don't hear you claiming her with such vigor. You may be their sire, but you haven't yet proven yourself their father. There is a world of difference in the meaning of the two words."

"You would not allow me the opportunity to be his father," he answered, ignoring the curious looks of the kitchen staff, most of whom had never seen the earl in their domain before, let alone arguing half-dressed with a woman who was also still night-attired, "And it is difficult to establish a relationship with Julie after you had hidden her away."

"Only after you had made plans of your own," she said, whirling and accusing him with the anger in her eyes. Any hope that his arrangements of a year ago would have escaped her knowledge died in that instant. "What were you planning on doing, Freddie? Fostering her out somewhere where she wouldn't bother you or embarrass you? I would not allow you?" she continued, not giving him a chance to answer. "Who was it who stole my children from their beds? Don't talk to me of rights, Freddie."

"What other choice did I have, Katherine, when you made it perfectly clear you would not tolerate my presence in their lives?'' He tried to keep his voice relatively calm, despite the irritation that grew with every moment. He met her glare with one of his own.

Twin spots of color appeared on her warm and already-flushed cheek, irritating him further. Memories of a year ago cascaded into his mind with the force of a river too long dammed, further infuriating him.

''Did it ever occur to you, my great and powerful lord of the realm, that you might have been wrong?''

''Goddamn it, of course I was wrong!'' The words, shouted at the top of his voice, shocked her. They froze the rest of the interested bystanders, halted in the action of preparing breakfast by this fascinating scene. ''Don't you think I know that?'' It had kept him awake all night, this guilt. An unwelcome feeling, but one too long denied. He had been wrong about Julie, wrong about taking the children. Too damned wrong about too damned many things.

''You force circumstances to fit your will, Freddie, never admitting that there may be times when you may not win.'' Her voice was gently chiding, her eyes would not meet his. In truth, he had diffused her anger with his own. And with that startling admission, so unlike him. ''Do you always get what you want, my lord? All the time?''

''Most of the time,'' he admitted, deliberate in his perusal of her. She nuzzled the top of his son's downy head with her lips, rocking from side to side in an age-old movement of calm, even though Robbie was far from being upset. Indeed, he looked from one parent to another as if the verbal contest was great fun.

What was it about her that made him alternately want to turn her skirts up and beat her soundly and even more strongly want to pull her into his arms and comfort her? By God, he had missed her.

Why did her eyes stray to his exposed chest, the curling black pelt against tanned skin, his rumpled hair and sleep-deprived eyes. What was it that made her want to scar him for life one moment and elicit passion from him in the next breath? Dear God, she had missed him.

It was a strange and unwelcome thought.

The countess had been summoned once again by the ever present Peterson. She stood wearily against the door frame and eyed the combatants. Without a doubt, she would be old and gray before this was ever settled. Perhaps it was just as well she was already a grandmother twice over. Now she had a reason to keep to her bed for the rest of her life. Her grandchildren could visit her weekly, crawl up into bed, and read to her, and she would wheeze at them with fondness. At this rate, she could expect to retire to her bed in a month or less.

"Children," she said in a voice not only weary but fast running out of patience, "can we not let Cook get on with breakfast?"

Both of them had been oblivious to their surroundings, and they each glanced around the room peopled with curious inhabitants and then at each other. An embarrassed grimace crossed both faces.

Katherine left Cook with instructions for Robbie's breakfast, then brushed past the earl. It was as if she were so sensitized to his presence that a pocket of air opened up around him, warm and darkly scented. Damn him, she thought, he's doing it again. Effortlessly, with the crook of an eyebrow, he'd somehow managed to make her pulse beat harder.

She knows what she's doing, he thought as she left the room. She knows and she revels in it, he thought with a feeling that was half delight, half pain. He watched her, wondering if she knew that no other woman of his acquaintance could look so seductive walking up a flight of stairs. She stopped and frowned at him from the landing, and he smiled, thinking that no other woman could look quite as wanton while holding a baby, either.

The countess sighed heavily, this time not so much in exhaustion as in exasperation, and ignored them both.

Miriam studied the note in her hand with a small, victorious smile.

It was time.

She rang for Peterson, asking him to summon both her son and Katherine to the sitting room. She seated herself amidst a rustle of taffeta skirts, composed her thoughts, and otherwise prepared herself for a tumultuous battle.

Katherine and Freddie met each other at the doorway, the earl entering from the dining room where he had finished a solitary and late lunch. Katherine emerged from upstairs, where Robbie had been put down for a nap and Julie was playing quietly with a collection of tin soldiers that had probably been her father's. Both children were being looked after by the young maid who had summoned her.

Seven hours had elapsed since the morning's confrontation. Seven hours in which both antagonists had counseled themselves to refrain from exposing their innermost thoughts and even more intimate emotions.

Katherine swept passed him and seated herself to the right of Miriam on the sofa. The earl stood by the fireplace, his customary pose, until his mother waved him into a nearby chair with an aggravated look. She would not have him towering over them. This meeting would be hard enough without the participants vying for positions of power from the onset.

"We have a situation here," she began, addressing them both, "with all the makings of a Greek drama. Quite simply, you two are on the brink of outright war, and unless something happens to stop both of you, only the children will truly suffer. Freddie, you will stop at nothing to keep your children about you. Is that true enough?" Her son nodded, not trusting himself to speak. "And you, Katherine, you would do the same, would you not?" Katherine nodded, a grim look tightening her lips.

"These children, illegitimate or not, are my grandchildren." Miriam placed a comforting hand on Katherine's rigid arm. "I am sorry to state these things so baldly, my child, but we must have no fabrications among us."

"I understand," Katherine said in a low tone, not noticing the look that crossed the earl's face and just as suddenly was masked.

"Therefore," Miriam continued, "their welfare is also my concern. You, Freddie, are quite capable of destroying Katherine's reputation in order to retrieve your children, while Katherine is quite willing to destroy this family in order to keep them. We have, my dears, an impasse. By the way," she said in an audible aside to Katherine, "that stupid contract is in my possession now, so it would do no good to threaten him with it." At Freddie's look of triumph, she admonished him severely. "So is your copy, my son. Your solicitor would do anything rather than have his wife find out about his not-so-legal affairs." She smiled at the looks on their faces—identical consternation.

"It does seem that I have your attention now, doesn't it? Which is just as well. You two have forgotten what it would mean to your children if you do not settle this. Freddie, you especially should remember what scandal feels like. Monique should have left that legacy, if nothing else."

"Leave Monique out of this, Mother," he said tightly.

Miriam ignored him. "Monique was Freddie's wife," she explained, turning to Katherine and pretending the look on her son's face was not one of towering rage. "She was a young, foolish woman who fell madly in love with a married man. She left Freddie for this man, without regard to society, the man's family, or Freddie." She patted Katherine's hand, looking down at the contrast between the two. "He was my husband," she said in a voice that echoed none of the pain of betrayal or hurt. "Freddie's father found himself madly in love for the first time in his life. Enough to leave me, his obligations, and everything else behind. It was a dark time for both Freddie and myself, even though society unfortunately seemed to blame Freddie most of all. As if he could control Monique. Or his father." The last was said with gentle humor and no rancor at all.

The countess seemed to read the question on Katherine's face. "It has been too many years, my dear, and many, many hours spent in soul-searching. I have not always been this calm about it. I spent too long blaming the world, society, anything but my family. They were the only ones exempt from my rage." The look she gave her son was fond, ignoring his frown. "Freddie was hurt more than anyone. I had known from the beginning what kind of man my husband was, so I was not overly surprised by his actions. Unfortunately, Freddie was still very young and believed himself very much in love. Consequently, he was devastated by her defection."

"Hardly devastated, Mother," he said dryly.

She smiled at the stubborn man he'd become. Despite all his faults, she loved him with a mother's ability to overlook less palatable aspects of his nature. To overlook, not to ignore.

The earl stood abruptly and strode to the fireplace, where he stood, leaning indolently against the mantel, feet spread as if braced against a strong wind. His hands were clamped on his hips—the style of the day eschewed such trivialities as pockets in the form hugging trousers—and attempted to reason with his mother by the simple expedient of signaling her with his stern looks and arching eyebrows. She ignored him.

Not so Katherine. Another time she might have felt a tremor of amusement at the silent battle being waged between mother and son, but now she only felt an unwilling empathy for the earl. How he must have suffered for his wife's betrayal, and his father's. It did not, however, make his actions toward her or his children any more understandable.

"Is there a reason you have chosen to illuminate Katherine on the more sordid chapters in our lives?" he asked sardonically, conceding victory in this skirmish to his mother.

"Only to refresh your memory as to what your children would feel, Freddie, should you act upon the course you are considering. For myself, I no longer care. Melissa is betrothed and no scandal will part her would-be husband from her inheritance. Jeremy is happily married, and I, frankly, don't give a farthing any more. The scandal you threaten with such impunity will only harm your children, innocent victims as you and I were. Can you imagine what it would be like for Robert to grow up hearing his mother called a whore? Or his father classified a bounder? What will it be like for Julie? You may be able to buy a husband for her, Freddie, but you'll never buy respectability or peace of mind. The wounds such scandal causes are deep; the whispers never cease, someone always remembers." She glanced at them both; neither had the courage to meet her look.

"Would either one of you actually do that to the children you profess to love?"

Katherine studied her hands as if surprised to find them at the end of her wrists. Freddie looked at Katherine, remembering twelve years ago when his innocence had truly ended and his cynicism had begun.

"Then, here it is," Miriam said, taking their silence as a good sign. "One of you needs to take the children, and the other must agree never to interfere again. No, Freddie," she said, at the sudden bright look that emerged in her son's eyes. "I will not play Solomon. They are brother and sister and will not be separated. They will be reared together. Think carefully about this, my dears," she urged them. "Freddie has the money, the power, and the title," she said, enumerating the points upon beringed fingers. "Robert would be the heir to a great estate. Julie would be an heiress."

She glanced at Katherine's stricken look and continued. "Yet, Katherine has a mother's love; a love that did not fail Julie when everyone else did, Freddie. You, myself, the entire family. Nor has she asked anything of us since Robbie was born." The earl shifted restlessly. "That should count for a great deal."

Silence.

"There is an alternative, however distressing, which you must also consider."

Both of them were beginning to wear bemused looks.

"Have you considered that you might actually be able to legitimize your children, Freddie? Legally?"

Now she had their attention.

"Not only that, but by the considering this option, you would be giving Julie and Robert the benefit of both parents' love, not to mention the wealth and power that could be wielded on their behalf."

She gave them her brightest smile while delivering the most egregious blow.

"However, to do this, you would have to marry."

"Certainly not!"

"Good Lord, no!"

Miriam smiled.

Chapter 18

"Who are you, Katherine," he asked as Miriam left the room with a sweep of her skirts and a soft, curving smile, "that my mother would defend you, that my children rage to be at your side? What type of woman are you really?" He stood idly by the fireplace, a deceptive stance if one only noted the indolent pose and ignored the hint of danger in his sea-green eyes. The flick of a muscle beneath a tan, lean cheek warned her as well.

"A simple one, my lord," she answered, standing and brushing down her skirts. Melissa's dress was much too short on her, but she had no garments other than the mourning dress she'd worn on her breakneck journey to London. It did not matter; she could have been dressed as impeccably as any duke's daughter and she would still feel frumpy next to him. Wasn't it strange that her fondest recollections were moments in which he was not so coolly perfect? Those times of winter truce, like the afternoon they had played like children on the snow-covered grounds of Mertonwood, the snowballs flying as fast as the threats for vindication, laughter highlighting the day as glittering as the sun glinted upon snow. Or the time he had hauled firewood into her room, so as not to disturb the maid in the dawn hours, a field mouse startling them both with its inquisitive nose peeking out from among the stack, then running like a dervish down his shirtsleeve. He had laughed then, like a boy, his hair falling over his forehead in that errant look, his amusement deepening when she had scrambled to the center of the bed and pointed an imperious finger at his chest, insisting that he find the mouse before returning to her.

Memories that ached, strangely.

"Not so simple," he said, wondering at the look in her eyes. "Were you simple, I would not be here now, contemplating a marriage I want no part of to gain control of a child I knew nothing of." He smiled wryly. "No, not so simple."

"I said simple, Freddie, not simpleminded. Pray, do not go on about your sudden paternal interest in my children. We have crossed that Rubicon before. I am not as certain about your love for my children as I am of your ire toward me."

"There is that," he admitted with a smile. "Yet, I see no other course open for us, as my mother so eloquently expounded. It's a pity the House of Lords does not admit women; she has been wasted on the domestic staff." His sarcasm was tinted with rueful humor, and Katherine cast a sidelong glance at him. He was shaking his head as if pondering the woman known as Miriam Lattimore. He caught her look and shrugged. "If you have any other suggestions, now is the time to voice them. Maidenly reticence will gain you little at this point."

"You forget, my lord, that I am not a maiden. Nor am I so insipid as to attempt girlish reticence with you. I would be better served to come armed with a dagger and a spear."

"Then we have both learned much, you and I. I, too, have learned not to underestimate you."

"Must we prod and pick at each other all the time?"

The question surprised him, as did the sober nature in which she asked it. There was something warm and dark in her eyes that stopped his easy refrain, his casual glib and mocking remark. Instead, he surveyed her, dressed in Melissa's borrowed garments, her eyes still weary from lack of sleep, her face pale. Exhaustion did not alter her beauty.

What was her secret, that she would be capable of such courage? Leaving Mertonwood in the midst of a violent snowstorm had taken a determination he had not known she possessed. To live as she had, simply and without fanfare for the past year, and to be happy while doing so, called for a strength of character foreign in the women he had known. To carry a child out of wedlock, to bear him, and to love him proudly were the acts of a woman with deep conviction, great faith, and formidable inner strength.

"You have still not answered my question," he said, moving from the fireplace with sinewy ease, crossing the expanse of carpet to stand in front of her. He was an incredibly handsome stranger. A man whose body she knew intimately but who had shared little else with her. Only today had she glimpsed a hint of his past, and that without his willingness. His plans for the future? He guarded information about himself with a miser's care. She had little idea what he wanted from life, but whatever it was, she had no doubt he would attain it, by dint of his will, if not his effort.

The past year had wrought too many changes in his face, she thought. His eyes were surrounded by crinkling lines, his mouth was too thin, his face even leaner.

Her hand almost strayed up to his cheek to stroke it before she caught herself. She flinched from the impulse and he thought it was because of his closeness.

"As I said before," she said, moving away from him, "I am a simple person. I crave peace and a certain measure of freedom. I do not seek to take advantage, either of situations or of people, but would prefer to make my own way in the world. My favorite color is yellow. I cannot draw and I do not dance well, never having had much practice. I loathe sewing and cannot even mend my own garments. I love Julie and Robert with all my heart. You seek answers, Freddie. Are these good enough for you?"

He stepped behind her and gently pulled her around to face him. She looked up, met his intent look and some impulse, not understood, told her to remain, unresisting, in the circle of his arms. The prey, convincing itself that the tiger wasn't truly a tiger after all?

"I, too, crave peace, Katherine. I demand freedom. I seek to help others in the world, I have already earned my way. I like books, music, and intelligent conversation. My favorite color is really blue. I have never tried to draw, but I dance superbly, having had too much practice. I do not want to sew, and if my garments become ripped, I trust it is for a worthwhile reason." He smiled and tipped her face up so that he could look into her eyes. She did not pull away, the prey entranced by the tiger. "Now you know more about me than most people, Katherine. Will that satisfy you?"

Katherine pulled away, but slowly, as if trapped by his gaze. She looked down at her clenched hands. "This will never do, my lord," she said, the words forced past the rictus of her throat. "It would never work."

"I had never thought to plead for a marriage that I have studiously avoided for twelve years," he said, his tone bemused. "Tell me what it is about me that you dislike so intensely, and I will tell you if it's something I can change. I will not give up my children, Katherine. Nor do you seem prepared to. Have you some way out of the matrimonial noose which binds us? Then, pray tell, expound on the idea, and I will be pleased as Punch!" The last words were spoken in a barely controlled shout.

"The only brilliant idea I possess is that you release me and the children." She unclenched her hands, smoothing them on the velvet of her skirt. Glancing up at him with suddenly hopeful eyes, she continued. "We will welcome you whenever you come to visit," she promised.

"How do you propose I explain to the world that my children are being raised in a hovel?"

She pursed her lips and wanted to shake him. Hovel, indeed. Bertha's cottage had been a delightfully snug place. Not the size of Mertonwood, true, but more than adequate for her and the children.

"Then choose the place, Freddie. Purchase a small home."

He disliked the fact that she looked so radiantly beautiful at this moment, as if the thought of being released from marriage to him was some sort of cause for rapture.

"Listen to me, my lovely little dolt." He peered down into her face, so close she could feel his breath on her skin. Until, of course, she raised her head to protest the insult and nearly broke his nose. He grabbed her face between his large hands to forestall another deadly blow. "There is one thing you are forgetting. Neither one of my children are legitimate, Katherine. They are bastards, not to mince words. By marrying, I can legitimize them both. Julie will be a fantastically wealthy young heiress, Robert can inherit the title."

"I thought Jeremy was your heir."

"Why should Jeremy be my heir when I have a perfectly good son? If you love these children, Katherine, you'll do what's best for them."

"That's blackmail," she accused, slanting a glance at him.

"You have wanted to sacrifice for my children. You have done so already. What better way to become a genuine martyr than to marry their father?" His smile was one of wry humor overlaid with genuine irritation. She decided to test the depths of both.

"It would be a sacrifice," she mused aloud, pulling away from him and walking to the other side of the room. She did not want to be touched by the earl. Something strange happened whenever he was too close.

"But marriage, my lord. It is so . . . so permanent!"

"I should hope so."

"What, exactly, do you give up?" she asked, a question that surprised both of them. She had thought it but had not meant to speak it aloud.

"Why the hell should I give up anything?" he asked warily. After all, he was sharing his name and fortune with her.

The way she looked at him did not bode well, he realized. Whenever Katherine smiled in that secretive way, he knew that the next words out of her mouth were going to be damaging. To him.

"I agree, the idea of marriage to you does have merit. But it seems as though all of the sacrifice is on my side. You get the children, but your life is not disrupted, your existence can go on just as before." A vision of him carousing from one London nightspot to another flashed before her mind, as did the thought of him reeking of perfume, staggering into his home as the sun marched across the sky.

"You honestly think that incorporating that little beast from hell and my son into my establishment is not going to alter my life?" The look he shot her could only be characterized as incredulous.

"They don't act badly around me, my lord. Just you. Either it is something in your character that brings out the worst in people, or it is being stolen from their home that brings out the worst in them."

Gone was the notion that she might have softened toward him.

"You did have, in your mind, thoughts of a real marriage, I trust?"

"By real," he asked wryly, not at all surprised by the source of the gleam in her dark eyes, "I presume that you mean conjugal rights and all that they entail?" He was not, after all, unfamiliar with being manipulated. The point was, how far was he willing to go for the two children he wanted?

"Exactly." She turned and faced him. "Should I be the only one to sacrifice for this grand notion, my lord? Is that entirely fair?"

Evidently, he was willing to go too damned far, he realized, and she was testing the bonds of his restraint. "Why do I think that the idea of fairness and marriage to you do not go hand in hand, Katherine?"

She frowned at him. "Therefore, I insist that another contract be drawn."

"State your conditions, my worthy adversary." How quickly she had tasted power and hungered for more. He was strangely disappointed.

"You will not touch me, my lord. Not on the wedding night, the following night, or any night in between the ceremony and death. Without my express written permission."

"Good God, are you going to send me a note?" He bit back a laugh. She looked so earnest, so sincere, so empowered by her own tentative foray into autocracy, that he didn't have the heart to ridicule her.

"That is one thing you must give up, my lord," she emphasized, not realizing that the boundaries of his patience had been reached. "I do not like that deplorable tendency of yours to be pompous."

"Katherine, listen to yourself, will you?" He could not hide his smile. It softened his face, making him appear younger. "You offer to send me a note when you're in the mood, and you don't consider that pretentious? Why not do without sex altogether? Although," he said in a suddenly cold voice, "I will not tolerate another repeat of my first marriage. If I find you warming another man's bed or even thinking about it, I will cause a scandal that will not be forgotten in a hundred years."

"By what, my lord? Shooting the poor innocent?"

"No, Katherine, by shooting you."

She shivered at the look in his eyes. Now she knew what it meant. Silent waiting. The wounded anticipating more pain? Steadfastly masked, yet discernible if one knew of Monique. She mentally shook herself. How romantic she was being to so easily ascribe suffering to this arrogant man. Katherine doubted he gave the women in his life much thought beyond the satisfaction they gave him. And yet, it was an intriguing thought. Almost as interesting as the one that followed on its heels: How could a woman want anyone but him? It flowed so easily into her mind that she did not catch the danger of it until it was almost voiced. She caught the words by their tails and hung on to them for dear life. She would not give Freddie the satisfaction of knowing she found him too irresistible. Still. Perhaps forever.

"You will never have the opportunity, my lord," she said instead, forcing into her voice all the coldness her near-miss had made her feel. "However, there may come a time in which I desire additional children, and I understand that is the only way."

"So, when the maternal mood strikes you, or the moon is full, or the omens are right, I will be summoned as stud?" Dear God, his mother was wrong. This was not a Greek tragedy they were acting out, it was a bawdy comedy.

"Precisely," she said, in a clipped voice.

"I presume, then, by the terms of your agreement, I am free to seek out my earthly pleasures in other directions?"

"Of course," she said airily, pretending indifference when it was not one of the myriad emotions she felt at this moment. "Please do so. But there are two requirements you need to remember. Number one, do not cause a scandal that will undo both our sacrifices, and number two, do not bring home any consequences of your alliances. You have the very bad habit of sowing seeds wherever you water your garden."

He didn't know whether to wring her neck or to kiss her soundly. He grinned instead, a wolfish, anticipatory grin that made the hairs on the back of her neck stand at attention.

"Conditions accepted, Katherine." He bowed slightly.

"Good," she said, still eyeing him warily. Katherine, she told herself, you're going into league with the devil. Impossibly handsome, ruthless, arrogant. Absurdly charming. Married to him, bound to him, protected by him, bearing his name.

So, he told himself, looking at the full-breasted curving figure of his soon-to-be wife, she's going to do it. Sensuous Katherine, who had obviously forgotten the weeks he recalled with such clarity. She would allow him to protect her, support her, be a father to his children, but not to bed her until she summoned him.

A marriage not exactly crafted in heaven.

Chapter 19

The marriage ceremony binding the fifth Earl of Moncrief to the impecunious daughter of the deceased Baron of Donegan Castle and his French wife was performed discreetly in the presence of the earl's family on the following Saturday morning. Also in attendance were those few friends whom Miriam trusted, and those of an official capacity whose sole purpose in attending was to witness the bond of matrimony between a calm and smiling earl and a sullen and less than radiant bride.

Katherine eyed the gathering with a wan smile and wondered what in the world she was doing. In her possession was the contract, duly signed, witnessed, and frankly, the only reason she had agreed to this farce.

This time, the document had been prepared by Duncan, who eyed with amazement the amount of money the earl was settling on a dowerless bride, and with shock Katherine's insertion of her terms. The contract would have been finished much sooner, but he had to stop and wipe the tears of mirth from his face at regular intervals. Even at the ceremony, the sound of chuckling could be heard from the rear of the sitting room.

Miriam scowled at him, distressed not so much by his unholy glee as by the terms of the contract itself. She had said as much to Katherine, who would not be budged.

"But, my dear, the marriage bed is an integral part of the institution. Can you honestly admit that Freddie isn't, well . . . adept?" Katherine could have no possible idea how many women she'd rescued Freddie from, servants and nobility alike. He drew them, like flames attracted moths, like roses enticed bees.

"He is very adept," Katherine answered calmly, adjusting the bodice of the new blue dress that served as her bridal gown. It was an extravagance the countess had insisted upon giving her. It made no difference to Katherine, except that she had wished, fleetingly, for the courage to wear black.

Katherine had no idea what Constance would have done, but her mother would have kissed her cheek and whispered some wonderful Gallic advice in her ear and her father would have wrapped her in a bear hug to give her courage. But they were not here, and she had to protect the children, even if it meant an alliance with the devil himself.

"The problem, dear Miriam," she said finally, shaking herself free of the past, "is that Freddie believes all he has to do is crook his finger and every available woman within three counties will throw herself into his arms. I won't be so easily controlled."

"And you think that if he has unlimited access to your bed that he will control you?" Miriam's forehead crinkled in confusion.

Katherine turned and looked steadily at the older woman.

"I don't know. Sometimes I think I understand myself less than I comprehend Freddie."

"Tell me, then, what do you understand of my son? It would seem that is the best place to begin."

Katherine stared off into the corner, as if seeing something far away. She remembered the earl at Mertonwood, striding through the grounds, sure and certain of his destination and his purpose. The kind steward who dispensed justice with an even hand. The arrogant lover who directed her passion with effortless movements but succumbed just as easily to her innocent explorations. She saw him extending an emerald ring to her, the same she'd wear in a few moments, a token of his esteem—or his purchase? The rage on his face the day of Bertha's funeral was burned into her mind, as was his tender expression as he hefted his infant son into his arms with clumsy care. Katherine looked at the countess, wondering how she could distill all those pictures in her mind into words someone else could understand.

"It is not that simple," she said. But Miriam was having none of it.

"Life is not simple, my dear. It is confusing, complicated, and messy. Just when you think you have it right, something else comes along to alter your destiny. It is never, but never, simple."

How did she describe him, then? Katherine shrugged, and let the words spill free. "He can be angry, cruel at times, tender, fair, humorous, intelligent, unbelievably obstinate, and yet, he is generous," she added, thinking of the settlement that had so startled Duncan and amazed her.

"Then you have just described a great many men in the world, my dear. What makes Freddie so different?"

How could she possibly tell his mother? That when he touched her, some answering chord responded in kind. As if there had been music made between them over the centuries. That he had the power to wound her with a look; that his presence in a room made it suddenly seem warmer and smaller; that she lay in bed at night and remembered times in which she had touched him with her lips and her hands. That she worried about falling under his spell again. Beloved conjurer. How did one tell that to a mother?

"My son is not a saint, Katherine," Miriam said, speaking into the silence generated by memories, "but neither is he as black a sinner as you might wish to paint him. Give him time to learn about you. Give yourself time to understand him. Most brides do not go to their marriages as familiar with their husbands as you are with Freddie. Please, Katherine, be obstinate, be prickly, be angry, but do not be stupid."

Miriam gently hugged the woman soon to be her daughter by marriage. She hoped that sense would come to them soon. She had no doubt as to the outcome of their union; she only wished, fervently, that it did not take as much time as she feared it would.

Their war, blessedly, would no longer be fought in her domain. They were free to slam every single door at Moncrief, to mumble dire warnings in their own home. If they chose to stride half naked in front of the staff, they were now free to do so. She would stay in London for the duration, if need be. No, she would remain in London for the rest of her life, in order to remove herself from the scene of battle.

Miriam stood behind the couple and a beaming Jeremy, who was thrilled to have been delegated into service by his brother. The ceremony was quickly completed, the contracts signed, and Katherine Sanderson became Katherine Lattimore, Countess of Moncrief, and wife to one of the wealthiest men in the British Empire. Katherine glanced at the enormous diamond on her finger. As if guessing her thoughts, the earl leaned over and whispered, "It's new, Katherine." She smiled at him, a wan, weak smile so at odds with her doggedly stubborn stance of the days before.

What had she done?

She turned to Miriam, who hugged her tightly. "Now, my dear, you may call me Mother. Only let's think of some other name but Grandmother. It sounds too ancient."

Katherine laughed, grateful beyond words to this dear woman. "I would love to call you Mother," she said, kissing the other woman's cheek. "And I shall endcavor to find something suitable for the children to address you by that does not put you in your dotage."

"Oh, I may well be there, my child, but I do not want to announce it every time one of the little darlings opens their mouth. As for the children, we shall have ample time to practice. Did Freddie not tell you?" She turned her censorious gaze upon her son, who smiled back calmly.

"No, Mother, I didn't. Not an oversight on my part as much as a prudent act. You tell her, though, while I prepare the carriage." He strode away with an impudent smile lingering on his lips and a gleam of mischief in his eyes.

"What did he not tell me?" Katherine asked, her wan smile rapidly transforming into something more reminiscent of the past few days.

"We are keeping the children, dear, just until you've had a chance for a honeymoon." She put her hand on Katherine's arm reassuringly. Katherine was not reassured.

"But, Miriam," she began, when Miriam interrupted.

"Yes, yes, I know. Your contract. Well, no one is saying that you have to bed him," she said in a whisper. "Just get to know him."

She didn't want to get to know him. She didn't want to be alone with him.

"But I haven't ever been separated from the children," Katherine sputtered as she was led firmly to the front door, past the small group of guests smiling fondly, past Melissa's sullen smirk, past Jeremy's fond and knowing look, past the arms of Peterson who held out a new yellow wool cloak, down the steps of the townhouse and into the carriage before she had time to realize that once again, she was being guided by Miriam's gentle, but firm, grip.

"It's only for a little while, my dear," she said to the astonished Katherine, who allowed the earl to press her close to his side, more out of bemused acceptance than actual realization of what he was doing. He covered her knees with a warm Indian shawl, and she let him pat her legs comfortingly.

"Have fun, my dears," Miriam called and waved as the horses pulled away in a sputter of gravel and an irate, but ladylike, yell from inside the carriage.

She was bloody furious.

What Miriam thought were only muffled gasps coming from inside the coach were the sounds of a genteel struggle taking place between the Earl of Moncrief and his new bride. He drew back his hand with an oath.

"By God, woman, now I know where Julie gets her taste for human flesh!" He stared at the shape of her teeth, beginning to appear on the reddened base of his thumb.

"If you hadn't put your hand over my mouth, my lord, I wouldn't have bit you," she spat. Katherine moved back on the edge of the seat and glared at her new husband.

"And if you hadn't been quite willing to scream so loud that not only all of our guests could hear, but half the occupants of the square—all too damn eager to spread the story, I might add—then I wouldn't have had to muzzle you." The look on his face contrasted sharply with the relatively quiet tone of his words.

"Muzzle me!"

"Exactly, my dear, like a recalcitrant bitch," he said silkily, as he leaned back on the opposite seat and eyed Katherine with some degree of caution.

She turned her face away. What a horrible way to start a horrible marriage, she thought.

"You should have told me about the children. You know that was unfair. After all, they are the very reason for this misalliance." He was not surprised to see the echo of Julie's mutinous look on her face. They might not be related by blood, but they were kin by temperament, it seemed. The earl smiled, which only fueled her anger.

"I see nothing about which to smile, my lord," she snapped. "The irony of the situation escapes me. Please, illuminate my feeble brain." She glared at him from the safety of the corner. She faced the rear of the coach, and with each step the horses took, she realized that she was doomed to remain there for as long as he deemed suitable. Physically, he overpowered her, and even if he did not, there was that look on his face that warned her not to attempt an escape. Besides, she was humiliated by having bit him in the first place. It was not the gesture of a rational woman. She sighed and closed her eyes. The things this man made her do!

"I but smiled because I thought of our daughter," he said softly. Her eyes flew open in surprise. His face was softened by a smile. She wasn't sure she cared for his sudden possessiveness. It disturbed her. Too much. Her heart beat so loudly that she was surprised he did not comment on the sound. "You and she are much alike," he added, the smile not leaving his lips, his eyes noting her sudden alertness. "She seems to have replicated even your gestures."

"Is that so unusual? After all, my lord, I did raise her from a baby. She thinks of me as her mother."

"After this day, my dear, you are her mother. Legally bound. You could not escape the children now if you wanted to." He smiled again, and that seductive gesture made her unaccountably irritated. Irritated and just a tiny bit nervous.

"I do not seek to escape my children, my lord, which is why they should be here now."

"But you do seek to escape me, then?" He laughed, then added more seriously, "Children do not belong on a honeymoon, my dear."

"This is not a honeymoon, my lord," she bit out.

His eyes were clear, brilliant, and the look in them was lethal. "It is in the eyes of the world, Katherine. For the children's sake, or have you forgotten so soon? Let us refrain from airing our problems in public. Our union will be romanticized, whispered about, cherished in the hearts of spinsters. We will not do anything or say anything or act in any way that will disabuse people of their fond notions. Is that understood?" Steel in his voice, poison in his eyes.

She nodded reluctantly. He was right; the children's future was at stake. But that did not mean that she had to like the pretense. Nor did it mean that it made her comfortable. In fact, the gleam in his eyes prompted her to feel just the opposite.

Nor was she relieved to find that instead of an extended wedding journey, they were going only as far as Moncrief. The earl finally imparted that information to her in a clipped voice. She would have felt more at ease dealing with her husband in the company of strangers. A lot of strangers.

She was also less than pleased to discover that a wagon containing the earl's working papers was following in a smaller and slower conveyance. The fact that the earl meant to continue to maintain his office at Moncrief did not augur well for their relationship. Somehow, she had thought he would either travel as much as he did before or work in London, thereby leaving her for extended periods with the children. Alone.

"Do you not think the children will be a distraction, my lord?" she asked in a futile attempt to make him reconsider. Good Lord, the idea of being in close proximity to him every day was a sobering one.

"Moncrief is not the size of Mertonwood, Katherine. I have a wing set aside for my business interests. They will not discommode me."

"Children can become very loud, my lord."

"So can irate husbands, Katherine, especially when they are always addressed as *my lord!*" He straightened, glared down at her from his aristocratic nose, then turned and looked out the window of the carriage, ostensibly carried away by the view of London. "Why is it you addressed me by name before we wed, but after the ceremony, all you can parrot is *my lord?*" He glanced at her. "I do not care to have one of those marriages in which we address each other by surnames."

"Freddie," she said silkily. She smiled, and he frowned at her. She was determined not to let his irritation disturb her. These weeks would test all of her patience. Not that she had much around the earl . . . Freddie. But she owed it to the children to try. If only he didn't make it so difficult.

They traveled in silence for a time, the scenery still occupying the earl's attention, her own discomfiture the focal point of hers.

Katherine slowly removed her gloves, one finger at a time. He turned his head, watching her. One did not sit caged with a tiger and tease it, she told herself later. It was a lesson she should have already mastered.

Freddie seemed fascinated by her actions. He watched her, his interest not at all covert. She grasped the tip of one gloved finger between her teeth and pulled gently, easing the tight fit. Two fingers of her right hand eased down the tight casing one inch at a time.

It was not a seductive movement, he told himself, as if he were not being driven mad by the scent of her, as if the memory of her willing participation in lessons of passion didn't infringe upon his every waking thought. And if he'd been able to bed a single woman in the last six months, he would have been able to ignore her. Or if he didn't feel the base of his thumb throbbing with the mark of her teeth, or if she didn't sit there with that soft smile as if she dared him to touch her, or to place his lips around one of those fingers and suck it deep into his mouth.

It was not a seductive movement, he told himself, as he reached out and, despite her squeals, dragged her hand, her arm, and the rest of her to sit astride him. He placed his hand over her mouth and, with a look, dared her to bite him. His other hand reached out and stripped the glove from her hand, tired of her teasing, her innocent wantonness.

One look at her bared hand chilled him. He held it out, nestled in his larger palm, examining it as minutely as he had his son's.

"You have done too much work, Katherine," he said as he noted the faint evidence of blisters. "You have the hands of a washerwoman."

She pulled her hand back angrily. "I have been a washerwoman, my lord. And a nurse, a maid, a hauler of logs . . . a myriad of positions deemed necessary for survival."

He frowned. "From now on, however, you will confine your activities to less strenuous pursuits."

"I will not be dictated to, my lord."

He sighed heavily. "I am not dictating, Katherine. I am simply concerned for your welfare. You are no longer required to do those things. There are servants whose sole job is your comfort. You have only to allow them to do their work, not assume it for them."

"Aha, the duties of a countess, you mean."

"Yes, but not those of a wife."

She ignored that. "What else are the duties I am supposed to assume, my lord? Exactly what does a countess, your countess, do?"

"If not for that stupid contract, my dear, you would be

too tired to do little else except care for me and the children. In that order."

He grinned that same daunting grin that had held such attraction for her in the past. She would not allow it to have any effect on her now, however. She scooted off his lap and returned to her own seat, but not before he gripped her hand and traced the scars on her fingers with a warm and talented tongue. Katherine shivered and drew her hand away quickly.

"I am not a sweetmeat, Freddie." She was conscious of the flush on her cheeks, but determined not to wilt in the face of his obvious challenge.

His eyes were unfathomable.

"Oh, but you are, Katherine, as delectable as any comfit I've ever tasted." He smiled at the flush that mounted on her face, the angry glitter of her eyes, and laughed aloud as she turned from him in a huff and forced herself to become fascinated by the sights of London.

As a baron's daughter, Katherine had been accorded the benefits of her rank, which, in her case, were almost nil. The peddlers always stopped first at the gates of Donegan, before traveling on to the village. The squire and parson always bowed slightly before speaking. The village girls, who sometimes acted as extra help when her mother infrequently entertained, addressed her as Miss Katherine. The visitors to Donegan Castle had been of mixed variety, mainly men of commerce who dealt in Donegan's horses or sheep, or the occasional prelate passing through. There was not ample occasion to note that her station in life was substantially different from the village children she played with as a child. Other than the castle, which proved to be drafty and cold in the winter, and stifling and without breeze in the summer, their conditions were the same. Truth to tell, the village girls may have had an easier lot, not having to contend with a roof that was three hundred years old and showing signs of caving in onto their heads any moment.

Therefore, neither her upbringing nor her past experiences prepared Katherine for the servile behavior of the landlord at the inn where they stopped for the night. She was not used to being called m'lady, and it was only the earl's small smile that prevented a start of amazement when she realized that the landlord's low bow was directed at her.

The fawning gratitude the staff exhibited toward the earl seemed a bit much to Katherine, but she entered the inn without comment. The day was not far advanced, it being only early evening, but the fact that her small trunk was being laboriously advanced up the stairs meant that the earl had made the decision to stay the night. She wasn't surprised that he had not imparted that information to her, few words having passed between them in the last three hours.

Nor was that likely to change, she thought as he bowed to her and mutely escorted her up the stairs. She caught his slightly uplifted brow at the sight of the buxom maid and wanted to elbow him in the ribs.

The reason the earl had not informed her of his decision to remain at the inn overnight was that it had been made impulsively. He had originally planned to drive straight through to Moncrief, which was only a few hours away. The master suite had been prepared, the late supper instructions already posted to the butler. His reasons for remaining at the cozy little inn were complex and disturbing. Too much so to be shared.

He had never lived at Moncrief with his first wife. Nor had his father stayed there much, preferring the life in town to a pastoral existence on their estate. Only after he'd acquired the title had Freddie returned to Moncrief to lick his wounds, pouring all his energies and not insubstantial wealth into its preservation and enhancement. He loved his home the way a trusting man loved a woman, with unconditional acceptance, peace, and a warm feeling of belonging.

He did not want it marred by anger, hostility, or barely veiled rage. If they were to have war, it would be fought on neutral ground and won right here.

He stopped to speak to the aproned owner and arranged for dinner to be served in an hour. That would give him plenty of time to set some new rules in effect. He strode up the stairs two at a time.

Katherine sat on the lumpy bed in the biggest room in the inn and chided herself for latent romanticism. Her children now had a father. More than that they had a future, one in which there might be whispers, but overt respectability. Not to mention wealth, an inducement to civility if there ever was one. Did it matter that her wedding night would be spent without a husband in a lumpy bed in the middle of a drafty room? No, Katherine, she told herself sternly, you've already had your wedding night. Despite her resolve, her caution that such thoughts could only be dangerous, she began to remember.

When the earl opened the door, his lust for battle was supplanted by simple lust. She sat huddled in the middle of a bed whose previous occupants numbered too many, her eyes not brilliant with the light of confrontation but lambent with remembered passion. Instead of being pursed stubbornly, as it had been all afternoon, her mouth was ripe, the bottom lip gently worried by her teeth, as if confused by thoughts not willingly hers. Her hands were clasped before her and her gaze was on the cold fireplace as if she remembered real fire and real flames. When she looked up and saw him, it was as if a year had not passed, and their bodies' wish was not overridden by the stubbornness of their wills.

He wanted to go to her.

She wanted him to come.

He shook himself and remembered his reason for storming into the room. She remembered that a year had indeed past, and too many things had happened to be easily dismissed. It was a moment lost forever, except in their minds. He would always wonder what would have happened if he had stepped forward and pulled her into his arms. If she had welcomed him, she often thought later, would the future have been altered?

"Dinner will be served shortly," he announced, with the formal intonation of a butler.

"Thank you," she answered, with the hauteur of a countess.

"We have some things to discuss, you and I." He entered the room fully, closed the door softly, and stood in front of her. "I have done all that you asked," he said, in a reasonable voice, he thought. "Do you not agree?"

"If you are referring to our agreement, then yes, you have acceded with graciousness. But then, I expected no less from the Earl of Moncrief."

"Do you mean to carry it on, then?" If his face had been hewn from granite, it could not have been any less immobile. His very stance gave warning. She framed her words with care, knowing, yet uncertain how she knew, that it would be by these words that her marriage was charted. Not by the words stated so tremblingly in front of several guests this morning.

"What would you have me say?" she asked instead, opting for safety.

"I would have peace in my home, not a battleground." I would have you come, warm and willing, to my bed. I would have your laughter and your gentle touch with the same gift of graciousness you bestow to my children. Too many words left unsaid, but perhaps not. His eyes spoke of things better left unspoken between them, and once again, memory stirred from the ashes and warmed the room.

"I, too, crave peace," she said softly, and he knew it was the only concession he would win this night. It was not the end, he thought, looking at her attired in her blue gown. He wondered if she knew how much effort it had taken not to pull her into his arms when she'd been made his wife, not to deepen the ceremonial kiss that had bound them. And to refrain, this long journey, from touching her in the way he knew she liked to be touched, with soft teasing kisses, and stroking, intrusive fingers.

She was his.

"I do not wish us to err in our beginnings," he said surprisingly, and it was that soft voice that was almost her undoing. She glanced at him and then down at her clenched hands.

"If we err," she said, tenacious to her damnable points even to the end, he thought, "it is due to your stubbornness, and not to our agreement."

"And you do not welcome me to your bed?"

Dear God, it was so much easier to speak when allusion was all that was necessary. How did she frame the words to deny him her surrender? Why did she fight this allure with such intensity?

Because he had nearly destroyed her before. This time would be so much worse. This time, she could not help but love him.

"The omens are not right, my lord," she said, forcing a smile onto her face. It was a weak effort at best. "Nor is the moon full."

"Be certain it is what you want, Katherine. Be very sure that pride or your stubbornness or some other fool emotion does not keep you from our marriage bed. Because I will not sit like a lovesick fool and howl at your window."

It was as much a warning as she was going to get, Katherine thought as she watched him leave. An announcement as stentorian as if he'd hired a crier. Perhaps not tonight, or tomorrow night, or the night after, but one night soon, he would lie with another.

The battle lines had been drawn.

The night grew colder, despite the newly laid fire, despite the warmth of the coverings, despite the fact that she lay wrapped in the heat of anger. The night grew colder because something froze inside her, lodged suspiciously close to her heart. The room adjoining hers was empty, and not a sound had come from it indicating his late arrival. Wherever he was, he intended to stay the night.

Newly wedded bliss.

It would kill her, this pain.

Her dinner had been brought to her by a serving girl whose ample breasts almost spilled over into the tureen. Nor was she shy about glancing at Katherine, a sly triumphant look glittering in her eyes. She had ignored the strumpet as much as possible, but the girl made a point of serving her with a flounce of apron, and then thrusting her breasts at Katherine as if displaying her wares.

Would she spend the rest of her life lying in a bed like this one, albeit richer, cleaner, and with less lumps, wondering at Freddie's nighttime occupation? Would each evening bring the onset of deep sadness such as she felt now? And if it did, whom did she have to blame?

Constance had often said that you could not butter both sides of your bread without making a mess. Well, Katherine had wanted to be able to say no when it came to sharing the earl's bed at the same time she'd wanted him to stay faithful. What a mess she had created.

This marriage would not have been easy even in the most perfect of worlds. Freddie trusted no one, and Katherine had shown her naivete by trusting too well. He was socially adept, well traveled, and culturally sophisticated.

She was used to talking to ghostly governesses and wet nurses, and she despised London with a sincere and utter loathing. He laid down onerous rules, and she, once so meek and malleable and willing to please, was receiving too much satisfaction from spiting him.

She had forgiven him the action of stealing his children. It was her incredibly uncomfortable ability to empathize with him that enabled her to understand. She would have done the same thing, Katherine thought. Nor did she honestly blame him for the idiotic contract penned at her insistence, or for his wholehearted tutoring of her in the passionate arts. She had welcomed her own downfall with barely hidden anticipation.

She did blame him for tonight, however. It was an action deliberately calculated to hurt her. As if he sought to wound her by bedding the first available body in sight. She had no doubt it was the voluptuous maid.

Her husband would have his wedding night, and if the bride giggled a little too much, or smelled of horse and ale, he would, no doubt, ignore it. If he ever noticed.

The innkeeper smiled at the earl, bowing low from the waist in a gesture that was servile enough for a king. He was no fool; he knew when to express his gratitude for money not rightfully earned. His Bessy was a tart, more trouble than the few coins she passed over now and again. Still, it was kind of the earl to pay for time spent, even though both of them knew the man had changed his mind and stayed by the fire all night, staring into the flames and refilling his tankard when it grew dry.

He gave the earl a leg up and rubbed his hands as the stallion bore its rider down the rutted road and out of sight. With any luck at all, the young countess would leave a large remembrance, too, and his fortunes would be double blessed.

Katherine didn't know to leave a tip for the innkeeper, nor did she realize until entering the carriage that her husband of one day had gone on without her. It was just as well. Right at this particular moment, it was doubtful she could remain in his company for more than a few minutes without succumbing to a fit of screaming or crying. She much preferred yelling at him, but realized she was too close to tears.

Freddie was exercising Monty and exorcising his demons at the same time. Katherine had won the first round, but she would never know it, not as long as he drew breath. He was emotionally, if not physically, incapable of committing adultery. He couldn't do to her what had been done to him; the ghost of Monique and his father held too tight a grip on his conscience. Yet, Katherine had looked at him as if he'd delivered a mortal blow when he'd left her room. She didn't have a clue, the little innocent, that she was the only woman he'd wanted in too damned long.

He was a man ruled not merely by his loins; his mental faculties were occasionally in tow, also. He could not disconnect one from the other. He like his bed partners clean, for example. He also liked them auburn-haired, intelligent, unbelievably stubborn, and downright bitchy at times. Other than that, he had few requirements. The fact that he had wanted, five steps from her room, to turn around and marshal his arguments once more only showed how close to the edge she was pushing him. God, how she would laugh if she knew.

He reined Monty in and waited for the carriage. An hour later, he tethered the horse to the rear, joining Katherine inside. Without a word, he lay his head back against the tufted seat and closed his eyes.

"Long night?" She could not keep the acrid edge from her voice.

He slit one eye open and realized his new bride was livid.

"Long enough," he said and smiled, a fond, reminiscent smile. It was enough, he hoped, to fuel the fire that was burning in her eyes without the expense of any further energy on his part.

Introspection and too much ale can make a man extraordinarily weary.

Katherine gazed at her husband between narrowed eyes, noting his fatigue with a curled lip. She wished she knew of some obscure poison that would render him motionless while still being able to see and to hear. Something that would paralyze him, and not allow him the luxury of speech. Then she would let him know exactly what she thought of him. Yet, even tired, there was an edge to Freddie, a threat in his manner that counseled prudence. For the first time since she'd met him, Katherine wisely refrained from saying anything further.

He dozed comfortably, oblivious to the barbed looks from his new wife. An hour passed and the two occupants of the carriage were each immersed in their own activities, Katherine in contemplating her future, the Earl in fitful sleep, awakening after a short nap to study Katherine beneath lowered lids.

Finally, when she could take the silence no longer, she spoke. "Will we reach Moncrief soon?"

"We've been on Moncrief acreage since a mile outside the inn," he said. She turned surprised eyes to him, but he shut his lids and pretended to sleep again.

It was not the first time she had unconsciously enlightened him as to her nature. She was not a fortune hunter, of that he was certain, else she would not have questioned the rather large amount he had bequeathed to her at their wedding. She had sent Duncan in to speak to him about it, to ensure herself that it would not diminish the Moncrief coffers. He had smiled at that, and even Duncan had chuckled at his bride's ignorance. His fortune was so large that at times it was incalculable. Certainly, it was occasionally unmanageable. The fact that Moncrief was one of England's largest private homes and boasted some of the most famous gardens in the world had evidently been withheld from his lovely new bride.

It was an odd feeling, he thought, to be wanted not so much for what he was as for what he had done. His role as father was of greater import to Katherine than his fortune, his title. Hell, even himself.

The carriage turned, lumbered through iron gates, and began to slowly descend between rolling hills. Moncrief was nestled in a valley of green. Even in the lateness of the season, with winter whistling down the valley, the trees had not shed their leaves. Instead, everything was lush emerald green and white.

Katherine had not been dazzled by Mertonwood. It was a stolid old house, buried in the woods, as the countess had said, with little culture in sight. This place screamed money and power. She gulped as she examined its sheer size.

"Moncrief was begun in 1620," he said before she could frame one of the hundred questions she longed to ask. His eyes were still shut, and his voice intoned the words not with the boredom she would have expected, but with a rich and loving quality. "By an ancestor who made his fortune in trade. It was rumored that Queen Elizabeth issued a land grant and the title in return for favors rendered." His eyes flashed open and pinned hers. "But we've never learned exactly what kind of favors." Freddie smiled. "The house was rebuilt around parts of an old castle that was here at the time. My ancestors did not believe in wasting anything. However, you will note that the shape of the original house is in an *E,* in honor of Elizabeth." He smiled, the smile of a young boy who is apt to be found doing mischief rather than doing his lessons. "I hope ghosts don't bother you, Katherine."

"Why? Do you have some?"

"The first earl's wife who died in childbirth, I believe, the old aunt of another, a youngish ghost thought to be the shade of a servant girl seduced by yet another scoundrel in the family." He winked at her. "It must run in the family. I think that's all."

"The only things I fear in the night, my lord, are human forms, not ghostly ones." She smiled, a totally benign smile, but he caught traces of devilment in it.

"Then you will have nothing to fear at Moncrief," he said, in the most utterly polite tone she had ever heard him use. It was the deft Earl playing host, the orator prior to an impassioned speech, a man satisfied with his life, his possessions, his peace.

It couldn't have been further from the truth.

Their entrance into Moncrief was dictated by tradition. All of the staff was assembled in a long line, facing each other, creating a path for the earl and his new countess. Katherine allowed him to hold her hand as they marched past the maids and the footmen, the stable boys and the grooms, the gardeners and the cooks. As the housekeeper intoned the names, she smiled nervously at all of them, but they smiled back unabashedly. At the head of the line was Newton, the butler, a man only a little older than the earl, firm of physique and not crippled with arthritis. That, at least, was a change.

She was escorted to her suite of rooms by the housekeeper, a woman as far removed from Mrs. Roberts as a beam of sunshine is from rain.

The countess's suite overlooked the park below, a bubbling brook intersecting a rolling meadow. In spring, she was told, the apple trees flooded the valley with white and pink flowers, and the scent was enough to think you were in heaven.

She was close enough as it was. Everything was in yellow, from the soft carpet beneath her feet to the canopy hanging from the frame of the bed. The curtains were yellow and the walls were papered in a soft yellow print. Only the plants provided a contrast, their leafy green placed on every available surface. Miriam had been here. Miriam or one of her elves. Beyond her room lay Freddie's, but she didn't venture farther than the door that separated their suites. She checked the lock and pulled on the door firmly. It was a solid barrier.

Abigail entered the room with a bubbling smile, and Katherine laughed at the sight of her. "Don't tell me you talked your way here," she said fondly to the maid she hadn't seen in over a year. The time had not made many changes in Abigail. She was still plump, still cheerful, and still bobbed a little too much, as she sank into a deep curtsy in front of Katherine.

All in all, this place, with its low wall and its four white turrets, was a fairy-tale place made for a prince and his princess.

A dream of a castle, a castle fit for dreaming.

Except that the prince and the princess were barely speaking.

Chapter 20

Freddie was frustrated and angry, and he suspected the condition was not going to improve appreciably.

He was intelligent enough to recognize the signs for what they were. For over a year, he had been celibate—he did not count those disastrous forays into drunken lust as anything but what they were—and now the object of his frustration slept two doors away. Undoubtedly, without a care.

Last night, she had not come to dinner, claiming the fatigue of the journey, even though they'd been on the road less than two hours. Tonight it had been a headache. Tomorrow what would it be? The megrims? Would she be like his sister, Melissa, and have vapors when she didn't get her way?

She was avoiding him, and if her actions were calculated to escalate this little battle between them into full-fledged war, they were highly successful.

Jack had been dispatched back to Scotland, and Freddie found himself having to work twice as hard to make up for what hadn't been done in the last week. If not for that, he would have said to hell with the work, marched out of his office, pulled her from bed, and demanded the answer to one simple question.

Was she trying to drive him daft?

Or was it simply something she did unconsciously, like humming to herself when she walked along the garden paths, or trailing her fingers along the wooden surface of every available piece of furniture as if checking for dust? Did she even know what she was doing?

She was the greatest of Moncrief's ghosts. When he entered the dining room, it was to see the sweep of her skirt as she left it. When he walked toward the garden, the ribbons of her bonnet flailed in the breeze as she strolled away. If he didn't know better, he would have thought that the woman he married was only a figment of his imagination.

Oh, he knew better, though, didn't he? He had the empty bed to prove it. Freddie laughed at the irony of lusting after his wife, lifted a signed agreement from the pile of those requiring his approval, and placed it on his "done" list. It was not growing to the extent it normally did when he applied himself to his work. He could only blame his inattention for that. His imagination was trying to distract his memory, with the result that what he could not recall about her he envisioned anyway, from scraps of conversations and stolen glimpses.

She had been concerned about the children's presence and how they might have interrupted his work. He wondered if she knew that her presence decimated his concentration. It wasn't the laughter of children that was driving him crazy, or even their tears or tantrums. It was, paradoxically, the insidious silence!

What was she doing to him?

If she had been more like the other women he knew, then perhaps he could have dismissed her as easily. Put his obsession with her down to a stint of prepubescent lust and gone on with his life. Yet, there was too much to admire about his wife. She drew people to her with her artless candor, her sometimes blunt speech, her way of viewing the world with acute democracy. Servant or squire, maid or marquis, they all elicited the same response from her. She did not have one set of manners to trot out for the titled and one used at home. If she were occasionally arrogant, it was attitude, not belief that sponsored it—she had not one autocratic bone in her body. If she knew how to dissemble, it was either done so well he could not discern it, or she trusted in the truth more often than not. In fact, her ability to trust was a characteristic he'd never thought important before. There was wide-eyed wonder in her smile, and her dark eyes hid nothing. She had a generosity of spirit that showed through her bubbling smile and warm eyes.

To everyone but him.

He found it difficult to believe she had married him for his money and his property, and almost as difficult to understand that she had wed him to protect the children. Such noble virtue was unknown in the women of his acquaintance. Yet, if there were underlying reasons for her actions, they were too deep for him to unravel.

Her stubbornness, her pride, her inflexible honor, all had the effect of eliciting a dual response in him. He wanted to shake her at the same time that he wanted to applaud. Her courage in seeking her own way in the world surprised him, when most women would have sought his help.

He knew she was a good mother, that was already proven. His mother liked her, and Miriam was a good judge of character. Jeremy certainly thought a lot of her, and if his sister was just a little jealous, it was because Melissa was jealous of every woman under the age of eighty. And Jack had championed her from the first.

Yet, it was not the opinion of others he found important, but his own. Freddie liked her, which was not a statement he would willingly repeat aloud. He could not remember ever actually *liking* a woman before.

If he discounted her appeal, he could not ignore her beauty. He liked her walk, not tiny mincing steps designed to enhance the sway of hoops, but long-legged strides that were more natural, hips swinging, hemline bouncing around her ankles. He liked the shape of her hands, those work-worn hands that had caused him such regret. And her laughter, lilting through the halls of his home.

He missed her.

It wasn't just her presence in his bed he craved, although he would have settled for the relationship they had maintained at Mertonwood—incredible passion at night, brooding silence by day. He missed their confrontations, her wit, her acerbic tongue. He had always known, until lately, exactly where he stood with Katherine.

Freddie picked up the memorandum and dismissed the face that appeared upon the parchment, imagination given flesh. He closed his eyes, willing her away, back to her room, back to her safely locked doors. Out of his mind.

Now, damn it.

If Katherine learned nothing else those first few days, it was that she would not be able to adapt to her role as easily as everyone thought.

She had spent the most useless two days of her life roaming through the halls of Moncrief. Never had she felt as superfluous as she did now. A figurehead countess with nothing to do all day. She didn't like it at all. When she walked down a hallway, two maids followed her. She entered the rose sitting room, the massive library, the music room, and was confronted with an eager staff, ready, willing, and more than eager to perform the slightest wish almost before it was uttered. She conferred with the housekeeper to find that meals had been scheduled a month in advance, in accordance, of course, with the earl's tastes. The cook had been scandalized when she entered the kitchen, the gardeners had been ill at ease around her.

The gardens encompassed over a hundred acres. Yet despite their size, and the varieties of styles, they were always in a state of perfection. From the pleached limes on the north lawn, to the canal, to the formal rose garden, to the hedges forming a concentric maze around a baroque bronze fountain, to the azalea dell and arboretum, it was nature as the first earl must have designed it. Everything was in massive scale, from the huge greenhouses to the three-mile grass walk around the perimeter of the garden. She knew the distance by now; she had walked it four times.

Not a bird sang out of tune, not a speck of dust was found on any of the enormous furniture that graced the massive rooms and halls. Not a leaf fell from the ornamental trees that two groundsmen didn't race to pluck it from the immaculate lawn.

Mertonwood had been no more than a country cottage compared to the well-oiled efficiency that was the earl's primary estate. If anything, there were too many people at Moncrief, all willing to assist her in any occupation she chose.

Of course, Freddie would have it no other way. His wish was a command before it was even voiced. The maids cleaned with efficiency and dispatch, but only after he left the dining room in the morning, so as not to disturb him. His lunch was prepared and served at his desk at noon. Precisely. The staff, meanwhile, tiptoed around the halls that led to the business wing of offices lest they unintentionally intrude. Even the rain appeared when he was finished riding in the morning, and not before.

Katherine had never seen so many people labor so long,

for the sole comfort of one individual. It was easy to see where her husband had obtained the rather odd notion that she would as easily acquiesce to his wishes.

What did a countess do all day? Dear God, was she doomed to be bored for the rest of her life? The earl's incessant drive to work occupied his time, but what would she do? Was this to be the tenor of her days?

He was trying to drive her out of her mind.

She missed the children dreadfully and wondered how they were doing, wishing she had them with her, not only because it felt strange to be separated from them, but because their care would have been an adequate antidote to boredom. As it was, she felt half complete, as if something vital were missing.

Time inched by on caterpillar feet. She could only stroll the gardens so many times, and her fingers already hurt from sitting at the pianoforte for so many hours. She did not paint, she would die of boredom before she would take up embroidery, and she was too restless to read.

She rose late on the third morning, in a desperate effort to ward off the interminable boredom, only to find that no one thought it strange for a countess to lie abed most of the day.

She found, unfortunately, that the time left her mind free. Free to wonder and worry and ponder the inscrutable owner of this palatial estate. It was not an occupation she particularly enjoyed, but try as she might, she could not get him out of her mind. She may have prevented him from entering her bed, but there didn't seem to be a deterrent to keeping him from her thoughts.

She spent too long in front of the portrait gallery, almost a duplicate of the one at Mertonwood. Here, though, the quality of the portraits was superior, and Moncrief wives were also portrayed. She stared at the petite, dark prettiness of Monique and wondered if the artist had rendered her true to life. Perhaps it was what she knew of the woman that made her think those tiny eyes betrayed a misery that money could not assuage. It was odd to feel a strange sort of kinship with a woman so long dead. She did not care for the portrait of the fourth earl, a face missing from Mertonwood's gallery. He was a large man, but not as imposing as her husband. His hair was thick and black like Freddie's, but his eyes were more like Jeremy's, hazel and unprepossessing. Although the portrait had been painted while he was still in the prime of life, a hint of jowl appeared below his cheeks, his mouth was drawn thin as if dissatisfied with his lot, his eyes narrowed as if not liking what he saw.

Would her husband look like this in twenty years? She could not help but think that time would not make these changes in Freddie. No, he would remain lithe and sinewy like the tiger he'd likened himself to. Nor did she think life would leave a look of cynical contempt on that chiseled face. If the past twelve years had not made their mark, she doubted if the next twenty would change him so drastically.

He was more likely to remain the same. Impossibly handsome, supremely virile, totally obtuse. She shook herself and wandered into the garden, where a contingent of workers stopped their labors, watching her stride over the newly raked paths. Katherine waved them off and continued walking.

She was becoming obsessed with the man. She wanted desperately to understand him, as if in solving that puzzle she would also settle the riddle of her future. Who was this man who could command his servants with a gentle look, who caused the maids to sigh heavily and the male servants to beam with pride that they worked for such a great man?

Was it only boredom that prompted the memories? She would listen to the sound of activity in the next room and recall moments preserved like summer flowers. How he appeared when stripped of his garments, tanned and muscular. In sleep, his face smoothed, his mouth relaxed.

Leaving her in the inn to pursue his own pleasures.

It was an effective deterrent to warm thoughts, that memory.

For the first time in her life, she had more than adequate funds. The settlement the earl had given her was the equivalent of a worker's moderate income for life. She no longer had to scrimp and save, or worry about the welfare of those in her keeping. She had a home that rivaled any residence of the king's. She only had to crook her finger and an army of servants would spring to her command. She had a magnificent diamond ring, a copy of her wedding vows, all the comfort she could ever have dreamed about, and no one to talk to.

And one memory that could make her miserable.

Four days later, on the week's anniversary of her arrival at Moncrief, boredom had rusted through her restraint. She could not picture the rest of her life this way—and Constance had always said, "Begin as you mean to continue."

Katherine had no intention of continuing in this fashion.

She strode down the hall the servants avoided with studied care, entered the wing that led to the earl's office, and pushed open the door to the room he maintained as the center of his empire.

Freddie was seated behind a massive desk, easily the size of her bed. One hand was buried in the thickness of his hair, the other scrawled rapidly on the paper before him. He was dressed informally, his usual working attire of linen shirt unlaced at the collar and his breeches tucked into knee-high boots. He did not look up as the door closed softly, but continued writing. Nor did he look up as she crossed the expanse of the room to stand directly in front of him. Piles of papers easily a foot high covered each corner of the desk. He signed his name with a flourish, sanded it, placed the quill in its holder, and finally acknowledged her. He had known the moment she walked into the room, and the last two minutes had been spent not so much in completing his letter as they had been in masking his emotions. In fact, he wasn't even sure what he'd written in closing, but hoped fervently that it wasn't drivel and that it hadn't betrayed his sudden uncertainty.

Not an emotion common for him.

She was attired in green, a dress picked out by his mother, no doubt. He had spent a fortune outfitting his wife in the few days before their wedding. She didn't seem to care about what she wore, but that apathy didn't detract from the way she looked. Her curls were tousled around her shoulders, her shawl clutched tightly against her body, hanging at the elbows. He couldn't help smiling. Had his Kat decided to take fate by the hand? Was she not intimidated by his orders that no one disturb his privacy? It was quite possible that his wife didn't know or didn't consider herself bound by his edicts. He had no intention, however, of turning her away at this point—he hadn't seen her for nearly a week.

"I can't take it anymore," she said, temper evident in the grip of her fists upon her shawl, the mutinous eyebrows that heralded a full-blown storm. His own response was to lean back in the chair and fix a rather paternal look upon the fiery vision that was Katherine aroused.

"It simply won't do, Freddie. This is really too ridiculous."

"I agree," he said, smiling.

"You do?"

"I do. However, it was upon your insistence. I merely have chosen to honor your desires."

"What are you talking about?" Her irritation had switched course and now was directed solely at him.

"That stupid contract. I had assumed that was the reason for your presence."

"Good God, no." She sat down on the chair opposite the desk and scowled at him. "I do not change my mind on a whim, my lord. Leave the contract out of this."

"Then what, may I ask, is simply too ridiculous?" He inclined his head politely, honor and a thousand other restraining emotions preventing him from hurtling himself across the desk at her, grabbing her by the arms, and kissing her soundly, thereby effectively neutralizing any clauses or relevant paragraphs in that damned agreement.

"I have never been so stultifyingly bored in my entire life. It simply can't go on, Freddie."

He looked at her with barely veiled irritation. Women didn't get bored; there was plenty for them to do. They had fashions, and charities, and each other.

"I'm afraid you'll have to remain bored for a while, my dear," he said, "I am simply too busy to engage in a social life right now." He would not squire her to an endless array of parties in order to keep her occupied. Nor would he spend valuable time listening to her complain about her wardrobe, or lack of it, in order to placate her. He mentally shuddered, thinking of the early months of his marriage to Monique.

"The very last thing I want to do is sit around chatting with a group of other bored women, Freddie," she said with a disgusted look. "Is there not something meaningful I can do at Moncrief?"

He looked, she thought, not at all interested in her plight. In fact, in the course of the last thirty seconds, his eyes had strayed down to the pile of paperwork aligned in military precision upon his desk, as if it were of more importance than she.

"What do you have in mind?" he asked, tearing his thoughts away from the new mill with some reluctance. He'd honestly thought she'd say something vacuous, like wanting to rearrange the flowers, even though the housekeeper did a more than competent job with the numerous bouquets changed daily throughout Moncrief. Perhaps, he'd thought fleetingly, she would even like to supervise the decorating of a few unused rooms on the fourth floor. He accorded her the supreme compliment by thinking her mind capable, and willing, of realigning his main library.

He was to be excused, he thought, for not thinking of her suggestion first. It was, after all, a rather novel idea.

"Isn't there something I can do for you?"

"For me?"

"I write a fair hand, I've some ability at ciphering, and I can certainly read."

"You want to work?" No woman he knew ever worked. The idea was ludicrous. The skills she'd just enumerated were primarily acquired in order to extend invitations, to calculate how many bottles of wine to decant and who should be added to a guest list. Not to be used to calculate square footage, acreage requirements, and a list of stores. Although his mother kept herself occupied with various charities, she certainly had never offered to assist him. Poor women worked, rich women . . . well, he was not certain he knew exactly what rich women did, except spend an inordinate amount of time on their appearance. Of course, Monique had solved her boredom another way.

He scanned her face, looking for a latent jest. It was only incidental that the look continued down across the full bodice, across softly curving hips. He made an abrupt decision. She would not last long at it. What harm could it do? At least for a day or two, or until the novelty wore off, he would see this bride of his.

"Here," he said, pushing a pile of papers across the desk. From the table behind him, he picked up a large book and handed it to her. "I need these sums transferred into the ledger. Can you do it?"

"Of course I can," she said, wishing he wouldn't stare at her so. It was unnerving to be studied by him as if he sought a way into her mind, some unguarded gate. She smiled brightly and took the ledger.

He, in turn, wisely ignored the impish quality of her smile, and pointed to another desk at a right angle to his own.

"You can work there," he said, abruptly dismissing her. He hoped, before he became immersed in the details of the new mill, that she wouldn't damage his records too badly.

It took Katherine a good hour to understand the earl's record keeping system—a period of time that could have been greatly reduced had she bent from her resolve not to ask him several pertinent questions—and another hour to become used to the routine of posting the entries into the large, red leather-bound book. After that, the rest of the afternoon seemed to race by, nothing like the past week in which every moment had seemed mired in mud.

Occasionally, he would glance over at her with a quick look, as if to assure himself she was still there. She would sometimes meet his wordless scrutiny with a small smile, then turn away. He couldn't know, of course, that she had done all the record keeping at Donegan the last year, and that the occupation was strangely reassuring and routine to her.

Eventually, however, she became so involved in what she was doing that she no longer noted his interest, consumed as she was by her own. The amounts she entered in the ledger were far greater than Donegan's meager profits, and their destination intrigued her. There was something called coal slag which was delivered from Leeds to Portsmouth. Glasgow and London seemed inexorably entwined by the purchase and repurchase of barrels, whose purpose was alcoholic, she assumed. There was no end to the amount of cloth stored in a warehouse near London, and if the figures were actual yardage, then it seemed as though there was enough surplus of finished cotton to clothe every man, woman, and child in England. Nor was that the only odd entry. Evidently, her husband had purchased a vast amount of slates, and books, whose destination was not readily apparent.

When he stretched, stood, and opened the door for one of the maids bearing a tray of tea, Katherine took the opportunity to satisfy her curiosity.

"Tell me, why do some of your purchases seem so odd?"

"Define odd," he said, his smile strangely content.

"Slates and chalk. Paper and books."

For a moment he said nothing, as if choosing his words.

"Which mill are you posting?" he asked finally, peering over her shoulder at the stack of paper rapidly dwindling under her dogged concentration. "Ah, Lincolnshire. I imagine it's for the new school."

If she had not grown to know him so well, she would have missed the slight hesitation in his voice. Her perusal of him had its roots in fascination, wariness, and simple curiosity. None of which explained, after all, this intriguing man.

"A school?" Her smile was gentle, inquisitive. It was like the devil stating he owned part of heaven. "You own a school?"

"I don't. The village does. It's a cooperative venture between the workers and the mill."

"Who owns the mill?"

"I do." His smile was oddly slanted. A boy's smile, with enough whimsy to be charming.

"So you do own a school. At least part of one."

"Not just one, if you must be exact. About thirty now, I believe."

"Why?"

"Why a school, or why a dissolute rake such as myself would be interested in education?"

She had never leveled the accusation at him, even

though she'd used the words. She frowned at him in mock censure, but he only smiled.

"Do you really want to know, or was that simply a polite question?"

They had long gone beyond polite questions. If they had not, wouldn't their lives be somehow easier? Good morning, my lord, how do you do this morn? Fair, and you, my dear? Tepid tea and toast questions, with less malice and more ennui. Except, of course, that they had never been tepid with each other, had they? They burned or they raged, and even now, when all was politeness and civility between them, when the day was bright with washed sunlight outside and comforting with only pockets of shadows emerging within, the heat was still there. Contained and molded into little braziers they each kept hidden but intact, inside, waiting for that moment when fire would meet fire and the inferno would consume them both.

"Genuine interest," she said, truthfully. He expected her to demur. Most women did not wish to be entrapped in detail. Instead, she had surprised him once again, as she poured herself a cup of tea and sat in the chair opposite his desk once more. Her eyes sparkled, her shawl lay forgotten in the other chair.

It was, he thought, a scene of domestic tranquillity. Pity it was only a temporary truce.

"When the mills first began, they were little more than huge barns housing pitiful equipment. As we learned to harness steam, we built better and better machines. However, as with most things, there was a detriment inherent in the advantage. Skilled workers are at a premium, men who not only understand the workings of the machinery they operate, but who could teach others, also."

"Then the schools are for factory training only."

"At first, yes. But there was a problem. Men could not be trained to understand written instructions if they could not read. Nor could they calculate the output of a certain day's work if they could not comprehend simple arithmetic. That's when the schools began to also admit the children and begin at the beginning."

"Then you've a crop of willing workers for your machines," she said, her voice hard. "Do you think it quite fair to use children?"

He smiled at her militancy. Didn't she realize that the newfound wealth she enjoyed could have been so easily a product of those children? Except, of course, that it hadn't been that way for a long time.

"I will not excuse myself from greed, Katherine," he said, his tone oddly self-condemning. "Perhaps it is not so much villainy that prompts other mill owners to use children as it is simple expediency." Children were often used to slip beneath the threading arms, their small stature an asset, their fate not as important as the production of cloth. Until, of course, something terrible happened. Tragedy is often the source of introspection and change.

He had toured his own factories with less concern than he should have, until the day a child had lost his life. At that point, he had investigated the rules set up in his absence by mill managers concerned more with profit than with safety. It was then he had decided to change the way his mills were run and institute a few different rules. Rules that prevented child labor and restricted the hours that could be worked consecutively by any employee. It was an innovative approach, and one not fully appreciated by other men in his industry.

Now he only shrugged, his gesture less one of modesty than of an odd sort of restraint. What he had done is what he wanted all of England to do by passing the Factory Act. If he explained it to her, would she understand? He didn't know, and he was oddly unwilling to put her interest to the test.

"I feel the same way about child labor that I do about slavery. Both conditions are abhorrent. People need to learn to govern themselves. In a free world, men work better, their lives are full of purpose and meaning. They can wake each morning with a sense of personal identity. The era of the serf is gone, although there are those in the government who would wish for it not to be so. It is easier to simply carry on that which has always been done. Even if it's wrong."

She curled up in the chair, her feet tucked beneath her, her chin nestled in the palm of one hand. She was fascinated by this side of the earl she had never seen. The impassioned speaker, the man who expounded upon his beliefs. It was rather bemusing.

It was also irritating.

When she had been a servant, he'd lusted for her body and ignored her mind.

As his wife, he challenged her mind and patently ignored the fact that she even had a body.

"You are referring to the Corn Law, I expect," she contributed, looking at the window rather than at him. It had gotten harder and harder to pretend that she didn't miss his touch. Miss it? Dear God, she was so lonely at night that sometimes she went to the door that separated them and nearly turned the handle herself. Only the last remnants of pride, and some innate caution, stopped her. He might have forgotten Mertonwood, but she hadn't.

"Yes, in part," he answered gravely, unaware of the conflict within her. "The greatest force for change would be the Reform Act, which at present doesn't have a ghost of a chance for passage. It seems there are some who are threatened by the idea that every man should have a vote."

Freddie couldn't believe he was discussing politics with his wife. The most in-depth conversation he ever had with Monique concerned her flagrant immorality. Even that, she had waved off with a laugh. Yet, here Katherine sat, eyes sparkling with interest. She had handled the chore he'd given her with diligence, had neither complained nor quit after a few moments as he'd half expected her to.

The earl was in hell.

She leaned toward him in artless candor, her eyes sparkling with interest, and he wanted to rip off her clothes and take her on the hard wooden surface of his desk.

So much for restraint.

He was going to have to do something about this. Too many more days like this and he would find himself howling like one of the hunting dogs kept from a bitch in heat. Yet he knew, damn it, that no one else would do. Hadn't he already tried that?

It was not quite fair, he thought, his eyes drawn to her curving mouth. Damn it.

Aphrodite with a mind.

Returning to her desk, Katherine finished transferring the rest of the figures from one stack of receipts, leaned back in the chair, and murmured softly as she pulled against tight muscles. She would not trade this quiet companionship with him for anything. Soon Miriam would bring the children, and their time together would be supplanted by the children's needs.

"Finished?" he asked, looking over at her with a small smile.

She nodded. "Now I know why Jack likes to travel so much. It is a full-time occupation just reconciling expenses, isn't it?"

He smiled, wondering if she would ever know the effort behind it, or the restriction he placed upon his own, not so noble, impulses. "It is, and you've done the chore so well that I will expect you at the first of every month. Tell me," he said, standing, "have you enjoyed your stint at working?"

"Very much. Besides, it was the only way I could determine the extent of your vast wealth." The look on her face was teasing, not acquisitive.

"At least now you know where all the money goes."

"Speaking of which," she said, hesitating. "What do I do with mine?"

He turned away, irritated. With a few words, she skillfully altered the atmosphere. She was becoming quite adept at teasing, his Kat.

"Have I said something wrong?" His mood had changed so suddenly she didn't know the reason for it. "It's just that I have never had so much money, before. I don't quite know what to do with it."

"Pin money?" he asked, his anger evaporating with her innocent question. His problem, he decided, was in ascribing normal motives to Katherine. She had never been normal, or usual, or commonplace.

"There can't be that many pins in the world," she teased him, "and I don't gamble. The children's needs are met. I haven't the slightest idea what I should do with it."

"Gifts? You could fritter it away or spend it on sweetmeats."

"Good heavens, I'd grow fat as a sow!"

"There is that," he said, his face softening at her smile. "Do you want to invest it, then?"

"In your ventures? Why not? If I cannot trust the source of my wealth, who else can I trust?" Her laughter sparkled through the room like summer sunshine. He found himself growing hard again, a damnable condition almost ever-present when he was with her. He cursed his loins, his mind, and most of all, his memory.

"I do charge for advice, though," he said calmly, walking over to her chair.

"Oh? What is your fee?"

He stood behind her, and she could feel his presence only inches away, as if the very air grew heavier and wavered to accommodate him. His hands rested gently on her shoulders, not pressing but restraining nonetheless. Yet she didn't tense at his touch, nor did she flinch.

Her skin welcomed the contact, her mind warned her away. Her mind, however, was silenced by something far more visceral, more needy. The world stilled in that moment, the only sound in the room their breathing.

He bent and his lips brushed the nape of her neck, his fingers toyed with the tendrils of hair escaping from her coronet.

"A kiss?" So tender a tease, so gentle a whisper.

"It might be enough of an inducement for me to consider your financial situation."

He walked around the chair and pulled her up into his arms. She hung there like a rag doll, her arms looped around his neck. Her lips opened readily beneath his, succulent and ravenous, as if he carried sustenance in his kiss.

Something dark and wondrous opened up, as if a cavern were created around them, a blessed secret place shared only by the two of them. A sweet corner of her mouth beckoned his touch and his tongue flicked there, tasting, luring. One of them made a sound, a wisp of wanting, of need.

It was remembered heaven and it was future hell, and he cursed himself for being twelve times a fool.

He stepped back. "Remember your virtue, Katherine," he said, the words sharp and slicing and torturous. "God forbid I should worship at your chaste altar."

"Damn you," she said, her arms falling to her sides and then as quickly wrapping around her waist. To keep herself intact, to stop from throwing herself into his arms?

"You already have," he said shortly, and left the room with barely leashed fury.

Chapter 21

She had not lost her taste for outrageous behavior, Freddie thought, as she slipped into his office ready for more tasks by the time he'd finished his morning ride. What had happened between them yesterday was evidently not important enough to concern her. Either that, or she'd learned a new version of torture. He could not ban her from his office. It was, he thought later with a touch of wry humor, like wearing a hair shirt—exquisite relief when it was removed. Like it or not, Katherine was both his penance and his delight, and as wise as it might have been, he could not say no to her.

She was not going to be forced into the boredom to which she'd been confined until now, she reasoned, as she knocked upon his door with all the brazen courage she had ever felt. All she had to do was simply pretend that yesterday hadn't happened, and that she'd slept perfectly well last night. She would immerse herself in the work, and in her burgeoning interest in his commercial involvement.

Each day exposed some facet of his far-flung empire.

On the second day she learned of the sugar cane plantations, on the third of the woolen mills and the sheep farms. With her respect for a mind that managed all of this came a growing understanding of the power he wielded.

It was not power in the traditional sense of the word, such as that assumed by the monarchy or by an autocratic ruler. It was authority over his own finitely created dominion. He employed thousands of people, and any decision on his part could affect their lives, either to their betterment or not. And he never seemed to forget it. This sense of responsibility was so at odds with his previous behavior, and yet such an integral part of him, that Katherine thought it the single most important discovery she'd ever made about the man she'd married.

Each morning found her eager to begin again, and each afternoon she was vexed by the feeling that he had exposed so much and yet revealed so little. There was the increasing knowledge of his business empire, of course, and because the two were so intertwined, of the man himself. He did not hesitate to answer her questions, nor did he make the assumption that she would not understand. When he discussed an obscure point, he explained it to her, not in denigrating terms, but with a natural ability to illuminate a topic.

It was an almost perfect time, distilled drop by drop and untinged by the taste of bitterness, regret, or the acrid taste of the future.

Except for the feelings.

She consented to join him for dinner, but always found a different man from the one who was beginning to intrigue her during the day. This man was always sartorially perfect, bestowing a flawlessly crafted smile not duplicated in his eyes. He did not have the habit of brushing his fingers impatiently through his hair as the daytime man did, nor was he possessed of the quick smile that appreciated her ability to grasp a point with lightning aplomb.

This withdrawn, uncommunicative man was not the same person who allowed her to peer into his mind from time to time, to experience the excitement he felt about the new steamship or the possibilities of increased trade with America's southern states. The man who had summoned a picnic lunch they shared on the floor of his office one rainy day was not the same one who sat in the formal dining room watching her with hooded eyes over the rim of his wineglass.

And yet, both lured her.

Except for the feelings, it would have been perfect.

"You're out early this morning," Freddie said, and Katherine spun around, only to nearly lose her balance. She hastily grabbed the flowers before they could fall, scooping up the ones that toppled from the basket, crushing a few with hands that trembled too much.

She was the embodiment of spring, he thought, leaning down from Monty's back and plucking a flower from the unwieldy bouquet. He brushed it against her nose and she smiled, the effort almost real unless you looked into her eyes and saw real sadness there.

"You're going riding?" A ridiculous question, really, since Monty was making a shambles of the daffodil bed.

"Care to join me?" A soft entreaty, promising more? A truce?

She looked at the blooms in her arms, the cotton of her morning dress, then beyond, to the sight of Moncrief dazzling in the early sun.

"Yes," she said, smiling, releasing the flowers to tumble to the ground. "I'll be just a minute." She brushed by Monty. Her riding habit was new, purchased the day most of her day gowns had been ordered.

"No," he said, his hand reaching down to imprison hers. Too much time, and she'd reconsider. Or change from the springtime sprite she was now. Or be caught by one of the maids, or the housekeeper, or someone who needed advice or instructions or direction.

"Have you missed riding my horse?" he asked, scooping her up and placing her in front of him.

"A little," she admitted, unapologetic. He was a different man this morning, her earl. Elegant as always, a charming rogue, but something shone through his effortless magnetism. It was as if he watched her, studied her, searching for signs of something. Katherine looked away, unable to bear his scrutiny for too long.

Freddie walked Monty slowly to the copse of trees that hid Moncrief from their view. He stopped and leaned back, stroking her left leg. She shivered, but she didn't move away. Without warning, he hooked her knee up and, bracing her with his other arm so that she wouldn't fall, turned her in the saddle.

So that she was facing him.

"The French have a word for this," he whispered.

"Oh?" Her heart was beating so hard it was difficult to speak.

"You're half French, my dear, don't you know?" Below her ear, her pulse seemed especially strong, and it was this spot he touched with the tip of his tongue. He pressed it there for a moment, tasting salt on her skin, the echo of her heartbeat as it quivered beneath his tongue.

"Do you hold it against me?" Breathless speech. What was he doing, and why did she arch her head so that her throat was exposed to that strange caress?

He chuckled. What he wanted to hold against her was not her heritage.

He leaned back and smiled into her eyes. It was not a comforting smile or even a tender one. It dared, and it challenged.

"Ride with me," he said, and dropping the reins from

his hands, urged Monty only with his knees, the stallion instantly obeying the effortless command.

She would have been wiser to refuse. She should have demanded to be put down. She knew she wasn't going to do either. Something dark and powerful raced along her skin, heating her flesh, destroying any thought or desire to escape. This restlessness had started with his kiss, been churned by her dreams, set into motion by the gleam in his eye.

The momentum of the horse forced her to lean close to him, her own will urged her even nearer, until not even a breath could have separated them. His shirt was white, without ornamentation or design. Yet the chest it covered gave it shape, definition. He was hard and strong; she was soft and perfumed with spring flowers. Her arms extended around to his back. One of his large hands raised her face up for his kiss. The other reached below her knee and lifted one leg over his.

Below them, muscle and movement.

He bared her other leg, repeating the positioning, until she was barely touching the saddle at all. He was the cushion for her thighs.

His kiss was not deep but teasing. A slash of lips, a flick of tongue, until she ached to have him end it and kiss her properly. She angled her elbows back and framed his face with her hands, feeling the abrasion of his unshaven cheeks with suddenly sensitive palms. She held him gentle prisoner as he surrendered to her demands, smiling softly until her mouth covered his. Then all thought of smiles disappeared as she became the aggressor. Her tongue dueled with his; she tasted him the way she'd longed to for months. There was ravenous hunger in that kiss, and newly unearthed need.

She barely noticed when one hand cupped a breast, gently kneading, then plucked the nipple into a thorn point. She only knew that her breasts were becoming too large and too hot, and that his cooling mouth would feel so much more appropriate than the confining and itchy cotton.

Monty obeyed an order and lengthened his stride, covering the ground with blurring speed. Muscle and movement.

She leaned against his chest, out of breath and dazed. He was the anchor in a world rushing by. There was only him, and she clutched his arms with a force she'd never used before.

Only then did she realize that one hand had insinuated itself between her bared legs. He had pushed her skirts aside and raised her chemise. She looked down and then squinched her eyes tight against the erotic picture. Tanned fingers stroking white thighs. Muscle and movement.

"Look at me." Command, not request.

She held on to his shirt, clutching fistfuls of it between trembling fingers, and forced herself to look up. His eyes were intent, hard, riveting shards of green, his mouth a thin slash. His hand cupped her, fingers pressing into her swollen, wet softness.

He raised her then, a silent command to Monty slowing his gait. His warm palms cradled her bottom, then pressed her against him as one hand readied himself for her. Only when he was poised just below her did he signal his horse again, and the stallion slowly increased his speed. She hung on to his shoulders, her forehead pressed against his chest, her breath fanning the fabric of his shirt. He would not allow her to move. Not up. Not down, but poised. Barely touching, but touching enough to feel his heat, enough to know her own wetness.

An incomprehensible sound emerged from between her clenched lips. He deciphered it well enough, and smiled. He felt the same. Close to screaming with a need he understood only too well.

"Soon," he promised, and she arched against him, flattening her cloth-covered breasts against his face as if by doing so he could bare them and suckle her. "Soon," he said again, and lowered her just an inch. Muscle and movement.

It was not enough. She wanted all of him. She wanted him to fill her and touch her.

"Oh, God," she said, and it was not a prayer, but an oath.

"Soon."

He raised her again, away from him, and she nearly clawed him to remain where she was. He smiled softly into her wide, dilated eyes, and licked the outline of one delicate ear. He lowered her again, and she reached up and dragged his face down to hers, kissing him, biting his lower lip, demanding and hungry.

He slid one hand into her wetness again, stroking with sure and certain movements, wet heat easing his passage. Each touch on the swollen petals of her sex made him want to impale her, to thrust into her so hard and so deep that she could taste him. But not yet. Not until. . . .

"Oh, God," she moaned again, and he nearly moaned with her. He slowed Monty again and raised her once more. She fought him this time.

"Oh, God, please." The oath had become a prayer.

"Not God," he groaned, his restraint nearly gone. "Me."

With that, he rose up as he pressed her down upon him, and the noise she made at their coupling was almost a scream. Monty stayed at the canter he'd commanded and, in a moment, the motion was nearly going to blow the top of his head off—if he lasted that long.

Muscle and movement.

With an effort that went beyond godlike, Freddie signalled Monty to stop. Rearing back, he raised Katherine from him and, ignoring the gasps from his wife and his own too-engorged, painful state, forced himself to look into her dazed eyes.

His smile was small, mocking, almost rueful, infinitely cruel.

"I'm sorry for forgetting, my dear," he said. "I require a summons from you, don't I?"

The hurt in her eyes did not shame him as much as it angered him. She was not the one who had paced most nights in order to sleep. She had not drunk enough brandy to open a grogshop, in order not to tear down the door between them. If she dreamed, her dreams did not obsess her, as did his. Nor was she likely to spend the next few hours in painful contemplation of this little scene. The opportunity, however, was too pointed to ignore. He wanted an end to this, a finale to the games they played, the skirmishes. He wanted, fervently, futilely, desperately, an end to the war.

"Will you clutch your virtue around you like a blanket until such time as we are both ancient, Katherine?" His voice was nearly raw with restrained emotion. It was, he thought, the greatest single act of will he had ever demonstrated. A saner man would have impaled her and thrust into her and found release and then preached this damned object lesson. Yet, he doubted he had been sane since Katherine first entered his life. "Who do you save it for?" he asked, discounting the crudeness of the question.

"At least I don't spread myself as thin as you, my lord," she said, pulling her skirts down. She would not look at him. The flush caused by passion had been replaced by one of shame. "Or have you forgotten the slut you bedded on our wedding night?"

"At least jealousy is a better reason than revenge," he said, his hand slipping behind her neck and cupping her nape. She tried to pull away, but he only drew her inexorably closer. "Unfortunately," he said softly, "either motive is incorrectly placed on my shoulders, my dear. My wedding night was spent in blissful contemplation of the tavern's fire. Now that we've dispensed with jealousy, how do you justify your avenging angel pose? What punishment do you accord me for the very honest pleasure I enjoy with you?''

She could feel the breath of his words on her lips.

''I want you now, my sweet wife, with all the youth I still possess. With longing, and certainly pain, and with the memory of your cries in my ears. I want you, but there might come a time when looking at you will be like looking at a stranger.'' He dropped his hand and moved her so that she could slide from the saddle. Better some distance between them, before he got down on his knees and begged her to take him.

''I am just a man, Katherine.'' His words seemed to come from very far away, much farther than the distance between them. ''I'm not a statue. Not a saint. But let me tell you something about yourself, my dear. Neither are you.''

''I've never claimed to be.''

''Yet you wrap yourself in angelic anger and drape yourself in chaste revenge, my dear.''

''Stop calling me that,'' she spit out. ''I hate it almost as much as Kat.''

He was gone before she turned around.

It had been the most jarring experience of her life.

Nothing else even came close.

Frustrated desire, she discovered, was actually painful. The throbbing deep inside had stopped only after hours had passed. Yet, it was as if everything thrummed, just below the surface, kept in a state of readiness for him.

Him.

Her husband.

It was difficult to decide whether she never wanted to see him again or wanted to chain him to her. Either option seemed more than what was necessary and less than what she wanted.

It was one of the worst mistakes she'd ever made.

She could lock her door, but she had not yet discovered how to banish him from her mind. How, then, did she balance this growing respect for her own husband with her absolute despair? How did she cease liking the man? How did she stop wanting him?

It began like a mouse might nibble its way out of a paper cage. A tiny question, really, an infinitesimal hole of a question: why should she try?

Why was she doing this? Why was she putting them both through this misery? If this marriage was what she had decreed it to be, before God and enough witnesses to make it legal, she was destined to remain wed to him for life.

She could barely tolerate one more day of this; how could she manage a lifetime?

Was it loving him she feared? To love and not be loved in return. She'd had a taste of it with the duke's second son, and despite her optimistic nature and her hopeful disposition, that hurt had cut too deep. Katherine picked apart her motives like a good little mouse still nibbling on its fragile cage.

Was he right, then, after all?

Had it been revenge that kept them apart? Payment for all his sins? Buried anger was so powerful a weapon.

She had risked her life, frantically fleeing from Mertonwood in the dead of winter, to save his daughter from his intolerance, and not once had he mentioned his regret.

She'd met the village women's censure-filled eyes with a smile and a prayer to be able to forgive them their judgement of her, and he had not been there to protect her.

She had nearly died bearing his child and he had not even known.

She'd borne his child in secret, and he'd stolen him.

Revenge?

Certainly.

Dear God, it was a tasteless dish, this meal of retaliation.

No, that was not quite true, was it? The mouse's beady little eyes protruded from its encapsulation. Soon, the truth of him would be free.

This revenge tasted bitterly of regret.

Chapter 22

Katherine watched the approach of Miriam's coach with gratitude and deep relief. The past week had been a miserable one, with only herself and the ever-present servants for company. She no longer went to work beside her husband. He kept to a strict routine, remaining locked in his offices for most of the day, dining at a precise hour each night, retiring to his suite of rooms at midnight. Only chilling silence lingered between them, punctuated by his glares of hot anger.

It had been a difficult time, this week. Not for the boredom, as ever present as the servants, but for the very real feeling of shame. She was guilty of so many more sins than the ones for which she had castigated Freddie. The sin of pride, for one, a thick cloak of self-righteousness she had draped around herself. And the sin of lying. To herself, mostly. She had not been brave, or admirable, or self-effacing. She had not wanted to raise her children alone because of some noble virtue. She had wanted to punish him. She had been angry, far more enraged than even Freddie had dreamed.

It was a week of self-illumination, and she did not care for the picture of herself that was slowly, but inexorably, revealed.

Miriam exited the carriage as Katherine descended the front steps. Her daintily clad daughter, dressed in a walking gown similar to her grandmother's, gripped her tight around one knee. Katherine swung Julie up into her arms, buried her face in the softness of her hug, and squeezed back.

"Were you a good girl for—what did you decide to call yourself?" she asked over Julie's shoulder.

"Grandmère, in honor of your ancestry, my dear," the countess said with a smile. "However, we are still practicing the pronunciation. She has been an extraordinarily good child. Discount the fact that half of Freddie's staff has threatened to resign. Spoiled by silence, I imagine." She relinquished her most precious burden. Katherine cradled her son in her arms, but he squirmed and reached out for his grandmother. She was dismayed and looked at Miriam helplessly.

"Fickle, aren't they?" Miriam asked, smiling gently. She mounted the stairs, ignoring Robbie's bellow for attention. He had been surfeited by it in the last two weeks, the young scamp. But she had not the slightest remorse about returning the children to Katherine spoiled rotten—after all, what were grandmothers for?

She sighed, removed the pins from her hat—an enormous creation crowned with cabbage roses—and gratefully sank into the only comfortable chair in the downstairs sitting room. Moncrief had none of the snug comfort of her own home, the Dowager's Cottage located at the far end of the estate. Miriam had gladly moved there over six years ago, and spent her time divided between London and the two-story house much more suited to her personality. Now that Melissa was almost settled, perhaps she would remain in London for a while. Perhaps the house was not too large, she thought, revising her estimate as she watched her oldest grandchild race from one room to the other.

One of the joys of grandmotherhood, she realized with a relieved smile, was that one could return the children to their rightful owners when one became tired.

One, in this case, was extremely tired.

"How is married life, my dear?" she asked Katherine fondly, noting the smudges beneath the younger woman's eyes. She sincerely hoped it was a sign that pleasurable nightly activity had supplanted simple sleep. Miriam had arranged this time alone to prompt some sane behavior between these two.

"Detestable, Mother, but thank you for asking," Katherine responded with a smile oddly balanced between acute happiness and deep despair. It was an expression, Miriam thought, that did not bode well for the rest of the story. She sighed again, wondering when the two of them would simply realize that they'd be better served spending less time arguing and more time enjoying each other's company.

When she said as much, Katherine shot her a startled look and then shook her head.

Deny it all you wish, my dear, Miriam thought. It will not change the matter. Nor will it change the way you feel about my son.

"He is a confusing man, your son," Katherine said, almost-accusatory.

Miriam smiled at her new daughter-in-law in perfect understanding. "He is that, isn't he?"

"He changes from one moment to the next. One moment he blows hot, the next cold."

"Like a human being, you mean?" Miriam nodded in satisfaction as the housekeeper entered the room on a softly veiled knock, bearing a large silver tray. Katherine poured their tea and handed the countess a plate piled high with a selection of sandwiches. "Katherine," Miriam said after a few moments, "people are not statues. We're all subject to feelings. Even Freddie, logical as he is, cannot deny his essential human qualities. We are an emotional animal, after all. Tell me," she asked offhandedly, as she reached for another of the tiny sliced ham and cucumber sandwiches, "do you truly not realize that you love him?"

Silence in the sunlit room.

"Does it matter?"

The words were injected with a curious sort of lightness, as though they wafted toward the ceiling on strings. A confession of sorts, or a final admission whose burden had proved too heavy to bear? The question answered so many questions of its own. Does it matter? What an odd sort of declaration of love. How futile those three words sounded on the surface and yet how filled with hope.

Yes, she thought with barely suppressed mirth, it does matter, Katherine. It matters very much.

"My parents loved each other dearly. But they did not seem as confused about their feelings as I feel at this moment. They were always warm and tender toward each other. They shared their days and their interests. They didn't battle from dawn until dusk."

"Love comes in different guises, my dear. It's not always a quiet emotion, filled with warmth and tenderness. Sometimes it's rocky, treacherous. The greatest loves are sometimes not those that are comfortable or easy. What becomes difficult is when both people refuse to admit it."

"I suspect that it would be dangerous to admit love for your son, Miriam. I think Freddie would use it as the sharpest, most painful weapon."

"And you? Does he not fear the same of you? There is Monique to consider, Katherine. He is not a stupid man, my son, but he is still human, fallible, capable of being hurt. Could it be that he is loath to grant you the same weapon?"

It was a troubling thought.

Miriam stood and extended a hand to Katherine, pulling her easily into a hug. She held her away from her finally, looked intently into those troubled amber eyes, and smiled. "Think on it, Katherine. When you truly know your own heart, then you will understand Freddie."

The children's arrival put a strain on an already-tense relationship. Katherine and her husband had not spoken more than ten words to each other in days, and those only when forced to by the presence of the hovering servants. She skirted his proximity as if he were plague-ridden. He avoided hers as if she were danger.

The earl insisted upon sharing his children's lives, not because doing so put him into direct contact with his ever-absent wife, but because of the children themselves.

He discovered that he was easily charmed by an infant who blew bubbles when he ate, and that his daughter had an inexhaustible supply of energy like himself. In fact, he and Julie shared a great many qualities, and the daily emergence of their similarities induced a novel and strong parental pride.

She was a natural equestrienne, having an affinity for horses in general and Monty in particular, which both surprised and pleased him. Before they had been at Moncrief for a month, he had found a small pony for her use. Every morning the two of them could be seen trotting in large circles around the paddock, the earl's large roan overshadowing the petulant Shetland, Freddie's smile an identical match to his daughter's.

She had a mind, his daughter. A mind of her own, he often thought, but one that could be channeled and directed and tutored. That brilliant little mind, which sparkled back at him from green eyes so like his, need not be filled with only frivolous pursuits, but trained in math and the new science. She actually liked to take things apart, a discovery he made one afternoon in his office, when he had looked up to discover her in the act of demolishing his desk clock. He hadn't the heart to upbraid her, and the two of them had spent the better part of an hour replacing all the parts.

She was brilliant, his daughter.

And his son. Who could ask for a son to match Robbie? Cheerful and smiling, as sturdy and wholesome and healthy as any father could wish. Robbie had learned to recognize him now, and howled for him when he entered the room. His favorite nighttime activity had become playing patty-cake and peekaboo with his son, and telling his daughter a story unearthed from a memory of his beloved nurse.

He disliked the idea of his children being raised by a succession of nannies and governesses, and did not demur when Katherine made a point of it during one of their rare dinners together. When they were talking. When he saw her at all.

None of Constance's admonitions came to mind.

Katherine sat in the magnificent suite that had not, according to the countess, been decorated on her instructions. Which left only one person responsible, didn't it? Only one person who remembered that her favorite color was yellow.

Damn him.

She sat, and then she stood, and then she paced, and sat again. It simply didn't matter what motion her body was in; her mind refused to budge from one thought.

She did not *want* to be in love with the Earl of Moncrief.

Granted, he had garnered her respect.

He was a good father; that had been adequately demonstrated over the past weeks. He was a caring employer—just ask any of the servants who seemed genuinely proud to be in his employ. He was generous. He was also well groomed, handsome—if you cared for tall, broad-shouldered, saturnine looks—and he was physically fit. He was intelligent, self-driven, and well respected by his peers. He cared about the world in which he lived, and he felt responsible for others.

He had ignored her totally for weeks.

She did not want to feel a stirring around the region of her heart when her husband walked through the gate, leading his daughter's pony, leaning his head back to laugh without restraint at something Julie had said. She did not want to look up from her walks to see him standing at the window of his office, watching her with an indecipherable stare. She did not want to note that he had unbuttoned his shirt one more button to reveal the mat of hair upon his chest. She did not want to see him in the hallway and yearn to reach up and smooth his hair back from his forehead. She did not want to long to sink into him, like his children did, leaning their heads against that strong shoulder. Nor did she wish to put her lips against the thick, strong column of his neck, or beg him to extend his arms around her, because there in his arms she felt safe and secure. She did not want to respect him, to miss him. She most certainly did not want to ache for him.

He had accused her of using their marriage contract as a weapon of revenge, an accusation filled with bitter truth. If he yearned for her as she did him, he hid it well. She was the only one reaping the fruits of the burnt seeds she had sown. If he were frustrated, angry, wanting, it did not show. If he had found a willing partner among the servant girls, she heard nothing of it. Nor had he left Moncrief for more amorous pastures.

Yet, he had offered her whoredom. She had retaliated by stealing his child and his horse. He had planned to send Julie away. She had hidden her for a year and denied him knowledge of his son. He had taken her children, and she had bound him legally to her, with chains forged not in passion, but in anger.

They had too much to forgive each other for.

Once, just once, what would it be like to be in his arms? To do so without bitter words or ramifications or promises neither wished to keep.

She stood again, walked to the door that separated their rooms, heard the movement within, and placed one palm against the wood as if to communicate by touch. Can't you feel me here? Standing and waiting. Hesitant, unsure. Waiting for what? Absolution, or only passion? She leaned against the door, forehead pressed upon the wood, lips against the back of her hand.

Forgive me, Freddie, for hating you. Once.

Nights of cold winter and hot anger recalled. She had lain in her bed and nourished this anger with the same fierceness she now wished forgiveness for it. She had been too young to know that she doomed them both by this rage. They could not fashion a life together if it was bonded by only fury. She wanted life and laughter and promises from him. She wanted the sweetness of waking up beside him and knowing that she belonged there. That society would not frown; that her parents would have been pleased by him; that it was right, and just, and good to be wed to him.

She had not been a proper whore.

She wanted to be a better wife.

He was strong and ruthless and hungry in his desires and his passions. He possessed an iron will that had created a kingdom from a modest inheritance, had allowed him to survive society's censure, to go against current standards and acceptable limits to create his own. Would he willingly give up his anger? Or were they doomed to remain as they were, she with her nose pressed against the glass of his life.

Wanting more than she had wanted originally, saddened by her impulsive rage, hemmed in by her inexperience, her youth, and her one taste of power. Would she forever be damned by that idiotic contract?

That stupid contract. No, her own stupidity. To have denied herself his comfort for some errant pride. Because of anger, hurt, the feeling of betrayal.

That stupid clause.

She sat suddenly, eyes wide, and wondered if she had the nerve to do it.

There was nothing in the world to stop her, except for pride. It seemed somehow lacking when all was said and done, didn't it?

She sat at the mahogany escritoire and penned the note. The first attempt was abandoned, as was the second and the third. Too demanding, too much a supplicant, too cheerful. Finally, truth seeped through the words and spread upon the paper, and she read the fourth effort with a growing feeling of exposure. As if someone had reached into her chest and pulled her heart free.

It was too short, this missive that betrayed her heart. Perhaps it said too little, although she was afraid it said far too much.

He was not a raving lunatic yet, and he could only thank God for the favor. It was not, he reasoned, because of anything he had done. He had not, although sorely tempted, left for London, or taken up spirits as a hobby, or foisted himself on one of the maids.

Nor had he beaten his wife, although the temptation was growing.

She was driving him to distraction, and it would be a pitifully short journey. She had already led him by the nose to a lack of sleep, which interfered with his daily routine—he found himself dozing at his desk, for God's sake. He was painfully aroused on a daily, if not hourly, basis, and what patience he had left was expended on his children.

She was the consummate earth mother, sweet empathy curving the lush fullness of her lips. She spoke to her children in a low, warm tone that set his blood on fire, imagining it used on him during dark, moonless nights. She haunted the Moncrief library to obtain an obscure book on heraldry, and played the pianoforte at dusk when the swans curled their wings and summoned their young to nest nearby. He could hear her laughter from the perfumed gardens, soon to be dormant, and her step upon the landing, both free and without restraint, both signs of youth not easily curbed. She had summoned loyalty from his servants, most of them London-bred and too jaundiced to give their affections lightly. She spoke to his housekeeper of verbena and beeswax, to his butler of entertainments and Molière, to his gardener of poetry extolling simple blooms and then, without a pause, questioned him on grafts.

She was, damn her, too attractive, and too tempting. He wondered if he should just bite the bullet and ask his tailor to increase the size of his crotch, in case he remained in this state for the rest of his life. He would never get used to it, but he was getting tired of being half strangled by his own trousers.

Dear God, why couldn't You at least gift to us poor mortal men the sense to understand women?

He wondered, finally, in one of those long nights devoted to thinking, since it was evident sleep was a luxury not easily obtained, if what Monique had felt for his father was in any way similar to what he felt for Katherine. And had the fourth Earl of Moncrief loved Monique so much that they had both been willing to deny their background, their rank, privilege, and social standing, in order to be with the other? Seen in that light, and with a rare understanding, he found himself pitying his first wife. And because forgiveness follows easily on the heels of empathy, he eventually found himself exonerating both of them for any suffering they might have caused him. It had not been greater than their own, he realized, with an insight too close to pain itself.

Was that passion? he wondered. Or was it love? Or were the lines too blurred between the two to really know?

He was not pondering any great questions when the knock came upon his door. He was divesting himself of the shirt Robbie had gummed while he had walked with his son. He opened the door to find one of the footmen—in full, ceremonial green and gold Moncrief livery—extending a silver tray. He picked up the embossed envelope resting in the center of it, frowned, and then thanked the young man absently.

It bore a single monogram, and he tried to dismiss the sudden pounding of his heart as he sliced it open impatiently.

I want to share your bed tonight. Will you welcome me?

How like her. Straightforward, demanding, terse almost to the point of rudeness, but prevented from that by the simple question. Will you welcome me?

Does the earth welcome the sun, Kat? He frowned at the note clenched too tightly in suddenly rigid hands.

He was too damned selfish to say no.

This was no scene of seduction, she thought, as she knocked on the door between them an hour later. There was no circular table filled with silver dishes, no wine cooling on ice, no scented candles.

There was no light at all, and it took long moments for her to discern his shadow, seated in the chair at the far side of the room. Her heart pounded as she saw his stance, arms laying straight upon the arms of the chair, feet planted on the floor, his head at exactly the proper angle.

He only needed a scepter and a crown to rival the king, it was so arrogant a pose.

He was not going to make this easy.

Or maybe it would be too simple, she thought, as she realized his attire. He wore a robe, tied tightly at the waist but showing too much long leg, too much furred chest to believe he wore anything else.

If she had once come to him as a whore, he sat before her now as stud.

Yet, his experience had been far wider than hers. He had been charmed by her innocence, by her offering. She felt inadequate against the latent anger in his pose,

"Are you just going to sit there?" she asked finally, when nothing passed between them but looks too filled with meaning to read easily.

"What, pray, do you wish me to do? I am only a servant to your needs, my lady. You command, I obey."

She walked toward him, her eyes glittering with something he couldn't decipher. Was it anger, or was it tears that sparkled those dark eyes of hers? He hoped, fervently, that it was anger. Her tears had too much power.

She leaned toward him, placed her hands on his shoulders, and closed the distance between them. He remained motionless, an immovable object of enormous proportions, especially that part of him which seemed to swell at her presence. He continued to smile, a mocking gesture she thought. A pleasant expression, he reasoned, and one infinitely difficult to maintain as long seconds passed.

"Put your arms around me," she said, and he placed both hands on her hips. He drew her forward and she straddled his hips with her knees, sinking into the softness of the chair with a small sigh. He wanted to howl at the hot, moist secret feel of her. Because she was as naked as he, barely veiled by lemon-yellow lace.

"Tighter," she whispered as she leaned her forehead against his chest. He complied, extending his arms around her, pulling her soft, fragrant form closer until there was not an inch remaining between their bodies. Not an inch, only scant silk easily conforming to sensuous limbs and hot muscle.

She leaned her face into his neck, as she'd seen her children do a hundred times, breathing in the scent of him, all male, all Moncrief. Her nose touched his skin, nuzzling, then her mouth touched the pulse beat there, a gentle kiss with the power of lightening.

"Kiss me, please," she said, gentle Atilla. She angled her head, pressing her lips lightly against his. He kissed her then, a sweet kiss devoid of passion. A grandfatherly kiss.

"This way," she said, demonstrating how she wanted to be kissed. She nipped at his lower lip with tender teeth, remembering lessons learned from him too long ago. She traced his lips with a quivering tongue, no longer as shy as she was needing. In her belly a fire had begun. A rain of passion drenched her womb and flooded through her. She rocked against him, unintentionally wanton, sending sparks of sensation floating through her. Sending him into torturous delight.

Still, he did not move.

Katherine breathed against his lips, tracing a path through his hair with shaking hands. Her palms descended finally to his chest, then wound around his shoulders until she clutched his back. She lay her head against his chest and heard the frantic beating of his heart, a staccato rhythm matching her own.

Her mouth moved against his skin, sucking gently. Soft kisses, a darting tongue marked her passage across his chest, up to his neck where bone subsided back into flesh and left a vulnerable hollow.

His eyes were closed, his face carefully shuttered. A death mask of determination.

"You aren't going to make this easy, are you, Freddie?"

His name on her lips was an aphrodisiac of its own. Breathless, honey-coated sound. He opened his eyes, grinned down at her, and shook his head slowly from side to side.

She remembered lessons he had taught her.

She licked her lips slowly, watching his eyes all the while. She smiled softly, seductively. Dark goddess of passion, shadowed by night.

He went taut from the effort of restraint.

"I want you in me, Freddie," she whispered. "In me. Filling me, stretching me."

She reached down with a courageous eagerness and stroked the fullness of him. He was hard and hot, days of unrequited arousal having demanded their price. He shivered with her touch, and a bead of moisture spilled from him and wet her fingers. She smiled, mischief lighting her eyes.

"Do you want me, Freddie?"

His arms tightened around her, his hands no longer lax upon her waist. He pushed aside the yellow robe with shaking fingers. She watched his eyes as they looked their fill, rested on the sight of her breasts, her nipples darker than before Robbie's birth. She watched his eyes sparkle with remembered passion, watched the effect her words had upon them.

"Touch me here." She brushed his hands aside. He'd never seen anything so pagan, so wanton, so daring, as the sight of her sitting astride him, her breasts in her hands, the nipples lengthening under his stare. She offered herself to him as if she were a delicacy, a feast of eroticism.

"I want your mouth here," she said softly, touching one nipple with a tender finger. It was a provocation that tumbled him over the edge, as the tiger was released from his self-imposed prison and captured his prey.

* * *

Well, at least her memories had not played her false, Katherine thought, as she lay in her husband's arms and watched the far-off, faint signs of dawn. He slept, his head burrowed into her armpit, both hands resting in places they had stroked and teased only a short time ago. She sighed against the silk of his skin, and thought that she was a decadent woman, indeed, to want him to awake so soon.

No, her memories had not been distorted by time. Inside her, the echoing tremors of passion still throbbed. She sighed, and stretched carefully, turning toward him and enfolding herself closer.

Chapter 23

It was as if the night before had never happened.

When she awoke she was in her own bed, alone, and it was quite evident from his treatment of her over the next few days that she was doomed to remain that way until she sent her husband another missive.

He was following the letter of their agreement perfectly. She could not have wished for greater compliance to her wishes. Except, of course, that she didn't wish it anymore. Freddie, however, seemed not to note the difference.

The earl seemed to change as she watched, growing distant in some inexplicable way, although never stinting in the affection he showed his children. It was a new side of Freddie, a relaxed and easy man who smiled often; she actually heard his booming laughter on more than one occasion. The pride he felt in his children was as surprising as the love he showed them.

It was as if she'd been rendered invisible.

Dear God in heaven, she was jealous of her own children.

What kind of mother did that make her? What sort of monster had she become?

At night, his was the last face they saw, as he moved beside her to add a final tuck to their blankets, touched Julie gently on the nose, and stroked his palm over the downy softness of Robbie's head. During the day, he made a point of being with them, too.

One day, in fact, Katherine had gone to the nursery to fetch Robbie after his nap, only to discover from Abigail that the earl had taken the baby to his office. She found her husband immersed in his papers, Robbie entranced with another stack at his father's feet. Shreds of paper lay around him in glorious disarray. Occasionally, Freddie would look down and smile at his inventive son.

"He will destroy your office," she said, removing Robbie.

"Perhaps," was all he said, as he returned to the letter he was reading.

After that, it became an undeclared tug of war. Julie would be missing and the servants would tell her that her father had taken her on a picnic. Robbie would be absent from the nursery, and Abigail would roll her eyes and say that the earl had come to get him.

One day, she was late rising. She had spent most of the night trying to sleep, attempting to ignore both the incredible feeling of sadness that had crept upon her lately and the anger that filled every other emotional crevice. It was as if she swung perched on a pendulum of pure feeling. She finally slept, and then awoke late. Hurrying into the nursery, she found her husband stretched out on the floor in the middle of the room, with a box of tin soldiers open at his side. Abigail smiled, stepped aside for Katherine, and closed the door softly behind her. Katherine stood at the door, watching as Freddie explained each piece to Robbie, seated on the rug beside him.

"Here is your captain, Robbie. He leads your regiment

into battle." A blanket had been placed upon the floor, mounded into billowing hills and sharp ravines. Upon each hill were two regiments of tin soldiers, placed as if the battle were about to commence.

Robbie reached out and tried to put a cavalry soldier from the opposing army into his mouth. Freddie laughed and removed it. "Well, I suppose it is a way to win the battle, son, but I really don't think Hannibal ate his enemies." He smiled fondly at his son. Each day Robbie grew so much that it was almost possible to see the change every morning. Already, he was trying to walk, gripping his father's hands tightly and struggling for balance. He was alert, his eyes darting from one spot to another as if absorbing everything he saw. He was good-natured, never whining or complaining, but voicing his needs just the same. Freddie had experienced the full effect of infant tyranny when Robbie was hungry. He was the most brilliant of children, the most promising of babies, the most wonderful of sons.

"Don't you think he's a little young for war?" Katherine asked with a smile. The earl half turned and saw her standing in the doorway. His smile abruptly disappeared.

"Perhaps," he said, as Katherine entered the room, "or perhaps there is no better time than youth to learn how to win." He stood, bowed with a slight gesture, and left the room. Katherine bent down and retrieved her squalling son, who reached out to his departing father with chubby arms.

"It's all right, Robbie," she crooned to the child. "Your father will be back," she reassured him, even though she knew that Freddie would not return, not as long as she remained in the nursery.

He was, she realized, the perfect father. He truly loved his children. To both of them, he gave all the unconditional love she craved so much. Katherine watched their bonds forming with pain and bittersweet tenderness, and not a little shame to know that she envied them their father's attention, devotion, and love.

Because, it was quite evident he despised his wife.

Abigail raised one eyebrow when she handed her the note. She looked at Katherine and then shrugged.

This evening would be difficult enough without the servants' gossip, Katherine thought, shaking her head and looking through the armoire for something intriguing, lacy, and incredibly alluring.

Because, she vowed, nothing would be the same in the morning.

As tersely worded as the first one, this summons left no doubt in his mind that she wanted him.

Or that she was furious.

He prepared for the evening with the same care he'd taken for their first night. Nor did it escape his attention that he felt as if he were sixteen again, when his father had taken him to his favorite bordello and had him initiated into manhood by two beautiful, willing, and expensive prostitutes. Frightened, but very, very eager.

There was no doubt in his mind that this evening would be difficult. His wife was a virago when enraged. Aroused and enraged was a tumultuous combination, but one that made him contemplate the hours ahead with more than mounting anticipation.

He hungered for the confrontation almost as much as he hungered for her.

"You're very prompt," he said, his smile revealing white, even teeth. It was a face, she'd often thought, too striking to ever forget. God knows she'd tried.

The peignoir was the one designed for her wedding night. Too much lace and too little else. What it didn't hint at, it revealed.

"I've never known the value of being sociably late," she said, crossing to the window. Outside, it was barely dusk. Inside, only two candles had been lit against the encroaching darkness.

A knock on the door surprised him, but she strode ahead, reaching around the door to take the tray from the same liveried footman who'd brought him her second note.

Katherine placed the tray on the small bedside table, then stood and faced him. Her gaze was neither embarrassed nor shy. Kat, surprising, resilient Kat, was not like any woman he'd ever known. Nor had she lost that gift of outrageousness.

"You seem to want to play cat and mouse, my lord," she said, her glance daring and full of challenge. "I've brought you a few toys."

He should have been prepared for her next action, but he was exquisitely incapable of anything at this moment but being captivated by the sight of her. Nor was that behavior apt to change as she removed the peignoir and draped it over a nearby chair.

She stood, letting him look his fill of her candlelit nudity without flinching, without her eyes straying from his. One corner of his mouth turned up in wry appreciation for her courage as well as her beauty.

"Meow," she said softly, tauntingly, and he smiled, bubbling anticipation turning his blood to hot fire.

She knelt on the bed in front of him, her soft white breasts bobbing gently, her rounded derriere twitching in a teasing motion. He walked closer to the bed, divesting himself of his cravat and his waistcoat with swift, economical movements. She sat on her haunches, arms hugging herself, a posture that pushed her breasts into prominent position. At least, that's what it had looked like when she practiced in the mirror. She licked her lips, another gesture that she had carefully practiced, and then smiled when he froze, both hands on the buttons of his already-straining fly.

"What are you up to, Kat?" he asked, not quite believing that this delectable harlot was the conscientious secretary or the doting mother. He wasn't about to tell her that she had the power to turn him into a rutting monster just by smiling at him or trading witty barbs. No, he would see just how far this charade led.

"Meow," she whispered again and he laughed, then finished stripping himself of evening clothes.

It wasn't fast enough, she thought, watching as the elegance fell to the floor, only to reveal even more beauty. She thought she would explode by the time he was finished. She was throbbing and miserable and she hurt, but she wasn't ready to admit it yet, or confess that if he didn't take her completely, and fill her absolutely, and make it last and last and last, she would hold a gun to his head and force him to perform.

When he reached for her, she slipped out of his grasp. One touch, and she would flame in his arms like a tinder box closed too tightly.

"No," she said, gently, "it's my turn." The look she gave him was fierce, but that was not why he lay back among the pillows and stretched out before her avid gaze. It was the sight of those magnificent nipples, straining and so engorged that it looked as though they were filled with milk. Not milk. Passion.

She was so hot, his Kat.

The porcelain bowl was covered, but he should have known the contents before she uncovered it, before she tipped it over his chest and let a few droplets spill onto his skin. But he hadn't, and desire raced through every nerve ending as she lapped the cream from his skin like a starving kitten. When she edged up to him, her knees brushing his side, he prevented himself from grabbing her only by gripping the coverlet with both hands. The touch of her teeth gently scraping his nipples almost levitated him from the bed, but the greatest shock was still to come.

Outrageous Kat.

The cold, thick cream should have cooled him, but it had an opposite, and immediate, effect. He'd been suffering too damned long, but he'd suffered before. He'd gone without relief in the months before their marriage, but nothing like the next few minutes. Nothing was like right now, with her breasts bobbing against his thighs, and her tongue licking up each droplet of cream from his engorged length. If she didn't make him explode in her mouth, he was a greater man than he thought.

He tasted, she thought, not like cream, but like salt and a not unpleasant metallic flavor. The cream mixed with his own fluid, and she chuckled as he arched his hips upwards, a small sound suspiciously like a moan emerging from clenched lips. He was hot and smooth, as silky as the inside of her mouth. She bathed him with her tongue, lapped at him, and took him between her lips and sucked, her cheeks hollowing.

She was suddenly upended, and thrown on her stomach. He entered her from behind, levering an arm around her waist and hauling her up until he could grip both breasts with his hands. He pulled her back, close to him, and then one hand upended the bowl's contents onto her bottom, rivulets of cream dripping down to mix with her own hot moisture and his.

Someone moaned, and Katherine didn't know if it was him, or if the sound came from her own lips.

His strokes, short and hard, lengthened, calmed, until they were too slow, too restrained. She wanted more. She must have more.

"Not enough," she muttered, and thrust herself backward, demanding, greedy. His hands clamped upon her breasts, her nipples peeking through his fingers. His breath was only a harsh rasp, hers interspersed with pleas and demands.

She screamed, finally.

He collapsed on top of her, knowing his weight was too heavy. Knowing, too, that he could not move even if the room was on fire.

It was a strange thought for a man so satiated, but he wondered right at this moment why he felt so damned disappointed.

Chapter 24

When she awoke, he was gone.

Not simply gone from their bed, but gone from Moncrief, riding away just past dawn, one of the footmen said, to London. He had no need to pack a valise, the servant had answered honestly and not unkindly, as the earl had closets full of clothes maintained at his townhouse. No, he didn't know when he was coming back. Truth to tell, the earl hadn't said a word from the time he'd asked for Monty to be saddled until he'd left like the hounds of hell were trotting at his heels. He'd just stood there on the front steps, looking out toward the east, as if he'd never seen a dawn before.

Julie asked about her father constantly; he'd long since become a hero in her eyes. Robbie chortled happily as they passed the entrance to the earl's office suite, then broke into tears when it was evident they weren't going to visit Papa.

Katherine felt like crying with her son. Why London? Why now? What was he doing, and with whom? Most importantly, why had he left? She had no answers to those questions, and no answer to the one question that kept her awake at night.

When was he coming back?

His letter arrived a week later, carried by a young courier she had seen once at Mertonwood. Katherine left him standing in the foyer as she opened it, read it once, and then paled. She turned and offered him refreshment, then excused herself and walked up the steps to her room. Once there, she closed the door and locked it with trembling fingers.

Once again, she unfolded the letter and read it.

> *I have begun steps to ensure the children's legitimacy and, for their sake, would prefer to maintain the illusion of an outwardly happy marriage. Moncrief is yours until Robbie inherits it.*
>
> *Froedrich Allen Lattimore*

She couldn't even damn him. She was oddly without energy, without will right at the moment.

The ennui lasted an hour, during which time she found herself growing curiously hot. She felt her forehead, and it was cool to the touch. She dribbled water on her wrists, but that changed nothing. It was only later, when she was dressing for dinner, that she realized the feeling she was experiencing was not so much physical as it was mental.

She was getting angrier by the moment.

She had been so incredibly stupid.

She had fought for Julie's well-being by running. She had protected Robbie by hiding. She had saved herself from the earl's deadly charm by simply avoiding it. She'd told Miriam that she was tired of running from her problems, but whenever there was a challenge, she had stepped aside, rather than facing it. She had sought Bertha's protection, or Miriam's, or she had hidden behind her children.

Even when she wanted her own husband, she'd not been truthful. She'd been willing to live the same way they had lived at Mertonwood, strangers in the daylight, lovers at night.

No one was going to rescue her now. Not Bertha, not Miriam. Her parents had long ago ceased to worry, and Constance's ghostly axioms were drowned beneath the voice of her own conscience.

By thc time she had finished her solitary dinner, eaten in great state in the dining room, Katherine had made her plans. She addressed her concerns to the butler, had Abigail agrcc to ccrtain conditions, then summoned the head groom from his quarters over the stables. By nine that night, everything was in readiness.

By dawn, Katherine and her two children were on their way to London, complete with coach and four, trunks tied to the top of the massive conveyance, Abigail tucked in beneath a blanket, Robbie clutching his tin soldiers, and Julie's pony trotting along behind.

If her husband was going to announce that their marriage was over, then he would damned well have to tell her to her face. Because she was going to do anything necessary to get her husband back. Not on her terms, but by meeting together as adults who know that they have everything to lose and nothing to gain by staying apart.

It was her father who supplied a gem of advice, a memory that caused her finally to smile. He had told her, when as an eight- year-old she stood in front of him, rubbing her bottom and demanding rather rashly to know why he had swatted her, that it was because she had refused to listen. If she was going to behave like a mule, then he would treat her as such, and the only way to get a mule to go the way you want it to travel was to get its attention. She had not cared for being likened to that stubborn animal, but now the comparison was rather apropos, she thought, smiling broadly.

Because she was going to get Freddie's attention. Even if it meant hitting him between the eyes with a club.

She didn't like London any better the third time than the second or the first. Yet she certainly was coming up in the world, she reasoned. The first time she'd entered the outskirts of the city, she'd been a paying passenger in a coach occupied by garlic-smelling men, one chicken, and an old crone who insisted on smiling and revealing blackened gums. The second time had been atop Monty, and neither she nor the horse had cared for the noise and the stench. Being transported in a specially constructed carriage was certainly better than her first two ventures, but not by much, especially since Julie had decided she missed her father enough to sob inconsolably for the last twenty miles, Robbie was suffering from a case of colic that made traveling with him a nightmare for everyone. Abigail would not stop sniffling for her temporarily lost love—evidently, the footman who had delivered the note to Freddie rigged up in ceremonial garb had done so because of Abigail's giggling kisses.

They arrived at dark and were greeted by Peterson, the all-knowing butler, who informed her that the earl had been called out and the dowager countess was dining with a friend. She dispatched him to prepare rooms for her traveling companions and dragged herself up the stairs holding Robbie, Julie in tow behind her. The nursery had been transformed since she'd seen it last into a fairy tale place with murals painted on the pristine white walls and all sorts of toys mounted on shelves beside the fireplace. A fire was quickly built, and the chill in the air dissipated in moments. Fluffy blankets lined the crib to prevent a chill, and Julie was ensconced in her bed only yards away.

Abigail, her tears subsiding with Katherine's promise to recruit the young footman to London, ate her dinner at the nursery table, promising to report quickly if either child developed the sniffles. The latter part of their journey had been spent racing through a cold and piercing rain.

Katherine descended the stairs and entered the room Peterson had earmarked for her. Unlike her previous accommodations, this room connected to the earl's. Poor Freddie, she thought. Between Peterson's interference and her own will, he didn't stand a chance.

"It's about time," Miriam said, sweeping into the room the next morning without knocking, and not looking the least perturbed by her lapse in manners. She did look, however, as if she would like to throttle her son, an emotion she readily acknowledged. "Do you realize what that idiot son of mine is doing? He says he is leaving for America as soon as the bill of legitimacy is passed. Dear God, will he never have any sense?"

"Neither one of us has shown much of that," Katherine admitted, looking down at her nails. She had chewed the second and the third almost to the quick on the journey here. At the rate she was going, she would be lucky to have fingers left by noon.

"What am I going to do with the two of you?" Miriam asked, throwing her hands up in the air and acting thoroughly French at that moment.

"Help me?"

If the fifth Earl of Moncrief had seen the look that passed between them, he would have hastened his departure plans. As it was, he was immune to any precognitive warnings, being immersed in trade negotiations for a lucrative shipping contract transporting rum. He was adamantly refusing to fill his hold with slaves on the outward-bound run.

He had a busy evening planned, and this meeting was not going well. Perhaps it was due to the intransigent nature of his partner in the venture. It could possibly have been due to his inability to concentrate. That had been his curse since he first met the woman—why should he think that simply because she was out of his sight, Katherine would ever be out of his mind?

Damn it.

It was a loud curse, a vocal imprecation, and something that had never previously occurred in business transactions with the Earl of Moncrief. He was known for his equanimity, even in the most delicate of negotiations. The fact that he had allowed his displeasure to be known was unlike him, and it greatly disturbed the men seated around the table. Evidently, this venture did not please the earl, and if it displeased him, then it bore further investigation. So, for one mere slip of his tongue, he spent two wasted hours recapping figures that had been correct from the beginning. It was not a lapse he would make again.

He strode up the stairs of his townhouse, late and irritated. It did not bode well for the remainder of the evening. He had planned rationally, logically, and systematically to rid himself of the ghost of the Countess of Moncrief by an evening of debauchery.

He had almost reached his rooms when his mother swept out of hers, dressed in an off-white gown that sparkled in the candlelight. She looked like a snow queen. He inclined his head in tribute to her beauty—his mother had aged well, he thought. She smiled back, then preceded to destroy his plans for the evening.

"I am delighted to inform you, my son," she said regally, in frosty tones worthy of the snow queen he'd likened her to, "that we have a visitor." She extended her arm out to her side, and a vision in gold and white stepped forward.

"Your wife," his mother announced, quite unnecessarily.

Katherine was beautiful, but not as radiant as she'd been two weeks ago when he'd awakened beside her and knew himself damned. She had come to him in need and he had found himself, absurdly, ironically, wanting more. He ached to keep her in his room until there were no more dawns, or the world stopped, gently imprisoning her until she admitted that there was more than passion between them, more than hot desire that erupted each time they touched. He wanted to hold her to him and beg for words she'd never said, words of love and affection that should have been shared between them by now. He'd wanted her then, on that morning, yet he knew that when she awoke nothing would be changed; they would be back to their games and their battles.

Damned.

He had pretended, while she slept, that it was different. That she had come to him out of love, not need.

In that moment, when he looked at her and saw the shining light in her eyes and the mischievous smile on her lips, he knew that he lived in a world of dreams to think it could ever be anything but what it was. She'd married him for the children she loved. As a man, he was superfluous. He was nothing more than a bank, a father figure, a companion on those occasions that called for one, security against the future. She would never forgive him for his sins, and he didn't know if he could ever beg for her clemency.

For the first time in his life, he had no control over his future. It was an odd feeling, this, to know that despite his efforts, any pleas he might make, any prayers he may utter, nothing would ever change. He had money, property, a title, health, acceptable enough looks, and none of it was worth a damn at this moment.

He would avoid her and pretend not to feel the need that was so much more than physical. She would avoid him until her healthy body craved release.

Damned.

"We won't keep you, dear," his mother said, as she followed Katherine down the stairs.

He didn't say a word as he watched them.

The ballroom was crowded, the air stifling despite the chilly weather outside. Katherine and Miriam sat on an overstuffed couch, enduring the heat in silence. Katherine sipped the warm ratafia with distaste. It was the waiting that was the worst. She had declined numerous invitations to dance, explaining that her husband was due to arrive soon.

She hoped she wasn't lying.

It had been an odd evening, filled with pleasant surprises that did little to offset the awful waiting. Jeremy and Beth had agreed to share the evening with them, and on the trip to the Raverston ball, she'd been regaled with the latest wonderful actions of the new ducal heir. She'd watched the devotion between Jeremy and his wife, feeling an odd sort of twinge around her heart at the obvious love between them.

It was Duncan McCorkle who surprised her the most, however. He'd leaned over to her after greeting Miriam and pressed a folded note into her hand.

"I thought you should have it," he said cryptically, before whisking Miriam off for a dance.

Inside was a short note, along with a second sheet of paper containing an address. The note was confusing, but not because it was written in French. She decided that she would solve this mystery later.

By midnight, it was evident that Freddie was not going to appear.

Miriam signaled to her younger son, and Jeremy wove through the crowd to be at their side. His wife was saying her farewells on the other side of the room and would join them shortly.

One look at Katherine's face told the tale well enough.

"I'm sorry, Kat," he said, adopting Freddie's pet name for her.

She had honestly thought he would come for her but he hadn't, and she didn't want pity right now.

Katherine smiled, but it was a weak effort at best. She truly wanted to reassure Jeremy that she was fine, but it was such an effort that she finally just shook her head and let them lead her toward the carriage, as if she were devoid of sight or incapable of movement. There was a bubble inside her chest, something she feared would break soon, and if it did, she would cry all the tears it held. She didn't want to cry in public, she really didn't, and it was the frantic look in her eyes that spurred Jeremy, Beth, and Miriam to nearly race to their carriage.

It was Peterson who told her that the earl required her presence as soon as she arrived home. She found him in his study, standing over his desk, carefully rearranging a sheaf of papers in a large trunk. Those that were not packed were set aside. He did not look at her but worked with great deliberation, completely oblivious to the sepulchral silence in the room. She concentrated on his fingers, his hands, their power and grace evident even in such a mundane chore.

He was dressed in his working clothes—a white linen shirt and black trousers. His hair fell forward over his forehead in artless disarray, and she longed to brush it back into place. Or to reach up to his face, and place the palm of her hand against his cheek. She did neither. It was not shyness that prompted her to remain still, but a sudden, horrible feeling that she should not stay to hear the words he would soon voice.

A premonition too soon given life in reality.

"You are leaving?"

"I am," he said, his tone oddly tender, his voice as soft as the smile he wore. Betrayal with a kiss.

"Where?"

"Does it matter?" His shrug barely dislodged his shoulder. He searched his desk as if it were of more import than the sudden, stricken look in her eyes. It would be too hard to look at her and then leave her.

"I tried, Katherine," he said, his voice still soft, his eyes still calm, "to give you everything you could want. All I asked for were my children. I thought they would be enough. Yet I find, somehow, that I want more." Much more. His tender smile altered shape, became self-mockery.

"I don't understand."

"No, you don't, do you?"

"Is it another woman? Do you love someone else?" He smiled at that. When had he the time, what with mooning after her for what seemed like years?

"No, Katherine, believe it or not, there isn't." There never really has been, my dear, which is my problem, not yours.

"Where are you going?"

He decided to answer her. Perhaps that knowledge would stem any further questions. "To America. Eventually to Indiana. A friend has started a community there. All for one, a dubious concept."

"But why now?"

"I have to, Katherine," he said somberly, the mocking grin suddenly stilled, his eyes chips of green ice. "Because if I don't, I will grow to hate you."

She flinched at his words, and if it were possible, her eyes widened even more.

The air was still, the room too quiet.

He eyed her with an appraising glance. His auburn-haired witch, too young to be the mother of one child, the protector of a second. She stood before him with pleading in those large dark eyes, her cheeks flushed with . . . what? Embarrassment, chagrin, torment? Beautiful, cold Kat. He had wanted her so desperately, and all she wanted was some obscure vindication. He hoped to God that absolution kept her warm at night.

"I have wanted you," he said softly, "craved your presence, sought your companionship. All I ever got was the rather chill, autocratic persona of Katherine. I miss Kat. Where did she go, I wonder?"

"She never left."

"Oh, but she did." His smile was tinged with self-deprecating humor.

"Don't you want to know why I've come to London?"

He smoothed one hand through his hair.

"To carry the battle forward? I've found that it's difficult to continue a war when one of the combatants refuses to further the campaign, Katherine. I don't want to play anymore."

"Why did you leave me that morning?"

She always cut to the quick, didn't she? Direct Katherine. Because what we had, my sweet child, was almost, but not quite, enough. What would she say if she knew he almost wished she'd stayed chaste and inviolate? To hold her close and feel her passion was, surprisingly, more painful than never to touch her. He wanted her heart, her trust, her mind. He was a fool to want more.

"Don't worry, you'll have as much money as you could possibly spend in two lifetimes," he said, not answering her question. "You will have Moncrief, a title. and two children who adore you. And you won't have the bother of a husband. But then, you don't now, do you?" An edge crept into his voice, nudging away the softness. He smiled again, as if in apology for revealing such crudeness. "We shall be the oddest of couples, Katherine. Married, yet not. A perfect solution for you, I believe."

"Can't we talk about this?"

"No," he said softly, gently.

She took a step forward, placing her fingers upon the edge of his desk. For balance? For connection? His rested in a similar fashion.

"But what about the children?"

"Ah, yes, the children. Do you know, they are the only reason I regret leaving. I have grown to love them, but not enough to live in an armed camp. I want peace. An odd commodity, to be sure, but if I have to fight a war, I do not wish the battlefield to be in my own home. We make love exceptionally well, Katherine, but I'm afraid it just isn't enough. I don't want my children to grow up like I did, with a father hell-bent on finding affection by bedding anything in a skirt and a mother bearing a perpetually martyred expression in her eyes. Better one loving parent, my dear, than two who hate each other."

"I love you, Freddie." Four words to seal her pride and cauterize around the edges. Four words to beg him to stay. Four words, dear God, how could she compress all of her sudden fear and always-longing into only four words?

He did not move, did not react to her words. If she had been blessed with darkness, she would have not seen the look of pity in his eyes. That, and something even more damning—the slight smile on his lips.

"Spare me the avowals of undying love. I do not believe you, you see. Words are so damned easy. It's actions that count. And our actions tell too much, don't they?" He turned, retrieved a book from a shelf, held it too tightly between fingers which felt cold and numb. "I wronged you, Katherine, and I'm sorry. For all my sins, I'm sorry." His smile was touched with an absurd tenderness, at odds with the words he spoke. "I've learned from my mistakes, my dear, but you keep punishing me for them."

"Is there nothing I can say?" Her voice was filled with supplication, her outstretched hand too beseeching a gesture.

She would always remember him at that moment, with his tender smile and deep green eyes. He folded his arms across his chest and looked at her, really looked at her, as if seeing her after a long absence. It was a gentle look, appreciative, soft, painful in a way she could not explain. It pierced her, this look, as if he memorized her.

"Katherine," he said softly, his voice low and stirring, just as it had always been, "did anyone ever tell you that you have a damnable sense of timing? You're too late with too little."

He strode to the door and opened it soundlessly, looking back at her one last time. She would not turn. She didn't want him to see the tears she'd been unable to restrain.

"I lost you once and bore the pain of it," he said, his voice still soft and without anger. "The second time will be easier, I think."

He closed the door behind him with a soft thud.

Chapter 25

"What the hell do you mean, she's left the children?"

The sighs, sobs, and caterwauling that greeted his innocent question was enough to wish him back into sleep. But he had been pulled none too gently from his bed at dawn by his mother, who looked like she wanted to plant her fist in his face. The same woman who now stood in front of him weeping like a banshee.

"If I don't get some kind of answer soon," he began, only to be silenced by a fulminating glare from his daughter, who then crawled up on his lap and sobbed into his neck.

"Mama said goodbye," she sniffled into his shirt, and something squeezed around his chest. He looked at his mother and she only nodded at him, wiped the copious tears from her cheek, and attempted to stifle her own sobs. She was not doing a credible job of it. Abigail was drenching Robbie, who was contributing to the melee by howling at the top of his lungs.

Where the hell was Katherine?

The answer to that riddle might be in the note his mother had thrust into his hands at the same time the door had opened and a herd of crying women—and one soiled baby—entered the room. He reached to his side and pulled the envelope free, staring at it with misgivings and not a little foreboding. It was Katherine's crested stationery. Why did he think that he didn't want to read it?

And why the hell hadn't he left yesterday?

Glancing around at the whimpering assembly, he sighed, nudged his daughter's head down an inch, and opened the envelope.

He was going to kill her, he decided. No, that was too quick. He was going to condemn her to the same hell he was currently undergoing.

> *Dear Freddie,*
> *You win.*
> *Tell them, please, that I love them.*

He was going to find her, and then he was going to kill her. But first, he had to get dressed.

"Out!" he demanded in a voice that even his mother obeyed. His daughter's eyes widened, and he kissed her gently on the nose. "I've got to go find Mama, puss," he said with a smile. She smiled entrancingly at him, her world returning to proper order with those few words.

His wife had a lot to answer, he thought with a frown as he locked the door behind the sobbing horde.

Not the least of which was why she had really left. Those few words were not as much a concession as they were a challenge.

It was a damned good thing his bags were already packed.

Winter in France was no more appealing than winter in England, Freddie thought, shivering for the five thousandth time in five minutes. But, the snow was letting up, he could see signs of occupation ahead, and she was only half a day in front of him.

Imbecilic woman. Damned female. Idiotic loon.

He had punctuated his journey with epithets he had every intention of repeating to his wife when he managed to catch up with her. Every damned one of them. From a roar to a whisper. He was thoroughly miserable, cold, wet, and so enraged that he could not hold on to the reins of his temper any more than he could the frozen leather leading strings of this pitiful mount he'd managed to retrieve from the last town. He'd probably rescued him from the stew pot, he thought, snorting in disgust and thinking of the dinner he'd purchased at that dreary inn the night before. Since then, he'd had something the French called cheese—even in frozen winter, it oozed—and bread that was as hard as his boots.

Yes, his wife had a great deal to answer for when he found her.

Which was only a matter of time, wasn't it?

His mother's lover—a confession of knowledge that startled his mother but made Duncan's eyes gleam with humor—reluctantly parted with the information that it was he who had sought out Katherine's family after conferring with Jack. And it was Duncan who had imparted the news that she had a grandfather alive, well, and overjoyed at the news that his granddaughter existed. Damned French. Damn Duncan. Damned horse.

He was not surprised to find himself at the crossroads in Verdun; the only thing good about the whole journey had been the directions. He turned left and followed the track as it wound upwards to the castle perched upon the hill. Even in the dusk, it was apparent that this was no ordinary house. He didn't give a damn if it was Versailles. His wife had no business traipsing around the French countryside. Especially when the French still hated his countrymen with a passion equally shared by the English for the French.

Not to mention the fact that he was damned tired of chasing her all over one country or another.

He squinted, but it was not a trick of the light. Up ahead, barely at the next turn, was a small black traveling carriage, its driver nearly folded over himself to ward off the cold.

He spurred the tired horse up the hill, promised him a meal of oats and ale if he didn't die on the next curve, and reached the door of the carriage as the driver turned curiously toward him.

Asking two questions in his fractured French, Freddie received an assent at the first and a short set of directions at the second. Without a pause, he managed to trade places with the driver, press a few gold coins into his palms, and gave him instructions on the care of the pitiful, but dependable, horse.

She felt the change in direction and thought nothing of it. She'd paid as little attention to the end of her journey as she had the beginning or the middle of it. She'd parted from the earl, and although she found that her rank, if not her money, had made the journey quicker, it had not necessarily been easier. That would require a peace of mind she did not possess. Peace for which Freddie had so longed.

She banished him from her mind the same way she had a thousand times in the last three days. It was laudable practice for the rest of her life.

She was very much afraid he was going to ignore her now, as studiously as he had the night of the Raverston ball. And she was even more afraid that her gamble had not paid off at all—perhaps he was right, and she was too late with too little.

When the carriage finally stopped, she peered out the heavy felt curtains, but could only see the outline of a tiny woodcutter's shack, misted by snow and mantled by dusk.

She was about to open the trap to question the driver when the door opened, and a mocking voice shattered her composure.

"Good evening, madam wife," he said, and sketched a low bow. She stared, openmouthed, at him, unable for once to find the words to greet him. "Kat got your tongue?" he asked, humor at his own pun showing in his shadowed eyes.

"Freddie?"

"The one. The only." A sardonic smile wreathed his mouth. "You disappoint me, Katherine. I was expecting a vitriolic insulting match. I've come primed and ready."

"I've nothing to say."

"Pity," he replied, reaching in and scooping her effortlessly from the carriage seat. She didn't think to fight him, so bemused was she by his presence, by the dark light in his eyes, by his growth of whiskers—an oddity for the sartorially elegant earl.

"I'll have enough words for both of us," he threatened, walking briskly to the hut and opening the sagging door. Thank God, he thought, as he saw the store of wood stacked outside the dilapidated porch. "Stay there," he commanded, and she did, not even removing her cloak or her traveling bonnet or her gloves until he had seen to the horses and returned. She'd done nothing about the fire, had barely looked around. All she could focus on was him.

He built a fire, returned to where she stood, her eyes wide and dark, and muttered to himself as he untied her bonnet strings. It was damned hard to yell at a woman when she was staring at you as if you were a ghost. Well, maybe not too difficult, he amended, as he remembered the hell she had put him through.

"What did you think you were doing, running away like that?"

"I wasn't running. I've decided I'm not going to run anymore. I simply quit."

"You quit?" She was trying to drive him daft; it must just come naturally with her.

"Yes." She fiddled with the latches on her cloak, and he brushed her hands aside impatiently and unfastened them for her. He lifted the sodden garment from her shoulders, then did the same with his own greatcoat. "You said that you wanted peace in your home. So do I."

"Not at the price you demanded, Katherine."

Her look was vulnerable, allowing him to see the emotions so painfully evident in her eyes. Regret. Shame. Something he could not quite identify, because he'd never seen it so openly displayed.

"If I send you a wagon full of notes, Freddie, one for each night of my life, would that be enough?"

Her words were softly spoken and he frowned at them. There was something missing here, something vital that he understand. He was not an obtuse man, but he had ached for what he saw in her eyes for so long that he doubted its presence now.

"And why would you do that?"

"Because I'm your wife."

Silence while he digested this interesting bit of information. It was the first time she'd announced it, and to do so with such fervor showed not that she was willing to quit the fray, as she had indicated, but that she was very much a part of it. He smiled, and she should have been warned. It was a smile devoid of mockery or bitterness. Instead, it was laced with a certain male triumph. Excusable, he thought, under the circumstances.

"Not under the terms of your damned contract."

She reached inside her reticule for something and then threw her hand in the air. For a few seconds, it snowed tiny pieces of paper.

"Why don't you ever do what I expect?" he wondered aloud, and it was a rhetorical question at best. "You are not at all like other women." A compliment coming from him. She slit a look at him that nearly seared him to his boots.

"And you, sir, are not like other men."

"You planned this, didn't you?" How quiet his voice was with the snow muffling each sound. How menacing.

"Yes," she said, admission coloring her cheeks rosier than the cold had managed.

"And you thought that I would come chasing after you, correct?"

"Perhaps," she replied, her smile wobbly.

"And what if I hadn't come?" He stepped one foot closer to her. One gentle step closer.

It had been a very real fear for her.

"You once asked what I would do for love. I would have returned, after a while."

"You took a great chance, Katherine."

"Did I, Freddie?" Stubborn to the end.

His smile was pure roguery.

"No more revenge, Kat? No more contracts?"

Her head was bent, her stare intent on the puddles of melting snow on the dusty wooden floor.

When she looked up at him, he nearly caught her up in his arms. In her glance was what he had dreamed of seeing. Not mischief as much as promise. Not dark secrets but the light of love.

"Forgive me, Freddie?" It was the only thing left to say. He had been so honest in his admissions to her that she could do no less. She asked expiation of this guilt she still bore, for once cherishing anger and pain and misery more than the greater gift of love.

His fingers were cold against her skin, or perhaps her cheek blazed with the heat of blood that rose to tint her flesh pink. A single touch, and yet it breached the distance between them.

He was very much aware that neither of them had won the battle that had raged so long between them. Because the cost had been counted as too dear. Because the battlefield had been quit.

"What will I do with you, Kat?" So the lecture was not to be postponed after all.

"What do you want to do?"

She darted a glance at the floor near the fire. A look part coquetry, part harlot, all Katherine.

A smile tugged at his lips in recognition of her outrageousness. His answer, however, was all seriousness. "Love you. Without being summoned. With no conditions. No reservations."

It was honesty distilled and precious, drop by drop. She savored it, and him, their kiss darkly promising. Sweet honeyed passion.

Until the door burst open and Freddie was facing the business end of a very nasty-looking pistol. Not to mention the man who was holding it. He pushed his wife behind him, a chivalrous gesture highly unnecessary as his indomitable wife began to giggle. The words the bulldog looking man and Katherine shared were too rapidly spoken for him to grasp—his French was of the schoolroom variety, consisting mostly of swear words and directions to the nearest bordello.

They were escorted to a massive carriage pulled by four of the finest white Arabians he'd ever seen. Only when they were in the carriage was he allowed to speak, the gun still being trained on him.

"Friends of yours, my dear?" he asked, a wiser part of him recommending that he should not lose such valuable time in sarcasm.

"My grandfather's," she said, smiling at the heavily jowled man who was convinced by prudence, or by Katherine's smile, to relinquish his death grip on the pistol's trigger. The trip upwards into the eagle's aerie was filled with fluent French.

"And the castle?" He knew the answer long before he asked it.

"His, too," she replied calmly, placing her hand on his thigh. He jumped at her touch, and the damned jailer smiled. It was such a Gallic gesture that he wanted to reach over and demolish his face. Only his wife's chiding look and a gentle squeeze held him back. That, and the feeling that his night was only just beginning, and he should not tax what reserves he had left.

A very long night, indeed.

His wife was a countess.

His wife was rich.

She was a countess, and rich, even *before* she married him.

It boggled the mind.

But what truly stunned him was the gentle laugh she gave him when he said as much. She had walked through the connecting door in their suite of rooms, having had a tearful reunion with her grandfather, a meeting he had left them both to, for privacy's sake.

"I love you, Freddie. Not your money, and certainly not your title."

She looked at him strangely, he thought, not realizing that his eyes sparkled with a curious light. "What are you thinking about right now?" she asked, coming to him and placing both palms on his chest.

"That you've never said it before," he admitted, smiling down at her.

"Nonsense, of course I have. You just didn't want to hear it."

"Stubborn witch," he said, nuzzling her hair.

"You, however, have been curiously silent on the subject," she teased.

"I love you, wife," he said, and it was a long time before she had enough breath to speak.

"Freddie?" It was a tentative voice, muted by fatigue. He looked down at her, lit by the glow of the beeswax candles. God, he loved this woman. A prayer in few words. She placed her palm against his cheek, reading his eyes and the tenderness of his smile. His arms enfolded her and he bent his head, nestling his nose between her breasts, feeling loved, and wanted, and prized. "Would you really have left?" The question did not surprise him. He had waited for it since he'd opened the carriage door. The answer must be truthful, not covered with artifice.

He raised his head and looked into her eyes, so solemn, so filled with love.

"Yes," he said, one hand reaching out and defining the features of her face. A beautiful nose, twin beseeching lips, a brow both noble and capable of the most ferocious frown. Dark amber eyes alight with emotion, lashes that rivaled fluttering fans. "We would have killed each other eventually. Little pinpricks of hurt, until we bled to death."

"And now?" Hopeful eagerness in her eyes, dread in the tightness of her lips.

"You will grow so tired of my company, my love, you will begin sending me notes to discourage me."

"Somehow," she said, her words enlivened by her smile, "I doubt that."

"I will endeavor to be up to the challenge, Kat," the Earl of Moncrief acceded, discovering that kissing his wife when she was laughing was a unique experience that he would have to repeat. Often.

It was rumored later that the Earl of Moncrief was the most attentive of husbands, but then, most reformed rakes are. It was also rumored that his wife, the charming countess, was never apart from her husband, often joining him on visits to one of their outlying estates. Their children, an unwieldy brood of nine, often trailed after their parents and, when they grew, managed to scandalize the ton with their outrageous behavior.

Had the Earl of Moncrief bothered to pay any attention to the whispers, he would have laughed uproariously. His children came by their natures honestly, he would probably have said, as he glanced at his wife. She would only have smiled, and winked, and said something lofty, like "Meow."

DON'T MISS THESE ROMANCES FROM BEST-SELLING AUTHOR KATHERINE DEAUXVILLE!

THE CRYSTAL HEART (0-8217-4928-5, $5.99)

Emmeline gave herself to a sensual stranger in a night aglow with candlelight and mystery. Then she sent him away. Wed by arrangement, Emmeline desperately needed to provide her aged husband with an heir. But her lover awakened a passion she kept secret in her heart . . . until he returned and rocked her world with his demands and his desire.

THE AMETHYST CROWN (0-8217-4555-7, $5.99)

She is Constance, England's richest heiress. A radiant, silver-eyed beauty, she is a player in the ruthless power games of King Henry I. Now, a desperate gambit takes her back to Wales where she falls prey to a ragged prisoner who escapes his chains, enters her bedchamber . . . and enslaves her with his touch. He is a bronzed, blond Adonis whose dangerous past has forced him to wander Britain in disguise. He will escape an enemy's shackles—only to discover a woman whose kisses fire his tormented soul. His birthright is a secret, but his wild, burning love is his destiny . . .

Available wherever paperbacks are sold, or order direct from the Publisher. Send cover price plus 50¢ per copy for mailing and handling to Penguin USA, P.O. Box 999, c/o Dept. 17109, Bergenfield, NJ 07621. Residents of New York and Tennessee must include sales tax. DO NOT SEND CASH.